ALISON SCOTT SKELTON

Alison Scott Skelton is the aut
Innocence and *Saving Grace*.
C. L. Skelton, under whose n
Beloved Soldiers and the bests
she lives in Drumnadrochit, Inv

By the same author

A MURDEROUS INNOCENCE
SAVING GRACE

Alison Scott Skelton

AN OLDER WOMAN

HarperCollins*Publishers*

HarperCollins*Publishers*
77–85 Fulham Palace Road,
Hammersmith, London W6 8JB

This paperback edition 1994
1 3 5 7 9 8 6 4 2

First published in Great Britain by
HarperCollins*Publishers* 1993

ISBN 0 586 21508 5

Set in Palatino and Bauer Bodoni

Printed in Great Britain by
HarperCollinsManufacturing Glasgow

For My Women Friends

AN OLDER WOMAN

I

Jacob and Esau were at it again. Liz stared at the blank screen, enduring the thuds and scrapings, until her concentration disintegrated. Then she got up carefully from amidst her books and files and notecards and went through to the living-room. They were sitting at either side of the hearth, silent as Egyptian gods. The blue pile of the carpet was snowed over with piles of beige fluff.

'Thanks a lot,' she said. 'You guys *know* I've got people coming.' She thought of hoovering but the blank screen nagged, and she only bent and clawed up little tufts of hair with her fingers before hurrying back to her study. 'I could use some support from you,' she said. They watched, twitching their chocolate ears.

Back at her desk Liz restacked her books, rearranged the file cards and laid her pen, pencil and notepad in a new order. Then she looked back at the empty screen. Half an hour later, a single line had crept bravely across it, when she heard Barry's key in the lock. Liz sighed. She laid her notebook down and her pen and stacked her file cards. That was that then. She looked at the sad little line and shrugged. Barry was moving about outside the study door, clinking and rustling on his way to the kitchen. She suppressed the urge to run and greet him until she thought of something, other than the truth, to say about the day.

She found Barry by the open door of the fridge, decanting things from a plastic shopping bag at his feet on to its shelves. Two more shopping bags sat on the bare pine table, with three bottles of wine and the two Siamese cats. The cats watched

the action and sniffed at each other with casual curiosity. Liz
scooped them off the table and dropped them on the floor.

'Hi, love.' She slipped past Barry to investigate the new
contents of the fridge. He kissed her ear, and drew a plastic-
wrapped package from the bag.

'Have a good day?' he asked, a cat-sniff of interest.

Liz said quickly, 'Oh, Moira rang and talked for hours just
as I was getting into the swing of it.'

'What did she ring for? We're seeing her tonight.'

'Apples.'

'Apples?'

'From their orchard. They've got hundreds still and she
thought we might want a couple of boxes of apples.'

Barry reached for another plastic bag from the table. 'Moira
never seems to remember *A*, that there are just two of us, or
B, that we live in a flat in London not a country house in
Hertfordshire. Where would we even put a box of apples?'

'She thought I might want to make cider.'

'You're joking.'

'*She* wasn't. I told her it was very kind but you're allergic
to cider.'

'I'm not allergic to cider.'

'I had to get her off the phone. Moira never will believe
that a person can be home and still working. She imagines
somehow that when I haven't got classes I lie here painting
my toenails . . .'

Barry set down his new plastic bag and then suddenly leaned
over and picked up one of Liz's feet like a blacksmith shoeing
a horse.

'Hey, what are you doing?' she shouted, clutching his shoulder for support. He was peeling off her white sports sock.

'Checking your toenails.'

Liz collapsed on the floor giggling and Barry sat down beside
her still stripping her foot. He tossed the sock on the table and
began nuzzling her unpainted toes.

'Stop it,' she shrieked. 'Your beard tickles.'

He worked the nuzzles up her ankle and under the cuff
of her tracksuit. Then removing his steel-framed glasses, he
clambered easily over her and lowered his angular frame down,
kissing her as he did. He stopped, looked at his watch, and

said, 'If you promise to be quick we can both have a delicious orgasm for hors-d'oeuvres.'

She stopped laughing long enough to say, 'What about Moira and John? And Andrew and Erica? They'll be here in fifty minutes.'

'Good God, woman, I'm not superman. Or bisexual at that.'

'Oh get off,' she said, still laughing. She gave him a happy shove and he sat down, mocking disappointment, on the floor.

'I thought it was a nice offer.'

'Wonderful. Come on, dinner for six at eight. It's ten past seven. Let's move.'

He jumped to his feet, tucking his loose shirt down into his jeans. 'Right. Action stations.'

Liz stood up and hopped across the vinyl floor, pulling her sock back on to her bare foot. She stopped in front of the cooker.

'Oven temperature?' Barry had his glasses back on and was peering at the small print on the underside of a rectangular, pastel-coloured box.

'Chicken in Tarragon Sauce, serves two, oven at 190, twenty-five minutes.'

'Check. You've got enough for six I hope.' Barry lifted two more pastel rectangles and laid them on the first. 'Main course OK,' Liz said, adjusting the oven racks. 'Soup?'

'Three double servings, Carrot and Ginger.' Barry held up three waxed cartons with line drawings of soup bowls in green and orange.

'Cream?'

'In the fridge.'

'OK,' Liz said, dragging out the orange Le Creuset casserole. 'Soup is go.' Barry opened the cartons and she dumped the contents into the pot. 'Hors-d'oeuvres?'

'You've had my offer on that.'

'Aside from that. Come on, Barry, forty-seven minutes to lift-off.' Barry dipped into the final plastic bag, and laid a covered polystyrene tray on the table. 'Crudités with Soured Cream and Chive Dip.'

'Right. Hors-d'oeuvres are go.' Liz stretched to the top shelf

3

of the kitchen unit and brought down a rough pottery platter. She laid it on the table and Barry removed the film wrap from the polystyrene tray and flipped it neatly on to the plate.

'Artistic,' Liz said.

Barry flicked rogue carrot sticks back into place and fished the plastic pot of dip out of the centre, turned it over and emptied its contents back on to the plate. Liz shrugged and pushed Esau off the table. 'We have three courses,' she said. 'All systems go. Salad?'

Barry lifted three plastic pots and a clear Cellophane bag from the fridge. 'Three-bean salad for two. Carrot and nut salad for two. Pasta salad for two. Mixed endive salad for six.'

'Well done. Chuck them in those.' She laid an array of wooden bowls in front of him, and stepped back. 'We're looking good. Where's dessert?'

'In the fridge. Chocolate and Cream cheesecake and Passion-fruit Pavlova. Accompanied by aforementioned cream.' Liz pushed Jacob off the table, wiped it down perfunctorily and began laying places with their battered early Habitat dinner service. She looked at the clock quickly while Barry stirred the soup with one hand and fished candles out of a cupboard with the other.

'Good stuff, we're going to make it,' she said jubilantly. 'Thank God for St Michael.'

'The Pavlova was Sainsbury's.'

'And St Sainsbury.'

'And,' Barry said with flourish, 'for the gourmets amongst us, three litre bottles of *Sunday Times* recommended plonk and *Spanish* cheese.'

'Spanish cheese?'

'Flavour of the month as they say in the US of A.'

Liz paused, her hands still busy, quickly polishing tulip glasses with a solitary flick and turn of the cloth for each. She said, 'I never heard anyone say that there.'

'They do now.'

'*Or* "have a nice day". Nobody said, "Have a nice day" when I was a kid. Nobody. Then one year I go back and *everybody*'s saying it. Everybody. Everywhere. *All the time*.'

'They're not saying it any more.'

Liz looked up from the last glass. 'They're not?'

4

'They're not. Even McDonald's doesn't say it any more. They have a directive against it. A kid in Chicago told me.' Barry opened the top oven and placed the ready-to-heat trays of chicken carefully in a row on the middle shelf.

'McDonald's have directives?'

'Sure. "Have a nice day" is out. It's considered tacky.'

'*McDonald's* are worried about tacky?'

'So it seems.'

'Christ. What's happened to my country?'

'Decadence. It happened to Rome.' Barry hung the oven gloves on their hook and began unwrapping his Spanish cheese. 'Is the bread ready?' He stopped and sniffed the air suddenly like a hound seeking scent. 'I don't smell anything.'

'I was working.'

'Didn't you make the bread?'

'I was working.'

'Liz.'

'Barry, I was . . .'

'Yeah, sure, I know.' Barry put the cheese down and looked away. 'But how long does it take to throw some bread together?'

Liz stiffened. She laid another place on the table and her voice went quiet. 'How long is not the point. The point is, it's a distraction.'

'A distraction.'

'Yes.'

'Christ, Liz, I wrote two books and managed to cope with the *distraction* of making bread.' Liz kept her head down and continued determinedly laying the table.

'So you were Superwoman and I'm not.'

'I wasn't saying I was super-anything. I just made bread when it was my turn.' Liz laid the sixth place and looked up, her eyes narrow.

'Oh let's not talk *turns*. It's so childish.'

Barry shrugged. 'Well, how else do you say it. We *do* take turns.'

'It's worse than childish. It's *married*. It sounds married.'

Barry leaped back from the table and raised his hands high, palms outward. 'Oh horror of horrors. The *Bogeyman*.' He caught his thumbs in the corners of his mouth, spreading a wide leer across his face and lunged across the table waggling his fingers beside his ears. 'Horrors!'

Liz turned her back and carefully transferred a stack of six dinner plates from a cupboard to the work surface beside the cooker. She said quietly, 'You don't want that any more than I do.'

Barry gave up trying to get her to look at him and dropped the face. 'Liz, let's just talk about the bread.'

'What's there to say? I didn't make it.'

'Sure. Look, Liz, we can get away with dinner for Moira and John, and maybe even Andrew and this Erica woman . . .'

'His wife, Barry. Andrew and his wife.'

'His wife. We can get away with hoovering up the shelves of Marks and Sparks *because* of the bread. The bread makes it work. The bread makes it acceptable that we never cook and sometimes forget to take things out of their plastic trays . . .'

'I've *never* done that.'

'You did with the taramasalata last time.'

'I didn't. I never did that.'

'But we get *away* with it because the bread tastes so good and makes the place smell like a farm kitchen in Northumberland . . .'

'Where?' Liz paused in the midst of unboxing the Pavlova and looked up at him, her chin tilted and her clear brown eyes widening momentarily in the way they did when something appealed to her.

'Somewhere. You know. Home. Hearth. Love. *Hospitality*. Bake bread and your friends know you love them.'

'*My* friends know I love them,' Liz said abruptly. Then, shoving the Pavlova box away from her she said, 'Oh for God's sake, Barry. Run down to Mario's and buy three white loaves, wrap them in tin foil and slam them in the oven. The place will smell like Northumberland, or Naples anyhow, and *everyone* will feel loved. I don't know what's got into you.'

'What?'

'Since you came home. You keep coming out with this rubbish.'

'*What* rubbish?'

'This dissatisfied . . . I don't know.' Liz turned away and

began twisting the pink candles into white pottery holders with determined concentration.

'What dissatisfied . . .?'

'Nothing. Forget it.'

'No. I want to hear this. What am I supposed to be dissatisfied with? Come on, you can't just *say* a thing like that and drop it.'

'I didn't *say* anything. Let's leave it. Come on, Barry. It's getting late.'

'Liz.'

'OK.' Liz made a sudden decisive twist of the last candle. She set the holder in its place on the table and looked directly at Barry. 'If you want to know. Since you've come home you've been . . . different. I don't know, restless, or preoccupied. *Dissatisfied. I* don't know about what.' She kept her eyes on his face. 'Maybe you should tell me.'

Barry sat down on the edge of the table, carefully avoiding her place settings. He slumped his shoulders and put his bearded face in his hands, pushing his steel-rimmed glasses up on to his forehead. He removed the glasses entirely as he looked up, meeting Liz's eyes with a look of candid disclosure.

'OK. May as well come out with it.' He sighed and rubbed his right eyebrow bemusedly with the knuckles of his right hand. 'I haven't been in Chicago for four weeks researching Carl Sandburg and American populism, Liz. Actually, I haven't been *in* Chicago at all. You see, it started in the airport. O'Hare. I was waiting at the luggage carousel and suddenly, beside me, was this six foot blonde Laplander.'

'Barry . . .'

'With six Siberian huskies.'

'OK, Barry.'

'She was waiting for her sledge to come off the carousel. On her way to Alaska to run that big race in the Klondyke.'

'OK, Barry.'

'Asked me to "hold the dogs".'

'They're going to be here in twenty-seven minutes.'

'Didn't *realize* then, of course, that this was a *Lappish euphemism* . . . now you, as an anthropologist, would no doubt have picked it up at once.'

'For Christ's sake, Barry, I'm sorry I started.'

'So, that's it, Liz. Four weeks of unabashed Nordic bedding
. . .' He shook his head sadly. 'Will you ever forgive me?'

Liz leaned back against the fridge, her left hand on her hip,
her right palm cupping her chin. She studied him carefully for
a long while. Then, stepping across the room, she nonchalantly
scooped Esau up from the floor and stood holding him under
one arm. 'You quite finished?' Barry nodded again. The corner
of his mouth twitched once. 'Right.' She looked down at the
cat. 'I'll forgive you the Laplander. I'll forgive you whingeing
about the bread if you go *now* to Mario's and get three Italian
loaves. I'm not sure,' she added, moodily stroking Esau's sleek
back, 'if I *should* forgive you for always avoiding serious issues
with silly stories.'

'Always.'

'Always.'

'When have I last . . .?'

'Get the bread please, Barry.'

'When?'

'You *are* dissatisfied. You're difficult and confrontational and
different. It's not just jet-lag. You've been home five days.'

'Jesus Christ. I make one *comment*, once, about some godforsaken bread and we're into the heavy stuff for half an
hour.'

'That's my point. You're confrontational.'

'Oh God, Liz,' Barry tilted his head and looked up at the
ceiling, 'that's so American.'

Liz put the cat down. She stepped back across the kitchen
and picked up the Cellophane bag of endive salad and gave
it an angry shake. 'Oh, really? It's American, is it?'

'Yes. It is. You people are amazing. You can't do anything,
vary anything, make the slightest *change* in routine, like maybe
have a cup of coffee one day and *not* have one the next, without
analysing it. Everything has to have some deep hidden *Freudian*
meaning.'

'And you're an expert on the American psyche?'

'You don't have to be an expert. It's so flagrantly obvious.'

'Four weeks in the States. Now you understand us
completely.' Barry nodded calmly, holding out the last of the
wooden bowls while she dumped the salad in.

'I've got a good surface picture.'

8

'I've lived here for seventeen years and I wouldn't presume to *suppose* what makes *you* people tick. But four weeks in the States and our soul is laid bare . . .'

'Oh come on, Liz.' Barry set the filled bowl on the table and surrounded it with the other three salads. 'You *do* understand us perfectly well *and* you know it. Don't be so self-deprecating. And it's not just four weeks of Americans. I've *lived* with one for more than a dozen years . . .' He looked around the table. 'Where's the wine?'

'In the fridge. Not one, Barry. You've lived with me. Don't generalize from one example. It's bad science.' Barry made a little light wave of his hand.

'Not my discipline, dear. We arts people, you know, muddy thinkers, the lot of us . . .' He shrugged whimsically, his eyes crinkling behind the glint of his glasses. On the floor, Jacob and Esau were rolling and tumbling, swatting at each other's flattened ears.

'Oh cut it out,' Liz said to them, but Barry got the point as well. 'The bread?' she said. He glanced at his watch.

'Better change first.' He backed off. 'Don't worry, I'll get it after. Plenty of time.'

Liz shrugged. 'All the same to me. You can stuff Northumberland for all I care.'

In the small bedroom they moved from dressing-table to wardrobes to chests-of-drawers in smooth coordination, dodging around each other with ease. Barry pulled off his Oxfam sweater and white shirt in one, disappeared briefly to the bathroom, came back with wet hair and beard and slipped on another white shirt and a newer Oxfam sweater. 'Should I change my jeans?' Liz looked, and nodded, and Barry undid his leather belt, dropped the jeans and stepped out of them. Liz stepped over them adroitly, undoing her hair. She brushed out a two foot cloud of black frizz and expertly rolled it up again. It curled, unprotesting, into its familiar snake, and she wrapped it in three smooth gestures back into its bun. The two grey streaks at her temples made distinctive exclamation marks on either side of her head.

'Moira says I look like a skunk.'

'She's a great friend. I have to hand it to her.'

'I think she's probably right,' Liz said, unperturbed. 'I

9

suppose I'd better change.' She looked down at herself in her grey fleece-lined tracksuit.

'You're fine by me,' Barry said.

Liz shrugged. 'Moira and John like to dress up.'

'Moira does. So. Let her. You wear what you like.'

Liz smiled. She paused, but stepped back to her wardrobe. 'It doesn't work if your hostess doesn't do *something*. I'd better help her out.' She reached into the wardrobe and extracted another tracksuit, this one of black velour.

'Yum,' Barry said, glancing over his shoulder while he combed his hair.

Liz smiled again, pulled the grey tracksuit off, the black one on, and hopped across the floor, slipping out of her sports socks and into gold lamé sandals. Barry was trimming his beard with small silver scissors in front of the mirror. She wriggled in in front of him, gathering up a fistful of delicate gold chains to drape over the black velour. Then she slipped in her plain gold studs and looked briefly at the effect.

'You look wonderful,' Barry said.

'I look like a university lecturer in anthropology,' said Liz.

Barry laughed aloud. 'You know, until I met you, *I* thought they were all forty-eight inches round the hip, in tweeds, horn-rims, and ethnic beads. Academic prejudices die hardest of all.'

'Some aren't dead yet,' Liz said drily. She adjusted one chain. 'Were you in to the department today?'

'Just briefly. Spent most of the day in the library looking out Mathieson's paper on Scandinavians in the mid-west. I went across for a coffee later.' He paused. 'The only thing I miss on sabbatical is the coffee breaks. Writing is lonely. I'm a social animal.'

'See anybody?'

'A couple. Everyone wanted to hear about Chicago. Of course I couldn't tell them about Elke.'

'Who?'

'Elke. The Laplander.'

'Oh, you,' Liz said. She cuffed his shoulder lightly.

'I met Lucy.'

'Oh.' Liz thoughtfully turned one of her gold studs, busying herself with the fastening behind her ear. 'How's she?'

'Oh fine, fine. I think she's better this year, with her new tutor. Though she *says* of course she misses me terribly . . .'

'I'll bet she does.'

'Oh it's just flattery, Liz. That's what she thinks I want to hear.'

'She's in love with you.'

'No. Not really.'

'Yes really.' Barry shook his head.

'Really no. I'm not the kind undergraduates fall for.'

'You're exactly the kind. I remember, my first year at Columbia I mooned over my Eng. Lit. prof. for the whole spring term. He was just like you. Gentle, a little tweedy, *fatherly* . . .'

'Bloody hell, Liz, I'll run and get my slippers and pipe . . .'

'No, no. You know what I mean. He was handsome, gorgeous as I remember, but *kind*, unthreatening.'

'I'm not sure I like being unthreatening,' Barry said. He stared morosely in the mirror. 'I sort of fancy myself as an axe-murderer. You know, like Jack Nicholson in *The Shining*. Yarrgh.' He leered hugely at Liz's reflection. She giggled. 'Anyway, it really isn't me they fancy. I'll tell you who they do, though.'

'Who?' Liz turned to him, interested.

'Pringle.'

'*Andrew?*'

'In droves, Liz. They fall in droves.'

'You're *joking*.'

Barry looked surprised. 'No. Why should I be joking?'

'*Andrew?*'

'He's bloody good-looking.' Liz laughed. 'Well come *on*, Liz, he *is*.'

'He's sexless.'

'*Andrew?*'

'He's a male Barbie doll, Barry. Utterly sexless.' She smiled placidly.

Barry looked genuinely offended. He said, a little stiffly, 'Well your friend Erica doesn't seem to think so.'

Liz looked away. She fingered her chains, and then lifted a scent bottle from the table and dabbed thoughtfully behind her ears. 'Yes, well,' she said.

Barry looked at her curiously, and when she said nothing more, he said, elaborately, 'Well, I'm certainly looking forward to meeting the famous Erica, the woman who swept Andrew Pringle off his feet and out of his marriage.'

'The marriage was over,' Liz said. She put down the scent bottle and turned away. 'As we all knew very well. I'm glad to hear you're looking forward to meeting Erica.' Liz looked briefly out of the narrow window that overlooked someone else's precise city garden. 'And a little surprised.'

'Why surprised?' Barry was sitting on the edge of the bed, tying the laces of an old pair of running shoes. His voice was mild.

'Because you've always been hostile about her.'

Barry looked up from his shoes. 'No I haven't, Liz. You've got that wrong. I haven't been hostile.' Liz raised one eyebrow. 'I may have been cool, but not *hostile*.' He paused, standing up. 'What I have been, if you want to know, is just a bit defensive . . . a bit unwilling to forget all about Fiona, who was our friend, and instantly embrace some little Swiss bimbo.'

Liz laughed, sharply. 'Christ,' she said, 'I'd hate to hear you when you *were* hostile. She's not a bimbo, Barry. So you can drop that approach for a start.' He turned one hand up, palm upwards and opened his mouth but Liz said quickly, 'Fiona wasn't our friend.'

'Yes she was, Liz. She was our friend.' Liz turned her back to the window and looked at him thoughtfully.

'All right. Maybe she was your friend. She wasn't mine. I never liked her.'

'Didn't you?' Barry said curiously.

'No.' She paused and then said smoothly, 'I didn't like the way she treated Andrew. I tolerated her because she was his wife, but that couldn't make me like her.'

'She was a bit off-hand with him,' Barry said vaguely.

'She couldn't abide his success. She was *always* like that. Always having to cut him down in any conversation. Then when he got the television thing and, after all, it wasn't *that* big a deal, then she was impossible. I hate that kind of jealousy.'

Barry laughed. 'Imagine being jealous over a few slots of Channel Four rent-a-don.' He laughed again.

Liz looked at him sharply. 'You jealous too?'

'Liz, for Christ's sake. I can hold up my head beside *Pringle* any day.' She shrugged. He said, a little harshly, 'Well, Fiona might have been a bit disloyal, but it was hardly an excuse for walking out of a twenty-year marriage.'

'She'd had two affairs.'

'*What?*'

'One with a merchant banker. And the other with some chinless wonder from the Counties.'

'I don't believe it.'

'Don't believe it if you like. It's true.'

'If you knew, why didn't you tell me?'

Liz picked her grey tracksuit up off the floor and stuffed it into a drawer. 'Why should I tell you? It's the worst kind of academic gossip. You didn't need to know it.'

Barry looked faintly hurt. He said, after a bewildered pause, 'Why are you telling me now?'

'To put you in the picture about Erica. So maybe now you'll drop some of your misguided loyalty to the first wife and find a little charity for the second. Andrew's *noticed* this hostility, you know. And you're not the only one. Why do you think it's taken a year to get him back into our social circle? They've avoided everyone since the wedding.'

Barry recovered slightly. 'Frankly, I thought they were too busy in bed.' He grinned. 'These twenty-year-olds need regular servicing.'

'She's thirty. And you *are* jealous.'

'Raging,' he moaned. 'All I can think of is naked fräuleins smeared in yoghurt and muesli. When I was a kid I used to read Heidi under the covers and masturbate.'

'You need help,' Liz said. She shrugged then and added, 'I don't care. That kind of jealousy doesn't bother me. It's normal. It's this other thing, dragging someone down because they've risen a fraction above you. Poor Andrew, he was so happy with his little bit of fame . . .'

'Success is hard to handle in a marriage,' Barry said cautiously.

'Not impossible surely. Look at Moira and John.'

Barry laughed. 'She *made* his success, Liz. Of course she's not jealous. The laurels are hers as much as his.'

'True,' Liz said thoughtfully, 'I hadn't considered that. That's a good insight.'

Barry looked pleased. 'Well, that's how I see it,' he said modestly. He looked at his watch. 'I'd better get that bread. Five to eight.'

He went out and in the four minutes he was gone, Liz lit the candles, stuffed the Pavlova box into a plastic sack under the sink, slid three ageing copies of the *Independent* under the sofa and removed Jacob and Esau from their central place on top of it. She carried them through to the bedroom and curled them up on top of Barry's discarded shirt and sweater on the bed. 'Stay there,' she said, 'Moira hates you.'

Back in the living-room she lit the log-effect gas fire and then hurried through to her study where, after a search, she found *The Dickensian Years: Britain under Thatcher* by Andrew Pringle under a copy of *Punch* and two coffee cups. She retrieved it carefully, rubbing a coffee-coloured circle off Andrew's photograph on the back, and was setting it in nonchalant prominence on the mantelpiece when Barry returned.

'Oh well done,' he said, 'I forgot about it.' He was holding a white paper bag from which protruded three long crusty loaves.

'Tin foil,' said Liz, 'on the bottom shelf.'

Barry nodded. As he went through to the kitchen he adjusted Andrew's book slightly. 'Thank God John doesn't publish as well,' he said.

Liz looked around the room with satisfaction. The silver carriage clock on the mantel, against which Andrew's book was now propped, read eight o'clock exactly. She flopped down on the sofa and curled her feet up.

'We're geniuses,' she called to Barry. He reappeared carrying two glasses of chilled white wine and the pottery dish of hors-d'oeuvres, and joined her on the sofa. 'Ten minutes to Northumberland,' he said. Then, after a pause in which his voice became carefully casual, he said, 'What about John? Is John sexless?' There was a moment's silence.

'John's attractive,' said Liz.

Barry laughed genially. 'Ah-hah, I'll have to watch him,' he said.

Liz sat up straight and looked at Barry without amusement. 'For God's sake. He's my best friend's husband.'

Barry's genial laugh expanded to absorb her anger. He said lightly, 'My heavens, Liz. I didn't realize the convention of marriage meant that much to you.' He reached an arm around her shoulder. She twitched free of it.

'Marriage doesn't,' she said. '*Friendship* does.' She glared, but then the street-door buzzer sounded.

Barry, happy with the distraction, looked at his watch, went through to press the door release, and came back slowly, smiling to himself. 'Here comes Heidi,' he said, 'punctual as a cuckoo clock.'

Liz stood up, and pointed a finger at him as she went to meet her guests. 'I warn you,' she said, 'don't try it on.' She opened the front door and found a cardboard carton of apples and, on either end of it, Moira and John.

II

'Liz darling, you look marvellous!' Moira said. She smiled sweetly and leaned around the apple box to make phantom kisses on either of Liz's cheeks. She was a tall, pretty woman, in her late thirties, dressed in a calf-length pleated skirt, a maroon blouse with a fluttery shawl collar and black court shoes. She wore a large gold bracelet, an antique cameo, and round gold clip-on earrings. Her hair, honey-brown and thickly waving, was tied back with a big velvet bow. It was a look, County and classic, that had once intimidated Liz. Now she found it vulnerable, tinged with a girlish timidity, as if Moira's mother was forever looking over her shoulder.

Moira's husband, John, stood patiently waiting at his end of the apple box, a slender, dark man, impeccably dressed in a charcoal grey, three-piece suit. When Moira was done with her greeting, he nodded and said, 'Hello, Liz,' tilting his head to one side with a small half-smile. He had very dark eyes, set just slightly too close together which gave him a look of impressive intensity. He shifted the weight of the apple box.

Moira said, 'We just brought a little box, darling. They're too good to waste. And you can always make apple butter with them. No one's allergic to apple butter . . . oh, Barry darling,' she cried, as Barry appeared behind Liz, 'you look *fabulous*. How grand to have you back. Did you have a perfectly marvellous time?' She made her little flying kisses for Barry, and then handed him her end of the apple box.

'A wonderful time, thank you, Moira. What do I do with this?'

'Oh just put them somewhere cool, darling. They'll keep for

16

weeks but they must be cool. And dark preferably. Though a *little* light won't hurt.'

Barry grimaced and shuffled backwards through the door with John following obediently. 'Where would you suggest, Moira? The billiards room? Or maybe the conservatory?'

'Excuse me?' Moira turned around and gave him a look between puzzlement and annoyance.

'Nothing,' Liz said quickly. 'He's just being witty.' With her back to Moira, she glared at Barry and said sharply, 'Put them on the floor in the study, please,' and then turning again to Moira she said, 'Thank you so much. They're absolutely gorgeous. That was so kind.'

Moira smiled again. 'Not at all. We do have masses.' She seated herself on the sofa and sniffed the air. 'Oh that wonderful bread. I've been looking forward to that wonderful bread all day.'

'Ah yes,' Barry said, rubbing his hands together as he returned from the study. 'Liz has been working her little fingers to the bone for hours, just for you.'

'Have you, darling?' Moira looked concerned.

'Of course not,' Liz said quickly. 'It's just bread.' She stood up, grabbed Barry's arm and steered him easily around John Harris, who had also emerged from the study, and into the alcove by the kitchen door. She said, 'If you're looking for a row with me, fine. But lay off my friends.'

He raised his hands lightly in front of his face, mouthing an apology. Aloud, he said, 'Of course, darling. I'll get the wine,' and dodged into the kitchen. He reappeared in moments, with a tray and glasses of wine for John and Moira.

Moira sipped from hers and said, suddenly, 'Did Erica phone?'

'No,' Liz said. 'Should she have?'

'Not really. But they might be late.'

'Surely not,' Barry said, 'she's Swiss.'

Moira looked up, her eyes briefly narrowed, but said only, 'It's not Erica. It's Andrew.' She turned to Liz. 'I was shopping all day, and I stopped in at the club before I met John, and had a perfectly delicious sauna. I saw Erica coming out of her late aerobics class. Andrew had an interview with someone from the *Guardian* and she was worried he

17

wouldn't get away.' She looked at her watch. 'I guess he hasn't.'

'No matter,' Liz said lightly. She raised one eyebrow to Barry and he disappeared briefly into the kitchen to put everything on hold. 'How are the children?' she asked.

'Oh fine. Looking forward to Christmas.' Moira looked down momentarily and then looked up and smiled quickly. 'Not half as much as I am, I bet. The house is so empty without the girls. William's a laugh. He's actually counting the days until Clare's school breaks up. After fighting with her non-stop all summer.' She smiled again, whimsically, and then looked sad. But when Barry returned she brightened. 'Now you must tell us everything about your wonderful American trip,' she said, patting the sofa. 'Come, sit by me.' Barry relaxed into a big grin, and crossed the room to settle beside her. Moira fluttered her discreetly mascaraed lashes and said, 'I'll bet they all thought you were marvellous.'

'Well, hardly,' Barry said. Moira fixed him with her most attentive stare. 'Hard to know where to begin,' he said, stretching his legs out comfortably.

'Try Lapland,' said Liz.

He raised his forefinger and pointed it at her, and gave his 'I'll get you after' look, but he was cheerful all the same. John Harris, who had been perched quietly on the arm of the sofa, got up as Barry began to speak and crossed the room to stand by Liz, leaning on the mantel and looking into the unvarying perfection of the gas log fire.

'And how's Liz?' he said.

Liz laughed and half turned away. She said, 'Don't ask. I just might tell you.'

'That's why I asked,' he answered with instant but honest chivalry.

She smiled. 'You're my favourite person to tell my troubles to. It's those one hundred per cent full attention eyes.'

He made his rare, crooked smile. 'What's the problem, Liz?' He looked wise.

She sighed. 'Work.'

'Not going well?'

'Not going. I've written a page and a half since Barry came home.'

'What about while Barry was away?'

'Oh.' Liz looked at him, surprised. 'Pretty good, actually. I got a lot done. No one to talk to in the evenings.' She laughed softly, but added abruptly, 'But that's past history. A week without work is a week that makes me feel like shit.'

'Just five days, surely, Liz. Barry only came home on Sunday night, didn't he?' He probed with his deep, inquisitive stare. 'Aren't you being a bit hard on yourself?'

Liz shrugged. 'As much as I'd love to accept all that delicious sympathy, no, I'm not. You're indulging me, you know, John. If I was a little temp in your office, you'd tell me to get my finger out.'

'But, Liz, this is creative work.'

'Oh balls.'

John looked puzzled. She said gently, 'To begin with, it's not. It's statistics and case histories and analysis. And even if it were, it doesn't deserve an ounce more respect than any one else's work. I'm lazy and badly organized, that's all.'

'I've never heard that before. Not from anyone you work with, or anyone you teach.'

'That's different. That's my real job. I know what I'm doing there.'

'So it's not laziness, Liz. It's lack of confidence. How strange. I can't imagine you lacking confidence in anything.'

Liz looked down at her hands and then glanced quickly sideways to the sofa where Barry was now telling, with animation, an anecdote about a Chicago restaurant that she had heard three times before. Moira watched fixedly, her expression of enthusiastic encouragement unwavering. Liz said, her eyes returning to John's face, 'It's amazing to hear what our friends think of us.' She laughed. 'I wish it were true, John. Well it may *be* true about teaching. And even writing straight academic stuff. But this is a new game and I haven't any confidence at all. If this book ever sees print, it will be a small miracle.'

'You sound fed up.'

'I am fed up.'

'Then why not quit?'

'Quit? You mean quit writing it?'

He nodded. His funny small smile was back.

'Christ, I'd love to.'

He was quiet, letting her own words carry weight. Then he said, 'So?'

'I can't, John. It's important.' She paused. John had always the arresting effect of making her think out motivations. 'It's important,' she began slowly, 'for several reasons. One, to prove to myself I can do it. Two, to actually *say* something about the world rather than just repeating for years what other people have said. Three . . .' She was quiet again, tapping the edge of the mantel and glancing quickly at the clock that now showed eight-thirty and wondering obliquely where Erica and Andrew Pringle had got to. 'Three, because I haven't any excuse not to. Barry's published two books. We're in different fields but aside from that our situations are the same. Now he's writing another.'

'He's on sabbatical to write it, not trying to fit it around a full schedule . . .'

'That's how he wrote the first two. He's paid his dues. There's no *difference*, John, it's not as if we had children.' She stopped suddenly and then said, 'I wonder what's become of Andrew and Erica.'

John Harris responded by glancing at his watch before he said, 'I had no idea you two were so competitive.'

'Oh,' Liz said, startled, 'oh, we're not. Not at all. It's just parallel careers.'

'I always looked up to you, actually, the way you can run two careers like that. No friction or anything.' He stopped and toyed with the jacket of Andrew Pringle's book on the mantel. 'It's interesting that you work better when he's not here,' he said.

Liz looked hard at him. 'It's not interesting at all, John. It's just practicalities. It's a small flat. I write better when he's not here to talk to.'

'Of course,' John said. He smiled charmingly, until Liz, pacified, smiled back. 'Tell me now,' he said, 'before they get here. What's Andrew's new wife really like? Will I like her?'

'Why don't you just wait and see?'

John looked hurt. She softened it with a smile. 'Of course you'll like her, John. *You* always give people the benefit of the doubt, anyhow.' When he glanced up, questioningly, she added, 'Barry's heavily into defending poor deserted Fiona. He has the most irritating chivalrous streak, you know; widows, and orphans, and abandoned adulterous wives.'

John laughed. 'It's hard when someone changes partners. You've just spent several years regarding two people as a unit. Then probably a year or two alternately consoling the pair of them while things are bad. Then you have to choose between friends when they do split up. And then readjust the whole circle when the new beloved arrives. And all the time you're looking at your own marriage in a whole new light.'

'You, John? I don't believe it.'

His dark eyes went suddenly bland. 'I'm speaking generalities,' he said.

Liz nodded. She said, 'Well, speaking generalities, new marriages succeed better when friends are willing to bury the old. Guilt and all.' The door buzzer sounded and she looked up. 'She's a really nice young woman. We have a lot of fun, Erica and Moira and I. I think Pringle's a lucky old sod.'

She excused herself and nodded to Barry. He went to the door while she slipped quickly into the kitchen and turned on the cooker. When she returned, Andrew Pringle was standing in the middle of the room, dominating it by his height and appearance, while Erica hovered at his shoulder. She looked slight beside him, because he was such a big man, but she was actually a tall woman, with a rangy, athlete's build, and a suntanned outdoor beauty. She wore no make-up and her hair was ingenuously curly and of the sunshine yellow of childhood. She was dressed in a navy blue skirt and a dark blue printed shirt buttoned firmly to the collar, and looked, beside her greying husband, like a serious schoolgirl.

Andrew, basking in the flutter of attention his arrival provoked, appeared to have forgotten about her. She was left to step briskly forward herself, extending her hand to Barry. 'Hello, I am Erica Pringle,' she said. Her slight accent added emphasis to the firmness of her voice.

Liz saw from Barry's face that Erica had confounded his fantasy of her. He rallied, taking her hand, eyes crinkling with flirtatious good grace. 'Well, Erica. Welcome to Britain,' he said gallantly.

'I have been here already a year,' said Erica.

Barry blinked behind his glasses and looked quickly to Liz for help.

'Good God, is that the time?' Andrew said innocently. He stepped closer to the mantel and peered at the carriage clock, giving Liz and Barry's copy of his book a fatherly pat as he turned back to the centre of the room. 'Dreadfully sorry.'

'It doesn't matter,' Liz said, but Andrew apologized again and then said, 'Had this bloke from the *Guardian* in all afternoon. Wanting my "expert opinion" on the hard ecu. Stayed on *far* too long. You'd think they'd more important things to do at the *Guardian*.' He shrugged in modest bewilderment.

Erica said suddenly, 'So what if he is from the *Guardian*? You are late. You tell him you are late.'

'It doesn't matter,' Liz said again.

'It *does* matter. It is very rude.'

Barry stepped in casually, his fingertips touching Erica's elbow. 'We don't mind, Erica,' he said. 'We're used to Andrew.'

'So?' she said sharply. 'I am married now a year to Andrew. I am used to him too. And it is bad manners to be late.' Her pretty, squared jawline hardened and her pale blue eyes went cold. Barry stepped back, rebuffed.

Liz said quickly, 'Erica, has Barry introduced you to John?' and when Erica shook her head, Liz led her across the room to the sofa where John Harris was standing beside his wife. Erica shook hands with John at arm's length, like a man. Her handshake was sharp and firm and she looked candidly into his eyes.

He said, shyly, 'I've wondered for months what you three get up to at that sauna club.'

Erica blinked. 'It is nothing,' she said. 'We sauna and we shower. It is good for the body.'

'That's all?' John said.

'Should there be more?'

'No. No, of course.' John looked flustered and turned hastily to his wife.

'We do talk a little,' Moira said helpfully.

'You, Moira? *Never*,' Barry said, but Moira didn't hear him. She had turned back to Andrew who, the attention diverted from him, stood oddly lost in the middle of the room. His handsome profile was turned away from the company and his gaze concentrated on a corner of the hearth rug on which the cat Esau had illicitly curled himself.

'Pretty cat,' he said. 'Yes, you're a pretty cat.'

'Andrew,' Moira said, 'tell us about this marvellous interview with the *Guardian*.'

Andrew Pringle looked up, his relief at being noticed again undisguised. 'Well I shan't bore everyone with that, Moira.' He smoothed back his thick, grey-streaked black hair, removed his heavy glasses, blinking his extraordinary blue eyes, and began talking at once. Barry touched Liz's arm and, leaving their guests circled appreciatively around Andrew Pringle, they retreated to the kitchen.

They stood side by side, Barry holding bowls while Liz ladled soup into them. 'It's gone thick,' Liz said.

Barry shrugged. 'Blame the *Guardian*.'

Liz set the plates out on the table and Barry went around them dropping a swirl of cream in each, out of a plastic tub. Liz opened the oven door and nudged the trays of chicken. She closed the door and drew one pastel package out of its hiding place behind the bread bin. 'It says eat at once and don't reheat. We've reheated it three times already tonight. They'll all get salmonella.'

'Probably not,' Barry said, chucking the cream tub into the bin.

'This meal's a disaster,' said Liz. She glowered morosely at the table. 'Why do you always make sexist jokes when there are men around?'

'What? What sexist jokes?'

'About Moira talking.'

'She does talk.'

'She *doesn't*. She asks questions and lets the men talk. She was doing it to you. *And* you were lapping it up. Now she's doing it to Pringle.'

'Thank God for that,' Barry said quickly. 'I thought Heidi was going to belt him with her alpenhorn over that *Guardian* stuff.'

'Will you cut out the Heidi shit?'

Barry raised both his hands in front of his face, laughing.

'That's some love match,' he said.

'She's right,' Liz said coolly. 'He's always late. It *is* rude.

23

Worse than that, it's deliberate. He likes making an entrance.' She lifted her shoulders in a shrug of annoyance and then went to the kitchen door, switched out the overhead light, and leaned into the living-room alcove, smiling warmly. 'Dinner, loves,' she said.

Over the soup, Andrew talked about the Exchange Rate Mechanism. Barry listened with the fixed attention that meant he was thinking of something else. Moira leaned forward and gave little nods of encouragement, looking, in her wide shawl collar, like a loving and placid dove. John Harris made pertinent points that allowed Andrew scope for enlargement, and Erica Pringle looked carefully at the patterned sleeve of her blouse.

She looked very young among them, and a little lost, her smooth brow furrowed gently as she sought to follow a conversation made baffling as much by old-friends-together intimacy as by any difficulty of language. Once, she asked John Harris a question, but Andrew answered it for him. Andrew reigned happily at the head of the table, where they had placed him the better to fit his big frame into their small dining area.

As Liz cleared the soup plates, Moira said, 'Darling, your bread is superb. John, grab me another slice before she takes it away. I come here for the bread alone.' She sighed, luxuriantly, buttering the new slice.

Liz smirked at Barry over Moira's shoulder. He got up and followed her to the serving counter. They made a discreet wall between themselves and the candlelit dining area while they decanted chicken portions and sauce from their containers. Liz slipped the foil evidence surreptitiously into the bin. Barry glanced at his talking guests and whispered in her ear, 'Smear yourself with yoghurt tonight or I'll spill the beans about Mario's.'

Back at the table, Moira was enthusing over Andrew. 'How fascinating,' she said. 'It's so amazing actually to *grasp* all that. Erica always *says* you're a genius, of course.'

'Do I?' Erica said, but Andrew beamed anyhow.

Moira said quickly, 'Do tell us again how you met, Erica. It's such a romantic story.'

'There is nothing for me to tell,' Erica said. Andrew smiled paternally, watching her.

'She's shy,' he said.

'I am not shy. I have nothing to say because you all know it, surely.'

'I don't know it,' John Harris said, softly. 'Tell me.'

Erica smiled and then did look a little shy. 'All right,' she said. She glanced quickly at Andrew before she began. 'It was in Davos, of course, where I am staying.' She looked down at her plate and then up at John Harris to whom she said, 'There is there my father's hotel, very big, and the ski school. When I was a little girl, always I am skiing and my father is angry because I am no good at school. He has no sons. I am the only child. The hotel will be for me. But then I fail the examinations and do not go to the university.' She shrugged. 'I am happy. I teach the children skiing. It is what I want.' She looked back to Andrew and her smile softened. 'So that spring, there are ten children in my morning class. Four of them are English. Three are very bold, very good at everything. One, one little boy, Daniel, is not good. He is afraid. Even his sister, Vanessa, who is younger, is better. I like this little boy. He tries very hard to please me. Not to be afraid. Still, every day, at the end of the lesson, he is so glad it is over. The other children ski to their waiting parents. They make fancy turns. They skid to a halt. Show-offs all of them. Daniel takes his skis off and walks. He is ashamed. I see, each day, the man waiting for him, his father. I know because they have the same blue eyes.' She glanced involuntarily at Andrew. 'He is English, of course, but he is a very good skier. And very handsome. I don't like this man. I know what he thinks: "I am very good. My son always must be very good too." He comes early and watches the lesson. I get angry. Each day, I get more angry. Finally, one day, when his little boy is busy with his sister, I go up to the man and say what I think. "It is no good. You push him to learn to ski, but he doesn't want to learn to ski. Children must do what they want to do. Otherwise, you make them afraid." I am so angry, I am shaking, thinking of poor little Daniel, trying so hard to please his big, handsome, show-off father.' She stopped, and looked suddenly at Andrew, and then they both giggled, remembering.

'Poor Andrew,' Erica said fondly. 'He stares at me. His mouth falls open. He is amazed, at me, at my anger, at everything. "It's not *me*," he says, like a little boy. "It's you . . . He comes every day to please you . . . At night he has nightmares, but every morning he gets dressed in his ski-clothes to ski with Erica. I think," he says, "he's in love with you." So,' Erica smiled, 'I am laughing, and he is laughing, and poor Daniel does not know what to think.'

She sighed, returned her attention to her dinner, and then looked up again. Everyone was watching her. She said then, 'So Daniel is in love with me, and in no time, I am in love with his father.' She paused, and took another bite of her chicken. 'And I am very sad all the time, because I know it is stupid. He is married. He is English and very important, my father says. I am jealous. It is very stupid because I never see his wife, I just imagine her. In no time, I know all about her, I think. She is very tall and thin and haughty. She wears always a white ski-suit and a white hat with fur, and big black sunglasses. And she stands around in the sun by the terraces with that bored look that I hate, because I think, if skiing is so boring, then why do they come? Oh, I hate her,' she ground her fork vehemently against her plate, 'I really hate her.'

Andrew Pringle laughed. Erica glanced sideways and gave him her schoolgirl smile. 'It is really very stupid. Then one day I get so angry that I say to Andrew when he comes for Daniel and Vanessa, "Why is it always you? Why doesn't your wife come for her children? Doesn't she care about them?" And again, his mouth falls open, and I learn that his wife is in England and they are getting a divorce.' She leaned back in her chair and stretched her arms out, remembering. 'Oh, I am so *happy*,' she said.

'I told you,' said Moira complacently. 'I love romantic stories.' She looked up suddenly then, to Barry and to Liz. 'What about you two?'she said. 'You were together already when I met you. You seemed *always* to have been together. I never heard . . . did you have a romantic meeting?'

Liz said, 'We can't remember.'

'You can't *remember*?' Moira looked stunned.

Barry shrugged again. 'We've tried. We just can't remember. It must have been sometime that first term when we started our PhDs. She'd come from the States that summer and I came up to Cambridge after my year off in India. And we were just *there*.

26

I had a bunch of friends, mostly postgrads, too, and so did she, and somehow we were always in each other's company. I can't actually remember meeting her.'

'Surely *you* remember, Liz,' said John Harris.

'Nope.' She grinned, getting up to clear the second lot of plates. 'He was part of the furniture. He seemed to come with the place. Like King's College Chapel, and the Cam. I do remember him falling out of a punt one day and coming up convinced he was dying of cholera. But it wasn't our first meeting.'

'What a shame,' said Moira.

'What, Barry falling in the Cam? He did it all the time.'

'No. Not having a romantic meeting . . . a memory. It's like there's something missing . . .'

'We cope, Moira,' Barry said.

'I can remember *exactly* when I first met John,' she said. Her eyes lighted as she went on to recite. 'It was Michaelmas term, our second year. And it was at the Union. John was speaking. "This House regards the admission of women to men's colleges as a travesty."'

'I opposed,' John Harris said hastily.

'He was *wonderful*,' Moira murmured. 'Afterwards, we all met for drinks, and a chap called Charles Stordy introduced us, and I decided, right there, this was the man I would marry.'

'Right then?' said Barry.

'Right then.'

'I met you before of course,' John Harris said.

'What?' Moria blinked.

'We met before. The spring before.'

'No we didn't, John.'

'It was May Week. Our first May Week. We were all very serious about it, determined to do it right. We got up an enormous punting party, and we punted up towards Grantchester and had a picnic in a meadow. Champagne, strawberries, wicker baskets . . . You were in another punt, with a couple of women and some big bloke from Clare. I remember you wore that wonderful dress I love. It was the first time I saw you in it. And you looked . . . I'll never forget how you looked in that dress.'

'What dress?' Moira said.

'The blue one. You know, your Guinevere dress.'

'Oh that!' Moira looked up at the ceiling. 'God, I got so sick of that dress. He was always asking me to wear it. Whenever we got dressed, for *years*, it was always, "Please, darling, wear the Guinevere dress." Well, it *was* pretty enough, but it was pure seventies, ankle-length, with a low, low neck and huge wide sleeves that came to points. I couldn't ever *eat* when I wore it, because the sleeves dipped in everything. And I couldn't lean over or my tits would fall out.'

'She looked so beautiful in it.'

'One day when he wasn't looking I stuffed it in a plastic bag and scurried off to Oxfam. What a relief.'

'You gave it away?' John's eyes opened wide.

'*Years* ago. For heaven's sake, John, I had babies by then. Where would I wear the thing? Anyhow, it was horrendously out of date.'

'I loved it. It was the first dress I ever saw you in.'

'Anyhow,' Moira said sharply, 'I don't remember any of that.' She passed her empty plate to Liz. 'I think you're mistaken.'

'That is very funny,' Erica said.

Moira looked at her. 'What is?'

'That you are both so sure of when you met. Only it isn't the same time.'

Moira said smoothly, 'John's mixed that up with the following year. I remember now.'

John dropped his eyes to his place mat, on which Liz was setting a dessert plate, and said nothing. Barry carried in the Pavlova and the cheesecake, and Liz went back to the kitchen, switched on the kettle for coffee and brought in the jug of cream. Moira and John were both pointedly not looking at each other.

Liz said quickly, to Andrew, 'I suppose you two lucky people will be off skiing together in a few weeks, again.'

'Not likely to have time this year,' Andrew said. 'Full schedule, plus all this hoo-ha over the paperback. Probably do a little tour. Publishers on to me about it, or otherwise, frankly, I couldn't be bothered . . .'

'What about you, Erica?' Liz cut in quickly. 'Will you go anyhow?' Erica looked dejected. 'No,' she said. 'I don't think so.'

'Won't your family want to see you?' Moira asked kindly.

'I do not like to go alone,' Erica said. She looked at Andrew but he was content with his Pavlova and said nothing.

John Harris said, 'I'd love to go on a skiing holiday.'

Liz turned, surprised. 'You ski, John?'

'John!' Moira hooted. 'John ski!' She laughed again, so loudly that Barry said, 'Sounds like there's a story behind this.' Everyone looked at John, who stared at his plate.

Moira said, 'Tell them, John.'

'What is it?' Erica asked. 'What is funny?'

John looked up, studied her pretty young face thoughtfully, and then made his small, ironical smile. He said, directly to Erica, 'My wife doesn't think I can learn physical things.'

'Well, John,' Moira said loudly, 'you can't just leave it at that. *Tell* them. Tell them about Aviemore.'

John sat up straighter. He had finished his cheesecake and now he crumpled his napkin up and laid it on his side-plate. 'No. You tell them, Moira, if that's what you want.' Barry raised an eyebrow to Liz. Liz stood up.

'Who wants cheese?' she said. 'Barry's got a lovely Spanish cheese.'

'All right,' Moira said, 'I *will* tell them.' Then she faltered, as the room went silent, everyone watching her. She fiddled with the edge of her shawl collar and then said quickly, 'Well, it was *years* ago. Before the children. Just after we were married, actually.' She looked around. John was watching her with cool, polite attention. 'Well, we had this group of friends. From London. We were still living in Islington then. And they all wanted to go skiing.' She looked nervously at John. 'Well John simply had to go skiing too. And he is right, he's never been good at physical things. He never did sports at school, or at Cambridge. *I* played tennis, even, but John didn't do anything. And so he decided he *had* to learn to ski.'

'I bet there was a woman in that party, eh, John?' Barry said cheerfully.

Liz gave him a cool look but John said clearly, 'No. I just wanted to learn to ski. That's all.' He spaced the words with careful control.

Moira looked uneasy, but began again, 'Anyhow, we got there, and we rented the abysmal skis and went up to that appalling place. *And* it was lashing with rain. And John's friends were all brilliant skiers, it turned out, and abandoned us immediately, and we spent the entire afternoon plodging up this stupid little slope in the rain and falling on our bums, with John pretending to have a wonderful time. I was soaked through and covered in bruises. And *then*,' her voice rose again with remembered fury, 'and then, Franz Klammer here says, I'm just going to go down that little steep bit there. And of course I told him not to, but he had to do it, and off he goes. Well, half-way down the slope is this stupid little fence, and of course he can't go around it because he can't turn the stupid things so he goes right into it and his skis go right through it and *he* goes over the top.'

'Were you hurt?' Erica asked quietly. John shook his head.

'*Luckily*,' Moira continued, 'he didn't break his leg. But still he was stuck in the stupid fence and *then* he realizes that he never asked his friends how to take the skis *off*. So there we both are. Him stuck in a fence and me stuck on those *bloody* skis, shouting for help; and eventually two little girls, about ten years old, come along and show my husband how to undo his bindings, take off his skis and stand up. I can see them still, two little Scottish girls fussing over him like he was somebody's *grand*father. "Are ye aright, mister? Are ye no' hurt?"' Moira closed her eyes. 'God, I could have died. We packed up our things, waited for our bloody *friends* and went home the next day.'

'How awful,' Liz said lightly, bringing through the cafetière. 'Put you off sport for life.'

'I had a wonderful time,' John said. 'I really did.'

After the cheese, they reconvened in the living-room and Liz and Barry raced each other for the dishwasher. Liz won.

'Christ,' Barry said, 'don't leave me alone with them. There's going to be blood.'

'Tough shit. I got here first. I load the dishwasher and you play marriage counsellor to Moira and John.' She smiled smugly.

'I feel like I've been doing that half my life,' Barry said morosely. 'Why *do* all our friends insist on getting married?' He leaned against the table, avoiding the rubble of the finished meal. 'And the joke is, they keep wondering why we don't.'

He heaved himself upright. They exchanged a brief kiss. 'Oh well, into the fray,' Barry said, lumbering wearily out.

Liz took her time over the dishwasher. She scraped plates into the bin and put the leftover salad in the fridge, the cats following her about quietly with question mark tails. She placed the last saucer in, shut the machine and switched it on, listening, over the sound of running water, for sounds of tears, shouts or hysterics. Hearing none, she paused to check her face in front of the little mirror by the toaster. She replaced two hairpins in her bun, and rearranged her gold chains, peering, as she did so, at the two streaks of grey in her hair. They did look significantly skunk-like. Bloody Moira, always accurate.

'Hi, everybody,' she said brightly, sweeping back into the living-room. It was very dim. Barry had turned the lights low, hoping perhaps that dinner guests, like cage-birds, quietened in the dark. It seemed to have worked. Erica and Andrew Pringle sat serenely side by side on the sofa; Andrew slouched happily, Erica very upright, her long legs neatly crossed at the ankle. Andrew had gathered a small fold of her blue skirt hem in one big hand and was holding it contentedly. On the floor, Moira sat in a prettily arranged pool of pleats, her back to her husband who stood with one hand lightly on the mantel, and her eyes on Barry who sat now in a corner chair. His legs were outstretched and his hands animated as he spoke.

'Of course,' he was saying, 'it's *nothing* like what they say about it. That's the first lesson, and you learn it the moment you step off the plane. Our *perceptions* of America are so distorted. By films and by magazines and, frankly, by sheer prejudice. There's an enormous amount of jealousy in the British psyche regarding the States. We may as well face up to that at the start.'

'True, true,' Andrew Pringle said amiably. Liz closed the door to the kitchen behind her and came in and sat down quietly on the hearthrug, patiently prepared to listen.

Barry went on. 'There's a dynamism about the place, it's hard to explain. You feel enthusiasm around you. In the academic world . . . well, frankly we haven't a look-in. The facilities are superb, the attitudes open. The *rigidity* of our system is simply not there. I must say, it was refreshing.'

'But surely,' Moira said, *culturally* it's lacking. I mean everything's *here*, isn't it?'

'Don't be so sure. Half the best manuscripts are over there. It's money. Let's just face it. Money. They have the willingness to put money in, and we haven't. We can either sit here complaining that our treasures are being leached away, or we can face facts.'

'Meaning?' Liz said quietly.

Barry looked surprised. He shrugged. 'It's worth considering,' he said slowly, 'that maybe there's where the action is.'

There was a brief silence in the room. Andrew Pringle straightened up on the sofa and said, quickly, 'Yes, well. When I was in New York . . .'

'New York doesn't count,' Barry said. 'New York isn't America. The mid-west, that's the real country.'

'Try telling eight million New Yorkers that,' Liz said.

'You know,' he continued, 'it's quite easy to forget New York exists when you're out there. They have this wonderfully self-sufficient culture. Complete unto itself.'

'Parochial,' said Liz.

'I wouldn't call it parochial. They have arts, and theatres, films, libraries. It's a whole world. A whole new world. I have to say, I haven't felt so excited about my subject for years as I felt talking to those American kids.' He laughed suddenly. 'You know, they would ask me to read Shakespeare. Because of my accent, you see. They would ask me to read. You'd think I was Laurence Olivier. Sitting there, with all those bright young faces looking up at me. I told them a bit about Britain, you know. A bit about London, and my time at Cambridge. They were so *appreciative*.' He shrugged.

'Well,' said Moira. 'That's to be expected surely. You can see how they go on when they get over here, about Stratford, and Oxford, and all those cute little thatched cottages.' She made a very bad American accent for the last.

Barry said coolly, 'Before we type the whole country by its tourists, Moira, would you like to be represented by the average Costa del Pisshead lager lout?'

'Give up, Moira,' Liz said. 'Barry's in the throes of Amerophilia. It hits everybody the first time – if they're not mugged or raped in the first half hour, that is.'

'Oh come on, Liz. That's a cliché for a start. Frankly, I felt safer in Chicago than I do in London these days.'

'Ignorance is bliss,' said Liz.

'And I'll tell you something else I liked. I liked their famous classlessness. And you can call that a cliché if you like, too, but it happens to be true. There I was, staying on Lake Shore Drive, with Pete Henderson . . . You remember Pete, John; he read Old Norse and then went back and took over his father's dog-food factory. Anyhow, he does all right and it's pretty posh, but one day, I'm riding up in the lift with one of his neighbours, and she's a beautiful woman, true, but she talks like a street kid. One of those Italian-American accents you can spread on bread. But is that stopping her living on Lake Shore Drive? No way. Now you find me the equivalent in Britain.'

He straightened up and looked Liz firmly in the eye. She said, 'I notice she wasn't black.'

'It's funny how expatriates are always their country's worst enemies. What is it, Liz? Are you afraid you made a mistake? That the promised land isn't here after all?'

Erica sat forward suddenly. 'I would like someday to go to America. It sounds very exciting.'

'*That*'s a nice attitude,' Barry said at once. 'Give it a try. Find out for yourself. Don't just buy the sour old party line.'

'I gave it twenty-three years. It gave me Vietnam, and I left,' Liz said. Then she shook her head annoyedly. 'Oh, it wasn't that. That's far too dramatic really. I came here by accident; I stayed here by accident. But I like it, and that's no accident at all. I have nothing against America, Barry. I just choose to live here.'

He was silent. Andrew Pringle said, 'Now the thing about America, of course, is that it's a flawed meritocracy. Now when I was in Washington, last year . . .'

Moira said quickly, 'Still, Barry, you had a wonderful visit, but surely *you* wouldn't actually choose to live there either.'

'I might,' he said.

Liz stood up and went through to the kitchen to make the last round of coffee. When she came back, they were talking about American food. She said, directly to Barry, 'You wouldn't you know. Not after the first few months. By then, you see, they'd be used to you. You wouldn't be the wonderful British guest, but just another immigrant trying to make his way. And they'd tire of you soon enough. They have a very short attention span, you know; look at their television. Your problem is you've fallen for the flattery. You just got too fond of being the master race among the colonials.'

'That's OTT, Liz.'

'Think so? Just be glad it was just a month, love. You'll have wonderful memories and no reality. A holiday romance. No time to get disillusioned with it all.'

'Well,' he said slowly, 'we'll have to see.'

She looked back at him as she stepped again towards the kitchen. 'What do you mean by that?'

'I was offered a job, Liz. Head of department. About twice what I earn here and facilities you wouldn't believe.'

Liz stared at him in silence.

Moira said, 'Surely you're not going to take it, Barry?'

'Actually,' he said, 'I am.'

III

Wednesday was sauna night. Wednesday was also cold and malevolently wet, as Liz emerged from the squat brick-and-stucco building that housed the Department of Anthropology into a raw December wind. *In a decent country it would snow at this temperature*, she considered, and then rejected the thought as a potential concession to Barry. Stoically, she stepped into the rain, her folder of lecture notes clutched against her raincoat, the Solomon sports bag Erica had given her swinging from her right hand.

The health club where Erica worked as fitness instructor and where, for the best part of a year, Liz, Erica and Moira had enjoyed a weekly ritual of self-indulgence, was on Gower Street, opposite the buildings of the university, and could hardly be more convenient. Still, Liz hesitated briefly, half-turned towards Russell Square and the Piccadilly Line, and then turned back. She felt exactly equally divided between a yearning for the warm comfort of the sauna and her friends' companionship, and a reluctance to face them in her painful new circumstances. She had seen neither Andrew nor Erica Pringle since Friday night and was acutely aware that Moira Harris had never telephoned her traditional 'thank you' for Friday's disruptive dinner party, a discomforting lapse in Moira's impeccable etiquette that added to her uncertainty.

Abruptly, she made up her mind and turned up Torrington Place towards Gower Street and the two staid buildings that sheltered the New Age Body Workshop. A small brass plaque on the nearer of the two identical front doors was the sole indicator of the nature of the establishment concealed behind

35

the prim four-storey façade. A serious renovation had knocked the two interiors into one, realigned walls and floors and made room for a swimming pool, work-out studios, sauna suites, squash courts and sunbeds; a haven of sensuality incongruously fronted by dour brick.

Liz ran up a broad flight of steps and entered the health club. The heavy door closed behind her, shutting out the rain and the evening traffic and she relished a blissful moment of relief as on sinking into a deep, perfumed bath. Shaking rainwater from her hair, she crossed the softly lit, musak-serenaded foyer to the reception desk.

The blonde woman behind it wore a white tracksuit with the Workshop logo, a lot of make-up, and a deep, artificial suntan. 'Good afternoon, Dr Campbell,' she smiled professionally.

'Hi, Joan. Is Mrs Harris here yet?'

'Yet? She's been here hours. She came in at four with a look of determination and a guilty tale about éclairs at Harrods. Hit the rowing-machine like a demon according to Erica. I think they'll both be in the sauna now.'

Liz thanked her, checked in her coat and her work folder and made her way to the sauna suite. The health club was decorated in shades of warm terracotta, splashed about with the greenery of improbably large potted plants. Water – pools, jacuzzis, fountains – was everywhere. Carpets were lush, seating plush, and a comforting backdrop of muzak cloaked the well-dampened sounds of exercise machines, squash courts and work-out studios. Fit-looking men and women in jogsuits passed her in the corridor. At the entrance of the sauna suite, the mingled smells of chlorine and hot pine drifted out like the incense of a sensual cathedral.

'Hi, Darren,' Liz said absently, dropping the Solomon sports bag. The sauna attendant handed her a fluffy peach-coloured robe and a matching towel.

'Hello, Dr Campbell.' He said it quickly, eyes downcast. Darren served also as a lifeguard at the pool, and Liz and Moira deduced he had been hired for his brawny swimmer's physique, since neither brains nor social finesse had been overly conspicuous in the choice. In the early days, his guttural Scots accent and a tendency to respond to all requests, comments, or criticisms with ingenious variations on the single word, 'aye', had threatened his tenure. But Darren had shown surprising invention. The Glaswegian glottal stop faded, the vocabulary expanded, and there were rare, uneven attempts at conversation. He would never quite fit the place, but he did his job conscientiously, and was a favourite with the younger female clientele around the pool.

Liz imagined his sort of good looks would please the very young; a well-shaped face, still a little unformed; those stunning blue eyes that Glasgow produced so readily, black hair, worn long on top with a loose forelock of curls, and shaved off short at the back and sides, the disparate lengths joined in an abrupt line, like the shaved winter coat of a racehorse. It was a style popular with her students, as was the single gold earring that decorated Darren's left ear.

'Mrs Harris is here?' Liz said.

'Aye,' said Darren. 'She went in wi' Erica ten minutes ago. You've got the place to yourselves.'

Liz smiled. She draped the folded towel and the robe across her arm and lifted the sports bag. 'God, I could kill for this,' she said.

He looked at her uncertainly and chanced a half grin. 'Is it that good?'

Liz stopped, surprised. 'Haven't you ever *used* the sauna?'

'No way,' he said, laughing.

'Why not?' she pursued. 'It's free. You work here. Erica uses it all the time.' But he shook his head, waving the suggestion away with one of his big blunt hands.

Liz gave up and went through to the locker room. Over the splash of the showers she heard Moira and Erica talking, their familiar voices a muffled blur.

'Hi, kids,' she called. The voices stopped too suddenly. Liz smiled wryly as she began to undress. Not surprising they had been talking about her, considering the other night. She was hurt a little, just the same.

'That you, darling?' Moira called back. 'We're just in the shower.' Moira's voice was perfectly unruffled.

'I'll be in in a minute,' Liz answered. She undressed a little slowly, bracing herself. Her working clothes, as she folded them to place them on a shelf in the beige metal locker, seemed suddenly dowdy; the grey wool skirt, blue flat-soled

Ecco shoes; even the grey cashmere pullover that Barry had given her for her birthday, looked oddly drab, as if the tweedy anthropologist of their jests was emerging at last. *Stuff Barry*, she thought with distracted vehemence.

She stripped off her tights and knickers and the sporty cotton camisole she wore instead of a bra, and tossed them on the pile, closing the locker door. Gathering up the towel and robe and her sports bag with her collection of shampoos, body creams and shower gels, she walked naked through the warm, wet locker room to the showers.

Moira stood directly under a showerhead, clothed in streams of water and shampoo, one small hand lost in her piled up, lathered hair. Fair, broad-hipped and small breasted, with a rounded stomach and long thighs, she had a classical, womanly shape. As Liz entered she was moaning to Erica, 'Look at this, isn't it disgusting,' prodding one white hip. 'God, I could die.'

Erica looked unimpressed. 'Women have hips,' she said. 'So?' It did not help however that Erica had no more hips than a boy. Erica stood outside the stream of running water, energetically scrubbing her pale blonde pubic hair as if to be naked was utterly, boringly normal. She was a lean, bony woman, her stomach absolutely flat, her tanned breasts narrow and easily swinging beneath her broad shoulders. When she turned to sponge her buttocks her body rippled with the golden fluidity of Liz's Siamese cats.

'Look at *that*,' Moira shrieked suddenly, twisting around out of the shower stream to stare horrified at the back of her thigh. 'Liz, look, oh I can't believe it. It's appalling.'

Liz peered curiously.

'Look at that *cellulite*.' A small dimple appeared under Moira's prodding pink nail. 'Oh I might as well give up,' Moira said.

'Is that it?' Liz asked uncertainly.

'I'll just accept it. I'm a fat woman. I'll learn to like it. All the women in my family are fat. Look at my mother.'

'Your mother is *elegant*,' said Erica.

'I'll grow huge and old and John will get fed up and leave me. God, I never should have eaten that éclair. *That* was my mother's fault, too. She dragged me to Harrods for tea, Liz.' Moira grabbed Liz's elbow, making her drop the handful of hairpins she'd extracted from her bun. 'Then she stuffed me full of éclairs. Just because *she's* huge . . .'

'Barry says your mother is the most handsome older woman he knows,' Liz said.

'Terrific. I'll be a Handsome Older Woman. That's a euphemism for Fat Old Cow, darling.'

'Of course it's not,' Liz said. 'Barry means it.'

Moira sniffed. 'Oh well. Barry has peculiar taste. He doesn't count.'

'Thanks a lot.'

'Oh darling, I didn't mean *you*. It's just that he's not . . .' she paused awkwardly, 'not very demanding. Not like John.'

'John did not seem demanding,' Erica said.

Moira gave her a sharp look as she finished rinsing her hair, and turned the shower off. She said only, 'He is.' She stood looking coolly at Erica a moment longer and then said abruptly, 'All men are. They may *pretend* to be casual about women's looks, but just let yourself slip a little and see what happens. Never mind that *they* grow a paunch and get jowly and leave their smelly socks around. *You've* still got to be the sylph-like nineteen-year-old they met. Sometimes I wonder if it's worth it.' She looked at Liz meaningfully but Liz turned away. She quickly shook her hair out and then clipped it up roughly as she got under the shower. When she came out, Moira and Erica were in the sauna and, dripping wet, she went to join them.

The sauna was generously roomy, its walls and ceiling clad with rich golden pine. Three of the walls were fitted with double tiers of pine benches, and the fourth held both the door and the neatly fenced off electric heating stove, with its surface of synthetic stones. Beside it, the old-fashioned wooden bucket and beaten copper ladle for wetting the artificial rockery seemed cheerfully anachronistic. On her first visit Liz had waited bemusedly for fat-armed Scandinavian women with birch twigs. None had come, but the heat and the aroma of hot pine had fetched up a complexity of memories, all American, of mountain cabins and summer beach boardwalks which, on each visit, still returned. Liz stepped up to the highest, hottest bench and stretched herself out full length.

There was a correct way of doing the thing – an orderly

succession from coolest to warmest benches, interspersed with refreshing showers – which Erica was following in strict routine. Moira however never progressed beyond the coolest seat, where even now her English rose complexion was rapidly reddening. And Liz plunged eagerly into the fray, soaking up all the heat available as if she might compress seventeen lost American summers into one half-hour.

'Oh heaven,' she moaned, stretching her toes towards the piney ceiling. Erica murmured agreement. She was lying flat on her back, her angular hipbones further reproaching Moira's éclair. Moira stretched herself out on the lower bench, lying on her side and moodily surveying her offending thigh.

'Of course the clever thing,' she said, looking resentfully at Liz, 'is not having children.'

'That is clever?' Erica said, raising her head to look at Moira.

'Of course. Children *ruin* you. Stretch marks, saggy tits, this great lump of a stomach.' She prodded herself angrily. 'That's what three babies does for you. After that, it's all over but the shouting.'

'You're not going to convince me you'd have it any different,' Liz said lazily. She leaned over the edge of the bench and smiled.

Moira smiled back. 'Of course not. But I would like to look the way I did. Or else,' she sighed, 'to just forget it and wallow happily in my fat.'

Liz laughed out loud. 'Oh Moira,' she said.

'It's not funny. I spend half my life trying to be – ' she paused – 'someone else. That other person I was. The one John married.'

'What I do not understand,' Erica said, 'is why you do all this for him. He doesn't do anything for you. You said so yourself. He doesn't do anything physical. So, he must be flabby and unfit. Doesn't it bother you?'

'Well, he works very hard,' Moira said vaguely. 'Anyhow,' she added, 'John's not the physical type.'

Erica made a ripply shrug and lay down flat.

'Cop out,' said Liz. 'Barry works hard too. But he plays squash twice a week and runs every day.' Before she finished saying it, she was sorry.

There was a brief, fertile silence. Then Moira said, 'Liz darling, I feel I never properly *thanked* you for that wonderful meal last week. I was just saying to Erica before you came, what a pity we had to leave so early. And apparently Andrew was in rather a rush as well . . .'

'Yes,' said Liz, staring up at the pine boards. 'Everyone was in a bit of a rush.' She laughed softly. 'There is that special feeling you get when your friends are all scuttling off early to let you fight.'

'Oh Liz . . .'

'It's all right, Moira. We had a real corker. I wouldn't have wished it on my worst enemy.' She paused. 'If there had been any possibility of me scuttling off somewhere, I'd have gone too.'

Moira sat up, swinging her legs over the side of the bench. She stared at Liz and when Liz said nothing more she said tentatively, 'Is it settled?'

'Sure.'

'And?'

'He's going.'

Moira's mouth opened. She sat staring and then said in a little girl's voice, 'Oh Liz. I'm going to miss you so much.'

'Me?' Liz sat up and smiled wryly. 'Why me?'

Moira looked hurt. She said softly, 'We've been such good friends.'

Liz laughed loudly and the hurt look intensified on Moira's face. '*I'm* not going anywhere,' she said.

'But Barry?'

'If Barry's determined to emigrate, that's his problem. I've got a job, a flat, two cats and all my friends in London. I'm not leaving everything just so he can be the leading light of English literature in Madison, Wisconsin.' Moira turned briefly even redder, and then shook her head, pushing back a loosened sweaty loop of hair.

'Well, then, the whole thing's simply ridiculous. You can't tell me he's actually going to go off with*out* you.' Liz made an elaborate gesture out of looking at her watch.

'As a matter of fact, at this moment, he's booking his flight.'

Erica, who had been lying with her eyes closed and apparently oblivious, sat up too. She said, to Moira, 'Is this a joke?'

'He faxed his acceptance this morning and received their reply just after four. He rang me to let me know.'

'He didn't,' said Moira.

'I think I was getting my one last chance,' Liz said quietly. 'If so, I flubbed it like all the others.' She stretched her arms and stood up. 'Christ, I'm sweltering. I'm going out.'

Liz turned the warm shower on full and stood under the deafening stream while Moira fussed about, rinsing herself and casting Liz questioning glances. When they came out Liz made a quick dash for the jacuzzi, almost colliding with Erica who had emerged from the sauna to take her stoical plunge under the cold shower, the closest the club could provide to a field of Norwegian snow. Liz sank gratefully into the haze of jacuzzi bubbles and closed her eyes. The water sloshed companionably as Moira joined her.

'Surely it's temporary?'

'Nope.'

'He's just *going*, like that, to a place he's never seen, and staying for ever?'

'He toured the campus while he was over there. The contract is open-ended, but it's understood he'll stay at least a year.'

Moira rearranged herself in the water. 'Well, I suppose you could weather a year . . .'

'He won't come back, Moira.'

'Are you *trying* to look at the blackest side, or what?'

'I'm being realistic.' Liz sat up straighter, the bubbly water cascading off her shoulders and breasts. 'He's forty. He's stuck in a rut here. He's bored with his courses, frustrated by the department, and sees himself going nowhere. All that American sycophancy must have felt real good.' She shrugged. 'Anyhow, once you get *off* the treadmill here, there's no guarantee you'll get back on.' Liz sank down until the water came up to her chin and the bubbles were at eye-level. She let her lids drift down until she was viewing Moira through a lash-framed bubble-strewn haze.

Moira was looking perplexed. 'I can't believe you're really so laid back about this,' she said.

Liz opened her eyes fully. 'Oh, I'm not,' she said, 'it's just that we've been through the mill about it. All Friday night. Most of Saturday, and then a pithy little re-run on Sunday.

I'm wiped out. Sorry to be a bore, but if you wanted to view the fun you should have stuck around on Friday.'

Erica came quietly from the shower, and stepped long-leggedly down into the jacuzzi. She glanced at Moira and at Liz and then looked down at the water with her schoolgirl deference. Moira said, 'Oh piss off, Liz.' As always when her cultured voice strayed into vulgarity, she won instant surprised attention. Liz and Erica both looked up. Moira said firmly, 'I'm sorry you felt deserted on Friday, but there was no way my staying could have helped. Now stop playing the brittle bitch. You're not very good at it and I don't believe any of it. You're surely not going to let your whole life fall apart over a flat and a career move. There have to be better solutions.'

'If there are,' Liz said sadly, 'we didn't find them Friday, Saturday, *or* Sunday. We finished where we started. He's going and I'm staying. Finis.'

'But, Liz,' Moira's perplexity slipped into anger. 'You've been together for as long as I've known you. Whatever you like to pretend, you're as married as John and I. *Surely* you don't split up because of jobs and property . . . God, if *you* two split up, who's safe?'

Liz was quiet for a while and when she did answer, she began speaking very softly. 'I don't know, Moira. I thought *we* were safe until last Friday.' She gave a quick shake of her head, dipping tendrils of hair into the bubbles. 'Oh, we'd always agreed in theory we were free to separate . . . no wedding, no *children* which was what really mattered.' She paused. 'Theories are fine until you have to put them into practice. I'm finding the reality pretty hard to face.'

'Surely, so is Barry,' Moira said urgently.

'Oh, he *is*. He is.' She looked directly into Moira's eyes, her own tired and confused. 'He *really* didn't believe me when I refused to go. Well, I mean, I didn't believe him either at first. Around about Saturday evening, I realized he was really serious. Around about *Sunday* evening he finally realized I was too. It was a pretty bleak moment.' She looked quickly away. 'Oh the *arrogant* sod.'

'Barry?' Moira said cautiously. 'Oh surely not?'

Liz looked back. 'He *is* arrogant, Moira. Fun, and warm, and great to be with, but oh, can he be arrogant. Just to imagine I'd simply leave everything because *he* wanted to go. Do you know he actually inquired over there about the prospects for me. A job?'

'Did they offer one?'

'Oh yes. They really want him. Enough to throw in some sop for the liability he was going to drag along . . .'

'Liz, I'm *sure* it wasn't like that.'

'It felt like that.'

'I think you're being over-sensitive.'

Liz dropped her gaze to the bubbly water. 'Oh, maybe,' she said morosely. 'But how would you feel?' She sat up suddenly in the water. 'Suppose John wanted to shift you out of your house, move the kids out of their schools, and drag you off somewhere. You'd just go? Leave everything, your garden, your friends?'

Moira looked pained. 'We'd talk about it,' she said.

'We *have* talked about it. All bloody weekend.'

'We'd talk about it and we'd reach some compromise.'

'Great. Barry and I will compromise. We'll both get positions at the University of Reykjavik.'

'Liz, it hasn't all been roses with John and me. We've had our disagreements. God, he was on about it just a month ago. You know, the old Yorkshire thing.'

'But that's not serious.'

'What is the Yorkshire thing?' Erica said. She stood up and the water flowed fountain-like from her body. Turning, she resettled herself, stretching her legs out over two of the water jets with a sensual sigh.

'My husband has a fantasy that he wants to give up law in the City and be a country solicitor back up in Yorkshire.'

'But it *is* a fantasy,' Liz put in quickly.

'It's a fantasy because I *show* him it's a fantasy. And lucky for him I'm there to do it. That's the point, Liz. They all have these fantasies. Back to the country. Or emigrating to Australia or America. It's the way men cope with boredom. But it's not *real*. John would be miserable in Yorkshire. And,' she paused significantly, 'Barry will quite likely be miserable in America. It's your job to show him that. Don't just give in and let him ruin his life.'

Erica raised one leg out of the swirling water and stretched her long brown toes. 'Does he agree?' she said to Moira.

'Does who agree?'

'Your husband. Does he agree this is a fantasy?'

Moira looked irritated. 'Of course not. If he agreed, it wouldn't *be* a fantasy. He has to *believe* he wants it.'

'So it is only you saying he doesn't.' Erica slipped her damp headband off with one hand, shook out her wet curls, and replaced the headband.

Moira's irritation had turned to suspicion. 'So?'

'So how is that a compromise, if you always get your way?'

Moira stood up. She reached for her peach terry robe by the side of the jacuzzi and stepped out of the water. When she spoke her voice had taken on the authoritative tone she used in addressing her own teenagers. 'Quite frankly, Erica,' she said, 'these are things that come with experience. When you've been married as long as John and I have, you'll understand what I'm talking about. When I met John he had no idea what he wanted out of life. He *needed* someone to show him. Sometimes he still does.'

'He wanted to learn to ski,' Erica said. '*You* didn't. But he *did*.'

'No he didn't, Erica.' Moira was coldly final. 'You didn't understand any of that at all.'

Erica made a small shrug and smiled and before Moira could get really angry, Liz intervened. 'It doesn't matter,' she said. 'I know what you're saying, Moira, but it doesn't make any difference. I've been over all that ground with Barry and got nowhere. He really means to do this. If it's a fantasy, he's going to find out for himself. I can't stop him. He's never turned to me for direction and I've never turned to him. We've always just gone our own ways and, as luck had it, the paths converged. Only,' she paused, looking down at the water, 'now they don't.'

Moira had wrapped herself in the terry robe and was now stretched out on a beige lounger behind a potted fern. When she answered, after some time, her voice was sad. 'Really, Liz?'

'*Really.*'

Moira's next silence was even longer. She said with none

45

of the confidence she had used against Erica, 'Well, if that's really it, I think you've got to see sense.'

Liz twisted around, looking over her shoulder. Moira's head was ducked low, behind the fern. 'What sense?'

Moira turned on the lounger and raised herself up on one elbow, her chin in her other hand. 'You have to go, Liz. You haven't any choice.'

'What?'

'It's not as if it's the end of the world.' Moira was suddenly warmly encouraging. 'It *is* your country. And if the job's as good as Barry says, you'll have stacks of money. And,' she swung her legs off the lounger and sat up, 'if the worse comes to the worse and you both really hate it, you can always come back. Barry's really well thought of. He'll always get another job.'

'But what about me?' Liz said. 'What about my job? What about the book I'm in the middle of, and all my *British* research? And what about us, for God's sake? What about all my friends?'

'Barry will be leaving friends too,' Moira said doubtfully.

'Barry doesn't have friends,' Liz said. 'You know what men are like. They all get together in some pub once a week and drink a couple of pints and make a lot of inane jokes and talk about the rugby. That isn't friendship. They don't know what friendship is.' She got up from the jacuzzi. 'I'm cold. I'm going back in the sauna.'

Both Moira and Erica followed her. They didn't say anything under the shower, but as soon as they were back in the piney heat, Moira continued her pursuit.

'Friends are fine. Friends are really important. Friends don't give you someone to come home to at night.' She stretched out on her towel on her low bench. 'What are you going to do for sex?'

Liz narrowed her eyes. 'I'll get a dildo for the cat.'

'Ha, ha. And after the RSPCA catch up with you?'

'I can live without sex for a while.'

Erica suddenly laughed loudly. 'For all the sex I get from Andrew, he might as well *be* in America.' Liz and Moira both looked up, surprised. Erica responded by making a little deprecating shrug. 'He is busy,' she said. She gave another little shrug and looked down at her fingernails. 'Not in the beginning.' She sighed and rolled over on her back, wiping the sweat down her body with both hands. 'In the beginning it was *wonderful*.'

'Well,' Moira said briskly, 'it's *always* wonderful in the beginning. Nobody's honeymoon lasts for ever.'

Erica looked sad. 'Shouldn't it last a year?' she said. She looked from Moira to Liz, her face uncertain and young.

Liz studied her with her eyes widening into alertness. 'I always imagined you two having a terrific time.'

'We did at first. In Davos, where it started. And when I came to London. And after we were married, too.' She relaxed, remembering and laughing girlishly. 'Sometimes, in London, we would be all day in bed. You know, never dressed, just in maybe a towel when we went to the kitchen for coffee, or some yoghurt or a little smoked salmon.' Liz thought of Barry and suppressed a smile. 'Andrew would get a bottle of wine in an ice bucket and pretend to be a waiter, standing up on the bed, wearing a black bow tie.' She began to laugh louder. 'Only where he would *tie* the bow tie!' She shrieked gaily.

'*Andrew?*' Moira's smoothly pencilled eyebrows arced.

'Not at the weekends when the children came,' Erica said primly. 'No, no. Then everything was very proper.' She paused. 'But I did not mind that. No, then I was very happy. Then we were a family. I love the children very very much.'

'They *can* rather get in the way,' Moira said drily.

'But that is no matter. The children come first. That was not the problem.'

'Then what was?' Liz asked. She was lying on her stomach on her towel, feeling the heat soaking into her back and the sweat trickling down between her breasts. She propped her chin on her hands, studying Erica. Erica raised her shoulder blades and looked away.

'I think it was the book,' she said.

'You mean when he was working on it?' Liz thought of Barry making a friendly grab at her leg whenever she brought a cup of coffee to his desk. Work never inhibited *his* sex drive, anyhow.

'No,' Erica said. 'When he working, that was fun. It was exciting. But later. When it was published and everyone paid him so much attention. Then suddenly he was too busy. There were always parties, not fun parties like we had in Davos, but boring parties with everyone talking about politics with Andrew. And suddenly, he is always annoyed with me; my dress is too tight, or I laugh too much, or I forget someone's name who is very important. He treats me like a little girl and lectures me on how to behave.' She sat up suddenly, drawing her knees up. 'I know how to behave. My father is an important man also. When I am a little girl, already I am used to dressing well, and meeting famous people. So, maybe it is not exactly the same as in England, but why should that matter? In Switzerland when Andrew did something different from the way we do things, we did not lecture him. We said to ourselves, "So that is the English way." That is all.'

'It is also the English way to think they have a monopoly on good manners,' Liz said. 'Don't let it worry you.'

'But it does worry me, because then we fight and he does not make love to me.'

'Just when you fight?'

Again Erica looked away. 'There are other reasons. He is studying. Or there is an early train or airplane the next morning. Or he is preparing a lecture. And then, half of the time he is not home at all. He is in Brussels. Or Geneva.'

'Why don't you go with him?' Moira said.

'At first, I do. But then there are the parties and the stuffy people and I never get it right. So finally, one night in Paris, there is a big fight. He shouts at me because I talk with a Frenchman. And why shouldn't I? But no, Andrew wants me to talk to the old wife of a banker. Then I want to make love and he takes to bed his word-processor. And I stalk out and sleep on the couch in the next room. And in the morning he says I am stupid and childish.' She put her head down on her knees, her long, yoga-trained back folding gracefully. 'So I think, if he wants a stuffy old wife, why did he not keep the first one. Why marry me?' She paused and said, almost inaudibly, 'So then, when I go home, I get a job, this job, and I let him travel alone. And sometimes, when he travels, he brings me presents home and makes love to me all night. But mostly,' she sighed, 'he sets the alarm, and reads the *Guardian*, and goes to sleep.'

'*Anno Domini*,' said Moira. She set her lips firmly.

48

'What is that?' Erica looked up, puzzled.

'Age, my dear. The years are telling. If you're going to marry a man old enough to be your father, you have to expect a little rust in the machinery.'

'That is not true,' Erica said indignantly. 'Andrew is not an old man. He is just fifty. That is not old.' Moira raised her eyebrows and Erica urgently shook her yellow curls. 'My father is sixty-three and he has two mistresses. One French and one Italian.' She stopped and looked around to Liz and Moira who were both staring. She tilted her head philosophically. 'He and my mother do not get on,' she added to explain.

'I'm not surprised,' said Moira. She stood up, reaching for her robe. 'I'll die if I stay here any longer,' she said. At the door she turned and put on her Woman of Experience face. 'As your mother could no doubt tell you, Erica, marriage is *work*. Why do you think I'm in here pedalling my bum off three times a week? To keep myself beautiful and desirable so if he ever again does fetch up the energy to make love to a woman, it's damn certain going to be me.'

'Why should I worry about that?' Erica said, eyes widening. 'Andrew doesn't want *another* woman. He doesn't want any woman. He wants books, and arguments and computers.'

'*I* wouldn't let him go to Brussels alone,' said Moira. She looked in at Liz before she stepped out, '*Or* to America,' she said.

Liz and Erica looked at each other uncertainly, and then grabbed their robes and towels and followed Moira to the showers and back to the jacuzzi. As soon as Liz had settled and closed her eyes, Moira said, 'I'll bet he met a woman out there.'

'He did,' Liz grinned, without opening her eyes, imagining the look on Moira's face. 'She's six foot tall and races sled dogs. Her name's Elke.'

'Are you joking or what?'

'Moira, Barry isn't leaving me for sex. We have great sex. He's leaving because he wants a better job.'

There was a dull bang behind the tiled wall of the jacuzzi. Liz jerked upright and turned around. 'What the hell's that?' Moira shrugged.

Erica said, 'It is nothing. The jacuzzi in the men's suite is not working. Someone is fixing it.' Liz slid back into the water. Moira got out and dried herself and pulled on her bathrobe. She sank down on a lounger and then at once got up and went to the exercise bicycle that sat in the corner, climbed up and began languidly pedalling.

'Oh no,' said Erica. 'That is not good. First exercise, then sauna. No exercise after.' But Moira pedalled on, glancing morosely from time to time at her bare, rounded thighs.

'You're going to really *miss* all that great sex,' she said to Liz. 'I mean it. You're a woman who likes sex.'

'So I'll *find* sex if I need it, OK?'

'Where?'

'Piccadilly Circus, for Christ's sake. I'll stand in front of Eros swinging my handbag. Jesus, Moira, you're doing my ego rafts of good.'

'You're not a casual sex person.'

Liz sat up. She leaned forward so the tips of her breasts brushed the water. '*Nobody's* a casual sex person any more. It still doesn't preclude forming relationships.'

'*With whom?*' Moira persisted.

Liz brushed a frustrated hand back over her forehead. 'Look, do you mind if I wait until Barry's at the airport before I get out my address book?'

'If you have an address book like mine, every man's name in it will have a woman's written beside it. Unless of course, it has a man's.'

'What are you getting at?'

Moira stopped pedalling. 'If you let Barry go, you'll spend the rest of your life alone. You're not going to find what you had with Barry. Not at our age. Not any more.'

'Crap. People divorce. People remarry. Look at Andrew. He just did.'

'Andrew's a man. And he didn't, you notice, marry another fifty-year-old. He went out and found a younger woman instead. Andrew proves my point, Liz, not yours.'

'Then,' said Liz, sinking back into the bubbles, 'I'll find a younger man.' She smiled to herself. 'I think I'll start with Stephen Lloyd.'

'*Stephen Lloyd,*' Moira said loudly.

'Who is Stephen Lloyd?' Erica asked.

'A colleague. Lecturer in African studies.'

'He is black?' Erica said curiously. Liz shook her head.

'*Stephen Lloyd*,' Moira said again. She stopped pedalling and glared at Liz.

'He's single.'

'I should hope so. He's barely out of nappies.'

'Oh come on, Moira.'

'He's about twenty-five.'

'He's twenty-six actually,' said Liz.

'Wonderful.'

'Yes.' Liz sat up and looked accusingly across at Moira on her stalled bike. 'It *does* sound wonderful. He's six foot two, brilliant, and looks like Michael Ignatieff. I've had the hots for him ever since he came to UCL.'

Moira drew her terry robe closed in as prim a gesture as she could make sitting half naked on an exercise bike.

'Does Barry know?' she whispered.

'Yeah sure. I come home every night and say "Pardon my wet knickers, I've been talking to Stephen Lloyd." Moira, can you ever believe people can experience a sexual attraction without acting on it? What did it matter if I fancied the bloke? Why should Barry know? I wasn't going to do anything.'

'But you are now.'

Liz leaned back against the tiled wall. The banging and thumping had begun again and she was tempted to thump the wall in return. 'I wish they'd cut that out,' she said, then added, 'I might. I hadn't really thought about it until this exact moment, but I might. All I was saying, Moira, is that a younger man can be an attractive proposition. I'd think you'd approve. You've just been declaring *older* men a sexual disaster area. Even *John* if I can believe you.'

'John works too hard,' Moira defended. 'He needs a holiday.'

'He needs to get fit,' Erica said.

'Rubbish,' Moira said. 'He needs a good long rest. Then maybe he'd get some energy back . . .'

'Fitness builds energy,' said Erica.

'Oh you. You're a fanatic. Just because you teach yoga, and aerobics and bloody ski you think everyone has to.'

'She's right,' said Liz. Moira looked wounded, but she continued. 'Exercise *does* help. As long as you don't go

51

overboard and run marathons every other weekend. It stands to reason. If you're fit you have more stamina. *Every*where.'

Moira looked disapproving, but she wasn't inclined to dismiss Liz the way she dismissed Erica. She said, 'Oh, I suppose so. But it isn't really a *physical* problem. He's overworked. He really is. That's what it's like if you're going to get on these days. He's *mentally* exhausted. He needs to relax, not dash about a squash court or whatever. I'd be afraid he'd have a coronary.'

'Why should he have a coronary?' Erica said. 'He is a young man. An hour a week of yoga and he would learn to relax and who knows?' She shrugged and looked uninterested, but her eyes were sparkly.

'And I suppose you're the one to teach him,' said Moira. She got off the exercise bike and settled herself on the tiled edge of the jacuzzi.

'It doesn't have to be me,' Erica said politely. She drew her knees up under the water and linked her arms around them innocently.

Moira stood up. 'Oh go on. You try. I'll send him in on Thursday. Only don't tie him in some inextricable knot the first day. He really has no aptitude for physical things. He never has had.'

Liz laughed softly.

'What's funny?' Moira snapped.

'You two. You're funny. You're like a couple of teenagers, all suspicion and jealousy.'

'I am not jealous,' said Erica indignantly.

'Nor I.' Moira looked imperious. 'You should talk. Teenagers. What about you, chasing after toyboys in African Studies?'

Liz laughed again, got up from the water and began to dry herself. Erica looked at her watch and rose from the jacuzzi as well.

Liz slipped into her robe. 'I'm really not about to leap in the sack with Stephen Lloyd. He was just an example.'

'Of what?'

'Of the "talent", as Darren would say. What's available in the sexual marketplace. And I don't honestly see,' she said looking once at Erica, 'why a younger man should be such an outrageous idea. Younger *women* have been in fashion for ever. Nobody jumped all over Andrew for marrying Erica.' Moira looked pained. 'Well, *did* they?'

'Well . . .' Moira's voice trailed.

'I do not mind you talking about me,' Erica said calmly. 'I know some people are a little shocked. But they get over it. Age is not important.'

'Then you agree with me,' Liz said.

Erica paused. She reached into her toiletries bag and withdrew her shampoo. Then, stepping under the shower and wetting her hair she said, 'Younger men are sometimes very stupid.' Before Liz could argue, she went on, 'When I am skiing in Davos, I know many, many young men. Beautiful young men. Beautiful bodies. Why not? All they do is ski all day. And in the summer, when they are done skiing on the glacier, they go windsurfing. Beautiful brown bodies. All muscles, broad shoulders,' she made a gesture with her hands indicating breadth, 'flat stomachs,' she patted her own, 'and here,' she laid her hand comfortably on her groin, 'here they are marvellous.' She turned away, splashed shampoo on her hands and massaged it into her wet hair. 'But *here*,' she held her hands one on either side of her head, 'here nothing. Empty. Nothing at all. *So*,' she scrubbed vigorously at her soapy curls. 'So, you make love, and you make love, and you make love. But eventually, *some* time, you must stop. And when you stop, you talk. Or you want to talk. And then, *nothing*. They tell you all the races they won. Which you know already. And how they won them. Every detail. Then they tell you all the beer they drank. All the women who loved them. And always, all the times they puked out the window or on the bed. That is romance? That is love?' She shrugged, sending cascades of shampoo on to the tiled floor. 'That is younger men.'

'That "make love and make love and make love" doesn't sound so bad,' Liz said cannily.

Erica looked sad. 'No. It was very nice. But I still want someone to talk to.' She looked at Liz with the slight awe in which she held her apparent on her face. 'And I am just a little Swiss girl who teaches in the ski school. But you! You are so educated, so intelligent . . .'

Liz laughed loudly, cutting her off. 'Oh hardly,' she said.

'Erica's right,' said Moira. 'You can't spend your whole life in bed. You'd be bored out of your head.'

'I doubt Stephen Lloyd would be boring, in bed or out of it, but even if he was just a little gauche or naïve, why should he stay like that? We're all a bit gauche when we're young. We all mature.'

'How long are you willing to wait?'

'Who says I have to wait? All that makes sophistication is experience. I can *give* him that. I'll *teach* him. That's my job, isn't it?' She grinned devilishly. 'Moulding young minds. Erica shapes bodies. I shape minds.' She laughed. 'We should go into business. Frankenstein Inc. The man of your choice, made to order.' Moira made a little suppressed snort and then burst out laughing. Erica joined her, giggling and then laughing so raucously that neither of them heard the knock on the outside door.

Liz said, 'Shh. There's someone there.'

The knock came again, three loud raps and then a male voice called hesitantly, 'Ladies? Can I come in? I have tae fix something.'

'Darren,' said Erica. Moira pulled her terry-cloth robe tight. Liz put down the hairbrush she had withdrawn from her sports bag. Erica said, 'Fine, Darren. Come on.'

'Erica!' Moira's eyes went round. Erica stepped out of the shower.

'You're not dressed,' Moira whispered.

Erica said, 'It's only Darren.' She picked up her robe, slipped casually into it and smiled, 'Better?'

Moira nodded vigorously towards her untied belt as Darren, in a grey boilersuit and carrying a big blue metal toolbox, stepped warily through the door. Erica made an easy loose loop of the terry-cloth belt around her waist. She sat down on a wooden bench beside the showers.

'Hi, Darren,' she said. He ducked his head and grunted something, and walked, eyes straight ahead, to the wall beside the jacuzzi. Moira settled on a lounger and Liz perched on the seat of the exercise bike, her legs dangling. They watched him as he removed a neat panel and began clanking actively among the exposed pipes behind.

Liz was startled to see a reddening blush creep across his

54

neck, up to the shaven hairline. She stood up. 'Come on, girls, let's sit down here.' She walked deliberately around the corner to the cluster of wicker armchairs and low tables at the far end of the sauna suite. She sat down, and pretended interest in a magazine until Moira and Erica joined her. 'We're terrifying the poor kid,' she whispered. 'Give him a break.' Dutifully they picked up magazines too, and glanced only occasionally in Darren's direction until he closed up the panel, dropped his tools hastily back into the metal box, and stood up.

'That's me done,' he said, and backed quickly to the door, stumbling into it and clattering clumsily through, toolbox in hand. After a momentary silence they looked from the door, to each other, and collapsed in fits of giggles.

'Daniel in the lion's den,' Moira cried. 'Oh the poor lamb.'

'He is Darren, not Daniel,' said Erica, but Moira did not stop to explain. Instead she said loudly, 'Well, there you are, Liz. There's the first job for Frankenstein Inc.'

'Darren?' cried Erica.

'Sure. What about it, Liz? He's a younger man, after all. Maybe just a *little* gauche, but I'm sure he's hot stuff in the sack.'

'Liz did not mean a young man like Darren,' Erica said.

'Why not?' said Liz.

Moira and Erica looked up together. Liz was brushing her hair again, thoughtfully, and her wide brown eyes had taken on their look of academic curiosity that preceded debate. 'Why not Darren?'

Moira paused, looked straight at her and said, 'Because he's thick as a brick.'

'He's not thick,' said Liz.

'Oh come on.'

'He's uneducated. He's not thick.' Liz paused, but before Moira could answer she went on. 'I know young people, Moira. He's bright enough. Look how different he is from when he came here. He can talk, for a start. Usually. I mean, you can hardly expect scintillating conversation from a kid that age in a room full of half-naked older women. But he's all right. I could do something with him.'

'With the best will in the world, Liz, that was not the stuff of great lovers just then.' Moira began massaging Body Shop

55

cocoa butter lotion into the skin of her calves. 'He looks a fright.'

'He is handsome,' said Erica. 'The hair and the earring are silly, but beneath, he is handsome.'

'I think so too,' Liz said mildly. 'But it doesn't matter. That isn't what we're talking about. Companionship. Right? Someone you can talk with, go out with, be friends with, *and* make love to . . .'

'*Darren?*' said Moira.

'Sure. Give me Darren for six months and I'll give you a perfectly presentable lover. Only you better square it with John first.'

'You're not serious.'

Liz laughed richly. 'Of course not, you twit.' She finished brushing her hair and lingered a moment with it on her shoulders. With her spread fingers, she pushed it up from the back of her bare neck, and trailed it slowly outwards. 'I'll tell you something, though. In another world, he might not be half bad.'

IV

The flat looked derelict. There were dusty holes in the bookcase where Barry's books had been removed, and pockets among the neat rows of tapes by the stereo. The records lay in a slithery picked-over heap, and on the walls three faded oblongs showed where his favourite prints had hung. In the centre of the living-room two large leather cases and a battered Gladstone bag held the more immediate essentials of his life. The rest, in bubble plastic and newspaper, was already entrunked and in transit, somewhere between London and Wisconsin.

'Barry?' Liz called. There was silence from the bedroom. 'Barry, it's getting seriously late for this flight.' There was still no answer and Liz, in winter coat, and with the car keys in her hand, sighed and settled down on the edge of one of the suitcases.

The flat was depressing, even without the signs of his departure. No one had found time to clean it in the preceding weeks, and the detritus of Christmas yet remained: brown pine needles prickled the carpet in the corner by the window, a stack of Christmas cards from once-a-year correspondents sat on the bookshelf requiring answers. A solitary silver ball stolen off the tree by the cats lurked under the sofa. On the mantel a small heap of trinkets from the Christmas crackers vainly awaited some child's fortuitous arival. Moira's children had always served in the past, but quite suddenly they had become adolescents with no interest in miniature water pistols, fortune-telling fish, and frogs that jumped at the squeeze of a rubber bulb. The absence of children at this Christmas preyed on Liz's mind, like an ill omen.

She got up from the suitcase and stood by the mantel, moodily piling up the heap of cracker toys, marking the dust with her fingers. She turned away, and stood studying the gaps in the bookcases. Leaning forward, she picked out a Penguin paperback.

'Barry,' she called. 'You've forgotten your Thomas Hardys.' There was still silence and she called louder, 'Barry, did you hear me?'

'I haven't forgotten them. I left them for you. You always liked to read them.' His voice, muffled by the closed bedroom door, sounded remote.

'They're yours.'

'You had *Tess* out the other day.'

'I was just looking at it. If I want to read *Tess* I can buy a copy.'

'Well, so can I. I don't have to take *every* book I own.'

'I want you to have your stuff.'

'I know, Liz.' There was something immobile about his voice.

She said, 'Are you *ready*, Barry? The traffic will be appalling.' He did not answer and she turned from the bookcase, laid the paperback on top of his Gladstone bag, and walked to the bedroom door.

'All right if I come in?'

'Sure.'

Barry was sitting on the edge of their bed, in his corduroy trousers and an open-collared shirt and pullover. He wore no jacket and his glasses were sitting on the bedside table beside his unzipped toiletries bag. The brown cat, Jacob, was curled up asleep on his knee.

'*Barry*. You're going to miss this flight.'

'I don't want to leave my cat. He settled on my knee. I don't want to push him off.'

Liz looked from him to the waiting suitcases outside the door, and then glanced in exasperation at her watch. She picked up the cat and dumped it unceremoniously on the bed. 'He's off now. He's my cat anyhow.'

Barry still didn't move. He said in a hurt voice, 'No he's not. Esau is yours. Jacob is mine.'

'They're *both* mine now. Come *on*, Barry, I don't want to

drive like a maniac to Heathrow.'

'Jacob's mine.'

'Right.' Liz picked up the toiletries bag and zipped it. 'I'll box him up and ship him over.' She paused as he slowly got to his feet. 'This is a bit rich, Barry. A while ago you were suggesting I just dump them on some hapless friend and come with you.'

Barry stopped half-way through pulling on a brown tweed jacket. He said stiffly, 'I never said "dump them", Liz. I said "a good home".'

'Same difference.' She turned at the doorway and saw he had picked up the cat again, and held it possessively against his chest. 'So drop the bloody sentiment, Barry. It's not as if you're really committed to them.' The cat wiggled to be free and after resisting a moment Barry reluctantly set it down again on the bed. This time it bolted underneath.

'Committed? Christ, Liz. They're animals. As long as they're well cared for, it doesn't really matter who . . .'

'It matters to me. They're my cats and I love them. You don't know what commitment means. You never have.'

Barry stopped. He put his glasses on and stared through them, his mouth opening in outrage. 'That's not fair.'

Liz turned away. She stuffed the toiletries and the Thomas Hardy novel into the Gladstone bag, closed the zip, and straightened up. 'I'm not going to argue. If you want to get *on* this flight, we're leaving now.'

In the car, Barry sat hunched up against the passenger door, the Gladstone bag at his feet, looking morose. Liz adjusted her mirror and then edged the car out of its parking bay, past the big white Volvo estate which habitually invaded three feet of their space. Its owner resided in the ground floor flat of their own building, but they knew him only as an automotive nuisance.

'You won't miss that, anyhow,' she said. Barry said nothing. Liz scraped past the Volvo and into the street, drastically narrowed by its double border of parked cars. She glanced instinctively up at the house they had just left, the end of a terrace of three-storey brick buildings, fronting directly on the street, doors and window-frames trimmed in white. Three windows delineated their top floor flat: two square ones – their living-room – and an arched window providing their bathroom with an incongruous street view. It was a sloppy conversion; not a great flat. They had bought it a little reluctantly, with the intention of soon finding something better. But they had settled, got comfortable, and never got around to moving on. They'd lived there eight years, half the time they'd been together. With the street it was set in, and those around, it made up the ordinary fabric of their lives. As Liz drove away she realized with a jolt that tonight she would return to it alone.

She stopped at the traffic light at the corner and looked around at the little cluster of shops; the Pakistani grocery where they bought their paper and late-night bottles of wine; Mario's, saviour of her baking reputation; the flower shop which in summer graced the pavement with potted shrubs. Down the street was the nondescript little restaurant that served great French food, in which they had been sitting with Moira and John when Barry announced he'd found a publisher for his book on Thomas Hardy. She imagined herself in Barry's place, leaving it all behind. She glanced across. He was staring at the Gladstone bag between his feet.

'We're really late,' she said, irritated by his lack of interest. She looked more seriously at him and said suddenly, 'What's that you're *wearing*?'

'What?' He looked at himself blankly.

'That jacket. Why are you wearing that jacket?'

'It feels comfortable.'

'It's ancient. I gave it to you for Christmas our last year at Cambridge. It's *antique*.'

'It's comfortable.' The light changed. Liz moved off. She glanced once more in his direction.

'Well if you want to look the tweedy English eccentric, you're well on the way.'

Barry looked at the bag at his feet. 'I don't care what I look like,' he said.

Liz sighed. 'God, Barry,' she said eventually. 'No one would guess this was your idea.'

He looked out of the window, and said softly, 'It's not exactly the way I envisioned it.'

Liz's shoulders tightened. She glanced quickly to left and

right and said brightly, as if he had not spoken, 'Take a last look at home.'

Barry turned to face her. 'Liz, I'm not being *transported*. I'm a seven-hour flight away. I'll be back all the time.'

'I'm a six-hour flight from New York. How often do I go back?'

'That's you,' he said. He refused to look but sat staring moodily at her instead.

At Heathrow they found his flight delayed an hour and a half.

'I could have sat with my cat,' Barry said.

They checked in his luggage and resignedly found seats in the departure lounge, directly under an uncompromising warning about unattended luggage. They put the Gladstone bag loyally between their feet and watched as two security officers walked by cradling sub-machine guns. 'And you people complain about New York,' Liz said.

'I'd rather have them than not have them,' Barry answered. 'Anyhow, there's a war on, old girl.' He looked at his watch and at a large and prominent wall clock and said, 'Or there's going to be next week. Maybe you should just go. This *isn't* the nicest place to sit around these days.'

'And hear you've been blown up on the car radio? I'd never forgive myself, Barry.' He smiled and she added, 'Besides, I always assume friends' planes will crash if I don't personally see them off.'

'In that case, do stay,' he said. 'You're such cheerful company anyhow.' She grinned, and looked around curiously at the crowds seated, standing and milling about. A large Asian family joined them on their row of seats, several men in dark suits, a cluster of women in brilliant saris, winter coats and fur-trimmed western boots. Two dark children in blue, purple and green shell-suits and Mutant-Turtle T-shirts ran around them shouting in Lancastrian accents.

Liz said, 'Barry, that Middle-Eastern-looking man has just left that briefcase.'

Barry looked up. 'He's left it with his wife. She's sitting right there.'

'Who? That woman? How do you know she's his wife?'

61

'They came in together. She just gave him some change out of her handbag, and he's over there making a phone call. If you'd like I'll go and ask to see their marriage lines.'

'No,' Liz said, as the man returned and took his seat again. 'I guess they're all right. I wonder if he's going on your plane?'

'Undoubtedly. And that chap over there who looks like Saddam Hussein's probably going too. *But*,' Barry leaned conspiratorially closer and whispered, 'the ones to watch are these two little guys in the T-shirts.' He nodded towards the two Lancastrians. 'I need hardly tell a woman of your education that Mutant Turtles are of course the acknowledged symbol of an ancient order of Iraqi bandit kings . . .'

She shoved his arm, laughing and said, 'I'll get us a coffee. You like a coffee?'

'Yeah, sure.'

She went off and returned with polystyrene cups from a machine. He was sitting, knees apart, head down over the bag between his feet, as morose as before. She sighed lightly, handed him his cup and said, 'Somehow, after seventeen years, I'm finding this last ninety minutes hard to take.'

Barry looked down again, over his big hands surrounding the small coffee cup. He said, 'You'll be late for dinner with Moira. Maybe you should just go.'

'No I won't,' Liz said brightly. 'I'll just go straight there. I was only going back to the flat to change and in to the department for a moment to pick up my mail and check out my ad.'

'Any replies?' he asked curiously.

'One. A second-year girl. Good student, but too shy. She won't cope with interviews. She says she will but she won't. She's fine as long as it's books in the library or old bones in the British Museum. People terrify her. This is social anthropology with the emphasis on the *social*. I'll need someone else.' She paused. 'Someone will turn up. I've got the ad up everywhere: Union, refectories, library. Bound to find someone.'

'I'm sorry, Liz.' She looked up. He said, 'I know you were counting on me to help.'

Her eyes were wide and honest on his own. 'No I wasn't, Barry. This was my project, I wasn't expecting you to help.' She paused and smiled slightly, 'Anyhow, you're too old.'

'Thanks.'

'No. I mean it. I'm too old too. I want a young person. A research assistant who can blend into the scene. That's who the kids will talk to. They won't talk to me and they certainly wouldn't talk to you.' Barry still looked hurt. Liz said again, 'I never thought, or expected, or *wanted* you to help me with this book. I just wanted a little moral support. A little return for what I maybe gave you over *your* projects.' He looked miserable, not inclined to fight. Liz said gently, 'I don't blame you for going. I certainly don't blame you for wanting to advance your career. The only thing I blame you for is the arrogant assumption that I would drop everything else in my life and go with you.'

Barry hung his head over his coffee cup. He said slowly, 'Liz, I honestly, *honestly* thought I was doing you a favour. I thought I was taking you home.'

Liz sat up straighter. She said, after a long silence, 'I'm willing to believe you convinced yourself of that.'

He raised his head to reply, and she quickly touched his knee. 'Barry, that Middle-Eastern-looking man has walked back and forth around that litter bin for ten minutes.'

'The one with the briefcase?' He looked to where Liz was watching with narrowed eyes.

'No. Another one. Look at him.'

'Maybe he's nervous,' Barry said.

'Maybe he's going to plant a bomb.'

Barry sighed. 'I hope you find your research assistant, Liz. You've a very good idea there. It will make a good book.'

'Don't condescend to me.'

His eyes brightened behind his glasses and for a moment he cast off the gloom in which he had wrapped himself. 'It's going to do you good,' he said loudly, 'to work on this project without me there to blame whenever things go wrong. That's half your problem, resenting me. The other half is your bloody inferiority complex about every damned thing.'

Liz tightened her grip on his knee. 'He's just dropped something in.'

'It's a *litter bin*, Liz.'

'Maybe we should tell someone.'

'Liz, he's still walking in circles around it. What's he doing, waiting for it to go off?'

'Maybe he's a crazy. He looks like a crazy. Look. He keeps

jumping around. Ask him what he's doing, Barry.'

'Liz.'

'Be a good citizen. Don't let him just blow up Heathrow.'

Barry held up his hands, palms forward, shaking his head. 'No,' he said. 'I'd feel a complete fool.'

'You British,' Liz said. 'You'd rather be blown up than embarrassed.' She stood up. 'I'll do it.'

'No.' Barry stood up quickly as well, and motioned her back. 'I'll do it.' He walked warily across the polished floor, and approached the man with one hunched shoulder forward, and a placatingly extended arm. He spoke briefly, as did the man, and then speech dissolved in a series of hand gestures, some of them peculiar. Abruptly the man turned and ran off.

'See,' Liz said, as Barry returned. 'Now he's bolted.'

Barry sat down and stretched out his legs either side of the Gladstone bag. He slipped his hands into the pockets of his tweed jacket and smiled within his beard. 'He's Bulgarian. Hasn't a scrap of English. Or French or German or any other language, I gather. And he was desperate for a pee. I pointed the way. Happy?'

Liz stared after the retreating man. 'There are international symbols,' she said tartly.

'Apparently obscure to a Bulgarian.'

'He *could* have had a bomb,' said Liz.

'My God, you hate to admit you're wrong.' She said nothing. Barry looked at his watch.

'You've got half an hour,' she said. He took out his ticket folder, checked it and returned it to his inside jacket pocket. He looked at his watch again, and the big clock on the wall.

'Oh, look, don't forget,' he said suddenly, 'the car needs a service. And get them to check that noise at the back.'

'I'll probably sell it,' Liz said.

'Sell it?'

'It's a nuisance in London. I'll use the train when I want to go anywhere.' Barry looked uneasy.

'You'll miss it. We've always had a car.'

'No I won't. I'll send you your half.'

Barry turned slowly to face her and lightly touched her arm with his fingers. He said clearly, 'Liz, I don't want any halves.

Not the car. Not the flat. Nothing. The least I can do is leave you the fabric of life.'

'Fair's fair. You'll get your half.'

'Stop being so bloody piggishly proud.'

'I don't need you to set up my life. I've got a job. I earn good money. Not as *much* as you, maybe . . .' A cold silence fell. They looked at each other bitterly and then Liz turned away. 'I have everything I need. My home. My work. My pets. And most of all, my friends. I can't believe,' she said slowly, 'that you thought I'd leave my friends.'

'You'd have made new friends,' Barry said. He was suddenly distant and calm.

Liz gave him a quizzical look and then said, equally calm, 'When I was a kid, my parents said that to me every time we moved. We moved all the time. Each time, I was *bereaved*.'

'Your father *had* to move. It was his work.'

'The great and implacable god.'

'Anyhow,' Barry said, 'you did make new friends.' He paused. 'If you hadn't come here in the first place, *moved* here, you wouldn't even *know* Moira.'

'There's a time for that,' Liz said quietly, 'for starting out and making your adult friends. When you're young. You can't keep doing it for ever. I won't find another friend like Moira.'

'Sometimes you don't even *like* her. You find her pompous and a snob. Admit it.'

'But I *love* her, anyway, Barry. Men are pathetic.' She looked away, as gloomy now as he had been.

He said cheerily, 'It *was* nice of her to ask you to dinner.'

'Nice?' Liz looked back. 'I suppose so. She owes me two actually.'

'I mean tonight. It was nice of her to think of it.'

'Oh, to comfort me in my abandonment. Yes, of course. Moira's got a whole slew of lame ducks. I suppose now I'll be one of them.'

Barry looked askance. 'Moira's hardly going to regard *you* as a lame duck.'

'Moira considers all single people lame ducks. I'll give you odds there'll be a spare man across the table.' She paused, her eyes narrowing. 'And if there is, I'll bloody kill her.'

Barry's expression drifted between immediate shock and

growing ill-ease. He said, 'Oh surely Moira would *never* do that.'

Liz raised an eyebrow and started to answer but an electronic chime interrupted and a female voice began an announcement that was drowned immediately by an uproar among the Indian family. Barry and Liz strained to hear over the shouts of Mutant Turtles.

'That's it,' Liz said.

'That's my flight.'

They got up from their enclave of seats, stumbling over each other in illogical hurry, both reaching for the Gladstone bag. Their hands met on the handle and they both dropped it. 'Liz,' said Barry.

'Right,' Liz said, checking his luggage tags with sudden urgency. 'Got everything? Passport? Tickets? Travellers' cheques.' She kept her head down over the case.

'Liz.'

'No time, Barry.' She lifted the case, and headed towards the departure gate, not looking at him. He caught up. He reached to take the case and she said, 'Barry, what about your duty free? Are you going to want duty free, or what?' He took the case out of her hand and set it on the floor. With both hands he reached for her shoulders. 'You're leaving it unattended, Barry. You can't leave it unattended.'

'Liz, there's something I have to say.'

Liz looked around him, at the case, her eyes darting reluctantly back, meeting his, and darting away. 'What's that, then?'

'You know that story about Elke?'

'*What?*'

'Elke the Laplander. That story. It wasn't true, Liz.' He paused, took a deep breath and swallowed. 'I mean, it wasn't quite the way I told it.'

She didn't watch his flight off. She meant to, but could find nowhere security-free from which to do so, and there was too great a muddle of aircraft to tell one from another anyhow. She made her way back through the lounge and glanced back at the two seats where they had spent their hour and a half. The Mutant Turtles had taken over. They grinned, bright white smiles in smoky faces, pointing red plastic guns.

It was raining when she got back to the car park. The air reeked of kerosene and huge aircraft rumbled overhead like punctual buses. 'Bye, Barry,' she said, to the general mass of them. She got in the car, turned the key and switched on the wipers. An oily smear of cold rain spread in an arc, filled, cleared, refilled. The sky was murky. She thought suddenly of the bright clear light of the American winter to which Barry rode on thunderous steel wings. For two insane seconds she was homesick.

The drive helped; her favourite tape on the deck, the invigoration of concentration, the fun of pushing the nippy little car a little too hard. She reminded herself she intended to sell it, and then, a little guiltily, put the thought to the back of her mind. She'd sell it in the spring. Winter was a bad time to sell cars anyhow.

She skirted London on the ring road and slipped easily into the Hertfordshire turn-off. A few more miles of urban-shark driving and then, quite suddenly, she was off the motorway, off the lesser dual carriageway, and on to a real road with a line down the middle and hedges at the sides. England, vanquished by concrete and tarmac suddenly reformed itself, timeless and beautiful.

She passed a tourist brochure church, Norman-towered, a jumble of red-brick tile-roofed cottages, an old estate spreading its clusters of fine old trees among the flat, winter yellowed fields. She drove instinctively, following a familiar route she could not, if pressed, describe. There was a row of poplars, a willow-lined river; the landscape conjuring old memories of cycling out from Cambridge with Barry when her English experience was young and romantic. The memory ached a little and then was jarringly shattered by an ugly, concrete and mud strewn building site, a line of completed, bald-looking new houses. Even here there was change and encroachment. She came unexpectedly upon the narrow arched bridge that was her landmark for the turn to Moira's converted farmhouse. The building site had undone her personal map. She slowed, took the bridge gently, swooping up and over its humped back. Beneath was a millrace and a solitary, cold-looking swan. A hundred yards further on were the twin red-brick pillars at the start of Moira's long drive. Moira had added the pillars with their black cast-iron lanterns and the black iron gates, and changed the house name from 'The Piggeries', to which the adjacent leased-out pig farm attested accuracy, to 'The Oaks', which were, unfortunately, conspicuous by their absence, the two old sentinels at the roadside having been felled to make room for the pillars. It was the sort of inconsistency that Moira handled with ease.

She was actually a superb, if unsentimental, gardener, and in the fourteen years of her occupation had totally recreated the environs of The Piggeries. In doing so, she had destroyed something charming and created something magnificent. The process was continuous and evolutionary; nothing in Moira's domain was guaranteed permanence. Even as friends sighed and applauded some new innovation, Moira was as likely planning its demise. Her tenure at the old farmhouse had reflected the changing mood and styles of the country and on its soil and shrubbery she worked out a social history in microcosm. In the fecund seventies, surrounded by babies and toddlers, she presided over half an acre of market garden: soft fruit, vegetables; apple, plum and pear trees. The children had grown; a tennis court had sprouted in the erstwhile cabbage patch. The good-life goat was replaced by rosetted ponies. As John's income expanded and his social life increased in sophistication, table flowers ousted the organic tomatoes in the greenhouse, and a sundial and herb garden replaced the potatoes. The vegetation narrowed to the more subtle and favoured delicacies of asparagus, celeriac, and mange-tout, and, briefly and unsuccessfully, wine grapes. Lawns and obscure old-fashioned roses expanded in the late eighties, and now, Moira moved ambitiously into the nineties with a dauntingly geometric parterre and, in front of the new Victorian conservatory, a miniature maze of Elizabethan box.

'The grandchildren will enjoy it,' Moira said, showing Liz around its foundations one chilly autumn day. She and Barry had laughed at Moira's pretensions to dynasty, but now, driving alone up the gravelled drive to the brick farmhouse, Liz felt suddenly rootless and envious and sad.

At the last bend in the drive, with the paddock and stable

on her right, she met a tall figure in grey sweats and a blue and white striped headband, jogging quickly up from the dusk of the stableyard. She stared a moment, then stopped the car, leaned over and rolled down the passenger window, and shouted, *'John?'*

The jogging steps slowed and then stumbled to a halt. He stood catching his breath and peering blearily at the car.

'Oh Liz. It's you. I didn't expect you yet,' he said in sharp bursts between intakes of breath. He shambled across to the car and leant heavily on the roof.

'You *all right*, John?' Liz said.

'Fine. Fine.' He looked down into the window and grinned weakly, wiping sweat off his chin. 'Mile and a half,' he said.

'You've just run a mile and a half?'

'Up the back lane to the Smythe-Hamilton's gate and then back and twice around the paddock.' He looked proud.

'You sure this is a good idea?' Liz said warily. John straightened up, drawing in his stomach and pulling up the waistband of his jogsuit.

'Sure. Why not?'

'You're not,' she paused, 'maybe *pushing* it a little?'

'Pushing it? A mile and a half. Good God, Liz, I should be able to run a mile and a half. I'm a young man.' He stepped back, removed his sweatband, brushed back his hair, and replaced the band neatly.

'You've been to Erica,' said Liz. He looked surprised, and then slightly offended.

'I've been doing some yoga,' he said evenly. 'The running is my own thing,' he added. 'Thought I needed something aerobic.'

'Aerobic.'

'Sure. Hey, why all the interrogation? You and Barry run. Why shouldn't I?'

'No, no of course, John. Great idea. Great.'

He looked mollified and then, obviously remembering, said, 'Oh, so that's Barry off then?' He sounded lame.

'Yeah,' Liz heard herself equally lame, 'that's him off.'

They looked at each other in silence, and then John tapped the roof of the car. 'Great, well, I'll just cool down a bit, and shower, and be in to join you. Moira's probably in the kitchen . . .'

'I'll find her,' Liz said. She rolled up the window and drove on. In her mirror she saw him jogging very slowly up the drive behind her.

The Piggeries/Oaks was a very pretty house. Red brick, with many-paned windows, a long sloping roof, crenellated chimney breasts and buff chimney pots; it had quirky attractive features added by numerous occupants over a couple of hundred years. A period double garage was attached at the left. There was a funny little extension to the right that contained but a single bedroom. The peak-roofed porch was tile-floored and large enough to hold two long benches plus the usual hall-stands and coat-racks. Hidden from view, as Liz parked in the semi-circle gravel drive, was Moira's addition, the large and luxurious conservatory that flanked much of the sunny southern wall.

Inside, the house had the low ceilings of genuinely old country properties, and a charmingly rickety staircase. Rooms were furnished in English chintzes or French Provençal prints and looked as if they awaited the *House and Gardens'* photographer imminently. Moira somehow managed to leave just the right wool scarf or straw hat, the perfect wicker flower basket, the appropriate Hunter wellies lying about. Even the children had inherited the knack; draping schoolbags and blazers decoratively over banisters, and leaving riding hats and crops ideally arranged in the hall.

Liz walked lightly in the open outer door, pushed open the interior one, and glancing once into the drawing-room and finding it empty, made her way down the dark polished corridor to the kitchen. The kitchen was modern. The Piggeries had presented Moira with a lean-to scullery which carried authenticity one step too far and her first act had been some major reconstruction: the removal of several walls (and the hasty replacement of one, found to be a retainer), and the creation of a totally new kitchen superbly decorated to look older than the original. Last year, however, Moira had declared the once beloved stripped-pine fittings *passé*, and they had been replaced with free-standing dressers, tables, and workbenches, hand-painted in shaded oyster and delicate pink.

Liz could not deny the effect was enchanting, though the

thought of John Harris's mortgage sometimes sent chills down her spine. Moira's response to her financial concern was unrepentant: 'This house is my showroom. It pays its keep.' And indeed, it was from the wide circle of friends and acquaintances who passed through The Oaks on social occasions that she drew much of her interior decorating clientele.

'Oh darling, you've made it,' Moira said, turning to greet her. 'I *am* glad.' She slung her oyster and pink kettle under the tap, filling it noisily. 'We can have a private cup of tea before anyone arrives.' Liz sat down at the broad kitchen table. Moira said suddenly, 'Did you see Sebastian Coe?'

'Out there working up a coronary,' Liz said. 'Whose idea was that?'

'You can thank Erica if I'm an early widow.' Moira looked genuinely worried. '*I* can't stop him. Ever since he started her yoga class he's got worse and worse. First it was finding him upside down in the bathroom with his feet up the airing cupboard. Now this.' She ladled tea in a flowered ceramic pot. 'Did he look all right?'

'I think he'll survive.' Liz paused. 'It's not a bad idea, Moira. He needs some exercise.' She looked around the room and then said casually, 'I can't believe Erica told him to run his ass off.'

'Oh no. Oh of course not. *Erica* says be sensible, a little at a time, you know. But he has to prove something. You know what men are like.' She made the tea before she said, 'So Barry's gone?'

'He's gone.' Moira poured the tea, brought milk and sugar and settled herself across the table.

'Are you sorry?' she said.

'I'm devastated,' Liz answered honestly. She paused. 'The funny thing is, so's Barry.'

Moira stirred her tea and laid the silver spoon down neatly beside her cup. 'I think you're idiots,' she said.

'Different values, Moira.'

'Oh crap.'

'I see you're going to be open-minded.'

Moira leaned closer. 'Liz, I just can't stand seeing two of my best friends ruining their lives. I can't stand it. If there was a *reason* behind all this.'

71

Liz straightened on her rush-seated chair. She placed the tea-cup neatly between her two hands and said, 'There *are* reasons. It's not our fault that none of them are reasons you can understand.' She paused and then said tentatively, 'There's one. One you might understand.'

'What's that?' Moira looked suspicious.

Liz smiled a little and, looking down at the tea-cup and her hands she said, 'You know what you said about a woman over there?'

Moira instantly turned wary. 'I was joking,' she said.

'I think you were right.'

'*What!*'

'I just think so. I don't know so.'

'The bastard. The sod.'

'I just *think*, Moira. I'm not accusing him of anything.'

'*Why* do you think so? Did he *say* so?'

Liz laughed, shaking her head. 'Barry never *says* anything straight. Not even trivial things. He hints. He jokes. He wraps things up in stories. Sort of parables, I suppose.'

'What would he do that for?'

Liz shrugged. 'Makes it easier to say? Who knows. He's a great talker, Moira, but not a great communicator. Anyway, I'm probably wrong.'

Moira stopped and thought and then leaned forward again. 'Why would he want you to go with him then? If he'd met somebody. Why was he so desperate for you to come?' Liz turned the tea-cup around and then lifted it and drank from it.

'Protection? Lashing himself to the mythical mast so he can listen to the Siren's song? Who knows. Middle-aged men do crazy things.'

'So,' said Moira, 'do middle-aged women. Now you've let him go off to his *Siren* with a carte-blanche. You *are* a fool.'

Liz smiled again. 'Actually,' she said, 'he's probably safer that way.' She finished her tea. 'Anyhow,' she added briskly, 'it's precisely none of my business now.'

Moira narrowed her eyes and settled her chin on her hand, staring at Liz for a long while. Then she quickly gulped her tea, put down the cup and glanced at her watch. 'Sorry. This is a bore, but they're going to be here in half an hour. Come upstairs while I dress.' She got up and darted expertly around the kitchen adjusting dials, like a pilot putting a plane on automatic. Then she led the way out and up the stairs.

Whoever had hand-painted the kitchen had done the same to Moira's bedroom the year before. Here, the colours were jade and ivory, attended by wallpapers, curtains, and bed-hangings in dark green regency stripe. Liz settled herself on the broad four-poster while Moira moved quickly about the room, gathering her evening clothes. She excused herself, disappeared briefly into the en-suite bathroom, and came out showered and perfumed, in a long frilled dressing-gown. She settled in front of the ivory and jade dressing-table and began quickly and perfectly doing her eyes. Liz watched, lying on her stomach across the bed, her elbows bent, chin on knuckles. 'The Making of Moira,' she said, laughing. Moira had moved on expertly to colouring her lips.

'It doesn't take me long,' she justified. 'I haven't masses of time to spend on myself. I never have.'

'I know. I'm not criticizing, I'm admiring.' Moira glanced at Liz's reflection in her mirror. She held up the lipstick. 'Want some?'

Liz shook her head, still smiling. It was a tenet of their friendship that Moira was beautiful and Liz, though individual and attractive, was not.

'Have you *never* worn make-up?' Moira asked.

'Nope.'

'Not even when you were a girl? You must have *tried* it.'

'I did a little. My *mother* sort of urged me to. Everyone else's mothers had been forbidding it for years, but I never wanted it, so in the end, she sort of pushed it. She must have despaired by then.'

'Your mother? She idolizes you. She positively glowed maternal pride when she came up that time to Cambridge.'

'She was always proud of the scholar. It's the woman she doubts.'

Moira considered that, combing out her soft brown hair and fastening it with one of her big velvet bows. She said tentatively, 'Don't you *ever* feel the need to do something? You know, spruce up a little?' She stopped and said hastily, '*I* feel it all the time. More and more, the older I get.'

73

Liz rolled over on her back and lay looking up at the green-striped canopy. 'Not really. I'm happy with me. Or at least, I'm used to me. And Barry never cares as long as I'm comfortable with myself. He's the same about *his* looks.'

'That's fine,' Moira said briskly. She had finished her hair and turned briefly on the stool to face Liz. 'Though it's not particularly relevant now, is it? Besides. Are you sure? Men are slippery as snakes. Particularly men like Barry.'

'*What's* "men like Barry"?' Liz said. She sat up on the bed, stretching her legs, in their red velour leggings and leather boots, over the edge of the bed.

'You know. Right-on, ideologically sound New Men. God alone knows what's really going on underneath all that suppressed machismo.'

'Suppressed machismo? Suppressed sexism. Whose side are you on?'

'Ours. Don't trust them. They're pigs in sheep's clothing. There's one in the village right here. Perfect New Man. Shared everything. Videoed every second of his wife's pregnancy. Played house-husband for ten months so she could finish her degree. Now it turns out he's been carrying on for three years with her best friend. All through the wonderful supportive lot.'

Liz laughed, swinging her legs, looking down at her red leather boots. 'Well, unless you and Barry are about to make a confession, I think we can let him off on that count.'

'What's your mother going to think about Barry?'

Liz sighed, 'Oh, she'll loyally condemn him to perdition, I imagine. It's a shame. They got on real well.' Liz stood up and walked around the room, touching the draperies of the bed, the silken paintwork of the wardrobe, the silver-framed family photographs on Moira's dresser. 'How are the kids?'

'Oh, super, Liz.' Moira paused, slipping into a loose-fitting sailor-collared navy blue dress. Her head emerged, utterly unruffled. 'Here zip me up, please. I miss them horribly now that both the girls are at St Anne's. I'm dreading William going off next year. It will be so odd, just John and me again. It's strange, when they were little, I positively yearned for a time when we'd be alone again. Now that it's about to happen, I don't seem to want it any more.' She paused, stepping into her navy

court shoes. 'It's hard to imagine us, now, without the children.'
She looked sad. 'Well, I'll have more time for work, anyhow.'

'How *is* work?'

Moira checked her reflection in the mirror, and, turning back
to Liz, put on her business woman's face, slightly grim. 'It's
lousy, Liz. Let's face it. We're in a recession and the first thing
to go is decorating the house. Even before the family holiday.
Fortunately, some of John's associates are so *filthy* rich, they
haven't noticed the recession. So, I'm managing, thank God.
Nothing's easy these days, even for John. We *need* this money
now. It isn't just trimming any longer.' She brightened briefly,
'I've got a nice cottage to do next week in Essex. Oh,' she said,
'on the subject, one of my potential clients is coming to dinner
tonight. So be sure to sing my praises.'

'Don't I always?'

'Yes,' Moira said fondly, 'you do.' Outside the darkened
casement window there was the crunch of gravel as a car
arrived in front of the house and a flash of headlights as
it swung around the semi-circle to park. Moira went to the
window and looked briefly out.

'Hadn't we better go down?' Liz said.

'It's all right. John's down there. He'll get the door.' She drew
the curtains over the window. 'Oh, this is a bore. I wish I hadn't
asked anyone. I get you out here so rarely, I'd rather have you
all to myself, just to sit and talk.'

Liz wasn't quite sure it was true, or a prettily composed
flattery. She laughed lightly and said, 'We do enough of that
at the health club.'

'Yes I know. But it's different at my own house.'

'I do try,' Liz said guiltily. 'But there's always something on.
Mine, or Barry's . . .'

'Barry never liked coming here.'

'Of course he did.'

'He didn't like the country and he didn't like my friends.
He was always sarcastic.'

Liz stared at her, amazed. 'I wish I'd known you felt this way
before,' she said at last. 'When I could have done something
about it.' She got angry. 'Sod Barry. What right had he to be
sarcastic?'

'It doesn't matter.' Moira had gone back to the window and

75

drawn the curtain slightly aside as another car crunched to a halt. 'I suppose we'd better go down.' She turned with apparent reluctance and led the way down the charming, fragile stairs.

The drawing-room was long and low, with plain cream walls, subdued flowered chintz curtains, and a pale Chinese carpet, all effecting to lead the eye to its star attraction, the vast brick inglenook that filled the end wall. The inglenook, like the kitchen, was recent, Moira's fanciful restoration of a probably imaginary early feature. As a result, the chimney, built for more prosaic use, never drew properly and the room was haunted by wisps of errant woodsmoke.

At the doorway, as Liz entered with her hostess, twelve-year-old William, in school trousers, a white shirt, and a bow tie, nervously held out a silver tray filled with sherry glasses. She took one, thanked him, and went further into the room, drawn by the warmth of the fire. Before it, John Harris, hair wet from his shower, was standing with an older couple; a white-haired, bushy-moustached, red-faced man in pale flannel trousers and a dark blue blazer, and a tiny woman in a long stiff skirt and a blouse laden with ruffles and frills. Liz recognized them as Major Smythe-Hamilton and his wife, Moira's neighbours and her favourite old reliables to be drafted in to dinner on awkward occasions. She was about to greet them when a big shape swooped out of the darkness by the bookshelves and into the firelight and a hearty voice exclaimed, 'Well hello, you must be Liz.' She turned warily. He was tall, blond, and improbably handsome. He flashed a huge white smile. 'Moira's told me all about you,' he said.

'Has she?' said Liz.

'All your little secrets.' He grinned. 'Charles Beatty.' He extended his hand, but when she reached to take it he turned his own and lifted hers, and raised her fingers to his lips. They brushed by, and Liz smiled sweetly.

'Then she'll have told you I'm a lesbian,' she said.

'Liz, how *dare* you?' They were in the kitchen together, midway through the meal, and Liz was ostensibly helping to bring through the sweet.

'How dare I? Moira, you shit, how could you!'

'He's my new client,' Moira whispered. 'Or he was. How

I'm going to get around him after that lesbian bit, I don't know.'

'Tell him I have a foul sense of humour.'

'*That's* obvious.'

'Tell him I'm menopausal and unhinged. And I've just been deserted by my lover. Only you *have* told him that, haven't you? *Haven't you?*'

'Of course not,' Moira said primly. 'I told him you were on your own for a bit. That's all.'

'Why did he have to know that?'

Moira stopped in the midst of pouring delicate streams of blackcurrant coulis over the perfect moulds of blackcurrant and redcurrant sherbet. She looked hard at Liz and said, 'Because he's lonely. His wife left him two months ago without any warning at all and took their two children. He's doing his best to play the footloose bachelor and hating every minute. I thought you might be understanding. I can see you're not.'

Liz was silent. She picked up the tray of desserts and said, 'Then I'm sorry. I didn't mean to hurt your friend. But it's not my fault. It's yours. You set me up. You set us both up. It's despicable.'

Moira turned aside and Liz saw, hugely guilty, that her mascaraed eyelashes were wet. 'I'm sorry,' Moira murmured. 'I did it for you. I thought you'd feel so horribly uncomfortable sitting at the table, all alone.'

Liz was pointedly well-behaved for the rest of the evening, though she left as soon as she decently could. A nine A.M. tutorial gave her the excuse for an early departure, by which time she had soothed the hurt feelings of Charles Beatty. He turned out to be a nice man, readily forgiving. He made Liz think of a large yellow labrador in his tail-wagging eagerness to please. She went out of her way to be nice in return, out of guilt and apology to Moira. Unfortunately, part of her apology involved allowing Charles Beatty to have her telephone number. She wrote it hastily and messily on a scrap of paper and, as she drove away from The Oaks, she was secretly hoping he would lose it.

The phone was ringing as she walked through the door of the cold, empty flat. The cats came running, mewing frantically. She glanced at her watch, stroking each of their backs in turn. Surely not Barry; he was only just landing in Chicago. Charles Beatty, *already*? She groaned and half thought of leaving the machine to take over, with the hope that Barry's gruff recorded voice would put him off. But superstition, with a friend vulnerably airborne, overruled. She lifted the receiver. 'Hello?'

'Is that Dr Campbell?' The voice was masculine, vaguely familiar.

'Yes, can I help you?'

'This is Darren MacPhee.'

'Who?'

'Darren. Darren MacPhee. From the health club.'

'Darren?' Liz paused, thinking frenetically. The plane had crashed and only *Darren* had heard about it? 'What is it?'

'It's about your ad.'

'My what?'

'Your ad in the Union. You're wanting an assistant?'

Liz sat down. She had a disjointed feeling that bits of her life had been shaken up, like a jigsaw in a box, and were falling into the wrong places. 'Why were you reading my ad, Darren?' she asked.

'I'm needing a job.'

'You have a job, Darren.'

'Aye, but I'm needing another. It's only part-time at the club y'ken. I need some bread.'

Liz distractedly pushed Jacob off her knee where he had climbed, still mewing for his supper. She said, thinking quickly, 'I see. Well I'm sorry to hear that, Darren. I thought you did all right at the club. Couldn't they give you more hours?'

'Aye, maybe. But I'd like your job.'

Liz was quiet. She said eventually, speaking slowly, 'Darren, do you know what a research assistant *is*?' There was an equally long silence on his end of the phone, and then his voice, young and exasperated, said clearly, 'Look, Dr Campbell, I may be thick, but I'm no' *that* thick.' She laughed softly. His voice came again, hurt, 'Is something wrong with me asking?'

'No, Darren.' She straightened up in the chair, working her boots off her feet, one and then the other. 'I'm sorry. You surprised me. I'd expected a student . . . I put my ad around

78

the college.' She stopped and then said, 'Darren, whatever were you *doing* in the Union?'

'I was with a friend. He said it was all right.' He sounded wary.

'Of course, Darren. Sure it was all right. I was just *surprised*.' She sighed, rubbing one tired foot against the other. She looked again at her watch; it was ten past eleven. The day felt endless. 'OK,' she said reluctantly. 'Do you know where the Department of Anthropology is, Darren?'

'I can find it.'

'Fine.' She was looking at her diary, open by the phone. 'Look, I've half an hour, from four o'clock. I'll be in my office. Ask the secretary. She'll show you the way.' She put the phone down and pencilled his name into her diary, hoping, as she did so, that he, like Charles Beatty, would miraculously forget.

V

Liz's office comfortably replicated her study in the flat. It was hugely untidy, with stacks of books in use, others in potential use, lava flows of papers spreading across desk, shelves, window-sill. With its used coffee mugs, electric kettle, jar of Nescafé and half-open milk carton, it resembled less a lecturer's study than an undergrad's bedsit. Still, Liz knew where everything was, all her books and files, and knew and resented if anything had been moved.

At three-thirty, Liz was at her desk, marking essays on polyandry in Tibet. A troubled first-year girl had again failed to turn up for a review of her stumbling progress, and Liz had resignedly written a note to pursue the issue next week, and put her extra half-hour to use.

She worked patiently, reading thoroughly and with indulgence, gently crossing through the worst of the excesses, letting others by. She finished an essay, wrote something encouraging in the blank space at the end, and stood up, tucking her cream-coloured blouse down into her tan wool skirt. She walked to the window, pushing aside a stack of journals so she could peer out.

The window overlooked an alleyway used as a short-cut by students. A girl walked by, lost in a book, oblivious of the cold wind that billowed her shapeless black skirt and tossed her red hair. Liz watched, charmed by her scholarly devotion. She did not share the disillusions that had prompted Barry's languor and perhaps his defection. Each year she found her new batch of undergraduates livelier, more intense, more honest, as if the world, despite all predictions, teetered on the edge of a happy revolution. The girl, eyes yet down, passed, like a secular nun, from her vision, and Liz turned back into the room.

It looked warm and pleasant, lit only by her desk-lamp, the rest in deepening shadows as the afternoon darkened. The walls were a pale dead green, but she had enlivened them with prints, posters, photographs and souvenirs. The wall to the right of the window was all but covered by an American patchwork quilt, which, by means of pine battens, she had transformed into a hanging. On top of a grey filing cabinet beneath it, a framed photograph displayed the same quilt spread out between the hands of a broad, smiling woman and an angular girl in jeans and dark plaits. The girl was herself, a final-year student at Columbia, and the woman, one of the subjects of her Appalachian field project. Liz's researches had amused her, and she had given the quilt, her own work, to Liz when she left.

On the bulletin board on the wall behind her desk were other photographs, mostly holiday shots of herself and Barry, together in Venice, in Milan, in Amsterdam. Among them, the most recent, a bright autumn picture of Barry looking terribly English in front of Lake Michigan, appeared startlingly out of place. Liz stepped nearer and studied it, trying to decide if its peculiarity was Barry alone, or Barry in the New World. Another peculiarity struck her then: that in seventeen years they had never gone together to the States. Her returns had been family oriented, except for one, to Boston for a seminar, and she had chosen distinctly not to waste holiday time on them. Holidays were for Europe. It was the way they had always wanted it, priding themselves on their expanding knowledge, linguistic ability, cultural achievements; regarding themselves as New Europeans, with a foot on either side of the Channel.

America just hadn't come into it, until of course Barry's extraordinary fascination with Sandburg; extraordinary because he was so unlike any writer he had cared about in the past. Always, the drier, the colder, the more English the better, and now this rambunctious Mid-western Swede. Liz smiled, looking at the photograph. She had always loved Barry in part for his inconsistencies, his ability to surprise. At least he hadn't let her down.

She picked up a Boots folder of glossy prints from which the one on the bulletin board had been taken. Barry on American streets. Barry in Pete Henderson's apartment. Barry amidst students and academics on the campus in Madison. She singled one out and studied it more carefully. Barry was holding forth on something, caught by the camera in his turbulent excitement. The back of someone's head blocked part of her view of him and of another figure she had barely noticed, a thin blonde girl, clutching a looseleaf folder, her eyes on Barry with rapt attention. Liz tilted her head slightly, moved the photograph into the light to see it better, and then rather hastily put it back with the others as the door to her office swung suddenly open. She turned, momentarily angry that Darren had presumed to walk in without knocking; it was not Darren, though, but Andrew Pringle, big, handsome, and as always, endearing. He knocked on the wide open door, smiling his beautiful smile. 'Am I welcome?'

'Of course, Andrew.' She smiled back and looked very quickly at her desk clock. 'At least for twenty minutes. I've got someone coming for an interview at four. If he shows up,' she added. 'Coffee?' She had picked up the kettle with its dangling cord.

'Oh please.' He came in, shutting the door, wandered about the room and eventually settled on Liz's desk chair. She made two cups of Nescafé, set his before him, and sat down on the supplicant side of her own desk. In that light, Andrew, prowling through the ruffled pages of her *Independent*, looked formidable.

The Gulf crisis filled the news. Andrew said, 'There was a report they've begun to withdraw.'

'Really?' Liz looked hopeful.

'Not likely.' He picked up his coffee still reading.

Liz said, 'We're having a peace rally on Saturday. Do you want to come?' Andrew laughed softly. 'What's funny?'

'You.' He looked up. 'The knee-jerk reaction. They say "war". You reach for your love beads and John Lennon. This isn't Vietnam.'

'Give it time.'

Andrew smiled to himself, still looking at her paper. 'You know what they say about cats, Liz. A cat who jumps on a hot stove will never jump on a hot stove again. On the other hand, it'll never jump on a *cold* stove, either. So much for feline intelligence.'

'Or mine, I suppose.'

'No, Liz.' He chuckled, still turning pages.

'I'm against war, that's all.'

'So am I, on the whole.' He paused, but before Liz could say anything more he said, 'Heard from Barry?'

'No. But I imagine he'll ring tonight. The plane got there, so it's logical to assume he did too.'

'You still angry with him?'

'Not angry, Andrew. Not precisely. If you want to know the truth I'm primarily baffled. It was all a bit sudden and all a bit – ' she paused ' – unlikely.'

'Do you miss him?'

'Yes I *do*, Andrew, which is silly, because there's hardly been time. I didn't miss him half as much when he was away for that month in the autumn. I actually *enjoyed* being alone.'

Andrew nodded solemnly. 'You know what Moira told Erica?'

Liz looked away, warily. 'What?'

'She felt abandoned. She and John. They felt like they might if their *parents* had split up.'

'Oh, for Christ's sake. You make me feel ancient.'

'No, no, Liz. It's nothing to do with age. She's as old as you anyhow, isn't she?' Liz shook her head. 'Well there can't be much in it. But no. It was about *security*. They looked up to you, as a *couple*, I mean. They depended . . . you were their role models, I suppose.' He paused, and then spoke in a different, querulous voice as if he blamed her for something. 'If you two split up, then maybe *anyone* might.'

Liz looked down at her desk, at her own papers, upside down. 'That's just silly,' she said.

'It's not. Each break in the marital chain makes others more likely. The first one overcomes the *idea* of fidelity. After that it's all downhill.'

'We weren't even married,' Liz said.

'You were better unmarried than most of us ever manage properly wed.'

'Is something wrong, Andrew?' she asked gently.

83

'No, no. Everything's fine.'

'Good.'

'There's just this silly business with Erica.'

'Oh?' Liz picked up one of her essays and pretended casual distraction.

After a while he said plaintively, 'She used to be so proud of me. Of my,' he stopped modestly, 'my achievements. Now she actually seems to resent them.'

Liz looked up from the essay and said, 'You mean the book?'

'Oh yes, well, there's the book. But no, it's more this new thing.'

'New thing?' She widened her eyes in helpful expectation.

Andrew leaned forward confidentially. 'Look, Liz, this is just between us and I'm afraid I'll have to be a bit canny about it all, but something rather special *has* come up.'

She sipped from her coffee mug, watching him over the rim. After a fair interval, she said, 'Oh, what's that, Andrew?'

'Well, you know I've always fancied a crack at Parliament?'

Liz hid her immediate surprise. Actually she *had* known and had completely forgotten. Andrew always imagined his hopes and deeds more vivid in the minds of his friends than they were.

Liz said, making her voice familiar, 'Yes, of course.'

'Well, I can't say just yet where it is, or anything, but it looks like I may be offered a seat. I was talking to the election agent last week . . . it's somewhere not too terribly far out . . . we would still spend a lot of our time in London though naturally we would need a *base* in the constituency . . .'

'That's marvellous, Andrew. I'm impressed.'

'Oh well, nothing *set* yet of course. But I'd say I'm in with a good chance.' He leaned back in her desk chair, expansively. 'You remember, this came up before once.' Liz nodded, though the memory was a few years old and vague. 'We got on quite well actually. Just pipped at the post by that young fellow who came over from the Greens. Rather a twit he turned out, too. I remember old Fiona made mincemeat of him at a dinner party without him even *realizing*.' He smiled fondly. 'She *could* be formidable.'

'I remember,' Liz said.

Andrew stayed briefly, nostalgically silent and then said, 'Anyhow, that's all over. The thing now is getting it right *this* time. And,' he looked down suddenly at one long leg crossed easily over the other, 'convincing Erica to play along.' There was a resigned unhappy tone in his voice.

Liz said quietly, 'The way you say it, I get the feeling you're not expecting a good reaction.'

'Well, how can I?' he demanded querulously, 'when everything I do in public with her she insists on messing up?'

'That's a bit strong.'

'Oh. Is it?' He leaned forward, uncrossing his legs, tapping three fingers, agitated, on her papers. 'Yesterday, we were at lunch with J.M. Haggerty, the historian.' Liz nodded. '*You* know what he's like . . . one of those dry old bachelor Anglicans who act as if they're in Holy Orders. So Erica turns up from work in those ghastly legging things.'

'They're very fashionable,' Liz said.

Andrew ignored her. 'Prancing around like a teenager, her hair all over the place as usual . . .'

'Also very fashionable,' said Liz.

'And she's all over the old boy. You know what she told him? She told him he had a "sensual mouth". Can you imagine?'

'I bet he loved it.'

'He was mortified.'

'Oh, Andrew.' Liz was laughing.

Andrew stiffened. He said, 'Well it may amuse you at the moment, but you *must* see I'm going to have problems ahead.'

Liz also sat up straighter and set her mug down amongst a small cluster of companions beside her telephone. 'Only if you make them, Andrew,' she said.

She looked cool and he protested with formal self-pity, 'Is it too much to expect her support in my career?'

Liz looked up, over his shoulder, to her bulletin board photographs. 'That depends, surely, on what, when you married her, you said your career would be.'

'It didn't come up,' he defended. 'She wasn't like this at the beginning.'

'Neither were you.'

He leaned forward, intent on justification, but there was a

heavy, clumsy knock on the door. Liz said, 'I'm sorry, Andrew. That'll be my interview.'

He was already standing, become instantly shy and awkward. 'I'm terribly sorry, Liz. I've been blethering . . .' He turned to go, and then added lamely, 'Ah, Liz. This is just between you and me, surely?'

'Of course.'

'Erica would hate to think I'd been talking about her.'

Liz shook her head. 'No problem.'

He backed to the door, opened it, and collided with the hasty entrance of Darren MacPhee. They fell over each other, disentangled, and both stepped back apologizing with equal vigour. They looked at once incongruous, Andrew so tall and sleek and impeccable; Darren short, tousled and dishevelled, and yet remarkably alike in their boyish discomfort.

'I'm awful sorry, sir,' Darren said, to which Andrew was muttering his monotone, 'No, no . . . all my fault, dreadfully clumsy . . .'

'I'll go out and wait,' Darren said, his eyes, panicked, meeting Liz's.

'No, no. Dr Pringle was just going.'

'Just going,' Andrew echoed and blundered out through the door. 'Thanks so much.' He waved a hand uncertainly and disappeared.

'Come in, Darren,' said Liz. He walked in slowly, looking once over his shoulder to where Andrew Pringle had so hastily vanished. He looked around the room cautiously, from window to desk, to each of the walls, taking in the Appalachian bedspread, the photographs, the shelves of books. He said, lifting one shoulder towards the door as Liz closed it, 'I ken him. He comes into the club to get Erica.'

'He's her husband,' said Liz, 'Andrew Pringle. He's actually quite eminent,' she added, feeling suddenly protective of him.

'Her *husband*!'

'Yes. Why?'

'I thought he was her faither.'

Liz paused, cast a quick, resentful look at his honest young face and then became businesslike. 'Well he's not. Please sit down, Darren.' She indicated the straight chair which she herself had recently occupied and settled herself back in her desk chair that Andrew had vacated. Darren sat down. He was wearing clean jeans, a white shirt, and a faded charity shop waistcoat. His shirt tail was disconcertingly left to hang out, under the waistcoat and over the top of the jeans. She wondered if the costuming was rebellious, or if he actually imagined it appropriate. He tossed back his thick tangle of hair with a familiar quick flick and looked candidly into her eyes.

'About this job,' he said.

'Yes. I've been thinking, Darren . . .' She hesitated, glanced down, fingering a grey fine-point pen. 'You're really going to have to convince me you're up to the task.'

'I cannae do that until you tell me what it is,' he said reasonably.

Liz sighed. She wanted it to come from him: she didn't wish to spell out his inadequacy. He showed no sign of perception. She said, 'Well, Darren, put simply, I'm writing a book and, by the nature of it, there's a good deal of plain donkey-work – collecting of information, distribution and collection of questionnaires, that sort of thing – time-consuming stuff it would pay me to have taken off my hands.'

'What's it about?' Liz looked blank. 'Your book. What's it about?'

She hesitated. Even in front of this probably illiterate boy she felt shy and vulnerable. 'It's a study of men and women. Their physical perceptions of each other, modified by changing social roles . . .'

He looked uncomprehending. Small wonder, she'd made it sound intolerably dull. 'It's no' a story then?'

Liz laughed. 'No, Darren. Not a story.' She smiled a little. The whole thing was a farce, but she liked his innocent honesty. 'Do you read much, Darren?' she asked gently.

'No,' he said, adding, 'I like videos.' She nodded, not surprised. 'And tapes. I like tapes.'

'Music,' she said.

'Story tapes. And plays. I've got some good plays. BBC tapes.' Her eyes widened with a small curiosity but she did not pursue it. He said, 'Would I have to read a lot to do your job?'

She smiled again at the incongruity of the question, but said,

'Actually, Darren, no. It's not that kind of research.' He was studying her, his blue eyes intense and she was aware of a tremendous willingness in them. She said suddenly, 'The book is called *The Female Adonis*.'

'That's weird,' he said.

'Weird? Why?' She bridled slightly.

'Adonis was a bloke. How can you have a female Adonis?'

'You've heard of Adonis?'

'Sure.' He sat comfortable in his knowledge.

Liz pursued. 'How?'

'When I did Latin. We had, you know, what they call Classical Studies part of the time. I had this really good teacher. Mrs Redfearn. I really liked her. She read us these stories. I remember Adonis. He was this great-looking guy, and there were two lassies after him.'

'Aphrodite and Persephone.'

'Aye. That's them.'

'You did Latin, Darren?' Liz said, her curiosity returning.

'Aye. O-Grade. I didna *get* it, mind. I just *did* it.'

'I see.'

'Do I need Latin to do your job?'

Liz laughed aloud. He looked puzzled, but she just shook her head.

'You were telling me about the book,' he said.

'Yes, well.' She leaned back in her chair, thinking – as she did when expressing a complicated idea to students – of a clear, appropriate approach. 'Darren, have you ever noticed how people in the last century dressed really, really differently?'

'Different from today?'

'Yes, of course. But different from each other. Men and women.' She fingered the pen and leaned forward. 'Think of some of the things you see on television: the costume dramas. The women in those huge, huge skirts, the men like straight black lines beside them.'

'Aye, you mean like *Gone with the Wind*?'

'Yes,' Liz said, surprised. 'Perfect example. Good God, are they still showing *Gone with the Wind* to people *your* age?'

'I've got it on video,' Darren said.

'*Gone with the Wind*?'

'I love to watch the acting. It's so funky. But it's great at the

88

same time. There's that scene when Ashley and Melanie meet and kiss and Scarlett's eyes are going, *doing*, *doing*, from one, to the other. I mean, it's *wild*.'

'It's very old-fashioned,' Liz said.

'It's not that. It's because they weren't yet fully out of the silents. It was silent movie acting still in the studios. All the eyes and eyebrows, and the *melodrama*.'

'You're a film buff,' Liz said, suddenly comprehending.

'Oh aye. I like live theatre better though.'

'*Do* you?' Liz was staring.

'Aye,' he said. He sat straighter, with a sudden dignity. 'Aye. I do.'

Liz was slightly unsettled. She took the cap from the grey pen and drew a small meandering line on her blotter. She said, tilting her head and looking up at him, 'Do you see much theatre, Darren?'

'I cannae afford it in London. I saw a lot up North. At the Tron. Or the Citz. And then there's all the things my friends are doing. I try to see all their stuff. And they try to see mine.'

'Yours.'

'Aye.'

'You act, Darren?'

'Aye.' He folded his arms in front of him and a faint belligerence crossed his face, response perhaps to her incredulity.

'*Where?*'

'Wherever I can. I'm in *Guys and Dolls* just now. We started rehearsing last week.'

'The *university Guys and Dolls*?'

'Aye. That one.'

'But you're not *in* the university.'

'So?' He looked more belligerent and a little wary. '*They* didna care.'

Liz drew back. 'Fine. Great. That's really great, Darren. I'll come and see it.'

'Wait closer to the time,' he said. 'I'll tell you if it's worth the bother.' He sounded cool and maturely self-critical. 'Can we talk about your book?'

She laughed. 'The perfectly tactful question, Darren. Just what every writer wants to hear.' She put her pen down.

'All right. Male and female dress codes are the visible expression of society's underlying perceptions of men and women. Nineteenth-century woman was perceived as a passive fertility, a great placid egg upon which her husband, slim and vigorous as a sperm was the moving active force. Late twentieth-century woman has become in every aspect an equal, often rivalrous partner to her man. And the ideals of feminine beauty have altered accordingly. All that softness, whiteness, *pliability* is gone. In its place: long limbs, firm flesh, slim hips, athletic, muscled shoulders. Even the face has changed: rosebud lips and downy cheeks are gone; instead, wide mouths, strong jawlines, tanned skin. In actuality it is an ideal that describes not a woman at all, but a perfect male youth: the Adonis of legend.' Darren watched in awed silence. Liz stopped herself and giggled, tangling her fingers in front of her. 'Sorry,' she said. 'You asked.'

'Aye. It's real interesting.' He stopped, thinking, and then said, 'You mean like when you go to a disco and see a guy and his girlfriend and they're wearing all the same gear. Same jeans, same leather jackets, same jewellery. Only his stuff is sort of loose and hanging, and hers is skin tight around her bum.'

'Excellent,' Liz said. 'That's it in a nutshell. The ideal male and female silhouettes, once naturally, even exaggeratedly divergent, are now virtually interchangeable. But, as you have perceptively observed, male and female bodies are not. A crucial difference.'

'You dinna have to be perceptive,' he said.

'Maybe not, but it's an observation lost on millions of women, Darren. For every tight bum squeezed into man-cut jeans there is an unhappy woman; appalled by her natural female shape, sickened by her padded thighs, her broad hips, her round female stomach.' Darren looked uncomfortable, shifting himself back slightly in his chair. Liz continued, 'A woman striving after an increasingly unattainable ideal. A woman convinced of the essential inadequacy of her body, because, quite simply, it is not a male body.' She leaned back in her chair and studied him severely. 'The price can be high. Depression, self-doubt; at the extreme, anorexia . . . It's an oft repeated fact that if Marilyn Monroe were alive today, she would be considered fat. That's how far we've come.'

'What about Madonna?'

Liz laid her pen down and looked thoughtful. After a while, she said, 'I *think* Madonna represents a nostalgic anomaly. But possibly I'm wrong. That's the sort of thing I hope to find out. Or,' she paused, standing up and taking down a folder from her bookshelf, 'more accurately, I want you to find out.'

'Me?' He looked terrified.

'It's quite simple, Darren. I've designed a pretty foolproof questionnaire. And then there's this chart of comparative secondary sexual characteristics. And a space for your own comments.' She looked up, a clutch of papers in her hand. He was still shrinking slightly in his chair. She said sharply, 'Well, do you want this job or not?'

Liz went straight home from work. It was a grey, cold day and she briefly considered a sauna. It would be nice, and with luck she'd meet Erica, too. But by the time she had closed the door to her office and walked down the two flights of stairs, she had changed her mind. She went out and turned resolutely towards the Underground. She didn't want to do anything to break her homewards momentum and suggest, even to herself, an avoidance of the empty flat.

It felt only a little odd not meeting Barry for the ride home. They had their own schedules and always maintained their personal social lives. Often as not, they journeyed home separately. The odd feeling came from the recurrent realization that he was not, however, somewhere familiar; in his office at the English department, or at his favourite table in the library, or rooting around the British Museum; and therefore she would not run into him by chance. That possibility had always lent a small romantic frisson to her movements about the university that belied the many years of their companionship. She missed it sorely.

Leaving the train at Parsons Green, she walked swiftly, stopping only briefly to pick up a single portion of cook-chilled lasagne and a French loaf at Mario's. At the Pakistani grocer's she added an extra newspaper and a magazine as armour against imagined loneliness, and two doors further on she paused in front of the brightly lit video hire, studying the gaudy posters.

This is ridiculous, she thought, and walked past. *I've been alone hundreds of times. I've enjoyed it. Looked forward to it even.* But her solitudes in the past were brief, and sheltered, like little quiet rooms in her life, securely sealed by Barry's return. This solitude was new, a long tunnel with a faraway, ambiguous end.

She walked up the far side of their street, because it had trees. In the summer it was leafy and suburban and even in the winter she liked their bare, city-worn branches overhead. The three windows of the flat looked blank and lonely. She crossed the street and stood outside the white door, juggling the newspaper and magazine, the food and her work folder, searching for her keys. She was not particularly good with keys, and had lost two sets within the year, one down a grating beside the car, and one mystifyingly in her office. She held the keys carefully now, aware of sole responsibility: Barry would not appear to rescue her any more.

Once inside, she climbed the dim stairs and repeated the whole balancing act outside the flat. At the first click of the lock, two solid thuds sounded behind the door; Jacob and Esau decanting themselves from the sofa. They were on the doormat, twin demand notes, as she opened the door, and at once set up a force field of meows. *Barry's damn cats*, she thought brutally, hurrying past. Though one had always been, at least nominally, hers, and now both were by default, they still were not precisely her idea, which, despite love and loyalty, had always allowed her to emotionally disown them when so inclined. 'They're baying again,' she would say blithely and he would feed them. Now, without that option, she went straight to the kitchen, dumped everything on the table, and reached for the tin opener and a tin of the ridiculously expensive gourmet tuna that was all they'd eat. 'They're patricians,' the vet said fondly. He didn't have to feed them.

'Dolphins have died for this,' she told them as they circled her legs in confounding brown rings. 'I hope you realize this is very un-Green.' They leapt upon their dishes without mercy. 'A lot you care.'

Jacob and Esau had entered their lives eight years ago, rather obviously, around the time when Barry's tests had made it clear that babies were not a possibility. Barry had brought them home, one in each pocket, as a consolation prize. She had made the expected and deserved fuss, though left to her own devices she would have chosen big striped moggies from the Cat Protection League. She would also have liked to be consulted. Trips abroad would now be expensively complicated by catteries; some of life's spontaneity lost. But Barry, rather more than herself, was feeling stunned and bereft by the lost potential of parenthood and, out of kind sympathy, she held her tongue.

Rat-like and incessantly mewing, his surrogate children were not promising. From small rats they grew, in sinuous stages, into small weasels, and then emerged as small pumas, with long dog heads, hideous voices and appalling arrogance; without ever actually passing through 'cat'. By then, however, like any offspring, they were beloved.

From birth their central motivation, aside from food, was a determination to dismantle each other, practised with furious intent in fur-scattering competitions all over the flat. Aside from that, though, they caused little trouble, were fastidiously clean, demanding fresh litter hourly, and slept in appealing tan balls deep in the folds of the duvet.

Barry was opposed to their exposure to the great outdoors, partly out of fatherly protectiveness and partly because, rat-like though they were, they had been inordinately expensive. 'Putting them out is like hanging a Picasso on the washing line. They won't last two minutes. Someone will nab them.'

Liz, not so certain that residents of Fulham could read pedigrees and feline price tags as readily as Barry supposed, clung to her conviction that even Siamese cats were natural creatures, craving the natural world. In Barry's absence she had delicately suggested an exit from the kitchen window on to some perfectly acceptable roof tiles. They were appalled, clinging to the sill with an apparently endless number of feet, mewling frantically, as if she were tipping them overboard from the *Titanic*. She gave up. They sat in regal splendour, softly inside the glass, dreaming no doubt of Siam, and practised their jungle skills among the bookshelves and curtains.

'So now I've got you,' she said, looking wryly down on their matched backs, their yin-yang curling tails. She wondered if she would become sentimentally over-attached to them in Barry's absence or, conversely, begin to resent them because of his failings. 'He'll probably sue for custody,' she said, 'just when I feel you're really mine.'

Liz went to bed early, to convince herself she wasn't avoiding that either. The cats, stuffed and placid, followed her sleepily. The bed seemed huge, but not entirely displeasing. She experimented with solitude, changing sides, stretching out spread-eagled, indulging a decadent diagonal. She read for a while, a crappy detective novel, luxuriantly enjoying it without the literary scholar beside her raising the corner of his moustache in an indulgent grin. When she put it down she splayed its lurid cover boldly unrepentant on the floor. Lying down to sleep, she missed at once the big curve of Barry's back, but became inventive, moving Jacob and Esau around like hot-water bottles, siting feline warmth in strategic places. She lay down again and put off the light, half intrigued, and half desolate in her new freedom. She thought of Barry, counting hours backward across the Atlantic, imagining what he would be doing, but stopped abruptly. She couldn't spend the rest of her life wondering what time it was in Wisconsin. She turned over, curling unconsciously into her habitual position and place, and delicately did not think of sex.

It intruded anyhow, at once, and perversely in a silly dream about Andrew Pringle and the sauna at the New Age Body Workshop. In the embarrassing midst, she was woken, rattled, at three A.M. by her bedside phone's insistent electronic chirp. She knocked the receiver free and dragged it, upside down, into the bed. Inverting it, she murmured muzzily, 'Yes?'

'Darling? Did I wake you?'

'Barry?' She reached to switch on the light.

'Is it late, Liz? I never get these time zones right.'

'Three.' She cleared her voice enough to sound aggrieved.

'Oh, I'm *sorry*, darling. I was with these people and the time just got on . . . I should have called before.'

'It's all right,' she said, waking further, sitting up and sending a seismic ripple of feet under the two sprawling Siamese. 'You OK?'

'Me? Oh great. Fantastic. Everyone's so terrific here, my feet have hardly touched the ground since I arrived. You know, welcoming parties, introductions . . . just been to a fabulous bar with some of the faculty and one or two

94

students . . . I must say I like the way they *mingle* here, Liz . . .'

'What time is it *there*?' she moaned.

'I don't know. Eight, nine . . .' His concern over her lack of sleep was short-lived.

'You certainly seem to have cheered up,' she said.

'Cheered up?' He didn't know what she was talking about. London, and his morbid departure, were forgotten. It made her feel forgotten too. She tried, a little desperately, to draw him back into her life, talking hurriedly about Moira and Andrew Pringle and things they'd said and done. He answered politely, without enthusiasm. His interest in everything there had faded already.

'I've hired Darren MacPhee for my research assistant.'

'Who?'

'Darren MacPhee.'

'Oh.' Barry sounded far away. 'Good, good. He'll be great.'

'You don't know who I'm talking about.'

'Of course I . . . well, not exactly . . .'

'He's the sauna attendant at the health club.'

'Liz? What's going on? You sound angry.'

'I don't care that you're not interested. Just don't pretend.'

There was a long expensive silence. Then Barry said, sounding formal, 'Look, I'm really sorry I woke you, and, well, I just wanted to tell you I was all right and – ' he paused ' – and see you were all right . . . Look, I'll call again . . .'

'No, Barry, I'm sorry.'

'It's all right.' Again a silence. 'I miss you.'

'I've got your cat on my feet.'

'You haven't changed your mind, Liz?'

'You changed yours?'

'No. If anything, I'm more certain than the first time. This is where I'm meant to be. I know it.'

'Good, Barry. I'm glad for you.' The silence descended again. Liz felt in it the ghost of the larger silence to come when she hung up the phone. She searched around for something to say to hold him, but there was nothing, nothing between them to talk about.

'Well, pat my cat for me.'

'Sure, Barry.'

'I'll be in touch.'

'Sure.'

'Goodbye, love.'

'Bye.'

She put the phone down, and the light out. Jacob got up, stretched, and turned around, his soft feet prodding her ankle. Sleep had left her. It was far too early to get up and she was too tired yet to read. She lay awake in the darkness, feeling lonely and sad and stroked Barry's cat which purred its private contentment, as remote from her, in its way, as he was. She lay like that for what seemed like hours, getting sadder and sadder, and then suddenly it was morning and the phone was ringing again. She sat up and stared at the clock, trying to remember what day it was, what her lecture times were, as she answered it.

'Liz, darling, did I wake you or something?'

'No. Or yes, but it doesn't matter, Moira. I've slept in. Barry rang at some insane hour last night.'

'How rude.'

'He got the time zones wrong. He was very sorry.'

'That's very forgiving of you.'

Moira's tone said she wasn't about to forgive Barry anything. It made Liz protective. 'You know what it's like when you're travelling. You forget that life is still going on at home.'

'How is he?' Moira said coolly.

'Oh fine. Fine.'

'And how are *you*?'

It was too early in the morning to put on a defence. Liz said honestly, 'Lousy. I feel *left behind*. Like when you're a kid and your best friend goes on holiday. Suddenly everything in your own life looks so plain and boring . . .' She stopped herself and sat up in bed, shifting the phone. 'Never mind. I'll survive. That was a super dinner the other night.'

'I'm sorry about Charles.'

'Oh, he was all right. *I'm* sorry, Moira. I'm too sensitive.'

There was a brief silence, and then Moira said tentatively, 'You haven't, uh, heard from him?'

'Not a word,' Liz said cheerfully. 'As a matchmaker you're shit, Moira, so give up.'

'I guess I shall.'

Liz brightened, waking up, and said suddenly, 'You'll never guess who *did* come to see me yesterday.'

'Stephen Lloyd?' Moira said quickly.

'Who? Oh for God's sake. No, dear. No. Darren MacPhee.'

'Who?'

'Darren. *Our* Darren. The Playboy of the New Age Body Workshop.'

'*Darren*? Where?'

'At the department. In my office.'

'Darren? I don't believe you.'

'Ask Andrew Pringle. He saw him.'

'But what was he doing there?'

'Answering my ad.'

'For a research assistant?'

'Mmm.'

'Darren? How ridiculous.'

'I hired him.'

'You what?'

'I gave him the job.'

'Oh, Liz, you didn't.'

'Why not? He has access to the people I want. Youngsters. He goes to discos. Pubs. All he has to do is help them with the questionnaire. Fill out the chart and make a few notes of observation.'

'A few notes. Liz, I doubt he can sign his name.'

Liz laughed genially. 'You'd be surprised actually,' she said. 'He has hidden talents.'

After a moment's silence Moira said, her voice very quiet, 'Liz, you're not playing with him, are you?'

'Playing? Whatever do you mean?'

'Only, it would be wrong. He's just a young person . . . like . . . like my girls.'

'Moira, I've just given him a job.'

'I know.'

'Good. I'm glad you know.' Liz swung her feet out from under the duvet and on to the floor. She got up, lifting the phone in one hand, flipping the curly cord out of the way with the other. She said sharply, 'Some people might think it's pretty good of me taking a chance on this *young person*.'

'It is, Liz. It's super of you.'

'You didn't sound like you thought it was super,' Liz said grumpily.

Moira answered in her most reasonable voice, 'Liz darling, why are we fighting about Darren MacPhee?'

VI

The long blue envelope, addressed in a graceful, calligraphic hand, sat on top of the morning pile of mail on her desk. Below were two academic journals from Heffers in Cambridge, a postcard of cross-country skiers in Wisconsin from Barry, and a thick brown manila packet with her name printed in odd childish letters. Liz picked up the blue envelope, turned it over curiously, and opened it first. She slipped out a single sheet of good notepaper, and unfolded it to reveal a printed Essex address, carefully crossed out and supplanted by a handwritten one in Butler's Wharf, and a handwritten note:

> Dear Liz,
> Unexpectedly, I find myself with two tickets for *Miss Saigon*
> Wednesday evening. Should you by chance wish to join
> me, I would be delighted to meet you at the Savoy Grill at
> six o'clock. Forgive this odd notice but I was unfortunate
> enough to lose your telephone number.
>> Yours,
> > Charles Beatty

Liz tilted her head, studying the letter, surprised. A fortnight had passed and she had forgotten about him entirely. He had slipped into the vast repository of faces and names of people she had met once and would not meet again. And now, quite suddenly, here he was again. Quite to her amazement, she was pleased. She thought of their meeting in Moira's house and found herself recalling him as attractive, a good-looking blond man with charming manners. *Ridiculous*, she thought, *two weeks without sex and everyone looks gorgeous*. She read his note again and looked up from it to the rain-dribbled window and her desk full of untidy work. An image floated up of her table in the flat, with a solitary place-setting graced with a slice of pre-packaged pizza. Oh why not? She hadn't been to the Savoy since her uncle had stayed there on the first leg of a European tour when she was still a student at Cambridge. She'd had to borrow clothes from Moira even to go. She'd probably have to do that now. That thought, of actually *dressing* to go out, almost had Charles's note in her waste-bin. But she reconsidered.

She checked it again, looking at the two addresses. The Essex one was home, no doubt relinquished now to the wife and children; the London address his new bachelor retreat. That's how decent men did it, got out of the way, least disturbance for the children's sake. She envisioned a house like Moira's, full of hand-painted furniture; Charles a mighty mortgage-bearer, like John Harris. She imagined John equivalently turned out from his fireside, and it touched her. Poor Charles. *He's probably a sod*, she reminded herself. *He probably had it coming.*

The Essex address had a printed telephone number, but there was none for Butler's Wharf. She would just have to meet him as he asked. The Savoy Grill at six. How romantic. And how idiotic she'd feel if he didn't show up. She glanced at her diary. 'Sauna with Moira' was written in a week-old scrawl in Wednesday's four-line box. She felt a mixture of disappointment and relief and was about to crumple the note. And then, with a sudden shake of her head, she picked up the phone and called Moira instead. Before Moira answered, on the third ring, Liz had a good clear reason worked out. It was even true.

'Moira, love, could we make it Thursday? I've just been thinking I'd like to do a yoga class first, with Erica.'

'Oh wonderful. You can untie John when he gets too enthusiastic.' There was a pause. 'I thought you couldn't be bothered with yoga.'

'Well, I have to do something, now that I'm not running.'

'You've stopped running?' Moira sounded astounded.

'Yeah,' Liz said, and then aggressively, 'look, I'm not going to run alone. It's dark when I get home. It's scary. Anyhow,' she added quietly, 'I hate running.'

'You *do*?'

'Yes,' Liz said, her conviction surprising herself. 'I do. I only did it for Barry.' An image of wet streets, pounding feet, shortened breath, and Barry always three infuriating strides ahead, came to her with startlingly unpleasant clarity. 'I hate running,' she said again. Then she made her voice cheerful, 'So we'll still have our sauna then?'

'Fine with me. I'm in town both days. I've a client in South Ken. And oh, did I tell you? Charles is having me do his new flat. So you weren't *too* awful.'

'I guess not,' Liz said innocently. She put down the phone and tucked Charles Beatty's note back into its blue envelope. Absently, she slipped the brown wrappers off the two journals and set them aside while she read Barry's postcard. There was nothing new. His telephone calls, three that week, had long since usurped it.

Her eyes settled on the fat brown packet. She felt a definite reluctance to open it, and quite possibly prove Moira right and herself wrong about Darren MacPhee. The awkward scrawl of her name on the outside was not encouraging. There was no stamp. The parcel had been delivered by hand and was slightly damp and dog-eared, as if it had been stuffed into a rucksack without much care. As she pulled up the half-stuck flap, her door swung open and Andrew Pringle leaned in.

'Am I welcome?' He smiled hopefully, leaning on the door like a very large, shy, schoolboy.

'Of course, Andrew.' She continued opening the envelope with one hand, reaching for the kettle with her other. Andrew's visits had increased in frequency since Barry's departure. He came to cheer her up and invariably ended morosely confiding his marital miseries. Liz got the reverse, a photographic negative, at the health club, from Erica.

'Heard from Barry?'

'Three times. I'm glad he'll be well paid. It's all going on telephone calls.'

'Missing you?' Andrew said, a little eagerly.

'Not exactly.' Liz put the fat envelope down. 'No, he's just *worrying* about me.' Andrew looked puzzled, and she said quickly, 'Because of the war, Andrew.'

'Really?'

She laughed. 'I keep telling him we're marginally out of range of Scud missiles, but he won't listen.'

'How extraordinary.'

Liz shrugged. 'Europe condenses from over there. It's so far away. They lose touch with geography. Also, they've flipped out completely about terrorism. Apparently nobody flies anywhere, nobody *goes* anywhere . . . they're not used to it . . .'

Liz made coffee for herself and Andrew and picked up the envelope again. She said, 'I just wish it were over, now that it's started. I can't stop watching the news. It's like when I fly and I have to keep awake to keep the plane in the air. I feel if I *don't* watch, something worse will happen.'

Andrew nodded. 'How was your peace rally?' He sounded friendly, not mocking.

She said, 'Lonely.' She slid the wad of folded questionnaires out of the envelope. 'We're having another this Saturday. Want to come?'

'Not a lot of point.'

'Who says?' Liz said with brittle brightness. 'Begin like we intend to continue after all?'

'It'll be finished in a fortnight.'

'God willing, it will. But if it's still going on next year, I want to be able to look this generation in the eye.' She waved her hand, encompassing the college in a vague way. Then she shrugged and unfolded her questionnaires. The familiar xeroxed A4 sheets were now wrinkled and marked. While Andrew drank his coffee and read her morning paper, she idly scanned through. Fine, fine. They were sloppy but effectively filled out. Then, at the bottom, she found, in the blank space labelled 'Comment', three sentences of tortuous handwriting: 'The subjecte, a gril of fortene, was whering desiner denim jeens, belongeng to her boyfreind . . .'

Liz stopped, stared, laid the paper down and said aloud, 'Oh *shit*.' Andrew looked up. 'What's happened to education in Scotland, Andrew? I thought it was good.'

'Best in the country,' Andrew said complacently. 'Why?'

'Oh nothing.' She put the questionnaires away in their mucky brown envelope and smiled. 'An anomaly, no doubt.' After Andrew left she rang the New Age Body Workshop and left a message for Darren MacPhee.

*   *   *

Liz had Wednesdays free that term, and spent the day, as usual, at the flat. She rose late and worked on the book. Darren's brown envelope sat on a corner of her study desk and served as a cushion for Esau. She had not looked at the questionnaires again.

She had meant to finish early, to prepare for dinner and the theatre, but in the later afternoon, just at the time she should have stopped, the difficult section on the post-war New Look regression began to come together and she worked on. Then, quite suddenly, it was late.

Were Barry there, it would not have mattered. They would have laughed and fallen over each other, throwing on whatever came to hand, and bulled it through with mutual eccentricity. But Liz had nothing mutual with Charles Beatty and she doubted eccentricity would charm him. Her wardrobe divided evenly between the sporty and comfortable for home, and the plain and sensible for work. She picked through it, thinking of Moira with her crisp dinner outfits, her pink sculpted mouth. She felt girlish and inadequate and yearned briefly for the easy comfort of Barry's well-worn companionship.

Finally she chose a severe emerald green dress she had never really liked and burrowed amongst her running shoes and boots for a boring pair of mid-heeled black shoes. When she had it all on and dressed up with gold jewellery, it looked all right. She was reminded that Moira had praised the dress in the past. But then, it was Moira's sort of classical costuming, into which she would slip swan-like, looking wonderful. It made Liz feel awkward and oppressed. She looked despairingly in the mirror, but it was far too late to change, only time left to grab her coat and run for the tube. As she clattered to their rendezvous amidst the plebeian crush of the District Line, she envisioned Charles Beatty cruising up the Strand, blondly immaculate at the wheel of his Porsche.

It was five minutes to six when she left the Underground and she ran the remaining distance, clumsily in the awkward heels. She arrived flushed and dishevelled and almost missed the recessed entrance to the Savoy in her hurry. The girlish feeling had returned and a faint sense of displacement, as she made her way, still breathing hard and tucking loose strands of hair back into place, past the limousines and uniformed doormen. She was ushered into the glittering foyer and brief panic descended as she tried to recall what Charles looked like. But then he stood up from a sofa, smiling eagerly, and unmistakable, though she had forgotten quite how enormously tall he was. He was as blond as she recalled but not quite as immaculate. He wore a grey two-piece suit, and his shirt was a little rumpled, as if he'd had his jacket off to do something. His tie was lopsided. He looked faintly uncomfortable, the way she felt.

'I was so afraid I'd be late,' he said, greeting her. 'It was my daughter's birthday and we took her to McDonald's.' He paused, embarrassed. 'It was what she wanted.'

'They all seem to.'

'The both of us, I mean. She just wanted both of us together.'

'Oh. I see.'

'My wife's taken them home now.'

Liz pictured him sitting on a yellow plastic chair, his knees up to his chin, his children (*A girl and a boy? What had he said at Moira's?*) in Ronald McDonald party hats. Across a table littered with polystyrene and paper, a woman, his wife. The air thick with the forced jollity of suspended estrangement.

'Did she have a nice time?' Liz asked politely. He looked puzzled.

'I *think* so. With Lucy you can never tell. Megan makes things obvious, but Lucy's a bit of a mystery.' *Two girls, that was it.* Charles remained looking puzzled and Liz had a sudden insight that the mystery of Lucy was a microcosm of the mystery of her mother. 'She kept saying, "Daddy's coming home now." We'd *told* her I wasn't. We both had. She kept saying it anyhow. Not sad exactly. Just insistent.'

Liz wished she were child-wise like Moira, full of pertinent advice. Instead, she nodded sympathetically, with a vague encouraging smile.

He brightened. 'Enough of me,' he said looking at his watch. 'Let's grab a bite and get along to this show, shall we?'

The pre-show dinner was lovely. The room dim and candlelit, the tables filled by well-dressed couples, destined for the theatre. It felt festive. Liz was glad she had worn the dress. It suited, and made her feel different from her old self with

Barry. She ate grouse and roasted potatoes and delicate thin green beans; all things she would never cook. They talked about work, hers first, and then his. He had a wine-import business and travelled regularly to France. He spoke modestly but he was obviously successful and accustomed to money. Liz had a brief indulgent vision of dinners and shows stretching out towards a summer of weekends in Provence.

Charles did not eat much. 'I had a Big Mac at McDonald's,' he apologized. He sounded depressed. 'I didn't *mean* to eat, but you know how it is when you get in those places. It's the smell or something. I have a friend who swears they put something addictive in the stuff.'

'Cocaine, I suspect,' said Liz.

'Never mind, I'll be starving after the show. We'll come back for coffee and a sweet.' He held her coat for her. She would have laughed if Barry had, but it was nice. She wondered a little meanly if he did it for his wife.

Going to the theatre with Barry was an intellectual experience; with Charles it was a social one. This was not the theatre of previews and standby tickets and café post-mortems among students and friends, but the theatre of money and style. She was swept past doormen and limousines on Charles's arm, subtly changed, half now of a glamorous couple. They walked to Drury Lane through West End streets crowded with fellow theatre-goers, keyed with pre-curtain excitement, at home in an enviable society. It was flattering and exhilarating and yet invoked a peculiar sense of betrayal that sharpened Liz's wits and made her aggressive.

She approached the show with a slight cynicism, but got swept up in it, and emotional. Afterwards, she wanted to talk, argue, milk it dry, as she would have with Barry. But Charles Beatty was one of those people who compartmentalized the arts in their lives and left them behind at the theatre door. They talked instead about Moira Harris and his new flat in Butler's Wharf. He spoke in an excited, forced way and half-way through coffee she was suddenly aware how painful it all was for him, how his thoughts were on his home in Essex, his children, his wife, and probably had been so all evening. She saw herself through his eyes, a pleasant stranger, incongruously in his company.

At the end of the evening, they slipped into a discussion of the war news, the first he'd mentioned of it, and then suddenly they were arguing with misplaced emotion about the Gulf, and the Americans, and Vietnam. It got quite heated and then, equally suddenly, they both stopped, mutually realizing that it was not with each other that they had quarrels. Charles resumed his courtly manners and found her a taxi. She saw him standing alone in the Strand, waving her away, and felt a pang of kindness for his big friendly shape, and with it, a small regret. The evening had the stilted feel of a limited success. Though now he did have her telephone number, she did not expect, this time, that he would call.

There were two messages on her machine when she got home. The first, from Barry, was his now familiar enquiry of her welfare in war-torn Europe. She smiled, listening to it, as she made a cup of Nescafé to return the evening to reality, and played it back once to hear his voice again. She had begun to wonder if they were never actually going to separate at all, only carry on exactly as before, but in a purely electronic sphere. Two celestial beings, she thought, a romance of angels. She let the machine run on. The second message was from Darren MacPhee.

'Sorry I didna call before. I was out wi' Sheila. I'll come in at ten like you said. If I get up.'

'That's the stuff, Darren,' Liz said cheerfully. 'That's what made Britain great.' She laughed to herself, switched off the machine, and wondered for an idle moment, while she fed the cats, what Sheila was in the life of Darren MacPhee.

Liz had a lecture at eleven and was in her office at nine-thirty, reviewing her notes. That completed, she braced herself with coffee and took out the brown envelope from Darren to read through the work once before he came. It was a depressing task. The childish script, the disastrous spelling, leapt out at her from every page. She sought for contradiction, for improvement, but found none. The boy was virtually illiterate. 'Oh, Darren,' she said, 'what were you thinking of? What was I?'

She forced herself to continue. Her mind was caught just occasionally by a train of thought, an insight that surprised her. *He thinks,* she considered eventually, *why can't he write?* She went back to the beginning and looked again. 'The subjecte was whering desiner jeens' . . . 'desiner jeens' . . . spelled three different ways in one paragraph. Oh yes. Oh yes, of course. That was it. She smiled, triumphant and fascinated, vindicated and challenged at once.

He was wearing the same extraordinary costume of waistcoat and trailing shirt when he arrived. It was obviously a favourite. He seemed already more comfortable in her presence, taking his seat across from her, his eyes on her face, not casting around for escape.

'You got the stuff all right?' He was looking at his envelope on her desk.

'Yes, Darren. I did.' She paused long enough, tapping a pencil thoughtfully against her forefinger, that he said, 'Was it OK?'

'Would you like a coffee, Darren?' He looked disturbed, but said yes. She made coffee and joked about the mess on her desk. He relaxed a little, holding the coffee mug between his big hands. 'Did you do well at school, Darren?' she said suddenly.

He laughed, a broad, man's laugh. 'Aye, covered myself with glory.' She looked up and he met her eyes. 'What do you think?' he said.

'I think you did very badly.'

'Aye, that's more like it. Maybe an understatement.' He grinned.

'You're dyslexic.' She expected surprise, even incomprehension.

'I know,' he said. 'It doesna matter.'

'It doesn't *matter*? Of course it matters.'

He shrugged. 'Susan Hampshire is dyslexic. It hasn't stopped her.'

'Yes. So are a lot of other successful people. But it still has to be *dealt* with.'

'Why?'

'How do you learn lines?'

'I *can* read. I'm just slow.'

'But it must matter being slow,' she pursued.

'I memorize a lot.'

107

'How much can you memorize?'

'Most of Shakespeare. From my tapes.'

'You've memorized most of Shakespeare's plays?' Liz said, incredulously.

'Well, the important ones. They're the only ones I can get tapes for.'

'Darren, I don't believe this.'

He shrugged again. Liz looked away, out of the window, thinking rapidly. Darren leaned forward towards her desk, 'Does it matter about the job?' he asked.

She looked back at him, distracted. 'No,' she said slowly, still thinking. 'No, I can cope with this. It's just the spelling. Your observations are good. You have a good eye.' She shook her head suddenly. 'Surely somebody, your parents, your teachers, would have done something . . .'

'Aye, that teacher, Mrs Redfearn, she tried. But nobody listened much. I dinna think I *helped* much mind. I wasna exactly cooperative.' He looked down and then raised his eyes slowly, revealing in them a small, wary hope. 'Can *you* teach me to read better?'

She was quiet, looking down at her desk, moving her cup, the brown envelope, to new positions. Eventually she said, her voice serious, 'I don't think so, Darren. There are things that can help. Sometimes it's to do with vision. There are special glasses . . .'

The look of interest faded. He was already turning from the idea. 'I get on all right. It's not *that* that's holding me back. It's more other things.'

A little relieved, she said, 'What do you mean, Darren? What things?'

'Other things.' He seemed reluctant now to talk. He looked almost belligerent as he said, 'You know.'

'I'm afraid I don't, Darren.'

'Yes you do.' The belligerence was clear, on the surface.

'Darren . . .'

'The way I talk, the way I look, the way I do things . . . because of . . . you know, where I come from. The kind of person I am.'

'Darren, if this is a class thing . . .'

'All the things you said.' His eyes were dark, resentful.

'*I* said?'

'Aye. You. And the rest. Mrs Harris. Even Erica . . . I thought we were friends because she was nice to me, but I got that wrong . . .'

'Darren, what are you talking about?' Liz stopped, her eyes widening rapidly. 'How would you know what I say to Mrs Harris?'

He shrugged, wary of the suspicious note in her voice.

'Darren? *How?*'

He turned aside and then, quite suddenly, turned back, flipped his curly forelock back defiantly, and looked right at her.

'I heard you,' he said.

'*What?*'

'I heard you. At the club.'

'You *listen* to us. In the sauna? You *listen*? Darren, I'm appalled.'

'No, no.' He looked shocked, perhaps by her anger. 'No, not like that. I dinna listen . . . I heard.'

Liz's voice went icily authoritarian. 'I fail to see the difference.'

'I *overheard*. I couldna help it.' He raised his hands. 'Look. I was fixing the plumbing. The plumbing's all connected. You ken how sounds travel where there's pipes, and there's just a wee wall between the men's sauna and the ladies . . .'

Liz glared at him, her mind racing over the suddenly embarrassing intimacy of their conversation, trying to remember what else she'd said. She felt stripped mentally naked. She said stiffly, 'I accept it wasn't deliberate, Darren. But surely even you can see that anything you heard, you should just have ignored, *forgotten*.'

'I *would* have forgotten about it . . . I hear a lot of things. I know I'm meant to forget them . . . but this was different. It was about me. The other thing you said. I couldna forget that.'

'What other thing?'

'That you could make me different. Teach me. Turn me into a different kind of person . . .'

'Oh, Darren, for God's sake. I was joking.'

'No you weren't.' Their eyes met and locked. She was astonished at the hurt, perceptive intelligence in his.

'Well, if not joking, I was fantasizing . . .'

'You could do it. You know that.' His assurance unnerved her and she laughed sharply and said with defensive sarcasm, 'What, turn you into the world's greatest lover?'

'No,' he said calmly. 'I didna mean that.' He paused. 'I dinna need help there.'

'*You're* cocky.'

'Maybe. But it's not what I meant. You *know* what I meant. The crack and the manners and all the things you take for granted that I dinna have.'

She looked down at her desk, bemused and a little touched. Her anger softened and she looked up at him with candid eyes. 'Darren, what you *need* is a drama coach. A drama college perhaps.' She laughed. 'There's a pretty good one around the corner.'

He said at once, 'I ken that. And I ken I'll not get in there until I'm different from what I am.'

'But that's not true, surely,' Liz countered, encouragingly. 'The theatre's terribly egalitarian. They love regional accents.'

'Aye. When you can turn them on and off like a tap. When you ken it *is* an accent and no' just yourself talking . . . I came to London eight months ago, and I thought I'd be a sensation.' He laughed. 'I know it sounds stupid but that's what it looks like from up there. That's why there's guys like me sleeping in the streets. I've learned better . . .' He looked with morose weariness down at his right foot, crossed across his left.

She noticed his shoes, worn and shabby. She said gently, 'Darren, have you thought of going back home?'

'Aye. I've thought of it.' His head came up, stubborn. 'I'm not going.'

She said carefully, 'Is this why you came for this job?'

He shrugged. 'Aye, maybe. I still need the bread. That was true.'

'Yes,' Liz said doubtfully.

He leaned forward. 'Look, the thing is, no matter what I can do, what talent I have, I never get past *me* . . . the way I sound, the way I do things. People don't expect anything of me. Look, you didna take me seriously. You were surprised I answered your ad. Surprised I was in the Union even . . . surprised about the acting.'

'No I wasn't.'

'Aye, well, you looked it.'

The awareness in his eyes made denying it further pointless. She looked down at her hands, still toying with the pencil. 'Well, if I did make that sort of judgement, I shouldn't have. It's my fault, not yours.'

He shook his head angrily. 'It doesna matter whose fault it is. It still has the same effect.'

'What effect?'

'They dismiss you, before you've a chance to show what you can do.' He looked at her bitterly and their eyes held for a long, unhappy moment before his slid away. Liz was quiet. She looked out of her window at the bar of cold morning sunlight on the brick wall beyond.

'All right, Darren,' she said, turning back to him with a quick, challenging smile. 'Show me what you can do.'

He looked up, startled, but not displeased. 'All right,' he said.

He stood up and stepped back from the desk and took a position in the middle of the small room, his back to the Appalachian quilt. He looked around himself quickly, as if setting an imaginary stage and then stopped, stood still, head bowed. When he looked up his face was entirely different, composed, firm, looking leaner and finer. '*Henry V*, Act Five, Scene Two, an apartment in the French King's palace. Henry to the Princess Katherine.' He turned his back to her, and then turned again to face her and once again his face was different, coarser, older and vigorous.

> '*Marry, if you would put me to verses or to dance for your sake, Kate, why you undid me; for the one I have neither words nor measure, and for the other I have no strength in measure, yet a reasonable measure in strength. If I could win a lady at leap-frog, or by vaulting into my saddle with my armour on my back, under the correction of bragging be it spoken, I should quickly leap into a wife.*'

He grinned suddenly, his eyes narrow and sexy.

> '*Or if I might buffet for my love, or bound my horse for her favours, I could lay on like a butcher, and sit like a*

> *jack-an-apes, never off. But, before God, Kate, I cannot*
> *look greenly, nor gasp out my eloquence, nor I have no*
> *cunning in protestation; only downright oaths, which I*
> *never use till urg'd, nor never break for urging.'*

He held out his big strong hands before him, looking down
on them solemnly. Then he raised his head, his eyes meeting
hers, wistful and brilliantly blue beneath heavy dark brows.

> *'If thou canst love a fellow of this temper, Kate, whose face*
> *is not worth sun-burning, that never looks in his glass for*
> *love of anything he sees there, let thine eye be thy cook. I*
> *speak to thee plain soldier. If thou canst love me for this,*
> *take me . . .'*

He stepped forward, extending his hand to her and the rough
fingers just brushed her cheek. She jerked back. He whirled
away, laughing, '. . . *if not, to say to thee that I shall die is true*
— but for thy love, by the Lord, no; yet . . .' he smiled gently, *'I*
love thee too.'

He stood silent as she stared. Then he straightened, took a
step back and inclined his head once, the ghost of a bow. His
shoulders relaxed, his posture changed, and he walked rather
clumsily back to the desk and sat again in his chair.

He became at once Scottish and shy. 'I hope you didna
mind me touching you. You see, it's part of it. I always do
that bit.'

'I understand, Darren. I didn't mind.' Liz was still staring.
Slowly she put down the pencil she was holding and sat back.
'That was brilliant,' she said, at last.

'Thank you.' He spoke with dignity, no false modesty, no
dissembling.

'I'm amazed.'

'Aye well. Like I said. You didn't expect anything.'

'No, maybe not, but it's not just *those* things. You *are* very
young.'

'I'm twenty-four. That's not young in the theatre.'

'I didn't realize . . .' She was thoughtful. He did look
twenty-four. Old enough to be a graduate, a post-grad. Two
years short of Stephen Lloyd, lecturer in African Studies. It was
not lack of years, but lack of education she had dismissed. Like

112

he said. She said quickly, 'But, Darren, you spoke beautifully then. You hadn't *any* accent, anything . . .'

'Aye, but that's no' me. I dinna have to find the words. They're all there.'

'Yes, of course.' She smiled. 'And not a bad scriptwriter . . .' She paused, thinking, and then said softly, 'Darren, if I was to, let's say, *advise* you a little . . . and I can't think really that I could do much more than advise . . . on your manner, your general *presentation* . . . you know, you might not like it. Most of us don't much care for being corrected. Having our faults pointed out. We resent it and resist, because it hurts our pride.'

'I can't afford a lot of pride right now,' he said solemnly. 'I won't resist.'

'All right.' She sat up straight, businesslike, shifting things on her desk until she found what she wanted. She handed him a new pack of questionnaires. 'This time write out your answers on separate paper and copy them cleanly. And use a dictionary if you have to. I want to see you trying.'

'Aye. All right.'

'"Yes, Dr Campbell", is more like it, Darren. And look . . .' He raised his eyes to hers. 'Tuck your shirt tail in. It looks like shit.'

VII

Erica wore a leotard and footless tights of luminescent green that shimmered like fishscales when she moved. A soft pink belt decorated her thin waist. She sat alone in a corner of the mirrored studio, legs splayed, back bent in delicious flexibility, face to the floor. The class came in and watched with the awe due a superior being. After a while, she straightened up, drew in her legs and relaxed the remote solemnity of her face.

'Hi, Liz! You joining us?'

'I thought so, until I saw you there and remembered what it was like.'

'You do only what you wish to do,' Erica said professionally.

'What I *wish* to do is go lie in the jacuzzi, but it won't keep me fit,' Liz said.

'Later.' Erica smiled. 'And it will feel so good when you've earned it, no?'

'Swiss work ethic, Liz,' said a male voice behind her. She turned. John Harris, in grey sweatsuit bottoms and a maroon sleeveless vest grinned happily. He jumped into *trikonasana*, and held the pose, legs stretching in a firm triangle, bare feet gripping the smooth pine boards. He had the comfortable air of an old hand and Liz felt clumsy. 'Moira said you were joining us,' he said, resuming a normal stance. 'Hey, what's this about quitting running? Barry will *not* be pleased.'

'Barry can run if he likes,' Liz said. 'I hate running.' She sounded sharper than she meant and John looked hurt.

'I didn't know that, Liz.' He paused. 'I'd thought maybe we'd do a bit together sometime.' He shrugged awkwardly.

114

'Oh sure, John,' she said hastily. 'I just meant the winter. I hate running in the winter. When it's dark.'

He looked partly comforted. 'There's a ten-K fun-run I was sort of working up to in March . . .'

'Well, I'm not sure . . .' Liz said vaguely.

Erica saved her, bringing the class together with soft-voiced authority. 'All right, everybody, *tadasana* . . . feet together, toes and heels in line . . . inner ankles touching . . . legs facing forward . . .' Liz found her quite different when she was working. The deference, the slightly girlish uncertainty, vanished. She was in charge; humorous, good-natured, but unrelenting. A shuffling of awkward track-suited bodies followed her first command. Liz creaked into an ill-remembered stretch. Erica talked them through it, holding them immobile with her soothing, melodious voice.

Liz had positioned herself comfortably at the back, between two well-padded matrons, and directly behind John Harris. The last was out of nosy curiosity. She had been so long accustomed to seeing him in the stiff formality of his sombre city suit, that she ceased to think of him as a physical creature at all. He seemed entirely composed of wit and mental resource.

Now, in his soft work-out clothes, he moved with surprising suppleness, and seemed vigorous and youthful, reminding her of the boy he'd been at Cambridge. She remembered him playing on the May river, scrambling up from a moving punt on to an iron fretwork bridge over the Cam, crossing it, and leaping back down to the passing punt, just before the stern slipped out of reach. She had quite forgotten that. He had been superb at it, better than anyone. Somehow, Moira's insistence on his ineptitude had permeated her recollections and all but blotted the memory out.

'Do you remember "bridging", John?' she asked, during a pause while Erica distributed foam blocks and webbing belts. He looked vague and then laughed.

'Yes. Yes I do. I seem to recall always landing in the river and nearly drowning.'

'But you didn't,' Liz said urgently. 'You were really good at it. Better than anyone.'

'Was I?' John said, still vaguely.

'You were great,' Liz said, but he looked away, his attention returning to Erica. The attention was reciprocated. Erica devoted a lot of class time to John; correcting his posture, encouraging, praising. She crossed the floor several times to readjust a leg, reposition an arm, smooth out his shoulders. She did it to everyone; Liz loved the wise, firm touch of her strong sensual hands. But she did most to John. Still, Liz could see why. She got the most back: he was her star pupil, eager, hardworking, readily responding. Liz imagined him practising heroically at home. Even when she had attended yoga regularly herself, she rarely managed more than a desultory shoulder stand between classes. Barry always tickled her. And the cats regarded the floor poses as a challenge, curling up on her stomach and going to sleep.

During the relaxation at the end of the class, when she was meant to be emptying her mind of all thought, curiosity about John and Erica romped playfully through it instead.

Afterwards, the three of them had cappuccino together in the club café, waiting for Moira to arrive for her sauna. John looked uncomfortable. He had changed back into his business suit; he was dining with a client. He kept looking at his watch. Eventually, he left before Moira arrived.

When she did, her eyes settled with uncanny precision on his empty cappuccino cup. 'I see my husband didn't bother to wait.'

'He had an appointment,' Erica said helpfully. Moira raised a beautiful eyebrow.

'He did,' said Liz.

'Why are you two defending him?' said Moira. 'I know he had an appointment. He could have waited to say hello.'

'You were late,' Erica said, unwisely.

'It's bloody rush hour.'

'Let's grab that sauna, kids,' said Liz with a determined smile. She walked between Erica and Moira as they left the café.

Darren was in his little attendant's cubbyhole, waiting to give them their supply of fluffy towels and robes. He said, 'Hello, Dr Campbell,' but made no indication that he had even seen her since her last appearance at the club. Liz was surprised at his instinct for discretion, but not displeased. Since his revelations in her office, she felt a little wary of verbally disporting herself within the sanctum of the sauna suite as she was accustomed to do. But, she reasoned logically, unless he was again mending the plumbing, as obviously he was not, there was no way he or anyone else could overhear.

'I don't think this yoga's doing John the slightest bit of good,' Moira said pointedly as she stretched out on her towel on the hot pine bench. 'He's stiff and sore all over. Of course he'd never *tell* anyone, but some mornings he can hardly get out of bed.'

Erica nodded sagely. 'Other things cause stiffness,' she said. 'Work, stress, emotional tension.' She sat up and looked at Moira. 'Sometimes sex is a good solution. Do you have good sex just now?' She nodded her head again encouragingly, her wide candid eyes on Moira's face.

Moira looked shocked. 'Well if we don't,' she said, turning her head aside and staring annoyedly at the dark shadows under the upper bench, 'it's not my fault. He's wiped out from the office, worn out from running, or asleep on the bathroom floor from bloody yoga.'

'It is very relaxing,' Erica said, unperturbed. Moira ignored her. She left the sauna first as always and was stretched out on a lounger, flicking through an old *Cosmopolitan* when Liz joined her.

'How's Barry?' she asked. 'Heard from him?'

'Fine. He sent pictures. I've got them somewhere.' She began fishing in her sports bag. 'I brought them to show you. There was a letter but it's mostly about the war.'

'So's everything,' Moira said. 'I keep trying to remember what the news used to be about. All that other stuff. You know – the government, and the recession, and motorway crashes, and Africa . . . what happened to it?'

Liz said, still searching, 'Coming to our peace vigil Saturday night?'

Moira looked pained. Liz found the folder of photographs. She opened them, took out a shiny clump and riffled through them, putting her favourites on top. She handed them to Moira who began looking through them.

'Good God,' she said, 'look at all that snow.'

'Barry's a bit disillusioned about that. Had his first serious encounter with a snow shovel trying to find his car. Talk about stiff and sore. He said he walked like a question mark for three days.'

Moira said, 'Who's that blonde girl?'

'Hmm?' Liz looked up.

'That blonde girl. She's in every other picture.' Moira splayed three out for her examination. 'There. There. And that's her again, surely, there, out in the snow.' Liz looked. In the picture, several young people faced the camera, but it was focused clearly on the central figure, a young girl with a narrow face, long blonde plaits of hair and a red woolly hat, holding up a snowball. 'Same girl,' said Moira, pointing to a serious looking scholar bent over a book in the background of a library scene. The blonde hair was in a bun. The face was unchanged. '*And* there.' Moira held out another, a snack bar, Barry seated with two older men, one bearded and serious, the other balding and chubby. The blonde girl was at Barry's side, listening attentively. Liz studied the picture, thinking suddenly of the one in her college office. She was almost certain it was the same face.

'American blondes all look alike,' she said.

Moira looked curious, but she did not pursue it. Instead she said quickly, her eye on the closed door of the sauna, 'Come to lunch Saturday. We need to talk.'

'I'd love to. But why not talk now?'

'I can't tell you.'

Moira looked meaningfully at the sauna door and Liz laughed. 'Are you *seriously* jealous of Erica?'

'She's not quite the picture of Swiss purity you imagine.'

'Oh, Moira. She's utterly straight. Erica's the sort of woman who would say "Please may I have an affair with your husband", before she'd make a move. You don't seriously imagine *John* is interested in Erica, anyhow.'

'He's utterly infatuated. He's like a small boy with his first teacher. He spends *hours* at that benighted yoga . . .'

'Maybe he wants to get fit.'

'Rubbish.' She looked up sharply as the sauna door creaked. 'Ssh.' Liz sat back feeling acutely uncomfortable. Erica showered and joined them.

'Isn't this lovely. Just us women together?' she said.

*   *   *

John Harris rang early on Saturday morning to suggest she brought her running shoes. Plodging through the wet lanes of Hertfordshire sounded almost precisely as appealing as pounding through the streets of Fulham, but he was so boyishly eager that she couldn't say no. She threw her Reeboks and a spare tracksuit on the passenger seat of the car and set out through the rain, hoping he'd forget.

On the way, she let the radio continue the commentary from the Gulf that breakfast television had initiated. Cruise missiles and surgical strikes rattled about the small interior of the car. A dismal feeling of loss grew upon her as she listened. She wished Barry were there to talk to and she was glad to see John, bouncy and cheerful in a navy and lavender shell-suit, waiting at the door as she arrived.

'Moira says we've got forty-five minutes if we start now and she'll murder us if we're late.'

'Well, perhaps we shouldn't?' Liz said hopefully. But Moira appeared behind John, in the tailored trousers and bat-winged designer knit that comprised 'casual' in her wardrobe.

'Go on. He'll be all twitchy and grumpy if he doesn't. Just be sure you're hungry when you get back.'

'I'm hungry now,' Liz said helpfully. She changed into her tracksuit and the Reeboks in the downstairs loo, feeling horribly guilty towards Moira. Coming out, she met Rachel, Moira's eldest daughter.

'Hi, I didn't know I'd see you.'

'Mid-term break,' she said glumly. She looked adolescent-moody and miserable.

'Coming for a run?'

'No way,' she said. 'Dad's stomach bouncing up and down all over the village. I'd rather die.'

'He looks pretty good, actually,' Liz said.

Rachel gave a long weary sigh. 'I've got a cold. *And* my period.'

Liz gave up and joined John. They jogged down the sweeping curve of gravel and out on to the narrow tarmacked road. John set the pace, hard and demanding. It was like running with Barry, only worse. After the first mile he slowed, and began to pant. Soon they were side by side in a companionable trot. They began to talk, slowing further.

119

'God, it's a relief to be away from the television,' she said. 'John, *you* don't think this thing is all wonderful and marvellous, do you?'

'I must say, the technology's stunning.'

'Technology. It's all I hear. People are getting *killed*, John.'

'Well, maybe not too many . . .'

'Every one of those surgical strikes. Dozens, maybe hundreds of people.'

'Military personnel.'

'Cleaning women, cooks, delivery men.'

'Look, Liz, I'm not *thrilled* about it . . .'

'But?'

'It was probably necessary.'

'I can't believe this. What's happened to us all? We used to believe in things. Now everyone's just going *along* with this.'

'We grew up, Liz. And the world stopped being simple.'

They were standing still in the wet grey lane that ran back to the paddock. 'Sorry, Liz,' he said. He looked sombre.

She shook her head, frustrated. 'Oh, it's not *you*, John. Come on, let's run. You're doing fantastically. I'm impressed.'

He brightened, put on a little burst of speed. When he slowed down next, he said, 'I feel really great. I haven't felt like this in years.'

'You don't find it –' Liz paused, seeking an innocuous phrase ' – a little *taxing*? It's all a bit new and you do *go* for it . . .'

'Moira's been on to you about my imminent collapse.'

'She mentioned you were a bit stiff . . .'

'Of course I'm stiff. I haven't *done* anything but sit in an office and make money since I left Cambridge.' He jogged a few steps. 'Somehow Moira never seems to worry about the harm *that* might do.'

'*Of course* she does, John. That's a dreadful thing to say. She worries about you a lot.'

He sighed and stopped jogging, turning to face her. 'I know. That wasn't fair I guess. Only when Moira worries, she just makes me feel old. You know, "Don't do too much, John. Better have an early night. Careful of your back . . ." You'd think I was seventy.'

'She loves you.'

'When Erica said to me I was a young man, I thought she

was joking. Teasing. And then I saw she meant it . . . it turned me around. It really did.' He looked down at his running shoes. 'Do you think I'm silly?' he said suddenly.

'Of course not.'

They walked the rest of the way back. At first she thought he was tired, but realized quickly he wanted to talk. He said diffidently, 'I rather thought it would be nice to have Erica down this weekend, too, but Moira wasn't very enthusiastic. She said you two had things to talk about.'

'Yes, I suppose,' Liz said vaguely.

'I thought you were *all* good friends.' He sounded defensive.

'Oh, we are.'

He looked sceptical, but he said only, resignedly, 'Wouldn't have worked out anyhow. The children are with them this weekend. Half-term or something. With *her* rather. Pringle's away somewhere. Brussels or Paris. She does love those children. Quite extraordinary. Such a young girl.'

'She always did work with children,' Liz said.

'Terrific girl. Pringle's an ass. He really *doesn't* appreciate what he's got there,' John said with chivalrous protectiveness.

You are *infatuated*, Liz thought. Aloud, she said, 'Oh, I'm quite sure he does, John. I'm quite sure he does.'

'We'll just be casual and eat in the kitchen. It's just pot luck,' Moira said. 'Hope you don't mind.'

Liz had showered quickly and changed back into her jeans and jumper. 'Wonderful,' she said. John came down from their en-suite bathroom, hair wet, face shining, in corduroys and a thick white jumper. He looked fit and handsome. Rachel drifted in to join them, pale-faced, hair freshly gelled into myriad tendrils.

Moira made a face at Liz. 'She always looks like she's just got out of the shower. She goes out like that.'

Rachel ignored her. She ignored her father as well and picked a lettuce leaf out of the salad, munching disconsolately. Her younger sister, Clare, rounded by puppy-fat, pink-cheeked, hair in thick amber plaits, bounced in, wearing jodhpurs and thick woollen socks. Her brother William followed, the headphones of his personal stereo clamped over his ears, bobbing glassy-eyed to private music. Moira lifted the headphones off with one smooth gesture. Clare kissed her father and flopped down at her place at the table.

'Peanut is going a treat. We had a super gallop.'

'Say hello to Liz,' Moira said, without turning from the Aga. William pretended not to hear.

'Hi, Liz,' Clare said.

'Hi, Clare.' Liz extended her hand. Clare shook it happily. She was in that blessed closing stage of childhood before the onslaught of adolescence with all its torpor and miseries. Liz remembered Rachel like that not long ago. Clare began gobbling bread.

'You *are* a pig,' Rachel said.

'Pig. Piggy,' William echoed. John silenced him with a look. Liz was impressed by the effectiveness of his fatherhood.

Moira's pot luck was the sort of sophisticated menu Liz clipped out of magazines during surges of optimism and never used. There was a subtle clear soup, lamb with herbs, a cluster of miniature vegetables. Moira apologized for not doing a proper lunch. 'We're tightening our belts a bit this month. And anyhow, I've been so busy. I spent two days getting this damnable dove-grey paint mixed. Charles and his "dove-grey". It *will* look stunning of course . . .' She looked up briefly to Liz. 'I heard you two had a smashing time by the way.'

'Well, did you!' said Liz, laughing. 'I thought Charles Beatty was meant to be the soul of discretion.'

'Oh, of course. He *is*. Only he does know me *rather* well. And I *knew* you wouldn't mind us talking about you. After all, why should you? You're free. He's going to *be* free. It's all terribly above board. His wife is quite aware he's dating. *Quite* aware. She *encourages* it, I suspect.'

'What's this Liz?' John said.

'Liz saw *Miss Saigon* with Charles Beatty on Wednesday,' Moira said.

'Oh how nice.' John was quiet and then added, 'I like Charles.' He looked puzzled, as if the reality of Barry's departure was not yet settled in his mind. 'I like Charles,' he repeated. He did not meet Liz's eyes. 'Tell me, Liz,' he said, helping himself from the vegetable tureen, 'how's the book going?'

'Oh fine. Great.' She was getting used to lying about it.

'Did you find a research assistant? Barry told me you were looking for a research assistant.' Moira laughed suddenly and John looked surprised. 'What's funny?'

'You tell him, Liz,' Moira said, smiling a little. 'I'll get the pudding.' She stood up.

Liz said, 'Yes I have. I've hired a young actor. He started working for me a week or two ago.'

'What?' Moira stopped half-way to the fridge. 'I thought you'd hired Darren MacPhee.'

'I have,' Liz said.

'He's not an *actor*,' Moira said. She turned to John. 'He's the lifeguard at the health club. You know, the Scottish one.'

'He's an actor, Moira. I told you he had hidden talents.'

'Darren? Since when, for God's sake?'

'Since quite a long time I gather. He's serious, Moira. And he's very good.'

Her voice was uncompromising but Moira said anyway, 'He *can't* be, Liz. And how would you know? He *told* you?'

'He showed me. He's *very* good, Moira. I was astounded.'

'Seems a nice enough boy,' John said in his peace-making voice.

'Liz,' Moira said baldly, '*I* would be astounded if he strung two coherent sentences together. But *acting*? It beggars the imagination.'

Liz shrugged, but her voice was faintly irritated when she said, 'I think you're overdoing his inadequacies, just a bit, Moira. He's a typical, shy, working-class kid. And as it turns out, he's extremely talented.'

Moira threw up her hands. 'Wait a moment. I'll get the dessert. Don't say anything until I get back. I've *got* to hear the rest of this.'

While Moira busied herself with dishes and cream jugs at the far end of the big room, Rachel awoke from the gloomy trance in which she had endured the meal long enough to say, 'Is he *really* an actor, Liz?'

'Yes.'

Rachel's eyes lit with interest. 'Is he good-looking?'

'Yes.'

'No.' Liz and Moira looked at each other across the room.

'He's good-looking,' Liz repeated.

Moira sighed. 'I suppose. In a sort of soap-opera pop-star way.'

'Great,' said Rachel. She looked cheerful for the first time all day.

Moira served dessert and sat down. 'I suppose,' she said reasonably, 'he does have the *looks* for an actor. I really do doubt he has the ability. Or the brains, frankly, Liz. Did you see that note he pinned up about the new rowing machine? He writes like a ten-year-old.'

'I saw it,' Liz said. 'He's dyslexic.' She felt a mixture of defensiveness and betrayal saying it.

Moira tossed her head. Her voice took on a note of incredulity. '*Dyslexic*. Oh really, Liz.'

'Really what?'

'When we were young there were bright children and stupid children. Now suddenly all the stupid children are miraculously transformed into dyslexic children. Half the dullards at school with William have parents claiming dyslexia. Learning disabilities. They all have educational psychologists when frankly – ' she paused – 'all they're probably needing is a kick up the arse.' She covered her mouth with two fingers, glancing at her daughters. 'Pardon me, but they do.' Clare giggled happily but Rachel looked curiously remote and turned back to Liz.

Liz said only, 'You don't believe dyslexia exists?'

'Of course it *exists*. But I don't believe half of humanity suddenly has it. I don't believe Darren MacPhee has it.'

'He might,' John said mildly. 'I don't suppose it only afflicts the middle classes.'

'Precisely,' said Liz. 'Frankly, as an educationalist, I find your attitude a little mystifying, Moira.'

Moira took her rebuff with good grace. She raised her chin, and nodded thoughtfully. 'Of course,' she said finally, 'I wouldn't presume to argue with you about education.' She tried her dessert, a sharply flavoured tart made with forced rhubarb from her greenhouse. 'That's not bad, is it, John?' she said absently. She turned back to Liz. 'I do think it interesting, though, that otherwise rational people will choose to dress up inadequacy in socially acceptable terms. Don't you?'

After lunch, John and the children loaded the dishwasher

and Liz and Moira walked around the wintry garden. It was raining again. Moira lent her a waxed jacket and old wellies. She wore something similar herself and looked like a magazine ad in it. Liz admired the miniature maze, already settling in and looking established.

'I thought these things took for ever.'

'Nonsense. Who has for ever?' Moira moved gracefully about her garden, removing unwary weeds from the clean wet earth with deft flicks of her fingers, nudging sprays of climbers back into place. Everything was controlled, disciplined and orderly. Moira leant over a trellis of roses, quickly nipping out two small dead branches with the clippers she always carried. She said, 'I don't know what to do about John.'

Liz was enjoying the cold silver light through the slanting rain, making jewels of the spider webs across the lavender hedge. She said absently, 'What needs doing?'

'I think I'm losing him.'

Liz turned quickly. Moira looked strained. Two lines, delicate as the spider webs, puzzled her forehead. 'I never thought I'd have to think of this. John was always so in love with me.'

'Of course he's in love with you.'

'Liz, you're my best friend. I don't need flattery. I need help.'

'You're really serious.' Liz put her hands in the pockets of the wet jacket and stood staring. 'I thought this was all a joke.'

'He's falling in love with Erica Pringle.'

'Oh, *Moira*.'

'Will you stop this denial? I can see it. Surely you can see it. He's utterly changed since he's begun seeing her at that yoga class.' Liz fiddled with a spray of lavender.

'Well, it was meant to change him,' she said awkwardly. 'Rejuvenate him.'

'He doesn't make love to me any more.'

Liz turned away. She was a little embarrassed, surprising herself. There had been a time when they shared every thought. But marriage, quite rightly perhaps, had long intervened.

'Surely that's not *that* significant. You said yourself he was tired a lot . . .'

Moira compressed her lips and looked away. 'This is different. He's withdrawn . . . he's turned elsewhere.'

'You're not suggesting he's sleeping with her,' Liz said sharply.

'No,' Moira murmured, 'of course not. Not yet anyhow . . .'

'I don't think any of this is very fair to Erica, you know. *Aside* from her being our friend. She's Andrew's wife and a very devoted wife. She puts up with a lot.'

'Oh, don't you start. I've had John singing her praises non-stop.'

'Then,' Liz said with a wise look, 'whatever he *feels* for her is pretty innocent. When the praises stop, maybe then you've got to worry. Not while he's sharing what he admires with you.'

She walked on a few steps, and appraised the cool precision of the orderly parterre with its mixed beds of lavender, rosemary and sage. 'I will agree he's a tiny bit infatuated.' She turned and smiled wryly. 'What's the harm in that? Barry used to fall for the occasional undergrad. You know, go a bit starry-eyed about her essays or whatever. It never *meant* anything.'

'Except that now he's in Wisconsin and you're here.'

Liz was startled and annoyed. 'You know as well as I do what that was about.'

'I suppose,' Moira said mildly. She sighed. 'I often think none of us really knows what's going on in our partners' lives. Never. No matter how many years.' She sighed again. 'It's depressing.' She walked briskly away. 'Come and see my greenhouse. I've been making geranium cuttings.'

The greenhouse was tucked away by the brick wall of the kitchen garden. It was old and the wood needed repainting. Liz followed Moira, ducking under the low door into the surprising clammy warmth. Moira prodded the wooden frame above the potting benches. 'It's ancient. This is the one bit of the garden I haven't changed. For the silliest reason, too.' She smiled sadly. 'When John and I first came to look at the place, the estate agent followed us around everywhere, like glue. We couldn't talk or even think. Finally we eluded him and hid here. This is where we decided . . .' Her fingers caressed the old wood. Abruptly she dropped her hand. 'I should knock it down before it falls down.'

Liz lifted a small pink geranium from the shelf. 'You gave me two like this and bloody Jacob ate them both.'

'Have some more. Take that one.'

'Oh I can't.'

'Of course you can. I have millions.'

Liz held the plant gratefully. She said, 'I remember when you first took me out here. It seemed so strange. One of *us* with a real house. Not a flat or something studenty. But a house. Land. It was like we were finally grown up. Only,' she looked down at the little geranium, 'Barry and I never really managed. I think that was what went wrong.'

'It's Barry's fault,' Moira said bluntly.

'Oh, of course.' Liz laughed broadly. 'It couldn't be *my* fault. I'm perfect.'

'No. All of it. Him going off . . . John getting this thing about Erica. Barry started it. Rocking the boat. Making everyone restless. *Bloody* Barry.'

Liz laughed. 'Oh that's *silly*, Moira.'

'It isn't. Ever since that night John's been restless. It's like a virus and Barry's infected him with it . . .' She stared angrily out through the rain-streaked glass. 'I thought we'd finally settled on what he wanted. Now he's casting around all over the place again. He's lost his anchor. We have. Oh, you two. We always relied on *you* at least to show sense.' She sighed wearily. The rain pattered on the glass roof. 'Come on, it's only getting worse.'

Liz followed her through the dripping garden carrying the plant. She set it beside the borrowed wellies inside the door.

'I'll have to be going soon.'

'Oh surely not already.' Moira looked stricken.

'I'm sorry. There's this peace vigil the students have organized. I want to show solidarity.'

Moira laughed. 'Well *some* things haven't changed.'

John was in his study, watching the war news. They perched on arms of chairs and watched with him, drawn in against their will. Scenes of besieged Baghdad alternated with footage of aircraft, brief shots of European protest demonstrations, and long tedious interviews with experts. Andrew Pringle made a short surprise appearance from a Brussels studio, analysing the economic effect. They all cheered.

The children came in, wanting to see a video, and were sent away, but William kept returning until Moira said, 'Oh, let him.

It doesn't make any difference. We'll hear it all ad infinitum on the main news tonight.'

John got up and nodded and William bolted for the television, pushing buttons with the consummate ease of computer-age children. The screen flickered and buzzed and suddenly filled with Sylvester Stallone in headband and fatigues. William crouched down, face ten inches away, mesmerized.

'Not *Rambo again*. I want *Dirty Dancing*,' Clare shrieked. They began to fight.

'You speak to them,' Moira said.

'It's William's turn, Clare,' John said. Clare was resentfully quiet.

'Don't sit so close,' Moira said as they left the room.

'You let them watch that?' Liz said. John shrugged. 'You don't maybe see a little irony?'

'What?' Moira sounded vague, her mind on something else.

Liz left soon after, driving away with the geranium wedged companionably in the front passenger seat. She felt lonely, and unsure who she was lonely for. She drove to Fulham, parked the car and ran quickly up to the flat, hurrying the geranium through the frost. She placed it on the kitchen table and bought Jacob off with double helpings of tuna. Before going back out she put leggings on under her jeans and added a warmer jumper, a padded ski-jacket and fur-lined boots. The rain had stopped and the sky was clearing. She rode the tube to Goodge Street and came out into a frozen clear night.

The small gathering was visible a short distance away, clustered around the steps of the American Church, their hand-held candles flickering like lonely, city-dimmed stars. They had draped two banners from the black railings of the brick walled staircase. One, STOP THE WAR, could have led any march in the sixties. The second was more pertinent: NO BLOOD FOR OIL. Put that way, Liz thought, who would argue?

People had gathered above the banners, on the stairs, and before the austere double doors of the church, and a larger group was scattered in candlelit clumps, singing a protest song, under the trees of the small, paved park beside the building. A scattering of posters proclaimed the interests of obscure political groups. Liz was warily conscious of her convictions being co-opted for other purposes, but the singing was innocuous and timeless, and she accepted a candle in a little paper collar from an eager hand. She found herself a place beside the low brick wall surrounding a small plot of shrubbery. Winter rubbish – sodden leaves, cracked polystyrene boxes, old newspapers – was piled in a wind-drift against the wall. Liz sheltered her candle with her hands and looked around.

There were a few young people, probably students, and a larger group nearer her own age. She recognized three or four as members of the university, but the majority were strangers. They looked gentle, and touchingly anachronistic: bearded men in homemade jumpers; women with scrubbed, hopeful faces, in droopy skirts, boots and ponchos; babies and children in Oshkosh dungarees, rainbow stripes, tasselled hats. They gathered under their banners, lit their candles, and listened politely while speakers denounced the war in the Gulf. A man from CND warned of nuclear holocaust. A woman from Greenpeace promised global warming, which Liz thought under the circumstances of a freezing London night sounded pretty good. A member of the Communist Party stood on the staircase and droned a while about the class struggle, until, drowned out by a wailing New Age baby, he relinquished the podium to a young woman in a Chilean hat who sang a song about the rain forest.

Liz stepped from one cold foot to the other and forced a smile of encouragement on to her face. The candle flickered, went out, was relit by a friendly man in dungarees, and went out again. A group of women with multi-coloured badges on their woolly hats linked arms with Liz and sang, 'All we are saying, is give peace a chance.' She sang and swayed with them in a mixture of nostalgia and despair.

'Where are the young?' she asked desperately. The grey-haired woman beside her shrugged and kept singing. Liz broke her link in the chain and stepped back, and, the dead candle still held in her hand, walked a small distance away. The little group looked littler and sadder from there.

'There was a great demo in Trafalgar Square earlier,' a man said. She turned and recognized the Communist speaker. He was broad and burly and kind-faced, with a bushy beard, a lined, weatherbeaten forehead and a Geordie accent. He lit her candle.

'I saw it on television,' she said. 'I thought there'd be more young people here.' The man had started singing 'We Shall Overcome' and did not hear her. Liz backed down the pavement, shielding her candle. Hot wax splattered on her hand. She stepped backwards again, still watching the fading stars beneath the banners, and collided heavily with a group of black-clothed kids who had emerged from nowhere.

Two girls giggled wildly. 'Sorry,' they cried, still giggling. They were juggling paper bags of Wimpy burgers and lidded polystyrene coffee cups, while trying to light fat white candles. The candles were the wrong sort, meant for indoor action only, and refused to perform against the strong wind. Liz handed the first girl hers.

'Ta.' The girl was blonde, white-faced, red-lipped, a Madonna clone in black tights and Doc Marten boots. Two boys with them were occupied unfurling a banner. When they had stretched it right out, blocking the pavement, the boy on the left tossed back a mop of black hair and suddenly ran his post of the banner around in a sweeping arc, encircling Liz and turning the lettering outwards. It said in huge, decorated script: PEACE.

'That's great,' the blonde girl shouted. She held Liz's candle up and handed it to the boy with the banner. The light flared, lighting his face, hers, and Liz's.

'Hi, Dr Campbell,' he said, clearly surprised. 'What are you doing here?'

'Darren! How nice to see you!' She looked happily around their little half circle beneath the wind-fluttered banner. 'How *very* nice to see you all.'

She stayed with them, linking arms with the two girls, joking with the boys, singing old songs that she knew better than they did, and new ones she had not heard of, until the demonstration began to fade, defeated as much by the cold as the indifference of passers-by. The block of protesters broke up into small circles as friends found one another. Children whined or fell asleep on adult shoulders. There was a sweet air of well-being and reminiscence. The Geordie Communist walked by with his arm around the woman from Greenpeace.

Darren and his friends rolled up their banner and drifted away with Liz now part of their group. Someone suggested coffee, as they clustered together outside the Underground in Tottenham Court Road. They ended up in a café in Earls Court, their banner draped behind a bank of seats, drinking coffees and sharing two boxes of chips. The other boy was called Mike, the dark girl Stephanie, the blonde Madonna, Sheila.

Liz introduced herself by her first name; anything more sounded stilted and ridiculous. They accepted the usage of it easily, but Darren refrained then from addressing her at all. He had been confident and cheerful among his friends out in the street, but in the intimacy of the café, her presence appeared to inhibit him. The others talked and he sat back, looking about nervously and not meeting Liz's eyes. Watching him, she was sorry she had gone with them.

'I must go,' she said to Darren, getting to her feet. He stood as well, surprising her. 'Aye. Me too.' The others looked but took little notice. They made the casual goodbyes of their age and turned back into their conversation. In the street Darren said, 'Which way are you going?'

'Home.' He looked blank. 'Fulham.'

'Fine.' He began walking with her towards the Underground. Curious, she said, 'Where do you stay, Darren?'

He said, 'I'll just go along this way.'

She felt awkward walking alone with him and to have something to say, she repeated how glad she had been to find him and his friends at the demonstration. 'It's so important that young people care. That young people *understand* how wrong it all is.' He nodded, seeming to agree. Then he said, 'Aye well, when they started talking about it, back in August, at first I thought I'd sign up for the army.'

'*What?*'

'Well, some of my mates were. First I thought I agreed with them. Then I decided I didn't. So I'm doing this instead.' He shrugged. 'Just now, anyhow.'

Liz was silent. Her conviction of solidarity with the young wavered. They rode the Underground without talking or looking at each other. When the train came out into the night at Fulham Broadway she wondered vaguely where he was going, but it was only after he got up to get off at her stop that she realized he was actually escorting her. She said quickly, 'Darren, you didn't need to do this. I'm often home late.'

'Aye well. It's no problem.' He looked embarrassed, but he followed her off the train and out of the station and walked her to her door. Standing in the cold streetlight outside the house, she thought of her flat upstairs, the warm kitchen, the cats, her new solitude. She wondered if she should invite him in, offer coffee, or whatever. As she hesitated, he said, 'Is your husband home?'

'I'm not married, Darren.'

'Oh.' He looked amazed and slightly stricken in the streetlight. 'Sorry. I didna ken. Erica said . . .'

'I used to live with a man called Barry Poore. He's in America now.' She paused. 'I live alone.' It sounded vulnerable and challenging at once. Asking him in was suddenly out of the question. She said, 'Goodnight, Darren. Thanks for seeing me home.'

'No problem.' He smiled quickly and then hunched into his thick jacket and walked away.

VIII

Just when she had again forgotten all about him, Charles Beatty rang.

He began apologetically, 'Sorry I didn't ring before,' surprising her with his sense of duty, surely premature. 'I've been down in Essex, sorting things out for Jane.' He paused. 'My wife. We . . . she, now . . . is putting an extension on the house. You know what builders are like with a woman alone. Always trying to pull a fast one.'

'That was nice of you, Charles.'

'Well, I wasn't going to leave her floundering.' He laughed. 'I'll be paying for it in the end.'

'How is she?'

'Who?'

'Jane. Your wife.'

'Oh.' He paused, embarrassed? annoyed? She could not tell. 'Oh fine.'

'And the children?'

Another, longer pause and a slip into intimacy, 'Not great. There was quite a scene when it was time to leave.'

'It must be very hard.'

'It's hell.' His voice was heavy. Abruptly he said, 'Sorry, Liz. I'm a bore. I did enjoy our night out. Would you care to repeat it? Maybe take in a film on Saturday?'

'I'd be delighted, Charles.' She heard her own voice, girlishly enthusiastic. *Have I been that lonely?*

'Oh good. I *am* glad, Liz.' He sounded very real and also as if he had feared a different answer.

She put the phone down with a feeling of gentle exhilaration.

133

Saturday had become pleasantly haloed in her week, an event, an occasion. It was so long since she had actually dated; not since she was an undergraduate at Columbia. With Barry she had never dated; they just were: friends, who became lovers in easy succession, without trauma, or even much discussion. But she still remembered the feeling of promise and excitement and slight uncertainty and found it startlingly unchanged. What would she wear? Would it go well? And, slightly uneasily, would more be expected?

This is silly. Old-fashioned. If I had so wanted to see him again, why didn't I just ring him? But the real truth was, she hadn't much thought about seeing him again until he rang her. He made the move, she responded; a pattern older than time. 'The hunt, pursuit,' she said dramatically, aloud, to Jacob who was sleeping on her desk. She laughed softly, stroking his curled back. It was difficult to picture gentle Charles Beatty as hunter and pursuer. 'He's a nice man,' she said, again aloud. Quite unbidden, the thought of being in bed with him crossed her mind. The idea filled her with shyness and, foolishly enough, remorse.

Jacob unfolded his Siamese length and strode around her desk on long savannah legs. 'I like you,' she said, still stroking him. Esau came to check out the action and prodded his smooth head against her shoulder. She stroked them both, in turn and in odd directions, amusing herself, breaking the rules, rubbing them backwards, or picking up their fastidious feet. Confounding her, they liked everything and settled eventually in two chocolate ellipsoids, feet stowed tidily out of sight. They stared at her with their eerie blue humanoid eyes. She could not look at them without immediate thought of Barry.

Her eyes widened in a flash of uncertain insight. 'Is that why he left you?' But of course, that wasn't the reason, but simple mundanities, like kennels and airplanes and hassle.

Esau had roosted with his usual accuracy on the exact page of notes she was transcribing. She used it as an excuse to get up and make coffee and get distracted in the kitchen. One small but definite reason for accepting Charles was the chance of an evening without feeling guilty about the book. She washed the coffee pot and then wiped the electric kettle, looked at it properly and got out scourers and began scrubbing yellowing grime from the stainless steel. It came up beautifully into a fine silvery shine, the most satisfying thing she'd done all evening.

She had struggled for three hours with the book. Nothing worked. One thought cancelled another. The sum of the parts never added up to a whole. Darren's questionnaires led nowhere. Not his fault. The information was copious and meticulously detailed, and revealed no prejudice on the part of the questioner. That was perhaps the problem. Unaware of her thematic motivations, he did no subtle winnowing, no selective choosing. He was the blank camera's eye and what he saw simply did not reflect her theories. It was good science. It just didn't make a book.

She finished the kettle, returned to the desk and picked up a heap of his papers. They were better, far neater, and the spelling, though still ludicrous, was better too. He had worked very hard and had indeed used a dictionary, not an easy task considering. The handwriting was still a child's laborious scrawl. She wondered suddenly if he could type.

She read a little, smiling slightly. Darren had a good feel for speech patterns, and an artless style, lacking in punctuation. Once she'd deciphered it, it read well, and a lively image of pubs, discoland, and karaoke nights emerged, more indeed than she had asked for.

'You're the writer,' she said aloud. 'Not me.' It was a strange thought, and unsettled her. She put the papers down and left the study. In the kitchen, she changed the cat litter and scrubbed the floor around the tray. The clock said eleven. She'd have a bath, practise her yoga, wash her hair, glance over her lecture notes. The book would have to wait. *As always.* She thought of Barry, when he was writing his first, the little study of Thomas Hardy that had once been the biggest thing in both their lives. Now he disparaged it, honestly; he had grown beyond it. But then it had been a loved, nurtured child.

She pictured him coming in from work, grabbing a cup of Nescafé, his mind already on the book, stirring the coffee as he walked to the study, absently leaving the spoon on a table or the mantel along the way. Ten minutes in the door and he was at his desk.

Of course, Liz thought sourly. *Easy for him. I had all this.* But her innate honesty intervened at once. No. They'd always shared what simple tasks their ramshackle domesticity required. Only he never let them get in the way. Never used them as an excuse, and she did. He had better habits. He worked harder. That was it, and nothing more.

On Thursday, when Liz arrived at her yoga class, Erica and John Harris were talking intently in a corner of the studio. He had a new, more stylish tracksuit. Erica wore her green leotard with the pink sash. They acknowledged Liz as she entered, but continued talking. Other people came in. John and Erica looked around, exchanged some further words, and stepped apart. A shell of intimacy seemed to remain a moment longer about them.

Then John noticed Liz again and bounced across the room to greet her. 'Been practising?'

'Once.'

'Naughty, naughty.'

Liz found his aggressive cheerfulness irritating. 'Oh,' he added casually, 'Moira said to tell you she won't be here tonight.'

'She's not coming to the sauna?'

'No. I think something's up. Work, or one of the kids.' He sounded surprisingly vague about a woman he'd presumably got up with that morning.

'Oh.'

'She'd have rung you, but she was busy.'

'Sure . . . fine.'

'Erica will be there anyhow.'

'I know that, John.' It sounded abrupt but she didn't feel like qualifying it and he walked away looking hurt.

The next morning, she rang Moira during a coffee break in her college office.

'Where were you yesterday?'

'Didn't John tell you?'

'He said you weren't coming. He didn't exactly say why.'

Moira's voice was airy. 'Oh I had so many things on. I just couldn't find the time.'

'Moira, you are always busy and you've always found the

time before. It's your treat and you make sure you have it. Now why weren't you there?'

'Liz, if you could see my schedule . . .'

'Is it because of Erica?'

'Erica?' The voice was still airy.

'Are you staying away because you're suspicious of Erica?'

Moira's voice dipped down to earth. 'Look, she isn't my favourite person in the world. I know you all think she's wonderful.'

'I think of her as a friend,' Liz said carefully. 'Our friend.'

'Well I don't.' There was a pause and then Moira said quickly and reasonably, 'Look, love, we don't always have to like the same people. You can be friends with her and friends with me. There's no *conflict*.'

'But no sauna night either, presumably.'

'Well,' Moira said slowly, 'maybe not just at the moment. Look, shall we have lunch on Tuesday? We could have lunch every Tuesday. We could be ladies who lunch.' She was sweet, cajoling.

Liz said, 'I just wish we could get this Erica and John thing sorted out.'

'So do I and I don't think we can.' Moira used the voice she used on the children to assert final authority.

Liz knew when to quit. 'Fine,' she said.

Moira said, 'Good.' And then, more tentatively, 'Tell me, Liz, have you heard from Charles Beatty?'

'Yes, actually, I have.' Liz was suddenly suspicious. 'Does this happy fact possibly have anything to do with you?'

'Don't be so self-deprecating, Liz. He asked you out because he likes you. It has nothing to do with me.'

'How do you know he asked me out?'

'Well, I don't *know* of course. I just assumed . . .'

'You put him up to it.'

'Of course not.'

'You've bloody well been match-making again.'

'I've done nothing of the sort.'

'You've set us up. Moira, I am *furious*.'

'Liz.'

'Furious.'

'Liz, listen.'

137

'No wonder I hadn't heard for a fortnight. He had no *idea* of asking me out again. Until you *pressured* him . . . Look, I'm not one of your lame ducks.' Liz's voice rose to an uncharacteristic shout and she glanced instinctively at the closed door to the corridor. All she needed now was Andrew Pringle on a coffee hunt. 'He told me he was helping his wife with the builders. *Rubbish.* The truth is he hadn't *thought* about me, until *you* reminded him. What did you tell him? I was sitting weeping by the phone?' Liz's face reddened.

'The *truth* is he was helping his wife with the builders. The truth is also that you intimidate him and he came to me for some Dutch courage. *He* came to *me.*'

'I don't *intimidate* him.'

'Yes you do.' Moira sounded very collected. 'He's a nice man, Liz. Don't chase him off. You could do worse.'

'You're a shit.'

'Have a lovely night, darling,' Moira giggled gently as she put down the phone.

Liz clattered her end down and glared at it. There was a little rap at the door and Andrew Pringle's hopeful face appeared sideways around the jamb. Liz grinned and reached for the kettle and the Nescafé.

He talked for a while about a meeting with the party selection committee and then said abruptly, 'Have you missed having babies, Liz?'

'Andrew, what an amazing question.'

'I'm sorry. I shouldn't have . . . terribly private actually.'

'No, not private. Not with us. Barry's sterile, Andrew. When we found out we told all our friends so everyone would know where we stood. I didn't know you then. It was before you came to London.' She sipped her coffee. 'What's amazing to me is that you thought about it. Why?'

He was evasive. 'Well, you know, being a family man myself . . . I just got to wondering what it was like *not* . . .'

'I couldn't speak for a man.'

'Well, for a woman then.'

'It depends on the woman.'

He nodded. 'Of course.' He looked uncomfortable.

'*Some* women mind a lot,' Liz said. 'I don't know how to say this without sounding awfully cold . . . I mean I *like* children a

138

lot. I just never worried too much about not having my own. We tried, of course. After some years that was. And then when nothing happened, we both had tests. The problem was with Barry, as it turned out, but I don't think it would have made much difference if it were with me. So that was it. We looked at ourselves carefully,' she paused, drinking again from the coffee, 'took a little holiday . . . Italy actually . . . I mean it did have some *impact*. And then we sort of re-geared our lives . . . *that* wasn't going to happen, but other good things were. Barry wrote the first book. I took on some extra courses. We put a bit more energy into our social life.' She laughed suddenly. 'We got the cats. I know it's a joke and a cliché, but they *did* help.' She paused. 'They still do. At least for me.'

Andrew looked solemn. 'Of course, now things are rather different.'

'Oh yes.'

'You could actually . . . I mean, you might meet someone . . .'

'I'll probably meet most of eligible London if Moira Harris has her way,' Liz laughed.

'Would you consider it now?'

'What? Children? At my age?'

'You can't be much older than Erica . . .'

'Andrew, you perfect charmer. I'm about ten years older than Erica.'

He looked genuinely, flatteringly surprised. He paused but said gamely, 'Even so . . .'

'Oh, no way. I'm long past that consideration. I'm thinking nice sophisticated holidays in Tuscany these days . . . not diapers and whatever . . .' She waved him away. 'I've got a lecture. I've got to go.'

Liz arrived five minutes early at the anthropology lecture room in Foster Court. She laid out her notes on the table at the front of the room, set up her box of slides, checked the screen and the projector and cleaned the big green chalkboard. Then she sat for a moment on the edge of the table, looking around the silent room. She lectured here regularly and the row of multi-paned windows, the businesslike clutter of functional wooden-topped tables, and brown and grey moulded plastic chairs, the unadorned cream-coloured walls, were the backdrop of her working life. But the familiarity she felt went deeper;

139

she had spent most of her adult life in rooms like this, first as student, now as teacher. It was her natural venue. And yet, she thought, remembering Andrew, things might have been different. She tried to envision herself with infants and pushchairs, schoolbags and blazers. Moira's image came to mind, but not her own.

Outside, footsteps and echoing voices sounded. She walked quickly around the table and sat down, bending over her notes, reading. The room filled up with the scrape and clatter of chairs and rustling of books and papers. When she raised her head her students were quiet, watching her. As she stood up she thought suddenly that *had* she had children, at even as early an age as Moira, one of those young but adult faces could be that of her own daughter or son. The thought intrigued, but did not trouble her. She smiled at the waiting faces and saw, as always, a few smiles returned.

'Kinship,' she began, 'is the mortar of human society, the stuff of lousy American soap operas – ' there were a few giggles – 'and an anthropological minefield . . .' The pens came out, the heads went down. She wished they'd listen more and scribble less, but never mind, she'd get through to them anyway, in time. She expanded into her subject, leading them in on a thread of ideas, coaxing, surprising, challenging. She felt happy, confident, utterly at home.

On Saturday morning, Liz went to the New Age Body Workshop to give Darren MacPhee a new lot of questionnaires. She'd never been there before on a Saturday. It was different, livelier, noisier, a different receptionist at the desk, different clientele in the corridors.

Darren was on lifeguard duty at the pool. He came out to meet her in his swimsuit, dripping water on the tiled floor. He had a nice body, firmer and more mature than she had expected, and an athlete's casualness about undress. She felt faintly self-conscious and was aware of their positions reversed from the occasion in the sauna suite.

'Sorry to drag you out,' she said. 'I'd have left these at the desk, but I wanted to ask you something.'

'Aye, what was that?' As always, he sounded wary.

'Nothing much, Darren, but I was wondering if you knew how to type.'

'Handwriting that bad, is it?'

'It's not wonderful,' she smiled. 'Do you?' He held up the forefingers of each hand. She laughed. 'Hunt and peck, is it?'

'Three fingers on a good day. Mind, I'm pretty quick.' He paused. 'I haven't got a typewriter,' he said.

'No, I didn't expect that. I've got a machine I could lend you. It's portable and pretty handy. Very handy for you actually; it has a spelling correction facility.'

'Aye, I've heard of those,' he said, interested. He looked down suddenly. 'But I wouldna want to borrow it, or anything.'

'Why not?' She was surprised. 'I don't use it. I've got Barry's word processor still.' He was silent, dripping quietly. Eventually he said, 'I havena anywhere to keep it.'

She was puzzled. 'Your flat?'

'Aye well. There's that. But you see,' he looked up, 'you see, there's Dudes.'

'Dudes?'

'Aye. Dudes. He's one of my mates.'

'In the flat.'

'Yeah. Well, often anyhow.'

'Would he mind you having a typewriter?' she asked. 'It's silent, you know.'

'He wouldna *mind*. He just might . . .' He looked baffled, as if trying to communicate in a foreign language. 'He nicks things, you see,' he said at last.

'He *steals*?' Darren nodded.

'He steals from you and you share a flat with him?'

'Oh no, no. I mean, not often. He's a good mate really. A bit druggie, but a good mate. Still sometimes he needs bread . . .'

'So he steals from you.'

'Not often.'

'Great.' She stared hard at his face. He looked quite undisturbed. 'Darren, why do you share a flat with someone who steals from you? Why don't you just throw him out? Good mate though he *undoubtedly* is,' she added sarcastically.

141

He smiled wisely. 'For a start,' he said, 'it's his flat. I've just got a corner of the living-room.'

'Oh.' She was aware of increasingly murky waters, and said quickly, 'Yes, I see you have a problem.' She paused.

He stepped restlessly from one bare foot to the other, glanced over his shoulder, through the glass partition that separated the corridor from the pool. The other lifeguard, a big blond Australian, was watching them. 'I've got to go,' he said.

'Yes, of course.' She hesitated and then said quickly, 'Look, Darren, you could work at my flat.' As soon as she'd said it, she hoped he'd refuse, and spare her the invasion of her privacy.

He hesitated too, and then said carefully, 'I think maybe that would be better.'

She was committed. Swallowing her reluctance she said briskly, 'Fine. Erica says you only work mornings and evenings midweek, right?'

'Aye, that's right.'

'I'm home all day Wednesday. Would Wednesday afternoons be all right?'

'Aye, fine.'

'I'll tell you how to get there,' she said.

'I've been there,' he reminded her.

She had forgotten. He had not. She nodded. 'Of course you have. It's the top flat. Just ring downstairs and I'll answer.' She started to hand him the questionnaires, but he shrugged, holding up damp hands.

'I'll leave them out front. See you Wednesday.' She left quickly, before the feeling of regret could settle, dropping the envelope with Darren's name on it at the receptionist's desk. As she stepped through the nearer of the twin front doors, she glimpsed Erica Pringle running down the alternative flight of steps, turning sharply right at the bottom, and hurrying up Gower Street, past the line of parked cars. Liz opened her mouth to call out and then stopped. Erica, blonde curls bobbing over the collar of her white ski-jacket, walked purposefully to the passenger door of a big grey familiar Jaguar. As she reached it, the driver's door opened, and John Harris, in his blue and lavender shell-suit and smiling broadly, stepped out. He walked quickly around to the passenger side, and opened the door, kissing Erica's cheek as he did. She smiled and slipped gracefully inside. John closed the door, walked back around the car, got in and drove smoothly away.

Liz stood still on the steps of the New Age Body Workshop. 'Oh *shit*,' she said, aloud.

She thought about them all afternoon, while shopping in the West End. Barry's birthday fell in early March, as did her mother's, and she took a long time choosing a present for each. Her mother's gift had long been limited by the demands of transatlantic posting and now Barry, too, shared the same restricted category. Mindful of the Wisconsin winter, she decided on a red cashmere scarf from a snobbish gentleman's shop off Curzon Street and, in choosing it, felt him slip from partner to simply friend, someone whose needs and desires were no longer made obvious by intimacy. She spent a pleasant hour in Hatchards and found a nice, newly published biography for her mother, and then, after selecting paper and cards, treated herself to lunch in a favourite café among the small tangle of streets around Shepherd Market.

At street level there was an Italian delicatessen and bakery that Barry had discovered years ago as a wonderfully reliable supplier of Christmas panettone, and every December they paid a ritual visit to select one for their Christmas breakfast from the cloud of domed paper boxes festooning the ceiling. Then they would celebrate its capture with coffee and pastries in the little café below the shop.

It seemed hardly more than a week or two since they had been here last, and Barry's presence accompanied her down the stairs and into the small dark booth where she took her seat. At a neighbouring table, a pair of demonstrative Italian lovers reminded her simultaneously of what she and Barry had lost, and what John and Erica had apparently gained. She was hugely guilty, simply because she had brought them together; unwittingly and in innocence, but she had done it all the same.

She felt misery for Moira, an equal misery for poor twittish Andrew, pity for lonely Erica, and for John, baffled dismay. How *could* he? Good, fatherly sensible John. She'd looked up to him for most of twenty years. *Hardly fair. Poor John, you've as much right to be an idiot, I suppose, as the rest of us.*

It might have been innocent, of course, she considered hopefully as she finished her espresso; though it was not easy to imagine how. Still, innocent or not, she could not tell Moira without betraying John and Erica, and she could not *not* tell Moira without betraying her. It was a conundrum with no solution; a burden of knowledge she dearly wished she'd been spared. Putting it from her mind, she spent the rest of the afternoon in Regent Street on an impulsive search for something new to wear for her date with Charles.

When she was a girl, she had dressed always in the fancied hope of pleasing some boy. Now, after so many years of choosing her clothes for her own taste and ease, with Barry's comfortable compliance, she found herself once more looking through the imagined eyes of another. Charles was a graceful, complimentary man. He had praised the green dress she wore to the Savoy, praised her hair, her jewellery. He noticed things. It set a standard, made subtle hurdles to be crossed. Her familiar, user-friendly wardrobe seemed unlikely to meet the challenge.

She wandered from shop to shop and grew increasingly morose. In Laura Ashley she tried on Moira look-alike frocks until struck by the frightening possibility of creating a false image for Charles that she'd then be obliged to maintain for ever. Rebelling, she retreated to Gap and found a thick white cotton tracksuit that flattered her dark hair. She looked in the mirror and saw herself again, instead of an unknown English county lady, and was relieved. She'd dress it up with a scarf. Wear a lot of jewellery and perfume. It was only a film, anyway.

She took the tracksuit to the cash desk and paid a pretty young girl with a thick mass of crinkly ringlets, like Moira's daughter Rachel. They bounced with each turn of her lively head.

'How do you *do* that?' Liz asked suddenly.

'What?'

'Your hair. I see that all the time. It fascinates me.'

'You like it? It's a perm. I just wash it and shake my head.'

'How wonderful.'

'*You* should do it,' the girl said, boldly. 'It'd look terrific with those white bits. How do you do *those*?'

Liz stared, and saw in the mirrored wall behind the desk the two white streaks in her tight-drawn hair. She laughed good-naturedly. 'By getting old,' she said. 'It grows like that.'

'Really?'

'My best friend says I look like a skunk.'

'It would be *fantastic* permed. And you could maybe do a couple of red or blue streaks too,' the girl suggested helpfully.

'What a wonderful idea,' Liz said, deadpan. She stared at her reflection, imagining it, and wondering wickedly what Moira might say. Or, for that matter, her students at UCL.

Charles loved the tracksuit. She wore it with a lot of gold jewellery and Je Reviens and when she opened the door to him, her hair was yet undone.

'Liz, you look wonderful.'

'I'm sorry I'm late.'

'I'm early,' he apologized. 'For once the traffic was actually bearable.' He was staring at her. 'That's so glamorous.'

'You like it?' She was genuinely surprised.

'I love that sort of thing. The white. And trousers. Sort of Gertrude Lawrence . . .'

'God, put it like that and I'm convinced.'

'I love women in trousers. Jane never wears them. I used to ask her to . . .' He stopped suddenly.

Liz said, 'I'll just get ready.' She turned.

'Liz, your hair is amazing. I had no idea there was so *much* of it.'

She laughed. 'Too much. I'll get it under control.'

He started to speak and stopped himself. She went off and came back with it tamed quickly into its bun and a red scarf tied around it. He cast her admiring glances all the way down the stairs. The Porsche was parked below. He helped her in, got in behind the wheel. She looked around and breathed in the scent of the pale blue leather.

'I could get used to this,' she said.

He turned and made his big, white grin. 'Good.'

Dinner was at an Italian restaurant in Soho where the head waiter made a sumptuous fuss of Charles and led them to his best table.

'You're a man about town,' Liz said, only half joking.

'No. I'm a wine merchant.' He smiled deprecatingly. 'If nothing else, I get intimate with a lot of restaurants.'

Liz liked the restaurant. The food was casual and good. Charles talked more freely than he had in the Savoy and he ate more heartily as well.

'No Big Macs this time,' she asked.

'No.' He shook his head slightly, smiling. 'I managed to resist. I tried for some variety today. Wimpy. Burger King. Pizza Hut. No luck. Ronald McDonald Rules.'

'You see them every Saturday?'

'It's so artificial. But in a crazy way I see more of them than I ever did. I was always working. I worked a lot of weekends . . . Jane used to say they'd forget who I was. So now I see them.'

'Quality time,' said Liz.

'I wouldn't call it that.' He twirled linguine expertly around his fork. 'McDonald's. The zoo. All the films. Every weekend a new treat and I know all the time the only thing they want is to be home doing nothing. And me there too.' He shook his head and poured her more wine. 'Oh, Liz. I'm some date. I'm amazed you agreed to come out twice.' She laughed.

'Actually, I was a little surprised you asked me again,' she said honestly.

He looked up, startled. 'Were you? Why?'

'I thought I'd bored you.'

'Bored! You! Impossible.' He was undeniably genuine.

Puzzled, she said, 'Things seemed a little strained at the end. I remember going on about the war . . . I suspected I'd gotten a bit tedious.'

He looked down. She saw him remembering too, and when he spoke again, his voice was tentative. 'It wasn't that. Not tedious surely. The truth is,' he paused, 'I was a bit out of my depth.'

'Out of your depth? *How* Charles?' She looked up, wide-eyed.

He shrugged. 'Education was never my forte, you know. I did a couple of business courses, but they were just something to please my parents . . . both my brothers have university degrees. I just scraped through a couple of A-levels.'

'So?' Liz said. 'You seem to do all right.'

'Oh, I make *money* all right. More than either of *them*, actually. But that's not the point.' He paused again. 'I'm a bit at a loss with educated people . . . I never know what to say without sounding stupid.'

'Charles, really, this is imagination.'

'You know,' he said, leaning forward suddenly, 'I shied off when Moira tried to tell me about you – you being a lecturer . . . I was sure it would be a non-starter. But then when I saw you in those red leggings and you made that joke about lesbians . . . I was so intrigued I forgot to be awed.'

'Awed,' she laughed raucously. 'In all my life no one I am sure has ever managed to be awed of me, Charles. The best I can scrape up, even from my undergrads, is a sort of temporary respect. And *that* wears off soon enough.'

'I doubt,' he said solemnly, 'that you have any idea how they really see you.'

She laughed again. 'Probably just as well.' But then, serious a moment later, she said, 'I wonder if any of us ever really resembles what the world sees? The older I get, the more my friends surprise me. And' – she paused, distracted – 'it isn't all nice surprises.'

They walked from the restaurant to the film theatre. The Soho streets were crowded but Charles was so big that crowds parted around him. He seemed self-conscious of his size, bending down to talk to Liz who, though not a short woman, was only at his shoulder height. As he moved through the streets he removed people from his path with big, gentle hands.

Liz laughed. 'It must be marvellous to be so tall.'

He looked doubtful. 'I feel I'm always in the way. I take up too much space.'

In the lobby of the theatre, women turned to admire him. He seemed oblivious. He had chosen Branagh's *Henry V*. After the conversation at dinner, Liz feared that exercising the Shakespearean option was an attempt to placate her mythical intellect, but they both enjoyed it and afterwards Charles even discussed it on the drive to Fulham. Liz answered, and elaborated as required, but her mind was oddly elsewhere; on Darren MacPhee courting the Princess Katherine in her college office, and the rough, startling touch of his fingers on her cheek.

*   *   *

147

Naturally, Charles came up to the flat for coffee. Any other end to the evening would be churlish, and yet, as they climbed the stairs together, Liz was fully aware of an advance in their relationship, a jump forward as inevitable as the click of a cog in a turning gear. The same inevitability seemed to settle upon the future. Liz saw it ahead, accurately now, without romance. Not the luxuriant succession of theatre evenings, the voluptuous climax in summery France that she had playfully imagined, but the true, likely progression: the friendly dinners, increasingly less formal, a few intimate lunches. The gradual assumption of the presence of the other. The 'we' and 'us' predominating. The recognition by friends and the gelling into coupledom. Gradually their lives would extend into each other's terrain: a shirt or two in her cupboard, her Body Shop shampoo on his bathroom shelf. And the real benchmarks: meeting the children, the former partner, the ageing parents, stiff with uncertainty over the new regime.

It happened. It happened all the time to other people. Andrew Pringle did it. So, appallingly enough, might John Harris. Why should she assume herself immune? And yet, she wondered, how often did people drift into love and even into marriage, simply for lack of a good reason not?

Charles admired the flat so enthusiastically that Liz said, 'Oh come off it. It's a mess. I don't *mind* it's a mess because I'm a slob, but it *is* a mess.'

'It's so lived-in,' he said, with emotion. 'When I go home at night to mine, now that Moira's finished it, I feel like I'm on a film set. I mean,' he said quickly, 'she did a beautiful job, but it's so *perfect* . . .'

'A little more perfection around *here* would be nice,' Liz said. 'What about your home?' she asked, and then regretted it.

'Oh, well, Jane always saw to that. She's a very precise person and I guess I'm not. We managed to strike a pretty good balance most of the time . . . I love those cats, Liz. They look like miniature lionesses.'

'They're male actually. I thought of tying ruffs on them, but I doubt they'd stand for it.' She began opening a tin of tuna to shut them up while the kettle heated. Charles leaned in from the alcove, filling the doorway. 'The trouble with me and Barry was *neither* of us were precise. We were both slobs together. A fatal combination.'

'Do you miss him, Liz?'

She crouched and set the cat food down and then stood up, meeting his candid blue eyes. 'Yes, Charles, I do.' She moved to the kitchen counter and scooped coffee from a crumpled foil bag into the cafetière. She poured the water on and said, 'I miss his company. I miss his conversation. And I miss him in bed.'

'Are you in love with him?'

'I lived with him for most of two decades. We were long past being "in love", whatever that amounts to. But yes, I love him. Enough, frankly, to know it was time for him to go.'

'But why, Liz? Moira said you were always so happy. So perfectly happy.'

'Nobody real is perfectly happy, Charles. We were like any other more or less successful couple. Happy most of the time. Unhappy other times. We agreed and we disagreed. We were mostly kind to each other and sometimes unkind. As far as I know,' she added slowly, 'we never cheated.'

'But why separate?'

Liz poured the coffee into two mugs and searched the fridge for milk. She started to search for a jug but then stopped and put the open milk carton a little defiantly on the table between them. 'Put it this way, Charles. We had come to a crossroads in life and wanted to go two different ways. Why not separate?'

He accepted the finality of her answer, but looked baffled just the same. In the living-room, sitting in Barry's armchair, he said suddenly, 'I can't comprehend a man leaving a woman like you.'

She laughed lightly. 'Wait until you've lived with me seventeen years.'

She grinned, but he reached across to where she sat on the floor and took her hand. 'I might take you up on that,' he said. He drew her closer and she was a little surprised to find herself making no resistance. He slid out of the armchair to the floor, reached his hand behind her head and leaned forward. His first kiss was light, discreet, and questioning. He slipped the scarf from her hair, loosened its fastening, and lifted it luxuriously in his hand, stroking her neck and kissing beneath the hair.

149

Her body stirred pleasantly in response and she knew in fifteen minutes they'd be in bed. She allowed herself a moment more of enjoyment and then pulled gently away.

'It's a little soon, Charles,' she said. He kept his hand beneath her hair but drew back obediently. He smiled, his eyes warm.

'Of course,' he said, acknowledging less a rejection than a promise. He kissed her lightly and got up and sat in the chair. She sat in the sofa across the room. They finished their coffee and, in fifteen minutes, he went home.

IX

He sent her flowers the next day – twelve uncompromising red roses – and they were still filling a tall blue glass jug on the mantel on Wednesday afternoon when Darren came to work. They gave the flat such a sumptuous air of romance that she had actually cleaned it up a bit in their honour, and straightened out her books, filling in the holes left by Barry's departure with strays from the stack in the loo, the pile beside her bed, and the heap on the floor of the study.

Darren stood in front of the bookshelves for a long time, staring. 'I guess you read a lot,' he said.

'It's my work, Darren. It wouldn't be much use if I didn't read.'

'Aye. I guess not.' He still stared. He looked at the roses, reaching out, his rough fingers almost but not quite touching one. 'Are they real?' he asked.

She laughed, amused. 'Of course.'

Her laughter seemed to puzzle him. 'Sometimes they're fake, y'ken,' he said.

'These are real.'

'Aye.' He looked a moment longer. 'They're awful grand to be real.' He seemed shy and young. He was wearing patched jeans and his favourite waistcoat, but the tail of his white shirt was neatly tucked in. Hard to believe he'd actually heeded her advice, but whatever, the result was attractive, revealing a sexy line of hip and long leg.

She said, 'I've set up the machine at the kitchen table, if you don't mind. That way you can work there while I get on in my study, and we won't get in each other's way.'

'Sure, great,' he said. She sensed relief, as if he'd feared working under her watchful teacher's eye. 'I've brought all my stuff.' He had a small green rucksack slung over one shoulder and he dropped it on a chair as they entered the kitchen.

Jacob and Esau were both asleep on the kitchen table, Esau with his chin on the edge of the typewriter.

'Just chuck them off,' Liz said.

'Oh, *great cats*,' Darren said. He reached over the table and casually scooped Esau off the typewriter, folding him in the crook of a muscular arm. The cat looked small and surprised there, his blue eyes blinking twice.

'They're not cuddly,' Liz said. 'They're a pretty stand-offish kind of cat.' Esau remained in a complacent brown ball on Darren's arm. 'That's unlike him,' she said.

'He's purring.' Darren held on to Esau and gathered Jacob up on the other arm. They both hung there, placidly making a liar out of her. 'I love Burmese. My grannie had one.'

'They're Siamese,' Liz said, a little miffed at their stupid defection.

'Same difference.'

'Better not tell Barry that. He was prouder of their pedigree than of his own. Not that his own was much to brag about.'

'Are they his cats?'

'Well, ours. But he chose them. I *thought* of them as his.'

'Why didn't he take them with him?'

'It's difficult . . . all that distance.'

'I've got a wee kitten in the flat. I wouldna just leave *it*.' He held the cats almost possessively.

Liz said, in Barry's defence, 'Well, he didn't *just* leave them. He left them with me.'

'Aye. All the same.' Darren carefully unloaded the cats onto a kitchen chair. They remained side by side and watched him with interest as he sat down in front of the machine and looked it all over before setting his fingers on the keys. He carefully pecked out the alphabet and then all the numbers with the forefingers of his right and left hands.

Liz grinned. 'Perhaps a little lacking in style, but no doubt effective. I'll let you get on.' She went back to her study, closed the door, and settled behind Barry's word processor. She had a good afternoon. Darren's presence in the kitchen had the same inhibiting effect as Barry's once had and she only broke from work twice to make coffee for both of them. On the first occasion she returned at once dutifully to her study, mug in hand, though on the second, at five o'clock, she paused to ask Darren when he was due at the health club.

'I'm not.'

'You're not working tonight?'

'I'm not working at all.' He looked up from his typewriter. There was a neat stack of typed questionnaires beside it. He stroked Esau who was now sharing his chair. 'I quit.' She was startled and a bit uneasy.

'Why, Darren? Surely you need . . . you won't manage on just what I'm paying you.' She half expected a request for more work or higher wages, either of which would be a problem.

'I'll find something.'

'I thought you liked it there.'

'I didn't *love* it,' he said. 'It was *all right*. It wasna that.' He paused, stroked Esau, and looked back. 'We fell out,' he said casually.

'Over what?' Liz said. She heard her own voice sounding alarmed. The health club had been a kind of reference; her employment of Darren had rested, at least in small part, on their previous judgement. Now, with that connection abruptly severed, she was left with a strong young stranger to whom she had given access to her personal space. She watched him with narrowing eyes. 'What was the problem? Money?'

He looked wary and also slightly offended. 'It wasn't anything bad, y'ken.' She nodded, a little ashamed to be so easily read. 'It was over time. I needed more time free and they wouldna agree. I suppose they had a point. I'd been getting Tuesday evenings for *Guys and Dolls*, and then when I asked for Mondays as well they were pretty narked.' He paused. 'And then I needed next week to work on my audition pieces. They said no and I quit.'

'What are you auditioning for?' she asked, placated but puzzled.

'RADA.'

'You've got an audition at *RADA*?'

'Anyone can get an audition. All you have to do is ask.' He smiled, stroking the cat. 'Getting in is the hard bit.'

153

She was still faintly astounded. 'Darren,' she said slowly, 'do you think you actually *could* get in?'

He turned. 'Sure.'

'Seriously?'

'Yeah, *seriously*.' He shrugged belligerently. 'What do you expect me to say? No, because I'm an ignorant git without any talent? What's the point, eh? The trouble with you older people is you're so bloody cautious. Don't *try*, you might fail. So Christ, I fail. The *world* won't bloody end.'

'Darren.'

'Oh what the fuck.'

'Darren. Cool down.' He glanced at her, eyes glittering, still protectively stroking the cat. 'Cool down.' She used her gentle, teacher's voice. 'I'm not criticizing you. I'm not saying you haven't got talent. I'm only saying RADA is a very very demanding goal.'

'You think I don't know that?' Their eyes met and locked, his aggressive, hers baffled.

She turned away. 'I'm going out for some milk, Darren. I'll be back in a moment. If that's all right.'

'Yeah, sure.' His anger was cooling rapidly into self-consciousness. He looked down at his work, embarrassed, and she went cautiously to the door. She took her time over getting the milk and, as she expected, when she returned the argument was over. He was typing industriously and when she came into the kitchen, he looked up at once.

'Somebody called for you. I answered it. I hope you didna mind.'

'No. Of course not. Did they say who they were?'

'Aye. It was your friend from America.'

'Barry?'

'Aye. I never talked to anyone in America before.'

'What did he say? Did he leave a message?'

'He asked who I was.'

She stopped in the midst of putting the cartons of milk in the fridge and slowly straightened up. 'What did you say?'

'I told him my name.' Darren shrugged. 'He said to tell you he'd call back tonight.'

'Oh good. Fine.' She finished putting the milk away and turned from the fridge. 'How'd he sound?'

154

Darren shrugged again. 'OK I guess.' He bent his head over his work. 'I'm almost finished,' he said as she moved towards the door.

'I'll be in my study if you want me.'

'Did he send you the roses?'

'What?' She stopped in the doorway.

'The roses in the other room. Were they from him? Interflora like? I thought maybe it was your birthday or something.'

'No, Darren. It's not my birthday.' She paused, and said slowly, 'The roses are from someone else.'

She was in the shower when Barry rang. Wrapped in a towel, she dashed to catch it.

'Hello, love, have I got the time right?'

Liz swept back a wet snake of hair from her shoulder, and looked at her bedroom clock. It said one. 'Improving,' she said.

'Great. I thought I'd catch you before I went out to dinner. I'm meeting some friends at eight.'

'I was in the shower.'

'Oh poor love,' he said without interest. He paused. 'Sorry I haven't rung for a while. I've been frightfully busy . . .'

'That's all right. I've been busy too. Anyhow, I wasn't *expecting* you to. I mean, you must be getting pretty settled in by now.'

'Oh yes. Of course.'

'It changes the focus, doesn't it?'

'Well, sort of. Liz . . .' He stopped, uncertain.

'Yes.'

'Liz, who was that who answered the phone?'

'When? This afternoon?'

'Yes. There was a man . . .'

'Oh that was Darren.'

'Who?'

'Darren MacPhee.'

'What is he, a student?'

'No, no. I never bring students home. You know that. I always think it undermines authority. No. Darren's my research assistant, Barry. I told you about him.'

'Oh. Yeah.' He sounded puzzled.

155

'You've forgotten, but I did.'

'He works at the flat?'

'He did today.' There was a long silence at his end and she added, 'He has problems at his own place. Besides, it will be handy as we get further along. We can discuss things.'

'You must get on well.'

'We do,' she said. 'Actually, I'm surprised *how* well we get on.'

There was another silence and then he said, 'That's great, Liz. I'm pleased for you. You'll get that book wrapped up in no time.'

He spoke with a confidence she did not share, but not wishing to reveal that doubt, she said, 'So tell me what's happening.'

'Oh, lots of good things,' he said slowly. He sounded tired, as if he had at last descended from the high he'd been on since his arrival.

'Still in love with the place?'

'Oh yes. Very much so. It has its faults of course, but what place hasn't?'

'Oh certainly.'

'I mean, London is hardly perfect.'

'Hardly.'

'Liz . . .'

'Yes?'

'You haven't reconsidered?'

'Reconsidered what?'

'You know. Joining me.'

'Oh God, no. I really thought that was settled, Barry.'

'Yes. Of course. I just thought, now that some time has passed . . .'

'If you're asking if I've missed you, well of course I have, love.'

'Oh, I've missed you too.' It sounded heartfelt and she felt sorry for him.

'Barry, it was only realistic to assume we'd miss each other. It doesn't change the basic situation.'

'Oh yes, I know. Of course nothing says it has to be a *total* separation. I mean we could still get together from time to time.'

156

'You planning a trip back?'

'Well, no, I mean I really couldn't just now. I'm just getting established after all and there's a lot of work. The pace is a bit faster, isn't it?' She made a small sound of agreement. 'No, I was just thinking if this war gets settled maybe and *I* don't know what's going to happen. It could be over in a fortnight. Or it could go on for years . . . but if it does get sorted out . . . would you like to fly over? Maybe Easter?'

Taken aback, she said quickly, 'I don't know, Barry. I'm not sure I want to give up the time . . . and I could hardly justify the expense.'

'Oh, I'd send your ticket, love.'

'That's very kind, Barry. I don't know how I'd feel about accepting it.'

'Oh for Christ's sake, Liz. You sound like a twenty-year-old worrying about her honour. I promise I'll still respect you if you accept this airline ticket. I'll book you your own room, too,' he added sarcastically.

'Barry, I would *expect* that.'

'Liz!'

'The door's closed, love, and you closed it. I'm not yours for life just because I used to live with you.'

'Liz, I don't see where all this finality is coming from. So I'm in Wisconsin for a while and you're still in London. It doesn't have to change everything.'

'No, but it changes a good deal.' She paused. 'Barry, I'm going out with someone.'

He was silent. After a long while, he said, his voice very quiet, 'Oh. I see.'

'Nothing terribly *serious* of course . . .'

'Anyone I know?'

'No. One of Moira's lame ducks, actually.'

'Liz, you didn't need . . .' He sounded indignant.

'No. I didn't *need*, but I've found I like . . .'

'I see.' He paused a long while, and then said evenly, 'Well that's very nice for you, Liz.'

'You see what I mean about things changing.'

'Yes. I see.' He sighed, then said slowly, 'I'm sorry, love, I seem to have jumped in with both feet where I really don't belong.'

157

'It's all right,' she said gently. 'You really couldn't know.'

'To tell the truth, I'm a bit unsettled tonight. This war thing's upsetting me.'

'It's pretty upsetting.'

'How does it look from your end?'

'Pretty much what you said. Anybody's guess.'

'Yes.' He sounded weary. After a long pause he said plaintively, 'It's hard to get a real picture over here.'

'I don't expect *we're* getting a real picture either.'

'No, but it's *different* here. They're awfully patriotic, aren't they?'

'Oh yes.'

'It's strange to find *young* people . . . I mean you *expect* dissent from the young, don't you? I've just had the most extraordinary argument with a young girl . . . and she's a super girl, usually . . . I couldn't believe we were fighting about this . . .' Abruptly he stopped. 'I'd better go, love. I have to meet these people.' He paused, and said with sudden warmth, 'Thanks for listening. You're a great friend.'

She said goodbye and put down the phone, getting up from the damp patch on the bed. The cats, having settled for the night, got up and turned around in irritated circles. She looked at the clock. *Christ, love, I hope they're paying you well.*

'Would you tell me,' Moira said over lunch, 'if my husband was having an affair?'

'Moira, I'm *sure* he's not.'

'That's not what I asked.'

'You mean I knew and you didn't,' Liz said with academic distancing.

'Precisely.'

'It's hardly likely, is it? I never really *believe* these stories about everyone knowing except the wife.'

'They happen,' Moira said. 'When Sebastian did the dirty on my friend Alice – you know, I told you, buggered off with her best friend and left her with the baby – it turned out that half the village knew about it the whole time. People they saw every day, people they entertained. *Good friends.* Everyone was too nice. They didn't want to interfere. That kind of thing.'

'Perhaps they didn't want to make it worse.'

'How much *worse* precisely could it have been?'

Liz looked away, out the window of the small dark restaurant, into the thin February sunlight. She said thoughtfully, 'When you say they *knew*, what did they *really* know? Everyone hears rumours, sometime or another, and they're usually false. The last thing anyone wants to do is spread gossip about a friend. Or,' she looked back at Moira, 'make some appalling mistake that knocks the trust out of someone's marriage.'

'I'm talking about facts. They were *seen* together. Often.'

'That could mean anything,' Liz said, a little desperately. 'That's not *evidence*.'

'What were they waiting for? *In flagrante delicto* in Sainsbury's? Oh come off it, Liz.' She tilted her lovely head sideways. 'People are convicted of murder on less evidence than they had on Sebastian.'

'Yes and there are a lot of wrongful convictions. Relationships are based on trust. They don't work any other way. Once suspicion gets in the whole thing's doomed to failure.'

'Were you never suspicious of Barry?'

'No.'

'What about now?'

'Now's a different story. He's a free agent. So am I.' She leaned forward. 'But if you're asking had I *cause* for suspicion, yes, on your definition. I suppose I had. He was often home late. He met alone with students. There was one he used to play badminton with. She liked badminton and I found it a bore. So? Was he bonking her under the net? Who knows? Who *cares*?'

'You'd care if you thought it was happening,' Moira said shrewdly.

'I'd want *evidence* first. Not just some PMT paranoia.'

Moira ignored that. 'I have evidence,' she said.

'*What?*'

Moira lifted her gold-clasped clutch purse from the banquette beside her, opened it and took out her green calf-skin wallet. She unzipped it and carefully withdrew a folded piece of tissue paper from its silken interior. She laid it on the white cloth between them. Liz was reluctant to touch it.

'Look at it. Go on.' Liz lifted the paper and turned it towards her. It was a VISA receipt for a hotel dinner in Brighton. John

159

Harris's strong signature was at the bottom. She studied it carefully and looked up at Moira.

'So?'

'What was he doing in Brighton?'

'Having dinner at a guess. Moira, what's this meant to be evidence *of*?'

'He's seeing her.'

'Who, *Erica*?'

'Of course.' Moira folded her hands on the table cloth and looked at Liz with unwavering certainty.

'You've found one dinner receipt and from that you decide your husband's having an affair with one of your friends?'

'One of my ex-friends. What was he doing in Brighton? Why is it dinner for two? Why a hotel? And why did he lie to me?'

'He lied to you?' Liz said uneasily.

'In effect. He said he was entertaining an American client. He would be late and might stay the night in town.'

'Maybe the American client wanted to see Brighton.'

'Oh don't be absurd. Who *ever* wants to see Brighton?' She picked the VISA slip up tartly and put it away.

'Moira,' Liz asked, 'how did you *get* that?'

'It was in his wallet. Of course.'

'*You went through his wallet?*' Liz's eyes widened with shock.

'Of course. How else am I to know what he's up to?'

'But to go through his wallet . . . his privacy . . .'

'I go through his wallet, his trouser pockets, his diary. I check his collars for lipstick and his jackets for female hairs. Sometimes, though not too often, I open his mail.' She smiled coolly at Liz's deepening look of shock and said, 'I regard it as marriage maintenance. A necessary evil.'

'You know, I'm appalled,' Liz said with a small honest laugh.

'I can see that. Look,' Moira leaned forward, her gracefully long fingers with their pearly nails brushing Liz's jumper sleeve. 'The world is full of older women living alone. I don't intend to be one of them.' She straightened up, with her sudden air of dismissal and signalled the waiter. 'Let's have coffee.'

Liz looked at her watch. 'I almost don't have time. I don't

think lecturers fall into the category of Ladies Who Lunch. Lunch hour's too short.'

'Oh, be late. I'm late too.' Moira ordered coffee. Over it, she said, 'Well, fill me in. How's Barry? Are you still seeing Charles? How's the toyboy?'

'*Who?* Oh, Darren.' Liz laughed gently. 'He's *all right.* He's doing the work and he's surprisingly good company.'

'Good company? Where?'

'He worked at the flat on Wednesday. Using my typewriter.'

'Good God, He-Man can type.'

Liz laughed helplessly over her coffee. 'You're really not fair.'

'At the flat, is he? I don't know, Liz.'

'Well *I do.* He's a very nice *boy.*'

'How old?'

'Oh twenty-something. I don't know.'

'So's Stephen Lloyd. The Michael Ignatieff of African Studies.'

'Yes, well. This is different. Anyhow, as a *working relationship* it's fine. I'm enjoying it.' She paused. 'You know he's left the health club.'

'I didn't know.' Moira's voice went flat at the mention of the health club and Liz regretted the reference.

'Yes, well. He was too busy rehearsing a play.'

'Is he paid for the play?'

'Oh no. It's a university thing actually.'

'What's he doing for money?'

Liz shrugged. 'He's managing, I guess.' She said quickly, 'Barry rang Wednesday night. He's fine. Sounded a bit down, actually, but I'm sure it's temporary.'

'Missing you?'

'A bit.'

'What about that girl?'

'Girl? What girl?'

'The one in the pictures.'

'Oh, Moira, now you're doing it to *Barry.* I have no idea about the pictures. He's never mentioned a girl.' She stopped abruptly in saying it and, after a thoughtful pause, she added, 'Well not any *specific* girl.'

Moira looked wise. 'What about Charles?' she said.

'Charles is great.' Liz raised her eyes to meet Moira's in cheerful challenge. 'Great time out, slap-up dinner, good film, straight to the sack, bonked all night.'

'Liz you *didn't*!'

'No, I didn't. Thought that would shake you up. No worries, darling. I'm just an older woman, living alone.' She giggled happily and picked up the bill.

They parted outside the restaurant on the corner of Great Russell Street and Tottenham Court Road. Liz watched Moira striding gracefully towards Oxford Street, a beautiful woman, beautifully dressed, utterly enviable in any stranger's eyes. She shrugged sadly and turned away and walked back down the narrow length of Great Russell Street, towards work. In front of the YWCA Central Club, she was happily surprised to see Darren MacPhee, in jeans and a long black coat, coming down the steps. His head was turned away and he did not see her. She called his name. He stopped, and turned towards her, squinting into the bright sunlight. He had a folder under his arm and looked neither surprised, nor for that matter particularly happy, to see her.

'Oh, hello, Dr Campbell.' His voice was subdued.

'Hi, Darren. What are you doing here?'

He shrugged and indicated with one shoulder a poster on the door. She stepped closer. It was a felt-tip notice: Royal Academy of Dramatic Arts, Auditions, one to three P.M. 'Are you auditioning today?' she asked.

'I've been.'

'Already?'

'Aye.'

'How . . .?'

He grinned sardonically and bowed towards her, his long coat sweeping the pavement. 'Good luck for your next audition, Mr MacPhee.'

'I don't . . .' Liz hesitated.

'I failed,' he said.

'Oh, Darren. I'm sorry.'

He shrugged. 'There's other colleges.'

'Of course. Can you try here again?'

'Aye. For what it's worth.'

She paused, sadly, and then said, 'Darren, maybe a little later, when you've got more sure of yourself . . . I'm sure a lot of it's what you said, your accent and all . . .'

'No,' he said lightly. 'That was nothing to do with it. I'm just not fucking good enough. That's all.' He turned his collar up, swirled the black coat around himself, and strode away.

She wasn't terribly surprised when he didn't turn up on Wednesday. She imagined him drowning his sorrows with his friends, perhaps the boy and the girls she had met at the peace demo, and going to ground for a day or so. Sympathy overrode any annoyance at the inconvenience to herself, though she did intend a slight but firm reprimand when they met again. Whatever his disappointments, a working contract was made to be kept, a lesson he'd soon learn in the theatre, so he might as well learn it now.

She hoped a little that Erica might have heard from him, but at her Thursday yoga class she found only that he had collected his things on the previous Friday and not returned.

Liz found the yoga class a strain. John was at his most oppressively jolly, teasing and loud. His progress was remarkable. He slipped in and out of stretches, wound into twists with supple freedom, drawing a stream of praise from Erica. Liz could not deny he earned it, nor did Erica's cheerful encouragement appear out of place. But her vision was coloured by Moira's revelations and her own suspicions, and in that view praise too readily became indulgence, physical instruction, caresses. Each quiet moment between them appeared a lover's confidence. When John bounced out after the session, his charming smile imparting cheer to the whole room, she was barely able to suppress a glower.

Erica joined her, blue Nordic eyes narrowed quizzically. 'Why are you angry?' she said.

Erica looked innocent and honest and Liz gave a sheepish smile. 'I'm getting just a little irritated by Super Man,' she said.

Erica laughed prettily. 'For so many years, he is the joke always, the one everyone laughs at and teases; poor clumsy weakling John. Now he enjoys a little revenge. Be kind. He will grow out of it.' She smiled winningly and the fond look

163

she cast after John seemed oddly maternal. 'Sauna?' she said to Liz, hopefully.

Liz's suspicions dissipated in the piney heat. Erica was friendly and sweet and chattered about Andrew's children and the games they played.

'You're great with them,' Liz said spontaneously. 'Like a big sister.'

'Like a mother,' Erica reproved. 'Doesn't a mother play?'

'Of course.' Liz propped herself up on an elbow, looking curiously at Erica. Erica was solemn, pulling at her blonde curls. 'Sure a mother plays. It's only, you seem so young. That's all I meant.'

'Too young,' Erica said miserably.

Liz laughed, stretching luxuriously. 'I strongly suspect that "too young" is one of those things like "too thin" or "too rich" that a woman can't be.'

But Erica seemed neither to understand nor to be amused. She said, 'I wish I was old and serious looking. Then Andrew would be happy with me.'

'I'm *sure* he doesn't want that. And I'm sure too he *is* happy with you.'

'He's not, Liz,' Erica said. 'Not any more. He would be happy now with Fiona. She is what he needs. At his parties. And with his political friends. He needs Fiona now.'

'Well he's a bit bloody late to think of that,' Liz said.

Erica lay down on her stomach and turned her face away. Liz reached from her bench and touched Erica's bare brown arm. She looked up. 'Oh, Liz.' The blue eyes were bright and girlish with unshed tears. 'I wish I was home in Switzerland with my parents and my friends and none of it had ever happened at all.'

X

The following Wednesday, Darren didn't turn up either. Liz worked in a desultory, restless fashion throughout the afternoon, listening for the door and the telephone. By five she realized he was clearly not coming, and she had half-wasted another day waiting for him. It made her angry. She heard herself mentally repeating all the things Moira said about feckless youth. They all sounded pretty accurate. What does a telephone call cost? Why not write a note?

But a current of sympathy undid her anger. She remembered too clearly youth's devastating depressions. She thought of the whole semester she wasted at Columbia, hanging around the library, hoping to see, who was it? That dark boy with the beard, his name eluded her. A whole semester of failed essays, missed tutorials, deserts of communication between herself and her parents and friends. If unrequited passion justified all that, shouldn't Darren's rebuff from the theatre entitle him to a small similar folly? Love was love.

Of course, she was making tremendous assumptions. There could be a dozen other causes, ranging from the trivial, a row with that girl Sheila, perhaps, to the ominous. What *was* that place he lived in, with his kleptomaniac druggie flat mate? Who *were* those people he mixed with? Indeed, a little echoing reminder of her earlier unease, who was Darren? Had he a home somewhere in the north; parents? Or had he come up from the mire of foster homes and institutions that set so many of London's itinerant young on the road? If she seriously needed to, where could she possibly find him, if he did not choose again to find her?

Fortunately, she did not need to. The solution was simple enough. He had, without reason, failed his side of the bargain. She owed him money, but he knew where to find her if he wanted it. Aside from that, she was free to readvertise the position, find someone else; someone conventional and sound this time, a student with a name, address, and history readily available. And that would be that. So much for her experiment in social welfare; next time she'd listen to her friends. She typed out another index card requesting a research assistant, but left it, for the moment, on the edge of her desk.

On Saturday she attended the now traditional vigil against the war in the Gulf. The numbers had dwindled to a few old faithfuls; the hardliners like the Geordie Communist with whom she was now on first-name terms, a few stalwarts from the women's movement, and a sprinkling of students. Uncertainty imbued even that remaining few. On the blank white wall of a shop beside the church, the spray-painted letters of FUCK THE WAR trailed unsteadily towards the pavement. Liz stood stubbornly in the windy night, beneath the bare rustling trees, cosseting the now-familiar candle and taking turns with a friend from the Gay Women's Peace Movement in holding the stanchion of a banner reading CEASEFIRE NOW. The talk, even the singing, was subdued. Liz was distracted anyway, rather more aware than she'd like to be that an additional motivation of her attendance was the off-chance that she might find Darren there.

He didn't appear, but after half an hour, a group of art students in their trademark vampire black joined the vigil; among them she saw the dark girl called Stephanie who had been with Darren and his friends. Leaving her banner in the charge of her lesbian companion Mary, she crossed to the foot of the brick-fronted steps, where the young people had gathered to light candles. She realized with a wave of self-annoyance that had it been Sheila she would not have had the nerve to approach. But Stephanie was a pleasant child, with no hints of intimacy about her.

'Hi, Liz,' she said, after a moment's puzzlement. 'I didn't recognize you. These are my friends.' She turned and reeled off a clutch of names. 'This is Liz.' They all said, 'Hi,' some juggling their candles to shake hands. 'Liz is a lecturer,' Stephanie said, a little proudly. They all acknowledged that.

'Is Darren coming?' Liz asked.

'Who? Oh Sheila's Darren.' She looked thoughtful. 'I haven't seen him for ages.' She paused. 'Are you looking for him?'

'Well no, not exactly.'

'He might be at Sheila's,' someone offered. 'They're both rehearsing.'

'Oh, I see,' Liz said.

'Yeah. They're in that play, aren't they?' Stephanie said. 'Would you like Sheila's number? I've got it somewhere.' She began rooting around in the black satchel she carried.

'No, no. Please don't bother,' Liz said hastily. 'Thank you anyway.' Quickly, she moved away.

She went back to her banner and relieved Mary, feeling oddly irritated. She knew at once that the possessive link of Sheila's name to Darren's was the irrational core of the irritation. It would have been utterly ridiculous if jealousy was the source of her annoyance, but it wasn't precisely that. It was more a feeling of foolishness, of having been used. For all her concern for him, Darren had a solid little world of his own, of friends, girlfriends, theatrical companions. She was a small and expendable part of it, to be deleted when, as now, his time was full. Far from having vanished into some unsavoury underworld, he had simply moved comfortably back into the sure, smug society of the young.

Stuff him, she thought sourly, and determined to pin up her notice for his replacement on Monday. At the same time, the thought crossed her mind that she did owe him money and the one easy anonymous place to find him was the rehearsal hall of the university production of *Guys and Dolls*. She rejected the thought. Why should she chase after him, even to settle a debt? If he wanted his money, he could come to her.

For the most part, the pedestrian traffic flowed by, happily undisturbed by their small demonstration, but occasionally people stopped on the pavement to watch, one or two briefly joining them before going on. A group of teenagers in denims and aggressive leather – boys and girls with cropped hair and pinched belligerent faces – slowed and lingered and then began to heckle, jostling the demonstrators and shouting about England and Our Boys. It sounded a bit forced, as if they were touched with the same uncertainty as their opposition. After a while they stopped shouting slogans from the *Sun* and mingled with the demonstrators, some arguing, some merely chatting. Liz wondered how many weeks or months it would take before the sides hardened into the kind of bitterness she remembered from the sixties. Maybe never; it was a different, more complicated world. She watched a group of the erstwhile hecklers settling down on a wall to debate with a tall man in a suit carrying a neatly printed sign reading NEGOTIATE NOW: WORDS NOT WAR. To her great surprise she recognized Andrew Pringle.

'Excuse me, Mary,' she said, 'I've just seen another friend.' She crossed through the candlelit crowd, and wormed her way through the circle of offended patriots.

'Andrew?' she said. He was wearing a three-piece suit and a wool overcoat and looked resoundingly out of place. He acknowledged her with a wave of his hand, but did not break his conversational, or rather lecturer's stride. Liz settled on the wall beside a short-haired youth in denims and listened too. Andrew continued to declaim, in relentless detail, the economic perils of a prolonged land war. Benumbed by facts, they listened with glazing eyes.

'I'm sure you're right, sir,' said a girl in black leather. Andrew was detailing the exact cost of a day's shelling, weapon by weapon.

'It's something to think about,' the denim-clad boy said, getting to his feet and rolling up his small Union Jack. Andrew started in on a price list of helicopters.

'We've got to be going now,' the black leather girl said. She began backing away, trying frantically to break contact with Andrew Pringle's mesmeric gaze. Eventually, catching hold of each other's hands, the couple fled. Andrew turned quickly to pin the rest of his audience, but they were melting hurriedly into the dark.

'Well done,' Liz said, applauding. 'You've won that lot for sure.'

'Do you think so?' Andrew sounded uncertain. 'They seemed a little baffled.'

'You weren't what they were expecting,' Liz said, adding

quickly, 'you weren't what *I* was expecting, as delightful as it is to see you. What's happened? Why the change of heart?'

'Oh not really a *change*, Liz. Just an adjustment. I told you I don't really *like* war.' He paused. 'It's *wasteful*,' he said, his handsome face grimacing distaste. 'I hate waste. Two weeks, maybe, was reasonable. But this is far too much, far too much. And a land war on top of it? Who's going to *pay* for this, I ask you?'

'We are,' Liz said brightly.

'No. Not us, Liz. The Third World. That's who'll pay. Higher oil prices, cut-backs on national budgets, you wait and see. Look at Africa. They're still starving. Where's the money going now? Into the bloody bonfire. Just *wasteful*. Appalling.'

'What about the Party?' Liz asked.

'Oh, I've never really been a Party man.'

Liz absorbed that and said tentatively, 'I would imagine they'd expect you to be in the House.'

'Hm? Oh that. Well that's not settled yet.' He sounded vague and uninterested, quite unlike his enthusiasm of the preceding weeks. She was curious at the change.

'How's Erica?' she said, rolling her extinguished candle absently between her fingers.

'Oh, fine. Playing squash with John Harris. More her sort of thing than this, I suppose.' He made a small gesture towards the dispersing crowds. 'Nothing much I do is *really* her sort of thing . . .'

'She sees quite a lot of John.'

'Hm? Oh yes. I suppose she does. A lot in common.'

Liz was silent, thinking. *Andrew are you really that thick? That innocent?*

He said, 'You know, I miss Barry. I really do. I say, Liz, we're having a little dinner tomorrow. Would you care to join us? John will be there.' He looked hopeful.

Liz said, surprised, 'And Moira?'

'No, actually. She had something on. Can't think quite what. John did say, but I've forgotten . . . What about you?'

'It's terribly kind and I'd love to, but actually I'm seeing Charles Beatty.'

'Oh are you, Liz? That's nice. John says he's a nice man. I'm glad for you.' He sounded fatherly.

169

'Yes, well, I'm meeting his children actually.'
Andrew nodded his head solemnly. 'Oh, I *see*.'
'I mean, just *casually*. We're going to the zoo, I think.'
'Ah, the zoo.' He nodded again, with portent.

Liz woke on Sunday to the rumblings of battle: Jacob and Esau
were mounting an offensive over her knees, the air filled with
feline growlings. The alarm went and they pounced on each
other. She buried her head in the duvet and let the tumult of
rolling fur ride over her until, with a crescendo of screeches,
they leapt from the bed, victor in pursuit of vanquished,
thundering like velvet buffalo to the kitchen.

Liz shut the alarm off and sat up muzzily. She'd promised
Charles she'd meet him at noon. If she got up now, she could
surface gently through the *Independent on Sunday* first. She was
ambivalent about the day, wary of Megan and Lucy who, by
Charles's own description, were not easy children, and wary
too of Charles in the unknown guise of Weekend Dad.

She followed the cats from the bedroom, switching on the
small television in the living-room as she passed, in the now
habitual craving for war news. Tanks and armoured vehicles
filled the screen. Land war tumbled into the living-room on a
torrent of commentators' words.

'Oh shit,' Liz said. She sank down on the floor in her pyjamas
and dressing-gown, staring at the screen. The cats made little
mewling guerrilla attacks from the kitchen but she pushed
them aside with impatient hands. She was still watching, an
hour and a half later, when Charles rang.

'Liz, look, I'm sorry. I'm running late . . .'

'Have you heard, Charles, it's started.'

'What. Oh. The land offensive. Yes, there was something
on the radio. Look, Lucy lost My Little Pony in the garden.'

'Your *what*?'

'My Little Pony.'

'She's lost your *pony* in the garden?'

'No, no. My Little Pony. You know, Liz, those ponies.
They're pink or lavender or . . .' A childish shout intervened.
'Rainbow. This one's rainbow. Anyway it was still lost when
I got here. Jane had been searching half the night.'

On the screen the prime minister's face appeared and Liz

strained to hear over Charles's explanation. There was a pause in his voice. 'So is that all right?'

'What? Is what all right?'

'What I just said. Meeting us at Regent's Park.'

'Is that what we agreed?' Liz said absently.

'No, Liz. It's what I just said. Liz,' he sounded querulous, 'are you listening to me?'

'Yes of course, Charles. Sorry, the television's on. This war thing's a bit distracting.'

'Yes, well. Look, I've got to go. I'm on Jane's phone. I'll see you at one then, right?'

'One.' Liz struggled to concentrate, her eyes still on the screen and the cats having renewed their attack. 'Fine. I'll see you there.'

'OK, Liz.' He put down the phone rather quickly. Liz returned hers to its bracket on the wall, shrugged slightly, and followed the two Siamese into the kitchen.

'Fine. Let Kuwait burn. Let Israel burn. What do you care as long as you get fed?' She reached in the cupboard for a tin as she switched on the kettle for coffee with the other hand. 'Next time it's big, sloppy, socially committed St Bernards all the way.'

Liz dressed to go out in leggings and jeans, wool jumper, Gore-Tex jacket, and boots. The zoo at the pace of small children was a chilly prospect. Images came to mind of sad little troupes of weekend half-families, dutiful fathers and their precise, solemn children, doggedly enjoying themselves. How odd to be joining them. Odder still to imagine herself in that world, with Barry calling to pick up shared-out children of their own. But of course, had there been children, everything would have been different. 'Come and take your bloody cats for a walk,' she said, dumping clean, dusty litter into their immaculate tray.

Before she left the flat she laid out dinner; pre-packaged duck and orange sauce, a frozen gateau thawing by the sink, two pleasantly ripe avocados. She had promised Charles candlelight and romance after the children's departure. He hadn't sounded all that romantic on the phone and she herself would now probably rather watch the news, but she stuck gamely by the original plan, and set forth warily to sample vicarious parenthood.

They were standing before the wrought-iron gates of Regent's Park Zoo when she arrived, great tall Charles with two minute little people, one clinging to either leg. His back to the entrance, he peered anxiously into the Saturday crowds, looking for her.

'There she is, there's Liz now,' she heard him say as she waved a greeting. And, as clearly, a small voice declaring, 'I don't like her. She looks like a witch.'

Charles, red-faced, gave her the smallest of kisses on one cheek. She looked down into two pairs of round blue eyes, widening with astonishment.

'Hi,' she said, her mind racing. *What do you say to them? What do they do at that age? What age are they? Lucy just had a birthday.* Which, *for God's sake, he must have said.*

'Liz, this is Lucy,' he gently propelled the older girl forward with his big hands on her shoulders. She was a perfectly self-possessed child, with a smooth, curved cheek, a well-formed smile, and English blue eyes of exacting honesty. Long buff hair, recently brushed but already tangling, hung down over her coat collar and to her waist.

'Hi, Lucy, how old are you?' Liz said.

Lucy treated it as the ignoramus question it was and refused to answer. Instead she said, 'Why's your hair like that?'

'Like what?'

'Those funny white bits.'

'Oh,' Liz laughed, 'because it's turning grey, sweetheart.'

'Liz has beautiful hair,' Charles said reprovingly.

'No she hasn't,' said Lucy.

Megan, her smaller sister, put tiny fat hands over a wide mouth and laughed explosively.

'Megan,' Charles whispered. 'Say hello properly.'

Megan snorted raucously again and then wiped her mouth and extended a wet hand to Liz. Liz shook it solemnly. Charles looked grim.

The children crowded around him as he bought the tickets, but then, released from formality, bolted on ahead, disappearing around the corner of the ape exhibit. He said, 'I don't know what's got into them. That's not their usual behaviour at all.'

172

Liz looked gently after their small running figures, remarkably agile in their stiff little coats and patent shoes. 'It's not a usual experience,' she said, wondering who had chosen the immaculately inappropriate costumes. 'Seeing their father with another woman. Not their mother.' He was quiet, but she saw no point in being coy with the facts. 'I somehow doubt those coats will last the course,' she added.

'No.' He looked confused. 'That's what Jane said, but I wanted them to look nice for you.'

She took his hand. 'They do look nice, Charles. They look lovely. Come on, let's find the rhinoceros. I love rhinoceri.'

The zoo was sunlit, but bitingly cold, a cutting wind whipping around the edges of buildings, scattering paper cups and chocolate wrappers along the pathways. Charles let the children choose their own route. Megan ran gleefully from one enclosure to the next, circling back, shouting at her sister, stopping wide-eyed to stare at some creature of particular fascination. There was a bewildering logic in her choices: the monumental elephants held her attention no longer than the small hoofed animals left seemingly by accident in the surrounding moat. Empty enclosures thrilled her most of all, their absent occupants wreathed in mystery. Lucy looked at everything and said nothing.

The animal houses were warm and rank, fierce with alien smells, recalling to Liz childhood zoo visits in New York. The appeal seemed timeless; these huge unlikely beasts tucked with Victorian primness behind moats and railings in the confines of a city park. Megan giggled gleefully at the colourful genitalia of primates, the thunderous urination of elephants.

Lucy stared solemnly at each exhibit for an apparently prescribed time, after which she would nod her head and say, 'All right. What's the next animal?' The experience seemed utterly joyless, but Liz suspected she was simply concentrating. Or possibly, like herself, thinking of two things at once. In her own case, the tanks and planes smashing through the Gulf; in Lucy's, what? Home, her mother, the curious upset in her brief, inexperienced life?

'All right,' Lucy said of the giraffes and turned to go, eyes thoughtfully questing a new animal.

'I'm not done yet.' Megan clung to a railing. 'I haven't finished them.'

'Well,' Charles said, 'finish them.'

'I'm *doing* it. Now I've lost my place.' She sighed with comic adult impatience. 'Now. One, two, four, five, seventeen.' Liz studied her quizzically. She was bent over her hands, clutching the rail and chewing at her thumbs.

'She's counting them,' Lucy said. 'She counts everything.'

'Seventeen. Finished,' said Megan.

At the elephants she again found seventeen. Liz managed four. There were a lot more than seventeen monkeys, counting all varieties, but Megan selected, apparently, the seventeen best. In the darkness of the aquarium, Liz watched her count out seventeen fish in the glowing tanks and abandon that.

'She doesn't *really* count,' Lucy said. 'She can't count.'

'Seventeen's a lot to count,' Liz suggested.

'Seventeen is the *only* big number she knows,' Lucy confided with impressive scorn. She added suddenly, 'I go to school,' and then, with a sideways glance from under her short, businesslike eyelashes, 'I'm six.'

'Why didn't you tell Liz when she asked you that?' Charles said, even as Liz jerked his arm for silence.

'Because I didn't want to then,' Lucy said. Her firm little smile added 'idiot' louder than words.

Charles apologized all the way to McDonald's.

'Look,' Liz said, 'don't worry. I'm an American. I *like* the crap.'

'Oh, you don't.'

'Sure I do. Within this staid British academic lurks a true-blue American philistine. Besides, if we eat a couple of Big Macs, it won't matter if dinner's a disaster. I'm a lousy cook, did I tell you?' •

It was a multi-level McDonald's on Oxford Street, one of the huge, urban variants that Liz couldn't get used to. While Charles got their order, she regaled the girls with folk tales of the early roadside McDonald's of her youth. They were fascinated, leaning in close to her, wide-eyed.

'What's got them so interested?' Charles said, settling uncomfortably into a small chair.

174

'Anthropology for the under-sevens. Thanks, Charles, that looks *wonderful*.'

The girls argued over who had the strawberry, who the banana shakes, but good-naturedly. They were happy, on home ground. Liz watched them unpeel their cheeseburgers, removing the pickle.

'The best bit,' she protested.

'Yuck.' Megan counted her seventeen french fries.

When the meal was finished, there was somehow more on the table than when they started; ketchup-stained papers, polystyrene boxes like square, empty clamshells, mouth-shaped crusts of bread roll and crescents of beef. Megan's coat was dribbled with milkshake and spotted with ketchup. Liz offered to take them to the loo but they refused.

'We'll go with Daddy.' He grimaced, leading them off.

'It's awkward,' he said, returning, the girls looking freshly scrubbed. 'It's OK here, but those public places . . .' He gave a little shudder. 'What do you do?'

'Have children of your own sex or don't split up.' Liz meant it as a joke but it fell flat.

Charles looked down. 'I wonder if you'd mind,' he said cautiously, 'waiting here while I return them to their mother. She's been shopping and she agreed to come by here at half-five. It's just that now.'

'Oh, no, of course not,' Liz said quickly. She envisioned the unknown Jane hovering outside in Oxford Street, double-parked on a triple yellow line. 'You'd better go,' she said. At the mention of Mummy the little girls became instantly animated, bouncing eagerly around Charles and hastening him away. Liz called a hurried 'Goodbye' after them, but they were already gone.

He was a long while. She sat awkwardly, sipping at the remnants of her coffee and then got up and cleared the debris of their meal. He still had not returned and she sat down again and waited, feeling awkward among the noisy pack of happy children and stoic adults. She picked out the other weekend daddies without much difficulty and felt sorry for them and for Charles. Another five minutes passed. Perhaps Jane was late. Perhaps they had things to talk about. They were married people after all, parents, like Moira and

175

John. Perhaps My Little Pony needed shoes, or the vet. Or the knacker's yard.

Charles came in, ten minutes later looking dishevelled and unhappy. 'Wheel-clamped, would you believe? In the five minutes it took to come to the door of McDonald's.'

'What is she going to do?'

'Oh, I gave her the keys of mine and told her where I'd parked. I've just been putting them in a cab. I'll sort it out later.' He paused. 'We can take the tube.'

'Sure,' Liz said, 'fine.' He looked quickly around the noisy patronage of the restaurant and shook his head.

'Come on, let's get out of here.'

He cheered up on the Underground back to Fulham, the cares of parenthood visibly receding. He joked about her good luck in avoiding it all. She gallantly defended his little girls, pleasing him.

Over a glass of chilled wine, she allowed him into the secrets of her culinary style. He unboxed the main course while she split the avocados.

'I like this,' he said. 'It's like being young again. Dinner's always so *serious* with Jane.'

'I bet it's good too.'

'Oh it's *good*. It's magnificent usually. It just isn't fun.'

She laughed lightly. 'Man doesn't live on fun alone.'

She set candles about the room as well as on the table, and lit the gas flame in the fireplace. Having got to Stage One on the last date, she was a little apprehensive about Stage Two, though a little excited as well. The slight discomfort of the afternoon, the outsider feeling that had haunted her at the zoo, was gone. Charles was back to his urbane and romantic other self, and she felt romantic too. He *was* a nice man. Why not? A few glasses of wine with dinner, a liqueur or two after, and carefree warmth enveloped her, defeating concerns for the world at war, and Barry in America.

She sat on the floor at Charles's feet and let him undo her hair and tease it out sensually, while he told her a long pleasant story about the owners of a villa he rented occasionally in France. They were already discussing the future with a vague mutual commitment and the route to it lay, she knew, through her bedroom door.

'I'm glad we didn't make love last time,' Charles said dreamily, sealing his assurance of the night. She murmured agreement, though not totally sure she was ready. *Oh what the hell. Just nerves. I'll never be ready if not now.* Her decision to tell him so was undone by the buzzer for the door.

'I can't *imagine* who,' she said apologetically. The intercom was in the tiny alcove by the kitchen. Aware that Charles could hear her she made herself sound sympathetically irritated as she said, 'Yes? Who is it?' There was a brief silence as, perhaps, the irritation had its effect. Then a male voice said scratchily,

'It's just me, Dr Campbell. Darren MacPhee.'

'Darren?' she said.

'I have to see you,' he said. She hesitated, glancing over her shoulder at Charles watching with benign curiosity.

'All right, Darren.' She pushed the button to let him in downstairs and went to open her front door, saying quickly as she did so to Charles, 'This won't take long.'

Darren came bounding up the stairs, as she watched from the landing, two or three steps at a time; not, she realized, because he was in a hurry, but because that was the normal way of mounting stairs at that age. He looked slightly scruffier than usual, his hair untidy, a battered, shapeless leather jacket over jeans with holes at both knees. He grinned when he saw her, innocently, as if he had not missed two appointments in the preceding two weeks. The grin faded when he saw past her into the candlelit flat.

'I'm sorry. I didna ken you were having a party.'

'Not a party. Just a dinner guest.' She would have liked to close the door behind her and deal with whatever he wanted from her out on the landing, but it was unacceptably rude. 'Come in, Darren,' she said.

'Is it all right?'

'Of course.' He picked up at once the sharpness of her tone and hesitated. She said more warmly, 'Come on, it's just my friend Charles.' She stepped back into the flat and Darren followed warily. He glanced instinctively past her, into the interior of the flat. Charles was standing by the mantel, carefully studying Andrew Pringle's book.

Liz stayed deliberately in the little alcove by the door to the kitchen and said, 'What can I do for you, Darren?'

'I'm sorry I didna come Wednesday,' he said.

She nodded gravely, allowing the earlier absence to pass unremarked. She said, 'A phone call would have let me know where I stood.'

'Aye.' He looked uneasy. 'I meant to. I didna get the chance.'

'It doesn't take long, Darren.'

He looked truculent. 'Look, I've had a lot of hassle.' She shrugged, neither accepting nor refusing the explanation. 'I'll come on Wednesday,' he added willingly. She had had a speech prepared for precisely this situation, about reconsidering the project, readvertising the position. But this was not the setting for an argument, or a lesson in the rules of life. She said,

'I'd appreciate that you do that or, if not, you simply telephone or write a note.'

'I will. I promise. Next time I'll let you know.' He sighed, looking uncomfortable, 'Look, Dr Campbell. This isn't the best time I guess, but you havena paid me.'

'Darren, I had no *opportunity* to pay you. You didn't come to collect your money. I had *no idea* where to find you.'

'I ken that.' He looked aside. 'That's why I'm here now,' he said awkwardly.

'Eleven o'clock Sunday night is hardly an appropriate time.'

'I *know*.' He looked angry, as if he wanted to drop the whole thing and walk out and he half turned but then turned back. 'Look, I wouldn't have come if I didn't *have* to.'

She looked blank and he said sharply, 'I'm skint, do y' ken?'

'You mean you don't have *any* other money?'

'No. I have eighty-seven pence,' he said with almost a smile.

'That's all?'

'Aye.' He tossed his head, a little defiantly. 'That's all.'

'Oh, for Christ's sake, Darren, why didn't you say? Of course I'll pay you now.'

'I was *trying* to say it . . .'

She stepped quickly through the living-room to her study and collected her bag, walking back through the room, conscious of Charles watching her. She didn't say anything. Back in the alcove, with her back to Charles, she got out her cheque book and, leaning awkwardly against the wall, began to scribble a cheque.

'Dr Campbell . . .'

'Yes?' She looked up, still writing.

'Dr Campbell, that won't help.'

'What?' She stopped writing, confused. He looked even more uncomfortable and then said hurriedly,

'Dr Campbell, I can't get any money for that for days . . .' She still looked at him, blankly, and he said, his voice strained, 'It has to clear and all . . .' She closed her cheque book and held it and the pen, both in her left hand, by her side.

'You want cash.'

'Cash is the only thing I can use.'

'Of course.' She sighed, leaning against the wall.

'Darren I don't *keep* a lot of cash.'

'You haven't got it?' He sounded a little desperate.

'I'm not sure.' She got out her purse and began looking through it. He said hurriedly,

'Look, even a tenner for now . . .'

'Darren, I have three pounds and fifty odd pence.' She looked up and shrugged. 'It's Sunday evening. I do my banking on Mondays.'

'Right,' he said. She could see him absorbing that quickly, his mind jumping ahead, thinking perhaps of other sources. What sources? She had a sudden glimmer of what it was like to be young and unskilled in a big city. He turned to go, 'Thanks very much anyhow,' he said, with dignity.

'I'll have it for you tomorrow, if you like,' she said. He nodded, still with that look of anxious concentration. She said quickly, 'Wait a moment, Darren. I'll be right back.'

Charles was still standing by the mantel, holding Andrew's book, open to the first pages. He looked up attentive. 'All sorted?' he said.

'Charles, have you possibly got thirty pounds in cash?' He looked startled, but at once took out his wallet, flicked through it, and withdrew three ten pound notes. Without question he handed them to her.

'Thank you. I'll write you a cheque in a moment.' He raised one hand, palm towards her in a gesture of quick refusal, but she nodded her insistence even as she turned back towards the door. Darren was waiting, uncertain. She handed him the money and said, 'We'll sort out the rest on Wednesday.'

He nodded, his face softened with gratitude and relief, looking very young. 'Thanks so much, Dr Campbell.'

'Not at all. Next time give me a little warning.'

'Aye, fine. I'll do that,' he said enthusiastically. 'I'll see you Wednesday.' He waved over his shoulder and ran lightly down the stairs. Before she returned to the living-room, she wrote out a cheque to Charles for his thirty pounds and handed it to him as she came through the door.

'That's hardly necessary. I could get it any time,' he said. He looked embarrassed.

'Easiest this way, before I forget.' She smiled brightly and for a moment their eyes met and the mood of romance flickered alive. But it was too late; the candles had burned down and gone out, tiredness had replaced dreamy sensuality. She flicked the light switch and the room sprang back to ordinariness. 'Like some coffee?' she said. He hesitated a moment and then nodded with a wry smile.

They sat at their earlier places at the roughly cleared table, surrounded on workbench and draining board by the wreckage of the meal. After the coffee was ready and poured, Charles, accepting the remnants of the cream from dinner, said, a little uneasily, 'Was that a student, Liz?'

'Darren? Oh no, Charles. I never have students to the flat.' The answer seemed to increase rather than diminish his concern. She said, 'He's my research assistant. I'm working on a book. He helps me gather material.'

'Is he a graduate?' Charles asked, startled.

'Oh no. No, he's an actor. Or trying to be. He used to work at the health club in Gower Street. Moira knows him.' He looked a little reassured at the mention of Moira's name.

'Does he come here to work?'

'Yes.'

There was a long pause and very tentatively he asked, 'Liz, do you really think that's wise?'

It would possibly not have made her as angry as it did had it not so closely echoed her own fears. '*Why* isn't it wise?' she demanded, eyes flashing. 'What do you mean?'

'Well, *Liz*,' he smiled kindly, as if nothing need be explained.

180

'Well *what*?'

Charles withdrew a little. He said in a studied voice, 'Well, frankly, he doesn't look the most *reliable* . . .'

'What's unreliable? How can you tell by looking?'

'He looks a bit unsettled.'

'You'd look unsettled too if you were twenty-four, alone in London, sleeping in the corner of somebody's flat and working for shit at some bloody menial job.'

The vehemence of her defence startled Liz. It shook Charles. He said querulously, 'All right. I won't deny that. But I do think a woman alone has to be careful.' He leaned closer. 'I'm just trying to look out for you.'

'I can look out for myself, Charles.'

'Of course.' He became very formal, polite and distant. He did not mention Darren again. When the coffee was finished, he offered to help wash up, accepted her refusal with grace, let her bring his coat. At the door he said, with warmth, 'Thanks so much for the day at the zoo, Liz. You can't know how much I appreciate the support.'

They kissed, on her doorstep, and he went away. She closed the door behind him and turned back into the flat with a mixture of regret and defiance. At once she switched on the television and, over the late-night news, washed up the dishes and fed the cats. Then she settled in front of the screen with a cup of Nescafé and Esau on her lap. She was still watching when Barry rang.

'Oh, thank God I've got you. I tried all morning and then I had to go out.'

'I was at the zoo.'

'Where?'

'In Regent's Park. At the zoo.' She added quickly, 'With some friends.'

'Oh. Yes. Of course,' he said without understanding. He paused and then said, 'Well, what do you think?'

She did not have to ask if he meant the zoo. She said at once, 'Oh, bloody awful, but at least it seems to be moving fast. Maybe it really will finish before too long.'

'Yes, perhaps. Of course they're all a bit delirious over here. I find the pride thing hard to deal with.' He sighed. 'I guess you can't blame them.'

'I can.'

'Yes, well. You would.'

'Andrew does too.'

'Pringle?'

'Turned up with a placard at the American Church.'

'Good for old Pringle.'

'I was proud of him.'

'Yes. I would be too.' He paused. 'I wish I was there to see it,' he said. There was another silence. 'How are my cats?'

'Oblivious of your absence.' He laughed a little hollowly.

'Liz?' he said. He sounded troubled.

'Yes?'

'Liz, there's something going on here I want to talk to you about.' She felt a premonitive chill but kept silent. 'Something . . . someone.'

'The blonde girl,' Liz said suddenly.

'What? Liz, how . . .?'

She said with calm logic, 'She's in all your photos. She's very pretty, Barry.'

He sighed heavily. 'Oh yes.'

'And very young.'

'Liz . . .'

'I don't think I'm the person to talk to, Barry. Perhaps you should ring Andrew.' She paused. 'Or better yet, why not try John?'

'Liz, this is really between you and me.'

'No, Barry. It's not. It's between you and her, whoever she is. It has absolutely nothing to do with me.'

She hung up quickly, before he could argue and before she could cry, switched off the television, grabbed Jacob and Esau and went with them to bed.

XI

Darren was early on Wednesday. Liz was just out of the shower. She answered the door barefoot, in her grey tracksuit, her hair wrapped in a towel. He looked stunned.

'Sorry,' she said, loosening the towel and mopping wet tendrils of hair. 'I wasn't expecting you yet.'

'I didn't want to be late.'

'Good, fine.' He hesitated and she smiled encouragingly, indicating the kitchen. He followed her warily. She dropped the towel over the back of a chair and filled the kettle. 'Coffee?'

'Aye. Thank you.' He set his rucksack carefully on the floor and sat down on the chair in front of the typewriter, still watching her. She made two mugs of Nescafé, gave him his and, taking hers, stepped to the window-seat at the far side of the kitchen to comb out her hair. Darren watched a moment longer and then quickly ducked his head, leaning over his rucksack, drawing out a stack of handwritten papers and laying them beside the typewriter. He took out a pocket dictionary and laid that beside the papers and began setting up the typewriter without looking at her. Liz finished her hair, stripped a knot of furry black from her comb and padded barefoot across the room to drop it in the bin.

'How are the interviews going?' she asked from behind his shoulder. He jumped and jerked his head around.

'Oh. Oh fine. I've got thirty.'

'You've been busy,' she said mildly, looking over his shoulder at his notebook open to a page of ballpoint scrawl.

He shrugged. 'I've had the time.'

She paused and then said, 'You found another job yet, Darren?'

'No.' He started to type.

Carefully she asked, 'How are you doing for money?'

He shrugged again. 'I'm getting by.'

She wanted to ask more but instinct stopped her. 'I'll be in my study,' she said. She went out, carrying her coffee mug and her comb. She returned the comb to the bathroom and stood in front of the misted-up mirror, braiding her still damp hair into a loose unfastened plait. Then she picked up the mug of cooling coffee and carried it back through the living-room towards the study, glancing at the mantel clock as she passed. It said one-forty and she switched the set on to catch the end of the extended one o'clock news. She had watched all morning. She settled on the floor again. On the screen the winter war thundered to its brutal conclusion. She kept the sound low because of Darren, but remained watching when the news was followed by a programme of military assessment and then a series of interviews. Forty minutes later, Darren tapped lightly on the doorframe and she leapt up guiltily. He was standing in the alcove, holding Jacob and Esau, one under each arm.

'Could I maybe feed them?'

She turned quickly. 'I'm sorry, I got involved in this thing,' she said, flicking the television off. 'What did you say?'

'You didn't need to put it off. I could do it myself.'

'I should be working. What did you ask me?'

'Could I feed them? I think they're hungry. They keep standing on the typewriter. I don't mind, only I feel sorry for them.'

'You're being manipulated,' Liz said. 'But I'll feed them. It's easier than arguing with them.' She followed him back into the kitchen, and reached into the cupboard for a tin. He took it from her.

'Fine. I'll do it. Go back to what you were watching.'

She sighed, leaning against the cupboard. 'It's voyeurism,' she said.

He looked baffled, his hand on the tin opener.

'Watching the thing. It seems indecent to watch. But it seems dishonourable *not* to watch.'

He nodded. She doubted he understood her, but when he

straightened up after setting the bowls of cat food down, he said, 'Dudes had it on the radio this morning. He kept shouting, "Get the bastards. Yeah, go for it." That kind of thing.' He paused. 'I wasn't sure if he meant our side or theirs. You canna always tell with Dudes.'

Liz laughed, tiredly. 'A wise man, Dudes.' She made another coffee for herself and Darren and carried the fresh cup through to the living-room. 'Shit,' she said, switching the set back on, 'I can't concentrate. I have to be in at the end.'

'Is it over, do you think?' he asked from the doorway.

'Oh yes. It's over.' On the screen a cluster of Iraqi prisoners appeared, bunched together on a truck.

'They look awful young,' Darren said.

'They'll be eighteen. Or less. Conscripts.'

'My wee brother's that age,' Darren said. He sounded awed.

Liz looked up, startled. 'You have a brother?'

'Aye. And a sister.'

She paused and then said cautiously, 'Do you see them, Darren?'

'No.' He looked at the screen. Then he added quickly, 'They're with my mother.' He gave no explanation and no invitation to further questions.

Liz was quiet. He had come into the room and stood, holding his coffee mug, intent on the war scenes on the television. She sat on the floor and said casually, 'Sit down if you'd like.'

He didn't at first, but after a while he settled cross-legged beside her. They watched together for almost an hour, the two cats, fatly contented, curled up between them. Eventually the coverage broke for the evening's children's programmes. Liz stood up and switched the set off, and drew the curtains against the late afternoon darkness. 'At least it's done,' she said.

'Aye.' He sat quietly for a while and then said, 'At the beginning like, I thought it would end up with all of us going. You know. Like Vietnam in America in the sixties.'

'That's exactly what I was afraid of,' Liz said. She settled on the arm of Barry's chair. She said, suddenly curious, 'You said once you thought of joining the army anyway. Surely you weren't serious?'

He shrugged. 'Well, y'ken how it is.'

'No, I don't actually.'

He looked up. 'It's my *country*.'

'Is it?'

'Aye. Britain. Scotland anyhow . . .'

'It's not exactly done a lot for you.'

He looked baffled. 'What's it meant to do?' he asked.

Liz laughed and put her head in her hands, her fresh washed hair, loosened from its plait, tumbling over her shoulder. 'I give up,' she said.

Darren was quiet, watching her. She looked up, expecting some kind of argument, or at least a query. 'I like your hair,' he said.

'What?'

'It's bonnie. I like your hair.'

She smiled quickly and looked straight into his eyes. 'Thank you, Darren,' she said. She leaned forward with friendly intimacy, 'To tell the truth,' she said, 'I'm thinking of having it cut.' He looked puzzled and she said quickly, 'I'm too old to wear it loose this long and it's a bit severe tied up. I think I look a bit of a witch.'

'No,' he said, 'you dinna that. But it's nice loose. You could cut some of it and still have the rest.' He was studying her professionally. He leaned forward, touching a loose lock at shoulder length. There was nothing intimate in the touch. 'About there,' he said. 'That would look great.'

'You seem knowledgeable,' she said.

'I like doing hair. And make-up. You do it a lot in the theatre. I was in a play up in Edinburgh last year. I did everyone's hair.' She laughed, charmed and surprised. He looked up.

'It's not my image of you,' she explained. 'A hairdresser.'

'I'm no' gay, if that's what you're saying,' he said abruptly. 'I just like hair.'

'Darren,' Liz said, laughing louder, 'I promise you, the thought of you being gay has *never* crossed my mind.'

'I wouldna *mind*, y'ken. Only I'm not.'

'I believe you.' She leaned closer and had a sudden urge to touch his shoulder in gentle affection. She straightened and stood up instead. 'I guess we'd better work,' she said. She didn't feel like working. She felt, rather, that she would like to make more coffee and light the gas fire and sit in front of it listening to the winter rain on the windows and talking in that easy way she had with Barry.

Darren stood up at once and moved towards the kitchen. At the door of the alcove he stopped, hesitated, and said, 'It's no' the way you said.'

'What's no'?' He looked up, startled, and then they both laughed together.

'Aye, great,' he said. 'We *both* end up sounding like me.'

Liz was still laughing. 'It's infectious,' she said. She paused and added, 'Traditionally, when two cultures meet, you know, only the strongest survives.'

'Guess we'll find out who's strongest.'

'I'm beginning to wonder,' Liz said. She smiled wryly, and then enunciated carefully, 'Now what's *not* like I said?'

'This whole thing. About the clothes and all. I mean, it's *sort* of right, but it's too simple. *Some*times they try to look like men . . . like in the jeans like. But sometimes they really don't. Sometimes they look really, really female. Like this here,' he stepped to the table and picked up his notebook, 'this lassie, Diana. Sure she wears jeans and DMs in the day but at night, here she is: "I like real clingy stuff, like, lycra and velour. My boyfriend says I have real nice tits so I want to show them, don't I? This top is real great, I mean it really *shows*, doesn't it?"'

'Did it?' Liz asked.

He looked up. 'Oh aye,' he said. He paused and added, 'You weren't going to mistake *her* for her boyfriend.'

'I imagine not.'

'She wasn't skinny either. She was a big lass. And pleased with it.'

'Secure in her womanhood,' Liz said thoughtfully.

'What's that?'

'Interesting. So you think I'm wrong?'

'I didna say that,' he said hastily.

'But the premise. The premise is wrong.'

He shrugged. 'I just don't think it's simple.'

She sat on the edge of the chair arm, thoughtfully replaiting

187

her hair. She coiled it up and, taking pins from her tracksuit pocket, quickly anchored it in its bun. 'Darren, would you mind if I went out with you?' she said.

'What?' The word was half-swallowed.

She said smoothly, 'When you're doing your research. Could I come too and maybe you could show me what you mean?'

'Oh. Oh aye,' he said quickly. 'I see. Aye, why not? Only,' he looked cautious, 'they're pretty grotty places some of them.'

'I'll cope,' Liz said. 'Yes.' She stood up. 'We'll do that. Let's think when . . .' She stepped towards the study to get her diary but the phone rang, stopping her. 'Sorry,' she said. She picked it up hurriedly. 'Yes?'

'Liz darling?'

'Oh. Oh, Moira. Hello.'

'You're busy.'

'No. Well, I'm working actually.'

'With Darren?' Moira asked.

'Yes, as a matter of fact.' Liz braced herself for the usual banter, but it didn't come.

'I won't keep you,' Moira said. She sounded depressed.

'No, that's all right,' Liz said, overriding her resistance to the interruption. 'Look, what was it about?'

Moira made her voice light and frivolous. 'Oh nothing, just chat.'

'It's more than that,' Liz said.

There was silence and a long sigh. 'I can't talk about it now. Not with . . .' She paused. 'Liz, come to Sunday lunch. Things have got serious. I really have to talk – ' she paused – 'it'll just be us. William's staying with friends.'

'John?'

'John has a client.' Moira's voice was brittle.

'On a Sunday?'

'Precisely.'

Liz was quiet. Then she said quickly, 'Of course I'll come. Are you sure you don't want to talk now?'

'Sunday will do. What's a few days more after sixteen years?'

'Moira?'

'Nothing, love. See you Sunday. Oh. Say hello to Darren. I haven't seen him in ages.'

Liz put down the phone. She turned back to Darren who was looking at his notebook. 'Mrs Harris says hello,' she said distractedly. He nodded, watching her. 'Right, where were we?'

'You were wanting to come out with me . . .' he suggested nervously.

'Of course.' She got her diary from her study and they agreed to meet the following Tuesday, after her last class, outside the British Museum. He wrote down the time and place carefully in his notebook and then went back to the kitchen to work. A little reluctantly she returned to her study to do the same. She read through her last chapter without enthusiasm. What he had said disturbed her and the ideas on paper seemed more fragile than ever. *This isn't working*, she thought clearly. But she bent over her notes to continue.

At half-five she permitted herself an honourable defeat, went through to the kitchen and switched the kettle on. Darren looked up from his typing and stretched his arms. A respectable stack of work sat beside him. The dictionary was open, face down on the table. He looked tired.

'Knocking off time,' she said cheerily. He grinned, pleased, and sorted his papers. Then he picked up Jacob from the floor and held him on his knees. Liz sat down across from him at the table. The cat snuggled in and closed its eyes to self-satisfied slits.

'Where's the other one?' she asked.

'On the chair behind me.'

'I don't know how you do it, Darren.'

'I like cats.'

'They *expect* that. It doesn't usually make them *nice*.' He shrugged, stroking smooth beige fur.

'Darren?'

'Aye?'

'What happened at your audition?' He looked confused.

'Aside from me failing?'

'*How* did you fail . . . I mean do you know . . . do they tell you . . .?'

'They dinna tell you.' He looked down contemplatively and carefully turned one of Jacob's ears inside out. The cat sat there looking deformed.

'You don't have to say.'

'No. It's all right. Now. I'm sorry I was rude that day.'

'You weren't rude. You were disappointed.'

'I shouldn't have been. I mean I wasn't *expecting* to get in.'

'Darren, I'm not expecting to get this book published. But when it gets turned down I'll still be upset.'

'You're not?' He sounded astounded.

'No. I'm not. It's a mess, Darren. I *know* it's a mess. I keep trying to make it work but I know inside it won't. I don't think I'm a writer, actually,' she said calmly.

'Well, maybe I'm not an actor.'

'I think you are.'

'*They* didna,' he said brightly. Then he added, 'No. That's not fair, really. They didn't like what I did, but, they were right. I didn't either. I blew it.'

'Nerves?'

'In a way.' He leant forward suddenly, still holding the cat close. 'You see, I went into this room and there was, like, a table, and three people . . .'

'Judges.'

'Aye. Audition judges. But in the middle was this famous actor. I mean, I didna ken his name, but I'd *seen* him. On the telly. I'd seen him. And there he was, sitting in front of me. I'd never been in a room with someone famous before . . .'

'It threw you.'

'Completely.'

She smiled gently. 'When can you try again?'

'Next year.'

'A long while.'

He shrugged. 'I've an audition at RSAMD next month.'

'Who?'

'The Royal Scottish Academy of Music and Drama.' He said it with exaggerated eloquence, for fun. 'In Glasgow.' He grinned. 'Maybe they'll no' be famous up there.'

* * *

On Saturday night, the final weekly peace vigil outside the American Church became spontaneously a memorial. A stark banner, hung between poles held by two Quaker women, was painted free-hand, in black: WE MOURN ALL THE DEAD. It set a muted tone of distress mixed with relief. The small crowd was quiet. There were no guitars, no songs. Liz sat on a low wall with Mary from the Gay Women's Peace Movement, their candles burning companionably side by side, while an ecologist recited a requiem for the wildlife of the Gulf. They listened politely, feeling helpless and defeated.

The little group of art students arrived, livening the atmosphere briefly before succumbing to the general gloom. Liz saw Darren among them with Sheila and Stephanie. He was absorbed with his friends, not seeing her. Liz did not approach; she felt alienated and sad, and wanted the company of her own generation. She was glad when Andrew Pringle appeared, anomalous in his Jermyn Street coat, and sat beside her. He took a candle from her and lit it and looked studiously around the gathering.

'*Ultima ratio regum*,' he said finally.

'Hm?'

'War. The last argument of kings.' He sighed, leaning back, stretching his long legs out in front of him, hands thrust in pockets. 'The trouble is, it works.'

'It depends on what you call working.'

'Oh indeed.' He looked at his feet. 'Heard from Barry?'

'I had a phone call yesterday,' Liz said. Her voice was flat. She didn't want to talk about Barry, nor elaborate Friday's stilted formal conversation, their first since his revelation about the girl. 'You know, the usual . . . glad it's over like the rest of us. Hoping things will get back to normal.'

Andrew nodded amiably. 'Ah yes. So do we all. Nice to think of just the *ordinary* old problems, again. And they'll all be there waiting for us,' he added reassuringly.

Liz agreed and then said, looking up, curiously, 'What about your political hopes? I haven't heard you say . . . but then, I suppose that's all been suspended until now . . .'

He laughed. 'Oh no. The cogs of politics click on oblivious. No, Liz, the truth is I*'ve* had some second thoughts. Told them to take my name out of the hat, actually.'

'*Have* you? Why, Andrew?'

'Oh you know. Getting a bit older, lot on at the university. Then there's the children . . . Might try my hand at another book too.'

'It's because of Erica, isn't it?' she said.

He took time to answer. Liz looked away, across the paved square. Darren and his friends were clustered on the pavement with their candles held at casual angles. Sheila was leaning against his shoulder, her blonde hair a halo in the streetlight.

'She said I was trying to turn her into Fiona.' Andrew paused again. 'It really brought me up short, you know? The last thing I'd want of course. Can't imagine what she was thinking of. I mean, the whole point was, I've just got *away* from Fiona . . .'

Liz said carefully, Sometimes what we want and what we *think* we want are different.'

Andrew looked baffled. 'Not that I've ever noticed,' he said.

Liz laughed softly. 'Don't worry about it.' She was watching Sheila's bright hair bouncing on her collar as she walked with Darren up Tottenham Court Road.

The sun in Moira's conservatory was spring-like and warm. Outside, daffodils tumbled in disciplined profusion and the dark line of holly trees quivered in a stiff bright breeze. Liz sat in a wicker rocker, her feet on a pink Persian rug. 'This is heaven,' she said.

'I'm thinking of taking down that line of hollies. They block the light,' Moira replied. She set down a cloth-covered tray with coffee, bone china cups and an array of delicate homemade biscuits. Her slender hand dismissed the fifty-year-old growth, merciless as an axe. Liz suppressed a protest. 'I thought we'd start with coffee,' Moira continued. 'I've just made a little quiche for later and we'll dash out and cut some broccoli in a moment. It's so nice just being ourselves. John always wants his hideous Sunday roast.'

'I thought he was watching his diet.'

'Oh he *is*. Now it's organically farmed low-fat beef. My Yorkshire pud is out of course.' She sniffed. 'How you're supposed to present a decent roast without it . . . but never mind. And then of course *before* he's running he *needs* starch, so I have to cook pasta for every bloody meal including breakfast now that he's *in training*.'

'Training?'

'Yes. Training. For his half-marathon next month.'

'*Half-marathon?* I thought it was a fun run.'

'It seems to have grown. He's a fool, Liz. He deserves the heart attack he's going to have.'

Liz leaned forward in the rocker to pour cream into her coffee and then stood up with the cup and saucer. The rocker tapped rhythmically against the tile floor. Liz walked to the window glass and looked out at the doomed hollies. She said, 'No he doesn't, Moira. And he's not going to have one anyway. He's not a fool. He's training carefully. Sensibly. He's a good athlete.'

'John's not an *athlete*.'

'Yes he is, Moira. Now.' She turned back. 'Open your eyes. *See* him for what he really is. Not for what *you've* decided he has to be. Let the man *grow*, for God's sake.'

Moira sat stiffly upright in her straight-backed basket chair. Her hands were crossed motionless in her lap, the frilled cuffs of her soft white blouse spread out on the lap of her navy pleated skirt. 'You sound like *bloody* Erica,' she said. 'Whose side are you on?' She looked coldly suspicious.

'I don't see why I have to take sides,' Liz said lamely.

'Because there *are* sides,' Moira returned. 'And I expect you on mine.' She got up abruptly and walked out of the conservatory, heels clicking sharply on the tiles. She was back in a few moments, carrying a neatly folded white terry-cloth towel. She laid it, without explanation, on the glass-topped wicker table, beside the tray.

'What's that?' Liz asked.

'Exhibit "B".' Moira smiled briefly, without humour. 'Look at it. Go on.'

Puzzled, Liz sat again in the rocker and set her cup down. She lifted the towel, watching Moira, and then looked at it briefly. She looked up again. 'OK? A white towel.'

'Name tag, Liz. Look at the name tag.'

Liz turned it over, unfolding it, examining the hems. Eventually she found a worn piece of beige tape of the type favoured by boarding schools. The name printed in a washed out girlish hand was 'Erica Van Hine'. She had an instant vision of a youthful, virginal Erica laboriously stitching. She looked up again at Moira, eyebrows arced.

'So?'

'In his sports bag. Locked in the boot of the Jaguar. After his *last* "country weekend with clients".'

'So maybe he was swimming? Or taking a shower?'

'It's *Erica's* towel.'

'I *know* it's Erica's towel, Moira. It looks ancient. It's probably been lying around a locker in the health club and he *borrowed* it.'

'Don't be naïve.'

'What's naïve?' Liz demanded. 'There are a dozen logical explanations for John having a towel with Erica's name on it.'

'A dozen logical, but one likely.' Moira took the towel from Liz and refolded it briskly, like an angry school matron. 'That's the mechanics of adultery, dear . . . lipstick on the collar *can* be a favourite aunt. Only, it never is.'

She sighed and leaned forward and abruptly her brittle calm broke. 'Liz, you can't imagine how much it hurts. I think about it all the time. Him with her, the two of them. My John . . . and then the children and what they'll think. And our parents . . . our friends . . .' Her face crumpled into her hand. Liz slipped hurriedly out of the rocker and crouched by Moira's chair. Moira clutched her shoulder. 'I worked so *hard* at our marriage. I always tried to make everything perfect for him. I worked at it so hard.' She gave a desperate breathless child's gasp. 'And it still wasn't good enough.' She sobbed again, hopelessly, 'Nothing I ever do is good enough.'

'Of course it is. Everything you do . . . everything's perfect. Your house, the garden, even the children . . .'

'But it's not true. It's not. It's a lie. I've made it all up. All my life . . . when I was at school, you know, boarding, my parents were abroad . . . they *worked* abroad, it wasn't anything they could help or anything . . . but I never saw them, except for holidays . . . and then it was all so crammed together and important . . . there wasn't *time* to be ordinary. I felt I had to *shine* if I was going to please

194

them. I had to do everything *perfectly*. Oh, I lived for their praise.'

'I know,' Liz said gently, 'I remember.'

'No, you don't remember. It was *all right* by the time I was at Cambridge. I had *some* confidence then . . . I mean I'd *got* there, hadn't I? And it wasn't easy. I wasn't clever like my sister. I worked all the time. *All* the time at school. And I played tennis too. I couldn't chance just being academic. My father was very sporty and he'd wanted a son anyway. My sister and I never *really* matched up.'

'But he *adores* you. He idolizes you.'

'Now. Now he's an old man. He's softened, Liz. He actually plays with the grandchildren. He was never like that with us.' She shook her head, touching her tear-stained face. 'Oh, he's not a bad man. He was a bit like Andrew Pringle, I suppose . . . *meant* well always but he hadn't a clue about emotional things . . . used to just pat my shoulder like a piece of wood, "Well done, old girl," that sort of thing. Oh I wanted *frantically* for him to hug me. He never did.' She shrugged, pensive and realistic. 'Then when I met John, it was like all the things I ever wanted were coming true . . . he used to hang on my every word. He'd just sit there, *adoring* . . .'

'I remember,' Liz said.

'I suppose it was silly, but I felt so special. Successful. Beautiful. I remember the first time we went to bed . . . it was quite soon, too, I hardly knew him . . . he just held me for about an hour. Just lay and held me . . . after that I was ready to do anything.' She twisted her frilled sleeve into a crumpled roll. 'Love makes you so strong . . .'

'And so vulnerable,' said Liz. She laughed lightly. 'The instant *I* ever fell in love, all *my* confidence went down the drain.'

Moira looked up, surprised out of her misery. 'I can't imagine you like that.'

'I was like that for years. Ever since I was a girl. All through high school. College. I was *still* a bit like that at Cambridge.' She paused. 'I've an awful feeling I'm still a little like that now.'

'I never saw you like that. You weren't like that with Barry.'

'No,' Liz was thoughtful, 'Barry was different. I always knew he loved me. He *let* me know. It takes courage to give love without dissembling . . .'

'And now?'

'Now I'm not so sure . . .' She got up from the tiled floor, easily athletic in her tracksuit and trainers. She went back to the windows. Wind had piled clouds up behind the hollies. The sun thinned and the garden looked wintry again. She said, 'You know, you were right about that girl.'

Moira blinked, tear-smudged and uncertain. 'Was I? What girl?'

'The girl in the pictures. There's something between them.'

'Oh, surely nothing serious.' Moira looked pained, affronted by the accuracy of her own prophecy. 'She's just a child.'

Liz shrugged. 'He tried to tell me about it over the phone. I wouldn't let him.' She glanced briefly at Moira and then back to the garden. 'I didn't want to hear.' She turned back into the room, leaning against the window-frame. 'The funny thing is, I did know. Right from the beginning. When he came back from the States. He was different. Excited, stimulated, challenged by a new environment, all that too, but *different*. And there's only one thing that makes a person different in that way. He kept trying to tell me, in jokes, hints . . . I kept shutting it out.'

'I *told* you, you should have gone with him,' Moira said stubbornly. 'What could that child offer him compared with you?'

'Youth, charm, intelligence, freshness, innocence . . .' Liz laughed, shaking her head. 'It doesn't matter. I didn't want to get into that again. Rivalry, jealousy, suspicion. Watching him all the time. Watching her . . . I wasted too much time when I was young that way . . . trying to hang on to some man who no longer wanted me. Seeing every woman as a rival. Never a friend. I'd rather live alone than live like that.'

Moira sat staring straight ahead, her face lined and bleak. 'I'd rather die than live alone.' Her voice dropped to a whisper, 'I'm so afraid.'

Liz watched her sadly. 'What are you going to do?'

'I'm going to divorce him,' she said clearly, 'while I'm still young enough to find someone else.'

Liz caught her breath, staring at Moira, who looked calmly back, her face once again composed. At last Liz whispered, 'Over a towel and a VISA receipt?'

'Over a betrayal of sixteen years' companionship and trust.'

'Of which you have absolutely no proof.'

'I'll get proof,' Moira said. She set her lips firmly and then she wouldn't discuss it any more. They went out to the garden and she sliced off firm wet heads of purple broccoli with a wooden-handled knife and talked about Rachel's O-levels. Over lunch, she asked about Charles and about the book. When the shadow of the hollies chilled the conservatory, they came in and had coffee by the drawing-room fire.

They were still there when John came home. Liz felt a small panic at the crunch of tyres on the gravel, but Moira stood up, smiled brightly, and met him at the door full of wifely solicitude. He looked tired and slightly weatherbeaten, as if he'd just come in from a run. He dropped his briefcase at the door of the drawing-room, and kissed Moira as she went out to make tea, and then came into the room and kissed Liz. His hair was wet.

'Is it raining?' she asked.

'Hm? No. Quite dry actually. Frosty.'

'Oh. Good,' she said. She felt awkward with him, as if she didn't know him any longer, and she marvelled at Moira's aplomb, the cool, placid way she served the tea. 'We've had a lovely lunch, Liz and I. And a lovely chat in front of the fire.'

'All right for some,' John said. He sounded utterly plausible, a tired man having spent his weekend at work.

Moira smiled charmingly. 'Shall we all have dinner next weekend?' she asked. 'Liz could come. And Charles. That would be nice, wouldn't it?' She glanced at Liz who looked uncertainly at John. She could not tell if he hesitated or she imagined it. 'You're surely not working again,' Moira added, gently disapproving.

'What? Oh no. Of course not.'

'Then that's settled. Just the four of us. And maybe the Smythe-Hamiltons. Oh, and Rachel will be home, I think. That will be lovely.' Her voice was smooth and domestic, the voice of a woman without a care in the world.

XII

On Tuesday afternoon, Darren was waiting in front of the British Museum, sitting on the broad steps, his rucksack between his knees. He wore his long black coat, a peaked navy blue cap, and jeans patched with purple cloth, and had a book open on his knees. He did not see her approach.

'Hi,' Liz said. 'Am I late?' He looked up from his book, still absorbed in it, blinking from concentration. He shook his head.

'I came early.' He turned the book over. It was a paper-back Shakespeare, well-worn. 'I thought I'd sit here and work.'

'Pretty chilly,' Liz said. It was a grey, still day, dry but with little else to recommend it.

'I was inside for a while,' he said putting the book in his rucksack. He gestured over his shoulder at the great pillared façade behind her. His face brightened suddenly. 'Hey have you got a moment?'

'Yes,' Liz said, curiously, 'why?' He grinned and stood up, slinging the rucksack over his shoulder.

'I've found a friend for you,' he said. Still grinning, he led her into the cavernous interior, hesitated briefly, and then turned to the left, past the bookshop and into the Egyptian exhibits. He walked purposefully between great stone statues, ignoring them.

Liz said, 'What are you working on in your Shakespeare?'

'An audition piece for Glasgow.'

'What about *Henry V*?'

'I'm no' sure I can face him after RADA.'

'I like your Henry,' she said. He looked unconvinced, but then he found what he'd been looking for and laughed delightedly.

'There he is,' he said. He pointed to a small glass rectangular display case. Within, remote with the placidity of age, sat a green-grey Egyptian cat, gently arrogant and vividly realistic, but for the incongruity of gold rings through its nose and one ear. Liz laughed softly, too, and came closer to the case to inspect it.

'He's got an earring,' Darren said. 'It's Jacob, with an earring like mine.'

'I think it's Esau, actually,' Liz said. She read aloud, '"Bronze cat, sacred to Bastet" . . .' She stood a long while admiring it, and wishing she could stroke its cool metal back. 'Thank you, Darren,' she said.

He was watching her. He said suddenly, 'I guess you'll have seen him before, won't you.'

'I've seen him before,' Liz said gently. She added, 'He's actually quite famous.'

'Aye,' his voice dropped. 'I haven't been in a place like this before.'

She turned to face him. 'Do you like it?' she asked, still gently.

He paused. 'I dinna ken. I like *him*,' he said, gesturing towards the cat. 'I like him a lot.'

'So do I,' she said. 'Thank you, Darren. I've never seen him quite like this.' He looked curious, but said nothing more and they went back out into the pale grey day.

They went up and down Oxford Street, in and out of the tatty, noisy, young people's shops. Darren hauled items of clothing off the cluttered racks, or stopped to point them out on people's backs, showing her with the acumen of youth what fell within the rigid invisible boundaries of fashion. In Carnaby Street he leaned against a shop front displaying extraordinary concoctions of leather and chains and catalogued attractive women as they passed.

'No' bad, aye, and that one. And oh *yes*, *all right*.'

'What about her?'

He looked, shook his head. 'Hopeless.'

'They all look the same.'

'They don't at all. *She's* a gothic. *She's* a hippie-goth . . . see, the scarf and the purple skirt.'

'They still look the same,' Liz said. 'What about her?' She pointed to a fresh-faced young county woman in a checked skirt, a blue blazer, and a silk headscarf knotted just on the point of her chin, walking purposefully in low court shoes, expensive leather shoulder bag swinging at her side. Liz smiled as he stared.

'I dinna ken *what* that is,' he said.

'I didn't think you would.' A girl walked by in black leggings, a skirt that was a shiny band of fabric pulled smoothly across her buttocks, and a short wool jacket over a skinny velvet top that bared an unwintry expanse of white skin. She walked quickly, hips swaying smartly to the music of her personal stereo. A maroon curled-brimmed hat sat on top of dark blonde curls.

'There,' said Darren. 'That's the look. Look at her. Now you're no' going to tell me *she's* trying to look like a man.' Liz studied the girl's retreating shape sceptically.

'It does help she's thin. You have to admit that. Those are thin legs.'

'Aye. But she's not thin up above. And look at them.' He pointed as two other girls strode by, again in the ubiquitous leggings, both with big off-the-shoulder jumpers and cinched-in waists. Lips were red, eyebrows painted and arced. 'Do you see what I mean?'

'All I can see is goose pimples. How do they *do* that?'

'Aye well, they'll no' be going far.'

'I hope not. I'm freezing even if they're not.' Liz clapped her woollen-mittened hands together. It was getting dark and her breath made puffs of vapour in the streetlight.

'Fancy a coffee?' he said.

She looked up and met his eyes. There was something appealing and protective in them. She nodded slowly. 'Yes. Yes, I'd love one. Let's find somewhere.'

They found a Pizzaland and ordered cappuccinos and Liz sat warming her hands around her mug.

'I suppose we can look at people just as well sitting here,' she said. But outside, it was dark and the café was quiet, and anyhow she felt a disjointed loss of interest. Faced with the reality of streets full of vigorous young womanhood, it was hard to see her theory at work. 'Maybe it's just my generation,' she said. 'Still, Darren, they don't exactly look like *women*, either. It's like the sixties again. They all look like little girls. Rather more *knowing* little girls maybe . . .'

'But not like men.'

'No. Not like men.' She looked around. '*They* do.' Two slim, flat-bottomed, jeans-clad blondes passed their table.

'Oh aye. Jeans don't count though. Jeans are *everybody*. It's like saying, OK, I'm *dressed* maybe, but I haven't *thought* about it.' She laughed. He said, 'We need to go to a disco.'

'Do we?' She sipped her coffee, smiling. 'Why?'

'To see real clothes. The kind people wear to say who they are. No' for work, or keeping warm like.'

'Self-expression.'

'Aye well. Clothes that say how you see yourself. How you'd *like* to see yourself. That's what you're talking about.'

'I suppose I am.' She finished her coffee. 'Right, Darren. You're on.'

'Serious?'

'Of course. Find me a disco. When'll suit? Saturday?'

He grinned slowly, looking at her steadily, easily. 'Aye, Saturday's fine.'

She called for the bill and when the girl put it down in front of Darren, she reached for it quickly, but he had lifted it first. 'No,' she said, in her adult-in-charge voice. 'I'll pay.'

'No. I will.'

'Darren, I know you're broke.'

He kept the bill, standing up. 'I want to pay,' he said. 'Anyhow, I'm not broke. I have a job.'

'Since when?' She stood up, also, her hand still out for the bill, not really believing him.

'Since last week. I'm working in McDonald's. The one up the end of Oxford Street.' Liz nodded. 'Do you know it?'

'All too well,' said Liz. 'All too well.'

There were two messages on her machine when she got home, both from Charles Beatty, each promising to ring later. He did, almost at once, sounding harassed.

'Liz, you're in at last.'

'Yes?' she said mildly. She was holding the phone between ear and hunched shoulder, opening a cat-food tin with both hands. Jacob and Esau orbited her feet, yowling. She strained to hear. 'Something urgent, Charles?'

'Oh,' his voice softened, the faint note of irritation easing. 'Oh, no, not really. It's just been one of those days. Trying to get things lined up and *nobody* in. Talking to these bloody machines all day . . .'

'What can I do for you, Charles?' Liz said clearly.

'Oh. Well, it's just this thing of Moira's.' The note of irritation was back. 'She spoke to you apparently.' Liz finished opening the tin, shifted the phone to the other ear and shoulder and began spooning tuna into two spotless dishes. For a moment she couldn't think what he was talking about. '*You know*,' he said, 'on Sunday.'

'Oh. Oh, yes. Sunday lunch. She did say something . . .'

'She said you were coming and I was to pick you up.'

Liz set the dishes down. She straightened up as the cats settled like lions at a kill, and took the phone into her left hand. She leaned against the wall and said carefully, 'Moira asked me to Sunday lunch. She did mention asking you too, but *nothing* was said about anyone picking *any*body up.'

'Oh,' he said hastily, 'I don't mind, Liz. I mean I'd love to pick you up.'

'It's not necessary.'

'Well if we're both going, why *not* go together?'

'You sound busy, Charles.' There was a pause. He gave a small tired sigh that made her think of their day at the zoo and the defeated, baffled look that came over him when the children proved incomprehensible.

'Not *busy* exactly. Or, yes, busy, but that's not the problem.' He was silent again. Liz waited patiently. 'Bit of a hassle with Jane actually. She's . . .' he paused again. 'She's seeing some *bloke*, I gather. Wants the weekend free . . . some late theatre thing in town and she's used up all her tokens . . .'

'Tokens?'

'With the circle.'

'Circle?'

'The *babysitting circle*, Liz,' he said, irritated with her obtuseness. 'You get tokens for doing nights for other people . . . *you know*.' Liz made a vague sound of agreement to please him. 'Of course it *has* been difficult. She can't really *contribute*

202

now that she's alone. She needs a sitter before she can sit.' He laughed, bemused by a private parental irony. 'Bit of a no-win situation.' He sighed again. '*Anyhow*, she wants *me* to stand in over the weekend. I told her that the flat's hardly suitable.'

'What's unsuitable?'

'It's a bachelor flat, Liz. One bedroom. One double bed . . . you know, what you'd expect . . . And of course Moira insisted on doing the whole thing in this *dove*-grey. You can imagine how that's going to stand up to crayons and Ribena . . . Anyhow, I told Jane, but she was pretty bloody determined, said she'd bring sleeping bags, all their stuff . . . Christ, I don't even have food in the place . . . there's three bottles of Claret and a couple of eggs in the fridge . . .'

Liz said, 'You could buy some, Charles.'

'Oh I know,' he said good-naturedly. 'And I will. I'm not that useless. I'm just . . . well it does rather blow my weekend. I had been hoping to see you . . .'

Liz paused, thinking, and then suggested, 'Perhaps you could bring the children to Moira's? She's certainly used to children. She'd probably love it. Why don't you ask?'

'Oh, indeed, indeed. Moira *said* that, of course.'

'Well?'

'I was rather hoping to see you Saturday . . . Saturday night.' He sounded wistful.

Liz said cheerfully, 'Well, actually, Charles, I have something on Saturday evening so there's nothing lost. Shall we meet Saturday daytime? We could do the zoo again.' She mustered as much false enthusiasm into her voice as she could manage, feeling sorry for him.

'Oh, I suppose. Actually they want a film this week. And *bloody* McDonald's. It'll be hideous, Liz. I can't impose this on you.'

'Of course you can. It was fun.'

'Really?' His voice gained a note of hope.

'Sure. You pick your film and let me know where to meet you.' She paused. 'If that's all right of course. With the girls. They might mind.'

'Of course not. Why should they mind?' he said defensively.

'They just might,' Liz said quietly.

*　　*　　*

'Why did *she* have to come?' Lucy asked in a ringing *sotto voce* in the lobby of the cinema.

Charles crouched down beside her, taking small shoulders in his hands. 'You *like* Liz. You told me.'

Liz carefully studied a poster for *Three Men and a Little Lady*. Megan made her hand-covered, spurting giggle, watching her father and then Liz.

'I *do* like her,' Lucy whispered, 'I just don't want her *here*.' Her voice was strained, tearful, her tiny perfect face scrunched in unhappiness.

'Well, she *is* here. And you're being rude. You're hurting Liz's feelings.' Lucy wailed, a soft, rising wail.

'She's not hurting my feelings,' Liz said clearly. She went to the kiosk and bought popcorn and orange drinks for the girls and when she came back, Lucy was sniffingly composed.

The film was not a success. Set in a chimerical world of medieval magicians and time-travel robotics, it revelled in sword fights and moulded latex monsters. Megan took fright at a small horned creature that was actually meant to be friendly and had to be carried out screaming during each of its appearances. Her departure, in her flustered father's arms, brought an increasing round of obscene protest from a row of twelve-year-olds behind them. Liz endured those and Lucy's stiff silent company until Charles and a whimpering Megan returned. Charles suggested leaving, Lucy broke sullen silence to set up a protesting howl. They stayed, wincing at every reappearance of the horned nemesis. Looking across at Lucy during one of their solo spells, Liz saw her smiling grimly at a decapitation. Blood poured over the screen. The producers held on to their PG rating by providing the muscular hero with a heroine of epic frigidity.

'Are they married?' Lucy asked, breaking silence.

'Not yet.'

'Will they get married?'

'Probably.' *When he's done cutting heads off*, she thought grimly.

'Are *you* married?'

'No.'

'*I* won't get married,' said Lucy.

* * *

Charles got the car and picked them up in front of the cinema. He began driving circuitous routes through Saturday traffic.

Liz asked, 'Where are you going?'

'Three guesses and it begins with Mac.'

'There's one right there.' Liz pointed helpfully to the politely refined but unmistakable façade. Charles looked straight ahead, grid-locked in place between two cabs, a delivery van and a crane-truck.

He said, 'They may seem similar. Head office may have made a considerable effort to create a certain uniformity. But the young ladies in the back seat will assure you there's only one worth going to.'

'Oxford Street?'

Charles sighed. 'After all, a little variety might creep in. A little originality. Father's aching brain might have some small relief.' Liz laughed into her hand.

'Don't you *like* McDonald's?' Lucy asked, severely humourless from the back seat.

'I love it, sweetheart. I love it.'

'Actually,' Charles said, when the girls were seated and waiting eagerly at a small moulded table and he and Liz went to the counter for the food, 'the psychologist says I should encourage it. Familiarity is good for children under stress.'

'Psychologist?'

Charles looked uncomfortable. 'Well, a *children*'s psychologist.'

'All the same. Why? What for?'

'They *are* under stress.'

Liz's eyes widened. 'Of course they are. Their parents have just split up.'

'I *know* that, Liz.' He turned away angrily, and stared at the leather jacket of the girl ahead of them in the queue. 'Hey,' he laughed briefly, 'don't tell me *you're* going to start passing judgement.' He sounded angry and also incredulous. It was the incredulity that hurt.

Liz said, 'I don't make it my business to pass judgement on my friends' marriages.'

He laughed again, still without humour. 'Particularly not when you're going out with the husband.'

'Charles.'

'Sorry . . . I don't . . .'

'Charles, when I met you, you were separated from your wife. Or so,' she added crisply, 'I was led to understand. You didn't present yourself as a married man. Accordingly, I don't wish to be presented as an adulteress.'

'Liz, for God's sake.'

'What's between you and your wife pre-dates me completely. It has nothing to do with me. If you ask my opinion about your children, I will tell you honestly that it's perfectly obvious that this separation is doing them damage. It may be necessary damage but it's still there and it's nothing a *psychologist* is going to cure.'

'Thank you, Liz,' Charles said coldly, 'but I didn't ask.'

'Can I help you, sir?' A girl in a maroon-striped shirt and a maroon cap over a pony-tail smiled a bright, trained welcome. Liz and Charles glared at each other. The girl waited.

'You'd better order,' Liz said.

They sat sipping coffee and not looking at each other while Lucy and Megan happily munched their cheeseburgers, squabbled over their chips, spilled their drinks. Charles sorted out each crisis like a weary automaton and Liz grew sorry for him. She smiled gently once when he looked up and he caught her eye and smiled awkwardly back. He was about to speak when Liz heard a familiar soft laugh behind her and turned curiously towards its source.

He was standing with his back to her, a mop and pail at his side. He wore the same white and maroon striped shirt as the girl at the counter, tucked into tight black trousers, stretched sexily across his bum. His maroon cap was turned back to front, allowing his tangle of black hair to fall forward over his eyes. He was talking with a pair of fat, cheerful girls in shell-suits who laughed at everything he said. Liz stood up, left the table with Charles watching, and tapped his shoulder. He spun around, looking guilty.

'Dr Campbell!'

'Hello, Darren,' she laughed softly, 'fancy meeting you here.'

'Ah, Christ. I thought it was the manager.' He winked at the girls. 'See y'around,' and turned to Liz. His smile broadened with open happiness. 'Hey. This is great. Are you alone?'

'Oh no,' Liz half-turned and pointed back to the table. Three pairs of blue eyes, all remarkably similar in their faintly suspicious curiosity, were focused on her at once. 'You remember Charles?' Darren ducked his head in acknowledgement. Charles nodded vaguely. 'These are his children.' Darren grinned at the children. 'Lucy and Megan.' They stared, awed, at both him and Liz. She realized she had pulled the ultimate rabbit from the ultimate hat; an actual acquaintance with a member of McDonald's staff. Darren shook hands with them and they giggled and glowed.

'Do you like the costume?' he said to Liz, standing back and pretending to model his new uniform.

'Very you,' she said.

'Aye. I thought so.' He glanced momentarily at Charles and said, 'Are you busy now, or is it still on for tonight?' He looked uncertain.

'The disco? Oh definitely. I wouldn't miss it for anything,' she said laughing. 'No, of course it's still on. Charles is dropping me at the flat when we're finished here. Is the flat still all right, or shall I meet you somewhere?'

'No, fine. Great.' He glanced quickly over his shoulder. 'Look, I'd better go. Can't afford to get fired my first week. Glad to meet you again, sir,' he said. He waved at the girls. They watched, round-eyed and in love.

When he had gone, with his mop and pail, Liz seated herself at the table beside Lucy and lifted her polystyrene coffee cup to her lips. Charles was watching her. She drank from the coffee and he still watched. The girls grew quiet too.

'You *do* remember Darren, don't you?' Liz said. 'My research assistant? Remember he came for . . .'

'I remember.' He sounded baffled and faintly hurt. 'You're going *out* with him, Liz?'

'What? Oh!' She laughed richly. 'Oh, Charles. Not *going out*,' she said then with melodramatic emphasis. 'Of course not.' She crumpled up her coffee cup, dropped it into the paper bag and began gathering the girls' debris.

'But what was that about a disco?' He looked no less baffled.

She laughed again, standing up. 'Megan, shall *I* take you to the loo this time?' Megan nodded happily. 'You coming, Lucy?' Lucy, suddenly conspiratorial, smiled and got up too, looking mysteriously at her daddy.

'*I* like discos,' she said.

'*Liz.*'

She led them off. Over her shoulder she called, 'Research, Charles. Just research.'

By the time Charles dropped her in Fulham, the girls had moved subtly into her camp. She invited them up to see the flat, and though Charles protested lack of time, the girls campaigned and won. Upstairs, she rooted about her un-child-friendly kitchen, seeking the sort of biscuits children eat, while she made coffee for herself and Charles. She divided a carton of milk into two reasonably sturdy glasses.

'They won't drink it,' Charles said. 'They never drink milk.' They both finished their glasses in huge, breathless gulps, grinned at their father and went off in pursuit of the cats.

Liz poured him coffee. 'I'm in their good books,' she said. 'Give up, you haven't a chance.' She felt smug and faintly dishonest, knowing that it was Darren, not herself, who'd worked the magic.

'I won't keep you,' he said, studiedly reasonable. 'I know you're going out.'

'Not for hours, Charles. I gather these things start late.'

'Where is it?' Charles asked.

She shrugged. 'I've no idea. Some club. Earls Court, probably. I think it's near where he stays.'

'Sounds rough,' Charles said pointedly.

'We'll survive.'

'Yes.' He looked unhappy. He was silent for a while but seemed unable to stop himself saying as he stood up, 'I can't really see what it can have to do with your book.'

Liz smiled easily, clearing the cups from the table. She turned to face him, her back to the sink. 'Well, it looks like you'll just have to read it and find out.' She raised one hand, palm upwards.

He smiled a little and then raised his voice, calling, 'Megan, Lucy, time to go.' There was some happy shrieking of protest.

Liz followed him into the living-room. The girls were lying flat on the rug, shading their eyes, peering into the darkness under the sofa.

'We can't go. They won't come out. Here kitty, here kitty.'

'You can see them tomorrow,' Liz said lightly, collecting their anoraks. 'They'll probably still be under there.'

'I'm sorry,' Charles said. 'They're too rough.'

'On the contrary. Just what the sods need. Teach them to appreciate the good life they have with me.' She thrust Megan's arms awkwardly into her anorak sleeves, taking for ever. Charles had Lucy parcelled up in twenty seconds flat. He took Megan's mittens from Liz's clumsy fingers and slid them over the fat waiting hands.

'Sorry,' he said, 'it just takes practice.' He bundled them apologetically before him, to the door. They were already full of questions: would he rent a video, where would they sleep, had he got their pyjamas? He answered each patiently. At the door, he turned briefly, a wistful smile crossing his handsome face. He looked past her, into the quiet room, where the fire flickered and the newly emerged cats licked their ruffled fur. 'God,' he said softly, 'I'd love to stay.'

'See you tomorrow, Charles.'

He nodded sadly. They made their arrangements at the door and in front of his daughters he chastely kissed her cheek.

Liz closed the door and turned her back to it, looking at her watch. She had just an hour before Darren was due. A surprising girlish elation filled her as she showered and dressed in her red velvet leggings, a long black turtleneck, and red suede boots. She stood in front of her dressing-table, brushing her hair out vigorously and bent forward with the mass of it falling over her face. She stood up, enveloped in a fuzzy cloud. For a moment she considered leaving it like that, but took fright and coiled it hurriedly into an obedient knot. She added long silver earrings, a bunch of silver chains, and a splash of Je Reviens and stood looking at herself in the mirror. She thought of Charles with a twinge of guilty pity. But then the buzzer sounded for the door and she went to answer it, her step bouncy and young.

Darren was waiting, head down, hands in the pockets of

his long black coat, when she opened the door. His head came up and, seeing her, his face lit quickly with a happy grin full of admiration. Their eyes met and he held her glance with comfortable ease. She had a sudden feeling of equality, as if a balance had shifted. 'Hi, Darren,' she said, her voice softened, almost shy. He stepped into the room, his hands still in his pockets. He was wearing his denim peaked cap, and a long impractical white scarf and looked like a glamorously archaic revolutionary.

'I brought you something,' he said. She thought he meant work, but he drew a small paper bag out of his coat pocket and handed it to her. She looked up, curious, as she took it. He nodded encouragingly. Carefully, she unfolded the top of the bag and drew out a small cardboard and cellophane box. Inside sat a small statuette of a cat, a miniature of the British Museum's deified feline. She opened the box, laughing, and the cool smooth bronze fell into her hand.

'He hasna got the earring,' Darren said casually.

'Maybe the earring's copyright,' Liz said, still laughing. 'He's wonderful.' She ran her fingers down the cold curves, examined the sharp ears and surprising, dog-like feet. 'He's perfect. Darren, how *kind*.' She leaned forward impulsively, her hand on his coat sleeve, and brushed a kiss against his cheek. He laughed, delighted, and unafraid. His hand lightly touched her arm, instinctively steadying her balance, surprising her again. 'I'll get my coat,' she said, turning away. She went first to the mantel and carefully set the cat there, moving Andrew Pringle's dusty hardcover aside.

The club was in a basement off Cromwell Road. Darren led her to it through a maze of Earls Court streets, pleasantly familiar to Liz from her student days. They passed the flat on Kenway Road where Moira and John had stayed with their Australian friend Mike before moving to their first married home in Islington. It looked much the same, the paintwork of the three second-floor windows grey and peeling in the streetlight. There was a new Thai restaurant down the road where their favourite Indian one had been. Before it, a tall sun- tanned man in a leather hat, his blond hair tied in a pony tail, talked in twanging antipodean accents to two admiring girls. He was so like Mike as to have been his brother. Liz laughed, thinking how little had changed. She said happily to Darren, 'Moira and John used to live down there.'

'Them? Here?' He looked amazed.

'It was a while ago,' she said, less certainly, and was startled to realize that in the year of the Kenway Road flat, Darren had been in primary school.

The street suffered a time-warp in her eyes, becoming suddenly raucous and alien, exotic with foreign smells, colourful with foreign costuming. Everyone they passed looked vigorously young. The suntanned Australian slouching against the curtained restaurant window was *not* Mike, but a boyish stranger. Mike was a paunchy executive in Melbourne now. What was familiar here was only the inheritor of what she had known, divided from her by a generation.

Newly wary, she followed Darren down a flight of steps and into a concrete yard. Music pounded out into the night. The bouncer, a big sweaty man, grinned at Darren and waved a tattooed hand. Inside they checked their coats at a tiny cubicle and went down a narrow corridor plastered with posters of rock stars and advertisements for concerts and karaoke nights. The corridor opened into a low smoky room with a bar at one end, a cluster of tables, and a tiny dance floor. The music was thunderous, a wall of sound made visible by flashing barrages of light. No one was dancing. The scent of hashish drifted amidst the reek of tobacco; Liz sniffed in wry reminiscence. Darren leaned over and shouted something that sounded like 'Drink?' and she nodded. She sat down at the nearest table, nodding uncertainly to the two girls occupying the other side. They were sipping drinks and leaning heads together watching a cluster of boys in the smoky distance and did not seem to notice her. She turned to watch Darren making his way through the scrum at the bar. Under the flamboyant coat he had been wearing just black jeans and a black T-shirt, a dancer's costume in which he moved easily and looked graceful and handsome. The girls at the table shifted their attention and watched him too. Liz was glad when he returned with two glasses of lager, and sat beside her, making the place seem safe and friendly again.

He pointed to the dance floor where a solitary girl had got up to dance. She wore a rust-coloured satin dress, skimming the tops of her broad thighs, clinging round her hips, and corseting her breasts into a Rabelaisian cleavage. She was fair and soft-skinned, with pale hair gelled darkly into a boyish bristle. She had a round happy face, folding comfortably into a double chin and a ring through her nose like the Egyptian cat. She danced, plump arms above her head, joyous and alone, until a girlfriend, in white leggings and a silver top joined her. They clutched each other, hugged and fell apart, still dancing. A row of boys watched from the side, drinking lager and wiping their mouths, lighting cigarettes, heads ducked low, laughing in sudden raucous outbursts. They wavered, like hungry shadows, but none approached. More girls joined the two on the floor, until the little square of open space was filled with bouncing, swaying happy female flesh, bright and multi-coloured in the throbbing moving lights, and the boys grew darker, more sullen and shadowy, by contrast.

Darren leaned closer to shout above the music, 'They dinna look oppressed to me.' She laughed, raising her hands in defeat. He stood up suddenly, caught her upraised hand and with his other waved easily at the crowded floor. 'Dance?' She shook her head and started to refuse, but the two girls at the table were watching and she shrugged suddenly and stood up too. The girls on the dance floor shuffled cheerfully aside as they joined them. Darren found them a little space, stepped away from her, caught the music for an instant and raised his arms above his head. He clapped twice, closed his eyes, hands yet upraised, feet planted firmly, swayed his hips in a sexy shimmy that brought a happy squeal from the nose-ringed blonde. He opened his eyes, grinned at Liz, and caught her hand. He whirled her around and then back, and across the dance floor. Caught in his sure rhythm, she could not but respond, awkwardly at first and then with ease. Whichever way she turned, he was there, laughing, clapping, embracing her briefly, flinging her free. He was a superlative dancer, showy, athletic and spectacular. The dance floor cleared; the girls circled clapping. The boys watched darkly.

Liz followed as long as she could, urged on by his happy encouragement, but at last cried, 'Enough!' and stepped back, laughing, and staggered to their table, collapsing on to a chair.

212

He danced a few more steps alone, and then clapped his hands once and leapt down to join her.

'Go on,' she shouted, 'don't stop.' He flopped in his chair, grinning. 'You're better without me.'

He smiled, raised his glass, wiping sweat from his face with the back of his hand. 'No,' he said and solemnly shook his head. The girls at their table were watching him, awed. He looked around, suddenly self-conscious. 'Come on,' he said, standing, 'let's go.'

Out in the street, wrapped in her coat in the cold air, still breathing hard, Liz gasped, 'Darren, you're *amazing*.'

'I love to dance,' he said. He sounded shy.

'Have you trained?'

'A little. Dance workshops. Community stuff.'

'You should do more.'

'Aye, maybe.' He looked away and she recognized the dismissal as the one he used whenever the issue of money arose. She had a dizzy urge to offer to pay, but better judgement prevailed.

'Well, where now?' she said, recovering her breath.

His happy grin returned. 'Let's try here.'

It was a bright noisy pub, packed with teenagers. They sat at a table in a corner, had two more lagers, and watched the crowd. Once again the girls seemed livelier, happier and more confident than the boys, and costumed with aggressive female swagger. In the next pub, Liz switched to mineral water and Darren drank lemonade. They argued about androgynous American film goddesses and were interrupted by a group of Darren's friends. Among them was Stephanie who shouted, 'Hi, Liz,' and bounced happily on to the bench beside her. She seemed totally unsurprised to find her in Darren's company. She admired Liz's red leggings and showed off her new patterned tights.

'Where's Sheila?' Liz asked, with faint perversity.

Stephanie held up innocent palms. 'Off *some*where.'

They moved on again. Darren said, 'There's a karaoke night in the place around the corner, if you'd like, Dr Campbell. You see some great gear . . .'

'Fine, Darren.' She smiled slightly. 'Look, maybe you should call me Liz? All your friends do.'

He hesitated. 'Aye,' he said softly, 'if you like.' She thought he wouldn't, but he did, almost at once, offering her a drink in the new pub while two black girls sang a bluesy song with stiff, self-conscious mannerisms.

'I'll get these, Darren.' She went to the bar, feeling light and young, moving comfortably among the crowd, and brought back their two soft drinks. He was watching the stage and only looked away when she returned.

The two black girls had been replaced at the microphone by a short, stout woman in silver lamé jeans and a fringed red satin shirt. A carapace of stiff platinum hair, topped with a big white Stetson hat, dwarfed a pleasantly pudgy, middle-aged face. Huge false eyelashes spidered outwards from wide blue eyes. She lifted her Stetson to a background of twanging country-and-western chords and shook her fringes. A bald, tubby man at a table near the front cheered and clapped. Husband or boyfriend, Liz imagined. He sat back smiling proudly and the woman batted her forest of lashes and began to sing in an American accent, heavily overlaid by Liverpool, about making love on a blanket on the ground.

'Oh my God,' said Liz, settling into her seat and looking at Darren with widening eyes. He dodged her gaze, almost sheepishly. 'You don't *like* it, do you?' she asked, alarmed. He shook his head.

'I like *her*,' he said. 'Oh I know she's terrible and all. But she *wants* it so bad. You cannae help but like that.' His voice was gentle. He seemed older, suddenly. The woman stopped at the chorus, removed the Stetson, and swung it in a rigid circle before replacing it on its platinum nest. The bald man cheered. 'Oh Jesus,' said Darren, covering his eyes.

The Liverpudlian Dolly Parton was followed by a pair of Cockney Madonnas in market-stall corsetry dyed bright red, who sang to shouts and foot stamping by their friends. When the applause died away, Liz turned to Darren. 'What about you?' she asked remembering the dancing.

'What?' She pointed to the stage. He laughed and shook his head vigorously.

'Can't you sing?' she asked, surprised.

He ducked and crossed his forearms protectively over his face, still laughing. 'No' to save my life.'

She smiled fondly. 'That's a relief, Darren. I was beginning to find you intimidating.'

He looked up, ready to laugh, and saw she was serious. 'You're *joking*, Liz,' he said slowly.

'No, Darren, I'm not.'

They sat looking at each other for a long while and then, their drinks finished, got up together to leave.

He saw her home. This time there wasn't any question about it, and this time, also, she asked him up to the flat. The cats met them at the door, yowling, circling as eagerly around Darren's feet as around her own.

'Look at that,' she said. 'They know you're a soft touch.'

'I'll feed them,' he said. He dropped his coat in a corner of the alcove, the scarf and hat on top of it, and went casually through to the kitchen.

'Put the kettle on,' Liz called, from the living-room. 'I'll just get my messages.' Through the open door to the study she saw the green light of her answering machine flashing desperately for attention. She slung her coat over her desk chair and sat down, playing back the tape. The first message was from Charles, his voice weary.

'Hello, Liz, it's . . . uh . . . eleven-thirty. I've been ringing since ten and now I'm going to bed . . . Tomorrow's off, I'm afraid. Megan's got some sort of bug. Vomiting half the night. *Apparently* she had it yesterday, too, but Jane neglected to tell me.' He paused, his voice brittle. 'I *hope* it's not infectious. Anyhow, I'm stuck for tomorrow. You'll just have to go alone, I suppose. I've rung Moira, so she knows. Sorry to give you so little warning, but I *did try*.' His goodbye was stiff, with a faint edge of hurt.

The next message was from Moira. 'Look, darling, I've just had a miserable Charles on the line, with a sick child. He *did* leave it rather late, and I'm afraid I'll be hard put to make up the table tomorrow at this hour. Will you mind *terribly* being on your own? It *will* be pretty casual. And, by all means, if there's anyone *you'd* like to bring, do feel free . . .' The last was formal and rhetorical, a hostess's formula. Liz switched off the machine.

She went through to the kitchen. The cats were hunched

over their dishes. Darren was carefully ladling ground coffee into the cafetière.

'How nice,' she said, sitting easily at her own table, pulling off the suede boots, while Darren got milk from the fridge and mugs from the draining board. He set the cafetière on the table, before her. 'You busy tomorrow?' she said.

Liz picked him up in Warwick Road in Earls Court, by his direction. She accepted his explanation of traffic convenience, but was still left with the faint feeling that he did not choose to show her where he lived. He was standing waiting in his long coat and cap. He had left off the flamboyant scarf, a concession perhaps to the conservatism of the venue. He had asked her, shyly, what he should wear and she had told him to please himself, curious what he would choose. He had played safe; jeans and a black sweatshirt with the name of a Glasgow theatre group in fine white print on the back. He'd shaved, too, and brushed his hair. He got into the car cautiously, and looked around. 'Nice,' he said, with a brief nervous grin, fastening his seatbelt.

She accelerated away from the kerb. 'Barry's,' she said. 'Barry's choice, I mean.'

'You dinna like it?'

'I love it. I like to pretend I'd have chosen something a bit more ecologically sound.' She smiled. 'I've a pretty good line in self-deception.'

He looked over the dashboard, the tape-deck; over his shoulder at the back seat where she'd flung her tracksuit and trainers. 'What's that for?' he asked.

'I've an awful feeling our host might be expecting it.' She looked quickly down, checking his footgear. He wore old, inexpensive trainers. 'As a matter of interest, Darren, do you run?'

'You mean for exercise?' He looked faintly incredulous.

'That's why most people run,' she said.

'Aye. I can run. I played a lot of football at school.' She smiled and said, 'You just might do me a favour. If John Harris appears in training gear, would you mind volunteering? Only,' she added quickly, 'don't *beat* him, whatever you do.'

'I wouldna do that,' he said. He looked uneasy.

He looked more uneasy as they slipped into the gentle Hertfordshire countryside approaching The Oaks. 'I'm still no' sure this is such a good idea,' he said softly.

'Of course it is. John's nice, and you know Mrs Harris anyway.'

'Aye,' he said, no more happy.

'Besides,' she said brightly, 'how can you expect to play Noël Coward if you've never had Sunday lunch in an English country house?'

'Aye, maybe.' He smiled a little.

She said, 'I seem to recall we made some kind of a deal.'

'I liked it better when it was theory.'

She gave him a gentle look. 'Are you really nervous?'

'I'm scared shitless,' he said, as they drove up to the gravel circle in front of the house. 'I don't belong in places like this.'

She reached one hand across and touched his shoulder. He turned quickly. 'You're an actor, kid, remember? *Act!*'

'Aye,' he said quietly.

John Harris was in the open doorway of his front porch, surrounded by pots of blowing daffodils. He wore a sleek black tracksuit and state-of-the-art trainers.

Liz said as she switched off the engine, 'Looks to me, Darren, like you've drawn the short straw.'

She got out of the car, waved to John and turned encouragingly to Darren. He was already standing beside his open door, which he leaned to close with an easy gesture. He looked around, one hand in his coat pocket, his shoulders relaxed, head tilted slightly as he surveyed the house casually. Surprised, she stepped towards John Harris.

'You've met my assistant, Darren MacPhee, haven't you?' she said uncertainly. But Darren was already beside her.

'I've seen you at the health club, sir.' He extended his free hand. 'A while ago. You'll maybe no' remember.' He shook John's hand with the confidence of an Oxbridge graduate. Liz stared. John looked amazed, casting a quick curious glance her way before Darren said, 'Liz said you'd maybe like someone to run with.'

'Why, yes. Yes, actually, I thought maybe Liz . . .'

'Darren runs,' she said smugly.

'Oh. Oh, well that's great.' Cheerful interest replaced his look of bemusement. He said, 'You've brought your kit?' Darren looked blank.

'He can wear my tracksuit,' Liz said quickly. 'It'll be a little short, that's all.' She returned quickly to the car and came back with the grey sweatshirt and trousers over her arm.

'But won't you want to join us?' John said solicitously. 'I'm sure I can find Darren something . . .'

'No, no. Fine, John. Twisted my ankle practising yoga the other day,' she lied happily. She handed the tracksuit to Darren. 'John, show him somewhere to change.' She glanced quickly towards the house. She had cherished the idea of getting John and Darren off together before Moira appeared from the kitchen. The day might prove easier if Moira was briefed in advance. Liz waited in the dark front hallway while John disappeared somewhere upstairs with Darren.

John came back down alone, and jogged in place for a few steps. 'Great idea, Liz,' he said. He stopped jogging and put his hands flat against the Laura Ashley wallpaper, leaning forward and meticulously stretching one leg and then the other. 'Frankly, it was about time I had a little *challenge* running. This'll do me good.'

'Sorry I never challenged you,' Liz said drily.

'Well, *Liz*. You can't expect to beat *men*.'

'Oh,' Liz said slowly, 'I *see*. I knew there was a problem. I just never knew what.'

'Liz?' John said. 'Did I say something wrong?'

'No, John. Of *course* not.' She smiled honeyedly. 'Oh, Darren, that's *great*.' He stood, slightly self-conscious, at the head of the stairs. Her grey tracksuit had taken on a strangely changed appearance, stretched tight across his shoulders and hanging loose and easy around his narrow hips. 'I think I like that better on you,' she said. 'In fact, I like it a lot on you. You can keep it.'

'I wouldna . . .'

'Who knows, John might need some *more* challenging,' she said sharply. Darren looked confused. He followed John out into the spring sunshine. John did two more stretches, his hands on the roof of Liz's car. Darren watched, and Liz

218

stepped up behind him and whispered, 'Forget what I said about not beating him. Run his ass off.'

'What?'

She laughed, raised both hands and waved cheerily from the door. They jogged off, Darren discreetly two paces behind John and looking once, mystified, over his shoulder at Liz.

Liz walked back into the house and slowly down the corridor to the kitchen, composing a small explanatory speech along the way. She opened the door and was greeted by a delicious scent of roasting lamb, and Moira, sitting alone at her kitchen table, in jeans and an old jumper. She was shaving thin slices off a courgette with a potato peeler and looked washed out and listless.

'Oh, hi, Liz. I *thought* I heard a car. Didn't you see John?'

'He's running.' Moira didn't get up, but continued morosely slicing her courgette. 'Something wrong?' Liz said.

'Why aren't you running with him?' Moira's voice was monotone. 'He was waiting for you.'

'I brought him a running companion.'

'Who? Charles?' Her eyes brightened. 'Did he manage after all?'

'Not Charles.'

'Oh.' She put down her potato peeler.

'You suggested I bring a friend.'

'Of course, Liz.' Moira managed a smile and stood up to switch on the kettle. She was wearing orange Garfield slippers. Liz stared at her feet. 'William's. I couldn't find anything warm. It's so bloody *cold*.' Moira shuffled across the kitchen. 'Christ, how are you meant to walk in these things?' She got out instant coffee and milk and sugar, undecoratively, in mundane containers. 'So who's the man, Liz? Someone I know?'

'You know him.'

Moira's interest engaged. She spooned coffee into two kitchen mugs, eyes on Liz. 'You're being bloody mysterious.'

'I've brought Darren MacPhee.'

'You've what?'

'He happened to be with me when I took your message. It just seemed a nice idea at the time.'

Moira put one hand on a hip, head tilted. 'How does it seem now?' she asked suspiciously.

'Great. I lent him my tracksuit and sent him off to run with John.'

Moira sat down. She still looked suspicious. 'Liz, what are you playing at?' she said finally.

'I'm not *playing* at *any*thing.'

'Liz, no. Wait a minute. Just tell me. Is this part of the great experiment, by any chance?'

'The what?'

'You know. The great experiment. You and . . .' she paused coldly. 'You and Erica and that rubbish about making a perfect man. Is *that* what you're up to?'

'Oh for Christ's sake, Moira. That was a joke. A long time ago and not a very good joke either.'

'Well,' Moira looked flustered by her vehemence. 'If not that, then what? What are you *doing* with this kid?'

'He's my friend,' Liz said plainly. 'I've brought my friend to Sunday lunch. Like you suggested,' she added a little sourly.

Moira nodded. 'OK, Liz. Fine. Whatever you like.'

'I'd appreciate if you'd be nice to him. He's young and he's a bit out of his depth.' She gestured quickly around the imposing kitchen.

'Whose fault is that?' Moira said, but before Liz could answer she added sharply, 'Of course I'll be *nice* to him. What kind of a cow do you think I am? I *like* young people, Liz. I *care* about them.'

'So bloody well do *I*.'

'You have to be a mother to know what caring is.'

'Bullshit.'

Moira looked uneasy and then slowly shook her head. 'Oh, I'm sorry, Liz.'

'As well you should be. That was appallingly arrogant.'

'I said I'm sorry.' Moira sat down at the table, curling her toes and standing the plush Garfields on their pink plastic noses. She looked up and tears tipped out of her eyes, flooded her mascaraed lashes and slid down her pale English cheeks. 'Oh *shit*,' she said, miserably.

'I knew there was something wrong.'

'I'm sorry, love. You're just getting the flak.'

'What's happened?'

'He called her.'

'What?'

'He called her. From here. From our house. From the phone in his office. He called her.'

'Erica?'

Moira nodded quickly, sniffing. She wiped her eyes.

'Are you sure?'

'I heard him ask for her at the club. He'd left the door to his study slightly open. I was in the corridor. I don't think he realized, but then he must have remembered the door because he got up to close it. After that I could hear him talking but I couldn't hear the words. He laughed a couple of times. I heard that. I know that laugh.'

Liz said carefully, 'Surely a man doesn't call a *mistress* from his own phone. That takes a hell of a lot of nerve.'

'Not at the beginning,' Moira said. 'But later. Towards the end. When he's sure of himself.'

'I don't think he'd *ever* be that sure of himself.'

'Oh yes, when he doesn't care any more if he gets caught.' She sighed. 'He's going to leave me, Liz.'

Liz reached instinctively for a denial but found suddenly she had none that she herself could believe. She sat down across from Moira and said seriously, 'Don't you think it's time to end the guessing?'

Moira looked confused.

'Confront him, for God's sake. Bring it out in the open. Who knows? Maybe it *is* nothing. And even if it's not, surely it would be better to know.'

Moira shook her head.

'Why *not*?'

'Because if I do, and I'm right, it's over. I can't face it yet.'

'So you'll live like *this*?' Liz said, exasperated.

'All over the world women live like this,' Moira said. 'Why not me?' She shrugged and turned away from argument, standing up, with her hands still on the table. She looked defeated and old. 'I suppose I'd better change,' she said.

Liz got up too.

'Can I do anything?' She waved towards the Aga.

Moira hesitated. She gathered her courgette slices into a bowl, and slid the bowl on to a work counter and then bent over to open the Aga door. She poked the roast with a carving fork and closed the door. 'I suppose you could do the salad.' Then she straightened up and said, 'No, stuff the salad. Come upstairs. I want company.' She picked up her mug of coffee and shuffled to the door.

Liz stood at the bedroom window while Moira wriggled out of her jeans and lifted a patterned silk dress out of her wardrobe. She sipped her coffee and watched down the gravel driveway for Darren and John. She said, 'You know, if anyone were to ask me, of all the men I knew, who was likely to have an affair, John would be at the bottom of my list.'

Moira's head emerged from a swirl of pink silk, newly painted lips carefully compressed. 'That just proves they're *all* shits,' she said. She had brightened slightly, cheered by the comforting ritual of dressing and making up. 'Frankly, I wonder I care.'

'There they come,' Liz said with a small smile.

Moira moved closer to the window. She peered curiously at the two men jogging side by side, talking companionably. 'He looks different,' she said.

'John?'

'Darren. He looks different. What have you done with him?'

'Lent him my tracksuit,' Liz said drily. 'Come on, the warriors return.'

They met Rachel on the stairs. She came out of her room wearing a grubby pink tracksuit, a personal stereo, and a look of glum detachment. Her hair was pulled back into a girlish ponytail and fastened with a rubber band.

Moira lifted the headset off her daughter's head and said, 'Are you dressing for lunch?'

Rachel shrugged.

'We have guests.'

Rachel glanced sideways and gave Liz a small sly grin. 'Liz doesn't care if I dress.'

'The Smythe-Hamiltons are coming too.'

'Oh bor*ing*.'

Moira shrugged, irritated, and dropped the headset down on her daughter's ears. 'Suit yourself,' she said, giving up. Rachel padded down the stairs in her thick white sports socks and disappeared into the drawing-room. Televised sound blared briefly from the open door and was muffled again as the door closed behind her. 'Wait for it,' Moira said. In moments the raised voices of William and Rachel burst out as the door was flung open again. William stood in the doorway, shouting something incomprehensible about a video. 'Settle it yourselves; I'm not interested,' Moira called over her shoulder as she led Liz back to the kitchen. 'Oh, why do we *do* it?' she asked wearily.

'Where's Clare?' Liz asked.

'On her pony. Thank God for ponies. Ponies give you a few years' grace at least. Then they start wanting something *else* between their legs and the idyll's over.'

'Moira!'

'Hmm? Oh, never mind. Where's that man of mine?' She was looking out the kitchen window. 'Didn't they come in?'

'There they are,' Liz said. Darren and John Harris were standing on the lawn, beyond the conservatory, dishevelled and sweaty in their running gear, looking up at the roof. Darren pointed at something. John shielded his eyes, staring upwards. They turned towards each other, talking, and began walking towards the house. They came in the kitchen door.

'Darren says it's just a loose flashing causing that leak,' John said, without preamble.

Moira looked straight past him. 'Hello, Darren,' she said. She made her sweet smile. 'This is a surprise.'

'I hope you didna mind,' he said at once.

'Of course not. I'm delighted to see you.' She held out her hand, rather formally, and they shook hands.

'Did you hear what I said about the roof? Darren says . . .'

'I heard you,' Moira said smoothly. 'You'll want to change,' she said, turning back to Darren. 'John, show him the guest bedroom. And oh, do have a shower if you'd like. I thought we'd have sherry in the conservatory, if it's warm enough, before lunch. Say, twenty minutes?' She glanced at her small gold watch. Darren nodded, looking a little awed.

'Have a nice run?' Liz asked him. He met her eyes with relief.

'Aye. Great.'

He glanced at John and John grinned. 'Good runner,' he said.

He was still breathing a little hard. 'Pushed me a bit. Just what I need.'

'I'm sure he did,' Liz said drily. She looked quizzically at Darren, but he ducked his head suddenly, not meeting her eyes. John clapped his hand companionably on Darren's shoulder and they turned together towards the door, but before they reached it, it opened and Rachel came in, her argumentative voice preceding.

'*Mum*, William says you said . . . oh!' She stared at Darren, eyes widening.

Liz said, 'Hi, Rachel. This is my friend Darren MacPhee. I told you about him. Darren, Rachel Harris . . .' Rachel's left hand scrabbled at her hair, pulling out the rubber band. She shook the hair out hurriedly, thrust the rubber band into her pocket.

'Hi, Rachel,' Darren said. She reached out stiffly and shook his hand, murmuring something unintelligible.

'Look, excuse me a moment. I'll be right back.' She whirled around and dashed out through the door, her stockinged feet thumping softly as she ran up the stairs.

'What's with her?' John said.

Moira just shook her head, ushering them out of the door after Rachel. When they were gone she burst out laughing. 'Well, I imagine she'll change *now*.' She turned back into the kitchen and then went to the window, looked out, and turned again to face Liz. 'God, John makes me sick.'

'*What?*'

'All that macho, come on m'lad crap.' She struck Liz across the shoulder in an imitation of her husband's camaraderie. '*Darren says it's just the flashing*,' she said archly, mimicking his voice. 'Twit. *He* doesn't know what a flashing is.'

'I'm sure he does.'

'Of course not. He's just being male.'

Liz stopped and then said evenly, 'Well, he *is* male, Moira.'

'Not *that* kind of male,' Moira said harshly.

Liz was quiet. Eventually she said, 'Maybe he'd like to be.'

The Smythe-Hamiltons arrived while John and Darren were changing. Moira brought them in to the conservatory and then went out in search of glasses and sherry and malt whisky for the Major. Liz and the Smythe-Hamiltons talked about the weather until she returned. She found it hard going and had a pang of concern for Darren about to be thrown into their company. But when he arrived with John, the three men launched instantly into a discussion of roof-tiles and joists, Smythe-Hamilton waxing lyrical about the advantages of good old English thatch. Moira, arriving with her silver tray of glasses and decanters, glared at them sourly and began to pour for her guests.

'Sherry, Liz?'

'No, thanks, love. I'm driving.'

'Oh yes. Of course. You're always driving now.' Moira looked perplexed. 'Perrier?'

'Lovely . . .'

'I'll drive, Liz.' She turned. Darren had broken off from the conversation and was looking across the room at her. 'If you'd like a drink,' he added a little uncertainly.

Liz looked back, curious. 'I didn't know you had a licence.'

'Oh aye. I've got that. It's just the car I dinna have.'

She hesitated briefly, glanced at Moira and then back at Darren. She smiled. 'Then, yes, thank you, if you don't mind.'

He shrugged easily. 'No problem to me.'

She smiled again. 'I'll have a sherry,' she said to Moira. Moira handed her a small golden glass and poured the Perrier for Darren.

'Hi, everybody!' Liz looked up. Rachel had reappeared in the doorway, a transformed Rachel in black tights, a minute black and white striped skirt, and a skinny black jumper. Her hair was frizzed and wet-look gelled, her eyes hugely framed in dusky charcoal and her lips bright red. She held on to the doorframe with one hand and leaned airily into the conservatory, displaying her pretty figure.

'What's happened to your eyes?' John said.

'Oh, *Daddy*.' She flounced happily towards him and clung about his neck, her glance flickering once to Darren and then away. 'I'll have a sherry please,' she said to her mother, fluttering her lashes.

'You'll have a lemonade,' Moira said. She ignored the costuming. 'Where are your brother and sister?' Rachel shrugged languidly. She released her father and wandered into the centre of the room, closer to Darren.

'Who cares?' She picked a solitary peanut out of a silver dish and slid it between her small white teeth.

'I care,' said Moira. 'It's time to eat.'

At lunch, Moira seated her eldest daughter between the Smythe-Hamiltons, as if a double wall of crusty propriety might keep her under control. She put Darren at the far end of the table, at her right, and Clare and William beside him. William looked Darren all over with open curiosity and then decided his roast lamb was more interesting, but Clare sat staring open-mouthed, her hands on her jodhpured knees.

'Are you really an actor?' she asked.

He grinned and looked shy. 'Aye. Sometimes.'

'*Really?*'

'Yes, really, Clare,' Moira said. 'Don't stare.'

'Are you on the telly?'

Darren laughed softly. 'No. I'm no' on the telly.'

'Are you Scottish?' she demanded then, with the same degree of excitement. Darren nodded. 'I met this boy once who was Scottish. He was really good-looking.'

'Aye,' Darren said grinning, 'we all are.'

'Yeah,' Clare breathed, awed.

Darren laughed and Moira said, 'Clare, stop quizzing Darren. It's rude.'

He was still laughing. 'It's no' rude,' he said softly. Clare looked at him with devotion.

'Clare, you're disgusting,' Rachel said sharply from her imprisonment across the table. 'You're so *obvious*.'

'I don't care.' She smiled happily. 'I think Darren's super.' She moved her chair closer to him and smiled at her sister. 'Would you like to see my gerbils, Darren?' she said.

'*Clare*,' Rachel said.

'As chat-up lines go,' John said, pouring wine, 'that's possibly my all-time favourite. Darren, excuse my daughters, they're at that age.'

'*Daddy*.' Rachel looked up appalled. She burst instantly into tears and, jumping up, ran from the room.

'Oh great, John,' Moira said.

'What do you mean? I didn't do anything.'

'You idiot.'

'Sensitive,' Mrs Smythe-Hamilton murmured. 'Sensitive age.'

Darren stood up, slowly, turning to John who was standing red-faced and miserable. 'If you dinna mind, John, can I have a word with her?' John looked around, his puzzled dark eyes settling on Darren's face. They looked at each other briefly and Darren nodded encouragingly, 'OK, sir? It's just I know what it's like . . .'

John nodded. Darren went out quietly and they continued their meal in uncomfortable silence.

After a few minutes, the door opened and Darren and Rachel came in together. She was tear-stained but smiled at him as they took their seats on opposite sides of the table. Rachel pointedly ignored her father, but she picked up her knife and fork and began to eat. Liz, from her seat beside John Harris at the far end of the table, caught Darren's eye, raised her glass to him and with a small smile drank a silent toast. He grinned and they looked at each other gently for a long while.

They retired to the conservatory for coffee. Clare and William dragged Darren off upstairs to see the gerbils. Rachel followed, a few paces behind, with a display of adult disinterest. Moira came in to the depleted company, carrying the coffee tray. She looked around and smiled lightly at Liz. 'Have we sent the children out to play then?' she said serenely. Liz gave her a cool quizzical look, but she said nothing more. The Major talked about when he was stationed in Scotland during the war and what nice people the Glaswegians were.

Moira said, looking out at her garden, 'What a shame Charles couldn't make it, Liz.'

'Yes,' Liz said mildly.

'Well, as for me,' John said, 'I'm thoroughly delighted Liz brought Darren. So far he's paced my best mile yet, charmed both my daughters, and in a moment he's going to show me how to sort out that roof. You can bring him *anytime*, Liz.' Liz laughed.

Moira said, 'Oh you're not going to mess about with that *now*?'

'Why not?' John retorted. 'Since I've got someone here who *knows* about it.'

'It's hardly fair to Darren. Ask him to lunch and send him out to fix the roof.'

'I don't mind,' Darren said. He came in carrying Clare piggy-back, her plump legs linked through his arms.

'Clare, for God's sake,' Moira said. 'You're far too big for that.'

'No I'm not. Darren's really strong. Aren't you? Come on, pony, come on.' She bounced up and down, face happily reddening. Rachel stood aloof to the side.

William shouted, 'My turn, my turn.'

But as Darren set Clare down on the tiled floor, John said firmly, 'That's enough. You lot can clear out now. Darren and I have something to do.'

They went out together and as Liz and the others watched from the conservatory, re-appeared from the direction of the garage, carrying an aluminium ladder between them. Moira opened the conservatory door and the party drifted out onto the lawn to watch. John set the ladder up against the wall of the house. Darren tested it lightly and then ran quickly up it, stepping easily over the guttering and onto the roof tiles. Rachel hovered, open-mouthed, watching. Liz felt a pang of protective concern. Darren scrambled up the roof tiles and balanced easily on the ridging, one hand casually. on the chimney-breast, utterly confident.

'He could have a nice little sideline in house-breaking.' Liz turned around, eyes narrow. Moira was smiling cheerfully. 'Sure beats working in McDonald's.'

'Aye, it's just loose, John,' Darren called down. 'I dinna think you need to replace it.' He worked his way carefully down the tiles and stepped lightly onto the ladder. John held it as he descended.

'Hurray!' Clare shouted as he stepped off, onto the grass. He bowed to her, eyes full of laughter, and turned to her father.

'I could fix it for you, John, if I had some cement.'

'No, no. Terribly kind. I'll have someone in. No, that's splendid. It's just knowing what's needing doing that's the problem . . .' He paused as Darren swung the ladder down, and then took up the other end. 'I really can't thank you enough.'

They walked off together, the ladder slung over their shoulders.

They were a long while returning it to the garage. Liz and Moira and the Smythe-Hamiltons had sheltered again in the conservatory when they returned. They came back slowly, Darren with his hands in his pockets, head down, listening carefully; John, his face animated, hands upraised, explaining something. They stopped for a while, deliberately, while John finished whatever point he was making. Then they looked at each other, Darren said something, John smiled and shrugged and put his hand lightly on Darren's shoulder. They walked that way back to the house.

When it was time to leave, the Smythe-Hamiltons climbed into their ageing Daimler to drive the few hundred yards to their house and the Harrises gathered in a semi-circle on the gravel forecourt to wave Liz and Darren off. Liz got into the passenger seat, Darren on the driver's side, and then Moira remembered the two pots of marmalade she had promised Liz and went off to get them. In the hiatus that followed, Clare stood outside the car, nudging Rachel who looked pointedly aloof, and William struck poses, imitating her, until Rachel clouted him. While John sorted it out, Liz said to Darren, 'You were brilliant.'

He looked surprised. 'What?' he said curiously. 'You mean the roof?'

'I mean everything. But yes, for that matter, how'd you know all that about the roof?'

He laughed easily. 'My uncle's a slater. I worked with him when I left school.' Liz nodded. 'That's what I was meant to be.'

'A slater?'

'Aye.'

Moira returned with four pots of marmalade in a paper box.

'That's lovely, but I'll never eat all of those. There's only me.'

'Oh, don't worry. They keep.'

'Sure,' Liz nodded, thinking of the sweet cidery smell of decaying apples pervading her study from the ageing box in the corner. 'Thanks,' she smiled. 'Thanks for everything; great meal.'

Moira looked happy. 'Bye, Darren,' she said. He looked up from checking the dashboard of the car and smiled nervously. He turned the key and the engine started.

Liz said quickly, 'You may need a little choke.' She pointed to it helpfully.

'No, she's fine.'

'There's your indicators and the lights are over here; that's the full beam . . .'

'Aye, I ken them.' He slipped the car into gear and pulled silkenly away. As he slowed at the end of the long driveway, she said, 'The clutch is a bit stiff . . .'

'It's fine,' he said mildly. He turned on to the main road and accelerated smoothly through the gears, reached up, adjusted the rearview mirror, and switched on the tape-deck, steering easily with his right hand.

Liz sat back in her seat. 'I hate men,' she said.

'What's that?' He glanced across, startled.

'Men. They all do that. Drive everything. No problem. They're all *born* knowing how to drive.'

He laughed. 'No' all men,' he said. 'Dudes wrote off four cars in four months.' He paused. 'But then, he was always stoned when he was driving them.' After a second pause he said, gently, 'I drove a lot of lorries. It makes cars easy.'

'With your uncle?'

'Aye.'

Liz said thoughtfully, 'What does your uncle think of what you're doing now?'

'What? The theatre?' He kept his eyes straight ahead, on the road.

'Yes. Did he mind, I mean.'

'He doesn't *mind*. He doesn't know much about it, but he doesn't mind exactly.' She wanted to pursue it, to ask the obvious questions; mother? *father*? But as always when his family was discussed, Darren offered no openings. Liz settled back in her seat, comfortably relaxed, enjoying being driven for a change.

'Hey,' she said suddenly, sitting up. 'What happened on that run?' She smiled playfully. 'You were meant to beat his ass, remember?'

He didn't look at her. After a while he said, 'I couldn't do it, Liz. It would no' have been kind.' He sounded reproachful and she responded with a small sigh.

'Oh, I suppose not. Not that he didn't *deserve* it.'

'Why don't you like him, Liz?' Darren said.

'I do like him. Of course I like him. He's my friend.' There was a long silence.

'He's worried about his wife.'

'*Is* he?' Liz turned to face him, her eyes widening.

'Aye. He kens something's bothering her. Only, he doesna ken what.'

'He told *you* that?'

Darren paused, uncertain. 'Aye, when we were putting the ladder back.' He added quietly, 'Maybe he didn't mean me to say it to you.'

Liz had a sudden feeling, as she had felt when he mastered her car, of the world of men shutting her out. 'No,' she said, 'maybe not. Well, at least he's worried.' Her voice was distant and cold.

'You angry with me?'

She turned hastily. 'No. Not with you, Darren. Not with you.'

XIII

The phone rang at seven-thirty in the morning. Liz had switched her alarm off twice and had her head under the duvet. Jacob was petulantly knocking scent bottles off her dressing-table. She reached a hand out and dragged the phone into a small duvet cave.

'Hello?'

'OK, Liz, what's going on?'

'What? Moira?'

'With Darren. What's going on?'

'Nothing's *going on*. He's my friend.' Liz sat up, pushed Esau off her pillow and began fumbling for the light switch and her clock. 'What time is it?' she asked distractedly.

'He's in love with you, Liz.' There was a small pause. 'I hope you know what you're doing.'

'Oh, *ridiculous*.' Liz snapped the light on. The cats both jumped on to the bed, staring with ravenous blue eyes. 'That's so stupid I'm not going to answer it.' She found her clock, looked at it quickly and set it back down.

'He never takes his eyes off you.'

Liz was quiet for a moment, and then she said evenly, 'He was *nervous*, Moira. That was heavy stuff for a kid like that.' She swung her legs over the side of the bed and said querulously, 'What have you got against him anyhow? You were sniping all day.'

'I was not. I bloody well was not. I was *charming*.'

'To his face. You were sniping behind his back. All that crap about housebreaking and "playing with the children".'

'I was joking. I was *not* sniping. What a shitty thing to say.'

'Well, it was a shitty thing to do. I thought you liked him.'
She paused. 'Your *daughters* certainly did.'

Moira was silent briefly and when she spoke her voice was
chilly. 'My point precisely, Liz. I rest my case.'

'Oh piss off.' She slammed down the phone.

It was a bad start to a less than wonderful day. Liz's morning
was taken up with a long urgent supportive meeting with her
best and most vulnerable student, a brilliant Bangladeshi girl
whose father had suddenly reconsidered the wisdom of her
degree course and was arranging a marriage instead.

In the afternoon, she met Andrew Pringle making his disconsolate way across the rainswept Front Quad, fine features
set in a now familiar expression of bafflement and dismay.
She had essays to grade, but instead had coffee with him in
the Lower Refectory. He shook rain off his tan trenchcoat,
hung it neatly over the padded plastic back of his chair, and
sat down, looking large and slightly misplaced amidst the
flimsy, functional furnishings, the utilitarian clutter of trays
and cutlery.

It was a quiet hour and Andrew had chosen an isolated table,
but he still looked around defensively before he spoke.

'Women are a puzzle,' he said, stirring sugar into his cup.

Liz thought of her morning of telephone conversations with
irate Asian males and said, 'And men *aren't*?'

'I don't think so,' he said innocently, 'do you?' Before she
could answer he continued, 'Men are consistent.'

'That's not always a compliment.'

'No,' he said thoughtfully, lifting his cup, 'but you know
where you stand. You know what, Liz? She wants separate
beds. Can you imagine? I mean she's . . . she's *Erica* after all.
I mean we all know . . . and I'm not complaining, not many
men of my age are so lucky, I dare say, and even if *occasionally*
it's a little . . . a little . . . *wearing* . . . I mean I'd hardly have
it any other way, would I?'

'Separate beds?'

'Yes,' he said, his forehead wrinkling. He pushed back
his well-groomed greying black hair. 'I mean, *Fiona* wanted
separate beds on our honeymoon but she was, you know,
English . . .'

'When did you make love to her last, Andrew?'

'Well. Well, *Liz.*'

'Oh c'mon, you can't get coy now. You've practically had me in the sack with the pair of you.' He turned red, but said, under his breath, 'Well *recently.*'

'Can you remember when?'

'Not exactly. I mean who does after a while when they're married?'

'I don't know, Andrew, I've never been married.' She leaned forward. 'Women who want separate beds *sometimes* aren't happy with their sex lives.'

'Well if she wanted *more* like she always used to say . . . surely she'd want a *double* bed . . .'

'We're not all quite as obvious as that, Andrew.'

He looked baffled. 'Damnedest weekend. Usually she's working, or away on one of those seminars of hers . . .'

'What seminars?'

'You know, those things she goes to. Yoga seminars. How you can have a seminar about tying yourself in knots . . .'

'Where, Andrew?'

He looked blank. 'All over, I suppose. I don't know. One was in Brighton I think . . . Anyhow, there *wasn't* one this week. And I was home as well. And the children weren't. It's always better when the children are there, but Fiona took them up to Scotland to see my parents. So it was just me and Erica. Shifting bloody beds.' He finished his coffee. 'Women *are* a puzzle,' he said.

In the evening, Liz rang Moira to apologize, but got no answer. Then she rang Charles to enquire about Megan, but he too was out. With no more excuses and the *Independent* read forwards and backwards, she sat down at her desk to work. An hour later she scrunched up three pages of notes and threw them in the bin, picked up a very un-erudite paperback, and went to bed.

She abandoned her book entirely the next night, on the justification that the following day being Wednesday, she'd work on it with Darren all afternoon. She got up early on Wednesday morning, cleaned the flat, did a wash and tidied her study. She laid everything out in carefully defined order; the print-out of her five completed chapters, the stacks of notecards, Darren's questionnaires, a heap of photographs that he had taken with her camera. She pinned the photographs on to a noticeboard, arranging them in groups to correlate with her chapter headings. She remembered Barry doing all these things, surrounding himself with a fortress of his own ideas, and was aware of consciously emulating him; but the exercise had a hollow feel, as of a failing argument buttressed with loud words. She was glad when the buzzer rang for the door.

Darren was early. He was slightly scruffy and looked guilty. As he came in, he said, 'Liz, I have to ask a favour.'

'Surely,' she said thoughtlessly.

'Aye well, you haven't heard what it is.' She stopped on her way to the kitchen and turned to look at him. He pushed the door closed behind him and stood with his hands in the pockets of his long black coat.

'Well,' she said a little uneasily, 'what is it?'

'It's this.' He pulled his right hand carefully from his pocket, and held it up in front of her. A small grey and black striped kitten hung uncomfortably across the palm of his hand, easily immobilized by his big fingers. Its miniature tail swished.

'Oh, Darren,' Liz cried, 'it's charming.' She reached for it.

'No' really,' he said. He turned it around with his other hand, and looked at it grimly. Then he handed it to her. Liz held it, childlike, to her shoulder. It scrambled up at once, out of her hands, and sprung from well-clawed hind feet on to the bookshelf. With two more scrabbling leaps it was on the top, staring down with bright amber eyes.

Liz rubbed her shoulder. 'It looks a bit wild,' she said.

'It's been shut up all day.'

'Shut up how?'

'Well in a box mostly. A big box,' he added.

'*Darren*. That's awful. You can't . . .'

'I don't usually,' he said hastily. 'Only, I've been with a friend.' He paused. 'And my friend has asthma. From cats.'

Liz nodded, watching the little animal tiptoeing along her bookshelf, stopping to teeter four-footed on the edge and then continuing with a whisk of its tail.

'Why'd you take it with you?' she asked. 'Why didn't you leave it in your flat?'

'I'm no' staying in the flat.'

'Not at all?'

He shook his head. He was watching the kitten as well, jumpily, like a nervous parent. 'Dudes chucked me out,' he said.

'He what? Why?' Liz asked sharply.

Darren shrugged. 'Well he didn't *exactly* chuck me out,' he corrected justly. 'He said I could stay if I got rid of him.' He jerked his chin up, indicating the cat. It leapt from the bookshelf to the mantel.

Liz felt a rush of sympathetic anger. 'Well he's a shit,' she said.

'No' exactly,' Darren added. 'I mean it *did* piss on his new personal stereo.'

'Oh,' Liz said, her anger briefly blunted, but then she added sharply, 'Well I don't care. It's still a shitty thing to do . . .' She paused. 'Darren, where *are* you staying?'

'Oh, that's OK. I've got a lot of friends.'

'But where?'

'I'm staying with Sheila just now. Until I find another flat. You met Sheila, right?'

'Yes,' Liz said, after a moment's pause. 'Yes of course I did. Oh well, that's nice of Sheila anyhow.'

'Aye,' he said.

'So there's no problem.'

'No.' He was hesitant, watching the kitten toying a biro to the edge of the mantel. 'Except there's her asthma . . .'

The biro slipped off and clattered on to the tile hearth. The kitten leapt down, worrying it. Liz watched it and said with careful clarity, 'I see. So you'd like to leave the kitten here?'

Darren looked startled but nodded. 'It wouldn't be for long,' he said helpfully.

The kitten caught the biro, bit it ferociously and flung it down dead. It scuttered sideways across the room, tail high in a victory dance, and disappeared, still sideways, into the study. There was a sudden silence of its pattering feet, a hiss and a hideous yowl. A striped streak shot at carpet level from the study and flashed up the bookshelves, treeing itself, panting at the top. Jacob stepped from the study, ears flat, back arched, blue eyes aglow with the retribution of the gods.

'I hope not,' Liz said warily.

236

The kitten roosted on top of the bookshelf for most of the four hours in which they worked. Eventually Jacob and Esau got tired of terrorizing it and went back to their older pastime of watching Darren in the kitchen. When Liz came out of her study at four-thirty, the kitten was curled in a small ring of stripes on a cushion on the sofa. She ran a finger down its back and it purred in its sleep.

'It thinks it's settled,' she told Darren as she filled the kettle.

'It's used to being moved around,' he said. He took a sheet of paper from the typewriter and said, 'I hope you dinna mind.'

She smiled and said, 'I don't mind.' He looked relieved. She wanted to add that it seemed to be the story of her life, but she feared upsetting him.

'How's your job?' she asked.

'OK. I'm doing "close" tonight.' He glanced at the clock. 'Six to two.'

'Sounds grim.'

'It's not too bad. A bit rough sometimes.' He shrugged, unperturbed. 'It's money.'

She nodded, getting mugs out for coffee. 'Where does Sheila stay?' she asked.

'Notting Hill.'

'Bit of a trek at two in the morning.'

He shrugged again.

She was quiet for a while and then said, impulsively, as she poured the coffee, 'Darren, I don't suppose this is really any closer, but if you *did want*, you could stay here. That's a sofa-bed in the living-room. We've put up quite a few people over the years . . .' He was looking at her oddly. She said quickly, 'Until you find somewhere. I'm sure it won't take long.'

'That's very kind,' he said, his voice neutral.

'I just thought it might be convenient.' She grinned and said, 'It seems a shame to separate you from your cat. What's he called?' she added, curious.

'Tiger.' He hesitated. 'That's very kind,' he said again, softly, 'Only . . .'

She felt his discomfort and said quickly, 'Well, whichever you like, Darren. It's all the same to me.'

He paused again and then said carefully, 'Aye well. I dinna think it's all the same to Sheila.'

'What's that?' she said, looking up.

'Sheila. I don't think it's all the same to her.'

Liz sat down. She looked across the table at him and said slowly, 'I think there's been something of a misunderstanding here.' Her voice was calm. 'So let me get something straight, Darren. What *is* Sheila to you?'

'A friend.' His face was impassive.

'A *good* friend?'

'Aye. A good friend.'

She studied him confusedly and then said, 'Darren, do you sleep with her?'

'I have done.' The vivid blue eyes met hers openly.

'And now?'

'No' usually. Sometimes. Sometimes you *have* to.'

'What do you mean, you *have* to?' She looked at him sharply but he returned the same reasonable gaze.

'Well, if a woman wants it, sometimes it doesn't seem right saying no.'

'And I suppose you *don't* want it? You sod.' She sat back, glaring at him.

He straightened also, his hands releasing the coffee cup he was holding. He folded his arms and said with dignity, 'No' if I dinna love the lass.'

The answer startled Liz. She dropped her eyes, and said without looking at him, 'You don't love her?'

'No. I don't love her.' She remained looking down at her hands on the table as he stood up and stepped back from his chair. 'I have to go,' he said awkwardly.

'I'm sorry, Darren.'

'It's all right.'

She looked up. He was standing in the doorway, getting into his black coat. 'That was really none of my business.'

'It's all right,' he said again, 'only,' he looked apologetically at the kitchen clock, 'I've got my shift.'

'Yes, of course. Sorry to keep you.' Her voice was even and friendly. She stood up and walked with him to the door. The cats followed and immediately began sniffing around the corners of the room.

'Are you sure it's all right?' He shrugged towards the sleeping kitten.

'It's fine, Darren.' She smiled and tried to be normal, but the tension in the room did not go away.

'I'll bring some cat food tomorrow after work. And some litter.'

'I've got plenty, Darren.'

She stood in the open doorway and gently waved as he ran down the stairs.

He didn't turn up with the cat food or the litter on Thursday and he didn't telephone to say why not. She was not surprised. She had overstepped and knew it. Any anger she felt at his irresponsibility was overridden by her own guilt and, also, a faint concern. It was the same concern she felt if any of her students found themselves in such tenuous circumstances. Only in Darren's case, she was not, as she was with them, part of the structure of support.

On Thursday morning, she had awoken at six to the sound of yowls and crashes and found that the kitten had knocked over three glasses in the kitchen, trying to escape from Esau. It had also dug a large hole in a crewel-work cushion to enhance its nest. She shut it in her bedroom with its tray and its food when she went to work. On her return she found litter all over the floor and damp patches in the corners of the carpet.

'You're a little shit,' she said, carrying it into the kitchen in one hand. She fed it in a corner while the two Siamese were too busy murdering dolphins to care. It sat on her lap while she ate supper, purring frantically. 'Where the hell's your master?' she said. It purred on, oblivious.

On Friday morning she dashed out to the Pakistani grocer's at the corner before work and came back with an extra sack of litter and four tins of gourmet kitten food. She suspected its diet was usually more mundane, but she could hardly have a second-class cat in the flat, whoever it belonged to. She gave up shutting it in anywhere, deciding to let it ruin the whole flat evenly. Besides, she had realized by late Thursday that it was actually the aggressor, starting all the scraps and stalking her two Siamese mercilessly.

239

'Fine,' she said, closing the door. 'If they eat you, I won't even apologize.'

She was preparing to leave her college office after her last tutorial when her telephone rang. She picked it up, expecting an apologetic Darren. The voice was female, soft, cockney, and uncertain.

'Liz?'

'Hello?'

'Liz, this is Stephanie.'

'Stephanie?' Liz slipped her shoulder bag off and sat down again at her desk. 'This is a surprise.'

'Yeah, well I hope you don't mind me calling you at work. Only I didn't know where else . . .'

'No, of course I don't mind, Stephanie. What can I do for you?'

There was a hesitance in the girl's voice when she said, 'It's about Darren MacPhee, really.'

Liz felt a jolt of concern, but said only, 'What about Darren?'

'Well, did you know Dudes threw him out?'

'Yes, I knew that.' Liz relaxed and leant back in her chair, her feet propped against the leg of the desk. She said calmly, 'It's all right, Stephanie. He's staying with Sheila in Notting Hill.'

'He's not.'

'What? He told me . . .'

'He *was*. Only she threw him out, didn't she? She's a real cow, Liz. She *knew* he hadn't anywhere to go. I really hate the bitch.' Her gentle voice was surprisingly vehement.

Liz sat up. She said carefully, 'Stephanie, when was this?'

'Wednesday I think. I haven't *seen* him or anything, but Jimmy says Malcolm saw him.'

'Where?'

'I don't know, Liz.' She paused, her voice unhappy. 'I said he could stay with us but Jimmy won't have it. I think he thinks I fancy him or something. Jimmy's awful jealous. Jimmy's my boyfriend,' she added quickly. 'Malcolm thought he was sleeping rough.'

'Oh terrific,' Liz said quietly.

'Liz, can you do something? I mean, I thought maybe you'd

know somewhere . . . I'm sorry to bother you, but you're like the only, you know, *adult* we know.'

Liz put her head in her hand, leaning the telephone against her ear, thinking fast. She said, 'This is a great world, Stephanie.'

'What?'

'Don't worry about it. I'll sort something out.'

'Oh thank you, Liz. Thank you so much.'

'Thanks for calling me, Stephanie,' she said gently. 'And look . . .'

'Yeah?'

'If there's ever anything else, you call me any time, OK?'

'Yeah, Liz.' The voice was shy. 'Thanks. Ta-ta.'

'Bye, Stephanie.' Liz put the phone down. She sat for a moment, staring bleakly at the rain on the window. Then she stood up, wrapping her coat around her angrily.

'The *bastard*,' she said aloud. She gathered her folders and walked out, slamming the door.

She had cooled down a little by the time she reached the Oxford Street McDonald's where he worked, but she was still angry enough that she was glad he wasn't anywhere in sight when she arrived. She ordered coffee and a doughnut and sat down at the table she had occupied with Charles and the children. When she had eaten the doughnut and drunk half the coffee, she caught the eyes of a pretty black girl wiping tables. The girl came over and smiled cheerfully.

'Excuse me,' Liz said, 'do you know Darren MacPhee?'

The girl looked blank.

'He works here.'

'Lot of people work here,' the girl said. She smiled again and tossed the cluster of minute beaded braids that hung down beneath her maroon cap.

'He's new. Black hair, an earring. Scottish.'

'Oh *Darren*. Yeah, I know him. He's real cute.'

'Yes,' Liz said icily. 'Real cute. Is he here just now?'

'Day off,' said the girl, tossing her cleaning cloth from her left hand to her right. 'You looking for him?'

'In a way,' Liz said, noncommittally.

'You'll find him tomorrow,' the girl said. 'I think he's on ten to six. Do you want me to tell him anything?'

'No,' Liz said. She smiled sweetly, 'Thank you very much. Nothing at all.'

She took the Underground to Fulham and emerged from the train into driving rain and wind, and walked quickly home, stopping only to buy a pizza and rent a video. She was in too vile a mood to work. She arrived back at the flat to find the pine pole that supported the curtains in the living-room tilted down at a crazy angle, its supports broken loose from the wall. The velvet draperies were pooled on the floor and dusted with loose plaster. In the middle, the striped kitten was curled contentedly.

'Oh *shit*,' Liz said. Jacob and Esau emerged from her bedroom and slipped into their piercing pibroch of meows, weaving in and out of her feet. She stumbled over them to the kitchen and dropped her folders, the pizza, and the video on the table.

'I hate cats,' she shouted, reaching for the tin opener. She fed them and looked around for the kitten. It was standing on top of the fridge, rubbing perilously against a bottle of wine. She snatched the tipping bottle down with one hand and put the kitten on the floor with the other. It looked up and opened a surprisingly large mouth in a surprisingly small meow.

'I hate *men*,' Liz said, opening the kitten food. She walked back into the living-room, kicking the fallen curtain aside and examining the damage to the wall. She climbed a chair and made rudimentary attempts at fixing it, jamming the plaster-coated ends of the screws back into the wall. They fell out immediately. She dropped the pole again and gave up.

She got her work folders from the kitchen and carried them into the study. The green light of the answering machine was fluttering unhappily. She ran the tape and found a message from Charles, his voice cheery.

'Hi, Liz. Looks like it's quality time again tomorrow. If you'd like to join us for Madame Tussaud's, we'd love to have you. Please ring me at the flat if you can.' She sat down and rewound the tape, her hand on the telephone. Rain spattered against the small back window of the study, streaking the dark glass. She sat thinking for a long time. Eventually she picked up the phone and called Charles.

He answered on the second ring and his formal tone brightened to friendly warmth at the sound of her voice. 'Oh, Liz, great. You coming? You're a brave soul . . .'

'Actually, Charles,' she said guiltily, 'I'm not. I mean, I've a lot on . . .'

'Oh. Oh I see. Well of course. Just phoned on the off-chance anyhow.'

'I mean, I'd love to, Charles, but there's a bit of a press of work.'

'Of course.' He laughed softly. 'Anyhow, you *must* get tired of a child's view of London every weekend.'

'That's not it at all, Charles. I've enjoyed our weekends.' She paused and said, 'I've enjoyed them a lot. Only *this* weekend, there's something I must sort out.' Her voice was firm.

He said, 'Liz?'

'What, Charles?'

'Have I done something wrong?'

'Not you, Charles. Not in the slightest. Look, ring me next week. Maybe we could have lunch.'

'Yes,' he said. 'Super. I'll look forward to that.'

'Have a good day tomorrow. Love to the girls.'

'Yes. Thanks. I'll try.' He sounded weary. '"Once more into the breach" . . .'

She laughed and said goodbye. As she put the phone down, the wind slapped rain against the window in a sudden gust that rattled the pane. She looked at it grimly, then got up and pulled down the blind. She went out and picked her way past the wreckage in the living-room to the bathroom and turned on the taps, poured in bubble bath and began to undress. The kitten wormed its way through the just-open door, and clambered on to her wicker clothes hamper, tipping the lid and falling in. She let it struggle out on its own. As soon as she was in the bath it jumped up on to the rim, staring at the deep layer of bubbles with fascination.

'Oh, don't even think of it,' she said. She turned around to reach for the shampoo and the kitten landed in the water by her feet. It was out in an instant, scrambling up her leg, leaping to the tile surround and then, in scrabbling haste, out of the door. 'Oh, for Christ's sake,' Liz shouted. She jumped up, rubbing the scratches on her leg and climbed out of the bath. Wrapping herself in a towel she followed the wet patches on the carpet and found it treed again on the top of the bookshelves, dripping and wild-eyed. Wrapping the towel tighter, she climbed up on the arm of the sofa, conscious of the view in through her uncurtained window, and snatched it down in one hand. It was ridiculously small deprived of its aura of fur, and looked like an unpleasant species of otter. She shook it lightly, and rubbed it with the edge of her towel until it looked the right shape again. Then she set it down.

It sat in the middle of the floor, ears flattened, and began disconsolately licking its fur, stopping to pick up and shake each of its feet in turn. On the last shake it caught sight of its transformed tail and pounced upon it hysterically, chasing it in a ring of visible terror until she caught it again, fluffed the tail into recognizable shape and cautiously set the kitten down once more. It opened its mouth and made a sound of utter misery. 'Oh you stupid ass,' Liz said, 'it serves you bloody right.' Shivering, she sat down, towel-wrapped, beside it, lifted it gently, held her face against its dishevelled fur, and began to cry.

On Saturday morning, Liz made a second failed attempt at fixing the curtain rail, tidied the rest of the flat, and went through her books collecting old paperbacks for a student AIDS charities sale. She filled a paper carton with crime novels, and began picking through the shelves for classier offerings. She lingered briefly over Barry's Thomas Hardys, untouched since his departure. She picked out three and carried them towards the box, but stopped, sitting on the edge of the sofa, thumbing through the top one. Its pages were marked at frequent intervals with notes in his strong black hand. She puzzled over a few, and closed the book, studying its cover briefly. She got up and put the three books carefully back on the shelf, and topped up the carton with glossy cookery books Moira had given her on Christmases past.

The striped kitten climbed in on top and Liz had a brief, wicked desire to tape the box closed. It had dried out overnight and, aside from its usual morning skirmish with her Siamese, was quite well behaved, though it still looked peculiar, as if it needed ironing. She picked it out of the books, deposited it on the sofa, and sealed the box.

In the afternoon, she carried the carton of books downstairs and set them on the front seat of the car. It was still raining, though the wind had dropped. She went back up the stairs and made the flat as kitten-proof as she could, removing breakables, stowing food and moving the litter tray into the bathroom. The kitten sat watching with golden-eyed innocence, its tail wrapped delicately around its feet. Liz gave it a warning look and went out of the door.

She drove first to Gower Place, parked illicitly, and hurriedly carried the carton of books up the stairs of the Students' Union. Retrieving her car, she turned down Gower Street and found an empty meter at the edge of Bedford Square. She jammed the car in at an impatient angle, got out and fed the meter, and then walked purposefully towards Oxford Street.

It was four o'clock and McDonald's was packed with birthday party children, shrieking adolescent girls and swaggering boys. She saw Darren the instant she came through the door. He was working a till, midway down the long counter, with a queue of five people in front of him and an argumentative man in a business suit at the head of the queue. He looked cool and collected, gathering together an order even as he responded to the man's complaints. Two small boys stood with the man, looking anxious. *Weekend Daddy*, Liz thought. Tough day at the zoo. She stepped quietly into the queue and became customer number six.

Over the tumult of the restaurant lobby she could hear Darren's distinctive strong voice, soothing and charming. The man cooled down gradually, became simply truculent, and then suddenly apologetic. Darren flashed a grin, the commiserative male grin he'd shared with John Harris. The dark-suited man picked up his paper bag of cheeseburgers and milkshakes, and nodded, walking away with a faint battered smile, his two boys following. The queue moved quickly then, and three people joined behind Liz.

'Can I help you, please?' Darren said politely. The two teenagers in front of her ordered Big Macs and fries and tried hard to flirt with him. He was too absorbed in the press of work to notice, calling their order over his shoulder, turning back, his eyes on the till, darting quickly along the polished machinery behind him, collecting cokes and fries.

He hardly looked up while he packaged their order. They walked away, leaving Liz facing him.

'Can I help you, please?'

'Yes.' He turned towards her absently and she said, 'You can tell me what the fuck's going on.'

'Liz!' Recognition flashed across his face.

'Where'd you sleep last night?' Liz asked clearly. There was a surprised shuffle in the queue behind her, and a female giggle.

'*What?*' Darren whispered.

'Just tell me straight,' Liz said reasonably. 'Where did you sleep?'

'Wi' Sheila,' he said hurriedly, under his breath, and then added more hastily, 'Well, no' *with* her, y'ken.'

'You did not,' Liz said, her voice rising. 'Sheila threw you out. Where the *fuck* did you sleep?' There was another giggle behind her and then a querulous male voice said, 'Look, are you going to *order*, or what?'

'Liz, I'm working . . . '

'Answer me!'

'You,' the man behind her pointed at Darren, 'do you work here or not?'

'Yeah, I work here,' Darren said quickly. 'Look, Liz . . . '

'*Are you going to take my order or am I going to call the manager?*' The irate man pushed his way forward and Liz stepped instinctively aside. The remainder of the queue formed an interested semi-circle at the counter.

'Yes, sir. How can I help you, sir?'

'Stephanie called me, Darren.'

'Stephanie?'

'I'd like a Big Mac, large fries, an apple pie and a coffee. If it isn't too much trouble.'

'She said you're sleeping rough.'

'Is that a large coffee, sir?'

'Regular.'

'*Are you?*' He shrugged, and called for the Big Mac and turned to collect the fries.

Liz caught his arm. He stopped and stared at her, uncertain.

'Are you getting my order or aren't you?'

'Yes, sir.'

'Answer my question,' Liz shouted.

'Let him get my fucking Big Mac,' the man said, turning red and pushing between Liz and the counter.

'You,' Darren shouted. He leaned over the counter, his eyes narrow, and his hand gripped the man's tie. 'Don't swear at her.'

The man jerked free, shocked, and then opened his mouth and bawled, '*Manager!*'

Liz stared as a crowd began to gather.

'You're a menace,' the man shouted at Darren.

'Aye, fine,' Darren said. He laid his hand flat on the counter and jumped up on to it, and down on to the floor on the customer's side. 'You want to discuss it?'

'Darren, calm down,' Liz said sharply.

'Calm *down*?' he shouted. 'You come in here grilling me about where I bloody sleep and *I* have to calm down? You bloody calm down.'

'I'm calm, Darren. I want one answer. Where *did* you sleep?'

'Christ knows.' He waved the question away and, looking up, said, 'Oh shit.'

A tall, broad-shouldered black man was walking towards them across the lobby. He wore a blue McDonald's shirt and a look of authority and he carried his big hands in fists. 'What's the problem here?' he said in a humourless, rumbling voice.

'No problem, sir,' Darren said quickly.

'There bloody well is.' Darren's customer was readjusting his skewed tie under his bright red face. 'First, I can't bloody get served because he's arguing with that bloody woman,' he pointed at Liz. 'And then . . .'

'Don't you *call* her that,' Darren lunged towards the man and was stopped by the manager's big left arm.

'You got woman trouble, Darren?' the manager said. His voice was softer.

'It's all right,' Liz said hastily, 'I'm his mother.'

Darren stared at her and then said loudly, 'You're *not* my fucking *mother*.'

'You *have* got woman trouble,' the manager said. He put his hand behind Darren's shoulder. 'Go on, clear out. I'll cover for you.'

'Am I fired?' Darren said cautiously.

'No, man, you're not *fired*,' the manager said. He grinned and vaulted the counter and stepped in behind Darren's till. 'Woman trouble, that *serious*.' He waved them away and picked up the red-faced man's order just where Darren had left off. 'Big Mac, large fries, apple pie, regular coffee. There you are, sir. Have a *nice day*.'

Liz grabbed Darren's arm above the elbow and walked quickly through the crowd to the exit. The curious watching faces blurred into a mass of unfamiliarity and then suddenly, in the midst of them, three sprang into instant focus. Three pairs of wide blue eyes settled on her and on Darren. Charles Beatty stood, a daughter on each side, staring in astonishment.

'Liz?' he said uncertainly.

She hesitated for a fraction of an instant and then just shook her head. 'Sorry, Charles, sorry girls,' she called, 'I'll catch you later.' She smiled weakly and without breaking stride, she propelled Darren past them and out through the door.

Out in the street, he stopped at once and turned to face her. He said, half querulous and half mystified, 'Liz, what the hell is this about?'

She slipped her arm back through his and started walking quickly towards Tottenham Court Road. 'We'll talk about it later.'

'Where are we going, for fuck's sake?'

'Stop swearing and stop arguing. I mean it, Darren. I'm really mad. Don't push me.' He followed, cowed. She realized he had never seen her angry before and she took advantage of the effect before it wore off.

'Just tell me where we're going.'

'To the car.'

When they reached it, he said, 'Right, we're here. Now tell me . . .'

'Get in, Darren.'

'Stop telling me what to do.'

'Just get in the car.'

He glared at her, but he did. He sat, one foot braced

248

belligerently against the dashboard, glowering out the window as she drove to Fulham.

He got out of the car as soon as she parked and started to argue again, but she ignored him. She locked the car and went into the building, leaving the outside door open. After a moment she heard him follow her, then the slam of the heavy door, and his quick footsteps on the stairs. He caught her at the landing, while she was finding the right key.

'Look,' he said, 'I'm no' coming in till you tell me what you're on about.'

'Fine,' she said. She opened the door and walked through, her back to him. The cats emerged sleepily from her bedroom, surprised by her early return. When she heard the click of the latch, she turned. He was standing just inside the alcove, his back to the closed door, watching her. She leaned against the kitchen doorframe, her hand on her hip. Darren stared, bewildered.

'You *shit*,' she said at last.

'What?' he whispered.

'Where'd you sleep last night?'

'Oh, for Christ's sake.' He jerked his chin up, hands raised in exasperation, eyes dodging hers.

'You slept rough.'

'Aye, that's right.' He looked back. 'So? What of it? A couple of fucking nights. It wasnae going to hurt me.' He paused and added, 'I've done it before.' She said nothing. 'Look,' he said loudly, 'there's kids of sixteen and seventeen out there doing it every night. If you want to worry about someone, worry about them. I can look out for myself.'

'I know you can,' Liz said quietly. 'I wasn't worried about you.' He looked startled and she continued quietly, 'I didn't mind that you preferred to go to Sheila's. She's young and you know her well and frankly I don't care what else is between you. That's not my affair. But to sleep in the *street* rather than come to me?' She paused and he continued to stare at her in such obvious bafflement that she wanted to slap him. 'It's an *insult*,' she shouted. 'It's an insult to our friendship. To everything decent. It's an insult to *me*!'

249

Darren shook his head slowly. He said softly, 'I didn't want it like that between you and me.'

'Like what, for God's sake?'

'That. Depending on you. You know, charity like.' She whirled around and slapped both hands against the wall.

'Darren, if *any* of my friends were in this kind of trouble I'd expect them to come to me. It *isn't charity.*'

'Aye well,' he said shrewdly, 'it's no' likely to happen is it? I mean Charles isna going to turn up with nowhere to park his bloody Porsche, is he?'

'Don't be so childish.'

'I'm no' being childish. I'm being realistic. Which is more than you are.' He paused, looking at her gravely. He said, 'I'm no' a wee boy, Liz.'

'Well you act like one. You have a stupid lover's spat with Sheila and you go sleep in the street. Not exactly mature behaviour, Darren.'

'It wasn't that.'

'What wasn't?'

'A lover's spat. It wasn't that.' He paused. 'It was over you.'

She stepped back from the wall, turning to him more directly. 'I don't understand,' she said.

'No,' he answered clearly, 'you dinna understand at all.' He paused and then raised one hand towards her. 'Look,' he said. 'I told you. I'm no' a wee boy. I'm twenty-four. I've been on my own since I was fifteen. I've worked a lot of places. I've slept a lot of places.' He paused again before saying, 'I've had a lot of women. I've seen more of life than you have. D'ye ken?'

Liz nodded, slowly, and said in a quiet voice, 'I think so. I still don't see how any of that makes it so impossible for you to accept my hospitality.'

Darren looked at her for a long exasperated moment and then turned aside and slammed a fist against the door. He leant his forehead against his outstretched arm and then suddenly looked up sideways. 'You *still* don't understand, do you?' He shook his head and turned towards her. 'Do you no' see, woman?' he shouted, flinging an arm out. 'There's only one place I want to sleep in this flat. And that's in there, in that bed, *with you.*'

Liz was silent, staring. He straightened up and slipped his hands in his pockets, met her eyes stubbornly and then looked away.

'Are you serious?' Liz said cautiously.

'No,' he said, 'of course not. Just my idea of a joke. Look,' he glared at her, 'do you mind if I leave?'

'Darren,' she said carefully, 'you do surely realize, I'm old enough to be your mother.'

He gave her one last exasperated stare. 'Well you dinna *look* like my mother,' he said wearily.

He turned to the door. She hesitated, watching him, and then drew a quick breath and said in a quiet, firm voice, 'I'd rather you stayed.'

He looked around warily, his hand yet on the doorhandle, eyes guarded. She smiled gently. The naïve restaurant uniform gave him an appearance of ingenuous vulnerability, but she saw past that. She stepped forward and laid her hand lightly on his shoulder. For a cautious moment, he did not move. Then he turned slightly to face her, and reached his hand out, and laid it, as lightly, on her own shoulder. The instant he touched her, she felt a flow of confident control and knew at once that this, like mending a roof or playing Shakespeare, was something he knew how to do.

The hand slid down her back, drawing her closer, his other tilted her head. His lips touched hers, and the hand reached her hips, tightened, drew them up against his own. The feel of his hard young body touching hers from thigh to mouth was shockingly pleasurable, and stunningly welcome.

He led her gently, sweetly, to the bedroom, as easily as he had led her on the dance floor. Only when they were sitting side by side on the edge of her bed did he relinquish his authority. 'Are you sure you want this, Liz?' he said. There was something startlingly assured in his voice.

'Yes,' she said, amazing herself. 'It's exactly what I want.'

'Oh, lovely,' he whispered. He stroked her cheek. She kissed the rough fingers. He unpinned her hair and very gently he kissed her neck.

'Oh shit,' she murmured, 'it's been so long.'

'Aye,' he said laughing a little. His hands were certain and unfumbling. There was nothing boyish about him, and any doubts she had about his experience vanished with the smooth familiarity with which he slipped a pack of condoms from his wallet and laid them on her bedside table. He pulled off his clip-on McDonald's tie and tossed it over his shoulder.

Liz unbuttoned his striped shirt. She giggled, 'It's like violating the American flag.'

'What?'

'Nothing.' She lay back luxuriantly, and pulled his strong, supple body down on to hers. 'Oh well, one up for Mrs Robinson.'

He drew back slightly, his hands knotted in her hair, his lips close to hers. 'Who's Mrs Robinson?'

'Never mind, love,' she smiled, locking her arms behind his back. 'Before your time.'

XIV

Liz awoke suddenly, alert and surprised. The flat was dark. Uncurtained streetlight crept beneath the bedroom door. Darren was asleep beside her. The kitten was asleep between them. She moved cautiously, sitting up, and switched on her bedside lamp. He didn't wake. The kitten opened amber eyes and immediately shut them, stretching its paws in ostentatious luxury. Liz looked at the clock. It said eight and the darkness told her it was evening, not morning. She stretched herself gently. Her body felt well-used, like she'd run a good few miles.

She looked down. He was sleeping, with the extraordinary soundness of youth, his face buried in his arm, black hair falling over it. He looked like a boy. She felt an onrush of tenderness, mixed with amazement and a small serving of guilt. She thought she would get up and make them coffee and something to eat, while he slept, but the moment she shifted her weight, he awoke.

He raised his head, blinking and bemused, like his little cat, and then sat up hurriedly. 'Christ, is it morning?'

'No, no. Nothing like it.' She smiled and said, 'Relax,' because he looked suddenly alert and agitated. 'It's eight o'clock. At night.'

'Saturday night?'

'Of course.'

'It's just I have to work early Sunday.'

'You're fine. You've got all night still.' He relaxed, smiled, lay back down and reached for her with both arms. They kissed and she said, 'That was wonderful, Darren. That was more fun than I've had in a *very* long time.'

He smiled again, his eyes crinkling sexily. 'Would you like more?'

'More. God. I'd forgotten what it's like being young. I'd like some *food*, actually, Darren. Aren't you starving? I am.'

'Aye. But I can wait, if you'd like.'

'I think food first,' she said. She kissed him lightly again and turned to rise, but he stopped her, holding her arms at the elbow, studying her as she looked back into his eyes.

'You're beautiful.'

'I'm not. I was never beautiful and now I'm getting old.'

'Beautiful,' he said again.

'Thank you for thinking so,' she said simply.

'I love you.' She turned away, taken aback. 'It's all right,' he said. 'You dinna need to say anything.' He sounded solemn, and anything but young. She did not meet his eyes. He let go of her arms and she stood up and walked across the bedroom naked, with the bold ease of body, the freedom from self-consciousness, that follows love-making. She gathered her underwear from the floor and dressed quickly, pulling on her sweatshirt and jeans.

In the living-room she lit the lamps and half-closed the curtains, dragging the fallen draperies part-way across the dark glass. Jacob and Esau leapt out of the sofa and stalked to the kitchen, demanding their belated supper.

She was feeding them when Darren appeared in the doorway wearing his black uniform trousers, and the striped shirt hanging open. He said, looking back to the living-room, 'How'd that happen?' He was pointing at the felled pine pole.

'Want to know?'

'I can guess,' he said uncomfortably. He crossed the room and leapt up on to the chair arm, barefoot, examining the broken fitting. 'I'll need some filler,' he said.

'Can you fix it?'

'Oh sure.'

'Oh great,' she said happily. 'I didn't know what to do with it.'

'Why didn't you ask me?' he said.

She shook her head. 'Oh no. I'd have gotten someone in or something. I can't start just depending on the men I know to do everything, just because I'm alone. I *should* do it myself really,' she added guiltily. 'It's so *unsound* asking you.'

He looked uncomprehending but, having propped the pole temporarily, he stepped down from the chair and said curiously, 'Would *he* have done it?' His voice was briefly hesitant.

'Who? Barry?' He nodded. 'No, actually,' Liz said. 'We're both hopeless. We'd just sit staring at it for weeks. Stupid, isn't it.'

He looked surprised, thinking about it, but said eventually, 'It isna stupid if you dinna know how to do the thing, is it? I mean, if no one ever showed you?' Their eyes met and shared a quick understanding.

'No,' she said. 'I suppose not.'

They worked easily together in the kitchen, making a meal of pasta and vegetables. He was neat and precise, long past the student chaos stage, and she suspected he could cook at least as well as she could, such as that was. She said, 'Do they feed you at McDonald's?'

'Oh aye. They do that.'

'You must get sick of it.' He looked up, startled. 'I mean, it's a bit the same, surely.'

'It's food,' he said quietly. She felt abruptly chastened.

She set candles on the table and laid linen napkins at their places at either end. He smiled appreciatively, watching her.

'I'm sorry I haven't got flowers.' She picked Moira's pink geranium off the window sill and set it between the candles. 'How's that?'

'Grand.' She nodded, and switched off the lights. The room was dim and pretty, her two oriental cats poised on counter and chair, washing themselves decoratively. They sat down to eat as naturally as if they'd lived together for years.

In the morning, she woke muzzily, to the sound of her name. Darren was kneeling beside the bed, dressed in his McDonald's uniform.

'Liz?'

'What time is it?'

'I'm sorry. I have to go to work.'

'*What* time?'

'It's six. I'm on early. I'm sorry.'

She woke properly and sat up. 'Darren, you haven't got a jacket or anything.'

'It's OK. I've got stuff in a locker there.'

'Take something. Something of mine. Or Barry's. There's some of Barry's things here still.' She started to get up, but he stood up and stepped back from the bed.

'No, really, it's all right. I wouldna have woken you but I needed to know . . .' He paused, looking uneasy.

'What, Darren?'

'Liz, do you want me to come back tonight?'

'Of course.'

'No' of course. Do you want me?'

She sat up straighter, pulling the duvet up to her chin, shifting Jacob with her feet. 'I want you. I'm not into one-night stands, Darren.'

'What?'

'Joke. Come back tonight. Please. Bring your things. Where *are* your things?'

He shrugged. 'Around. I'll no' stay. I'll find a place, Liz. Only, it may take a day or two.'

'I don't care, Darren. You can stay as long as you like.'

'Aye, well maybe it's no' wise.'

'Oh don't be silly,' she said quietly. She was fully awake and aware of the solemn uncertainty with which he addressed her. He seemed very different from the night before. She shook her head. 'Look, it's too early to talk about anything. Just get your things and come back after work. We'll talk then. And take something to wear. It's cold. You can't go out like that.'

'I'm fine,' he said. 'Go back to sleep.' He smiled for the first time and went quietly out through the door.

They didn't talk about it that evening. Darren arrived at four, wearing his street clothes and carrying his small rucksack and the sort of sports bag John Harris used for his trainers and a towel.

'Is that all?' Liz asked.

'There's a few things with Sheila yet. I can get them later.' He left the sports bag in the alcove, by the door.

'Did I get you into trouble?' she asked.

'At work?' He laughed. 'No. I got teased a bit,' he added. He didn't sound as if he minded. They ate dinner together, and washed up together and went to bed and made love. On Monday morning they went out to work like a married couple.

On Tuesday, she met him outside McDonald's and they went to a film. Wednesday afternoon they spent in bed, the word processor and the typewriter forlorn at the ends of their fat grey wires. Liz neglected to phone Moira all week, and on Thursday she skipped her yoga class with Erica. She forgot completely that Charles Beatty was meant to meet her one day for lunch. On Friday she had a spare key cut for the door. Darren had Saturday off until six and on impulse they drove to Eastbourne and walked along an empty strand while he recited audition pieces for RSAMD.

On Sunday afternoon, Darren repaired the curtain pole, while Liz read essays. When he had finished, she looked up from a ring of papers and said, 'Will you do something for me?'

'What's that?'

'Cut my hair.'

He sat down on the carpet beside her. She stacked her papers.

'You sure?'

'No. So do it fast before I lose my nerve.'

He looked doubtful, but then he grinned and said, 'Aye. If you'd like.' He got her hairbrush from the bedroom and scissors from the kitchen, and sat down on the floor beside her. He undid the fastenings of her hair, like he had when he'd first made love to her. Carefully, he brushed it out over her shoulders and down her back. She sat cross-legged, enclosed in a silken tent. He was a long time brushing and arranging her hair, his hands deliberate and sensual. 'When was it cut last?' he asked.

'When I was fourteen.'

'Oh *right*,' he said, laughing. 'Hey, this is an honour.'

'It is indeed. The last of my hippie youth.'

He laughed again, picked up the scissors and made the first, long, certain clip. A curtain fell from beside her ear and landed, startlingly black, on the pale carpet.

'Help,' she said, 'I've changed my mind.'

He sat back on his heels, facing her, grinning. 'Aye fine, I'll just leave it like that.'

'Go on, get it over with.' But he wouldn't be hurried, studying her carefully between each cut, walking around her, and settling again to view her at a new angle.

'Do you want a fringe?' he said, lifting a lock forward over her eyes.

'I don't know. What do you think?'

He studied her carefully again and then shook his head. 'No.' He drew the two shortened wings of hair down smoothly either side of her face and stroked them flat. Then he moved around to the back and clipped the last long hanks of hair from the nape of her neck. 'Shake your head.' She did, and a light short fluffy cloud enveloped her face. Her neck felt cool and airy and free. 'I love the curl in it,' he said.

'It's so *frizzy*.'

'Oh, it's *great*. You dinna have to do *anything*. I had a lassie once spent hours making it like that.'

'Really?' Liz looked up from within the fluffy cloud, uncertain.

'I'll show you.' He brushed the shortened hair firmly, made a few last clips and stood up. He went through to the bedroom and came back with the hand mirror from her dressing-table. Liz sat still, cross-legged within her circle of cut tresses, and took the mirror warily. She saw her own face, looking younger and smaller, half hidden by soft hair. The white streaks, so prominent when swept back into her familiar knot, were tangled amongst their darker sisters, making a gentle frame. She studied herself carefully, liking what she saw. 'That's *super*, Darren,' she said. 'You did that awfully well.' She paused and smiled at him and then said, 'Should I colour it? You know, the grey.'

'No.'

She nodded, glad. She lifted the mirror again, tilting her head whimsically. The kitten came down from its seat on the sofa and began to toy with the cut hanks of hair. She grabbed the kitten and bundled it up against her face, nuzzling its soft spotted belly.

'You,' she murmured, 'you're a devil.' The buzzer rang for the door and she called casually, 'Answer that, Darren, will you?'

He went through to the alcove, spoke briefly and came back. 'It's your friend from the university.'

'Who?'

'Dr Pringle?' he said uncertainly. 'Erica's . . .'

'Andrew? That's a surprise. Ask him to come up, Darren,' she said, plucking up tufts of hair from the carpet.

'I did.' He hesitated. 'I guess I should have asked?' He paused again. 'Do you want me to . . . you know . . .' He nodded towards the bedroom and study.

'What? *Hide?*'

'Well, no' exactly hide . . . you know, maybe look like I'm working or something . . .'

'No, Darren,' she said clearly. 'I don't.' The door chimed. 'That's him now; would you like to let him in?' As he walked away from her, barefoot and tousled, in jeans and a baggy jumper, she saw clearly that he had the indefinable but undeniable look of someone only recently out of bed. She shrugged as he opened the door. She doubted if Andrew was perceptive enough to see, and anyhow, she did not care.

She glimpsed Andrew through a corner of the alcove, standing in the open doorway, in the corduroy trousers and tweed jacket that comprised his version of Sunday casual. He carried a brown calfskin briefcase and had a red scarf around his neck and looked classically handsome but as always, bewildered.

'Oh, I say, it *is* you,' he said to Darren. 'I *thought* it was you, but then I said to myself, well it *is* Sunday, I mean, well, I say, this *is* nice . . .'

'Yes, sir,' Darren said, stepping back to let him in. They both moved jerkily, in equal awe of each other. 'Come in, sir. Liz is in here.'

She remained sitting like a buddha in her ring of shorn locks, which she casually gathered while she said, 'Hello, Andrew. This is a surprise.' She smiled to herself, amused by their mutual consternation and their comically opposite appearance.

'Sorry to be a nuisance, Liz, but . . . oh.' He stopped, staring. Her hand rose involuntarily to her hair, and she met his gaze, boldly but with trepidation.

He stared for a long while, then a broad smile broke across his face. 'Why, Liz. *That's* nice. Oh yes, I *do* like that.'

'Do you, Andrew?' Her voice was squeaky with cautious uncertainty.

'Oh yes indeed. It's . . .' He searched for words. 'It's *stylish*,' he said at last. The word sounded odd, like a foreign phrase uneasily pronounced. 'Oh I *do* like that.'

'Darren did it,' she said, nodding to where he stood, barefoot, in the doorway, watching them. 'Just now,' she added, a little unnecessarily.

'*Did* he?' Andrew turned and looked at Darren. 'Well isn't that clever?' He sounded genuinely amazed.

'Would you like something, sir?' Darren said suddenly. 'Coffee or tea, maybe?'

Andrew looked happy. 'Well, *that* would be nice. If I'm not detaining you . . . I actually came on the scrounge, Liz . . .' He held up his briefcase. 'I've the first section of the new book all ready to go; editor waiting on it, and my *machine* has packed in. Of all times. And then I remembered Barry's. You do still have Barry's?' he asked hopefully.

'Of course you can use it, Andrew. I'll just take my work out . . .'

'Oh, I hate to have you do that.'

'No problem, Andrew. I promise you. The muse is a bit quiescent just now. Moribund, actually,' she added grimly, getting to her feet. 'Do you want to work here, or take it with you?'

'Oh here will be fine, if that's all right. It's only a few pages.' He glanced uneasily at her and then at Darren.

'Fine with us,' Liz said deliberately.

He worked all afternoon, surrounded by watching cats. Liz and Darren brought him replenishments of tea and biscuits at intervals. The flat focused inwardly upon the study; Andrew reigning there, a bumbling royalty, to whom they became cheerful minions. Liz helped him order his paragraphs. Darren went out to get tobacco for his pipe. Later, they both made him spaghetti and listened to a reading of his introduction while they ate. When the work was finished, they opened a bottle of wine to celebrate. Liz said casually, as she poured it into glasses, 'How's Erica?'

'Oh, splendid. Fine,' he said distantly. 'One of her seminar weekends. Thought I'd get this finished while she's away.'

'Things OK between you?'

Andrew glanced briefly at Darren. Darren got up quickly and went into the kitchen and began washing up. Andrew watched him go and then said to Liz, 'Rather odd actually. She's quite, you know, perky, these days. Rather good form to tell the truth.'

'Oh?' Liz said mildly.

'Yes. Ever since we moved those beds actually.' He looked totally mystified. 'Not doing my back a lot of good, though, you know.'

'What's not?'

'Well, they're *narrow*, aren't they?' he said. 'Like a British Rail sleeper every night. Still,' he blinked his film-star eyes innocently behind his black-rimmed reading glasses, 'if that's how she likes it, I suppose . . .' He paused. 'All right for *her*. She's *used* to tying herself in knots.'

After he'd gone, with the print-out of his work in his briefcase, Liz shut the door and went back into the kitchen where Darren was feeding the cats. She began to giggle and burst out laughing when he looked up.

'What's funny?'

'Andrew. I'll never figure him out.'

Darren looked confused. 'I thought you knew him real well.'

'Oh, I don't know. Do you ever know *anyone* really? I've known him for nearly ten years and frankly his sex-life is still a total mystery to me.'

'Well, yours is no' a mystery to him,' he said.

'What do you mean?' she asked quietly.

'He knows,' said Darren.

'About us?' He nodded. 'Oh of course not, Darren. He might wonder, but he wouldn't know.'

'Aye, well, I think he knows,' he said unconvinced. 'Does it matter?'

'To me?' She shook her head. 'No. But anyhow, it would make no difference. He's an absolute gentleman, Darren. He wouldn't tell a soul.'

'Andrew,' Moira said.

'*Andrew* told you?'

261

'No.' Moira slipped a delicate piece of sole into her pink painted mouth and looked calmly about the dim interior of the little restaurant on Great Russell Street. 'Andrew told Erica. Erica told John,' she grimaced briefly, 'and John told me.'

'That I was sleeping with Darren MacPhee,' Liz said with loud annoyance.

'Shh,' Moira said, instinctively. 'Not at all, actually. *Andrew* said to Erica something along the lines of "that nice young David what's-his-name is staying at Liz's flat, just now. What a nice chap."' She replicated Andrew's clipped befuddlement perfectly. '*Erica* said to John, "That is good for Darren that Liz is so kind to him."' She mimicked Erica's Germanic naïvety equally well, though with a harsher tone. '*And*,' she paused and took another bite of sole, '*John* said to me, "I'm really pleased what Liz is doing for Darren. *Such* a nice lad, isn't he, love?" And *I* said, "She's sleeping with him."'

'You said that to John?'

'No. I said it to myself. And I'm saying it to you. And I'm right, right?'

'Right,' said Liz.

'Oh, for God's sake.'

'Well don't look shocked. *You* just told *me*.'

Moira put her head in her hand. 'Liz, *what* are you thinking of?'

Liz smiled whimsically and shook her new-shorn head. 'What's anyone thinking of when they fall in love? Don't be so serious. Do you like my hair?'

Moira looked pained. 'It's a bit frivolous.'

'Oh great. You were the one always telling me to get it cut.'

Moira said quickly, 'Well, of course. Only I always imagined something a bit more . . . structured.' She paused and said suspiciously, 'Was that Darren's choice?'

'It was Darren's haircut, actually.'

'Darren? You let him cut your *hair*?'

'Well, why not? After everything else I let him do, cutting my hair seemed pretty minor. Besides, he's good at it.'

'It's a good cut,' Moira said fairly. 'Liz, what are you going to do?'

'What do you mean, do?'

'In the future. What are you going to do?'

'Who knows?' Liz said vigorously. 'Look, Moira, I'm just a fortnight into this love affair. It's sweet and it's fun and yes, it's different. But I haven't begun to think seriously and neither I promise you, has he.'

'You'll both have to some time.'

'Then we will. Who cares, Moira? I could die tomorrow.'

'People always say that when they aren't facing reality. The truth is more likely you'll live for forty years and have to make sense of this mess.'

'It isn't a mess.'

'It will be. It will probably be very messy indeed.'

'I don't see why it has to be. He's a nice decent young man. And I'm fairly decent, too, I think. I can't see why we can't work something out.'

'Oh c'mon. Where's he going to live? With you? Who's going to pay the bills? While he works in *McDonald's*. Oh sharpen up, Liz. What does that make him?'

'As a matter of fact, he's looking for a flat because *he* wants to be independent. Which he has been, may I remind you, as long as we've known him and a *long* time before. Quite frankly, I'd rather he stayed with me. I *like* having him there. But the choice is with him.'

'So you're going to live in middle-class comfort in Fulham and he's going to doss in Notting Hill, or somewhere. Interesting basis for a relationship.'

'Charles Beatty has a home in Essex, a very upmarket Docklands flat, drives a Porsche and holidays in the South of France. And nobody ever found *that* odd when I went out with him.'

'It's different.'

'It's *not* different. Face it. Nobody would think twice of *any* of this if I were a man. Barry could have moved a twenty-year-old in with him and no one would say a word other than "lucky old dog". So why should I have to apologize?'

'Because you're *not* a man. And this is the real world, sweetheart.' Moira finished her fish and took a sip of her wine. She leaned back, arms folded. 'What *about* Charles Beatty?' she said. 'Have you told him?' She looked grim.

'I haven't *seen* him, to tell the truth,' Liz said, a little guiltily.

'We were supposed to have lunch a couple of weeks ago, but he never called.' Her mind flashed to her last view of him, watching open-mouthed as she marched Darren out of McDonald's. 'He must be busy,' she said lamely.

'This is going to do him the world of good,' said Moira. 'Would you like coffee?'

'No. I mean, yes, coffee. What do you mean? Am I responsible for Charles's welfare now? Because I went out with him a few times? For God's sake, Moira. Charles had problems before I ever met him. Big problems.'

'Well, he's got more now. And so has Darren MacPhee. Maybe you're *not* responsible for Charles. But you most certainly are for Darren. I find it impossible to believe that you're in *love* with this uneducated, unformed, socially inadequate boy. Which leaves only the possibilities that you are brutally unkind, or an irresponsible romantic fool. Since you're my friend, I'll choose the latter, if you don't mind.'

'Fine. I'll buy that. Maybe I'm not *in love*, whatever that is. But I do think I love him. I enjoy his company. I look forward to seeing him. I like to listen to him. He teaches me things.'

'*He* teaches *you*? *What* can he teach you?'

'All sorts of things that nobody ever bothered with, while I was busy collecting degrees. Like how to mend a curtain pole. Or a roof. But that's not really what I mean. He teaches me – ' she paused and turned away from the table while the waiter poured coffee – 'about youth,' she said, looking back. 'That youth is kind and optimistic. That youth lives in hope and has not learned cynicism. That youth pleases the heart and refreshes the soul. If that's foolish, well fine. I'll be a fool.' She smiled implacably. Moira returned the smile, her own bruised and brittle.

'Oh be one, then,' she sighed. 'I suppose it can't be any *worse* a mess than I'm in, for all my planning and good sense.' She smiled again, prettily. '*Well*. Since you *are* a couple now, would you like to come to dinner?'

'The two of us?'

'Of course. *John* will be thrilled. He can *male bond* up on the roof again.'

Liz smiled back. 'That's sweet of you. *Very* sweet. I thought

264

when we started this lunch I was about to be drummed out of the friendship.'

'Hmm? Oh don't be ridiculous. I may think you foolish, and I do, Liz, make no mistake, but it doesn't affect our *friendship*.' She looked down and tapped the silver spoon delicately on her saucer. 'Friendship's far too important to lose over *men*. And I do *like* Darren, Liz, I just see him in another light, that's all.' She paused and said drily, 'A motherly light.'

'I don't think you'd be inclined to mother him if you knew him the way I do.'

'I should hope not,' Moira said under her breath. 'Oh, never mind, what about this dinner? When are you free? When's he free? Weekends best? Sunday lunch again. *God*,' she said, 'Rachel's in for a surprise. Better be a weekend she's *not* at home. Let's say, a fortnight on Sunday?' She had her pocket diary out and was consulting it briskly.

Liz looked at hers. 'No, sorry, we'll be in Glasgow.'

'*Glasgow*?' Liz nodded. 'Good *God*. Don't tell me you're going home to meet Mum?'

Liz smiled, but said quietly, 'I don't think Darren comes from that kind of a family.' She was still, thoughtful, with Moira watching her. She shook her head quickly, the thick frizz bouncing. 'No, he's got an audition on the Monday. We thought we'd go up the day before.'

'What's he auditioning for?' Moira asked, interested in spite of herself.

'Drama College. The Royal Scottish.'

'Oh. I *see*.' She sounded impressed. Then she said, 'What will you do if he gets in?'

'What?' Liz said, surprised. 'Well, I'll be delighted of course.'

'You'll be delighted in London while he's in Glasgow? Or what?'

When Liz returned to the Department after her lunch with Moira, the secretary stopped her to say, 'Dr Pringle was looking for you. I told him you were at lunch.'

Liz thanked her and said, 'Is he coming back?'

'He didn't say.' She prepared herself for a forthcoming gloom session and wondered what Erica was up to now. But entering her office, she found instead a huge box of chocolates, a bunch of yellow carnations and a beautifully word-processed note:

> Dear Liz,
> Editor *loved* the work. Thanks so much for all your help, and Darren's.
>
> > Love to you both,
> > Andrew.

She lifted the carnations and sniffed their clean freshness. 'How kind, Andrew,' she said to herself. She felt warm, vindicated by his thoughtfulness in including Darren in his gratitude, and surprised. When she rang him later from the flat, he was even more effusive.

'What a nice Sunday that was, Liz. I did so enjoy it.'

'So did we, Andrew,' she said honestly. 'How's Erica?'

'Oh fine, fine.' He paused. 'She said she's missing you,' he added quietly.

'Me?' Liz said. 'Why?'

'Well, you haven't been to yoga for a while apparently. She says she never sees you.'

'Oh, Andrew,' Liz said, stricken. 'I *am* sorry. I've just been so busy . . . and quite frankly I hadn't realized it had been so long . . .'

'She seemed to feel you were angry with her.' He paused again. 'You're not, Liz, are you? I mean, I told her it was nonsense. What would you have to be angry about, you and Erica . . .' His voice trailed uncertainly.

'Of course I'm not. Really, I feel rotten . . . look, you tell her I'll be there Thursday and we'll have a sauna maybe after, OK?' He seemed happier then and after they'd said goodbye, Liz sat at her desk thinking it was time to get her life back in order. She hadn't written to Barry, or her mother. Regarding Barry she could be excused. He had phoned only once and not written at all since the occasion of his abortive confession. She was not surprised; she had effectively shut him out by refusing to listen. But neither did she feel a great obligation. Her mother was different however. And she'd forgotten her friends and she hadn't *looked* at her book.

The fortnight with Darren had passed in an adolescent haze of sex and emotional exploration. It was lovely but it couldn't go on. She had a life to live and, for that matter, so had he. But when he came in the door at seven o'clock, they were in each other's arms and in bed before she remembered to object.

Later, when they had had supper, a pizza he had brought home with him, and a green salad she made herself, he said suddenly, 'I've found somewhere to stay.'

She was startled, mostly by the suddenness of it, and said, 'Stay? You mean a flat? Already?'

'Aye.' He was watching her.

She looked down at her empty plate and said, 'I see.' After a moment she said, 'Where, Darren?'

'Holland Road.'

'In Kensington?'

'Well, sort of. Near Olympia.'

She stared and then said, 'Can you afford that? It can't be cheap.'

'Aye well. It's a squat actually.'

'A squat.'

'A nice squat,' he said encouragingly. 'I mean, it's no' been empty *too* long. And they look after it real well.' She was still staring. 'It's no' *free*, y'ken. I have to pay my share of the gas and electricity. And the maintenance.'

'Maintenance,' she said carefully.

'They'd no' like it to get run down or anything.'

'How socially conscious,' she said, only half in jest.

'Liz?'

'Nothing, Darren, I . . .'

'You dinna like the idea.'

She was thoughtful. At last she said, 'Well, frankly, Darren, I'm not *wild* about squatting . . . I mean, I can see both sides, but it's not legal for a start . . .'

'It's no' illegal either. It's somewhere in the middle.'

'Property owners *do* have rights, Darren.'

'Aye. And they get their rights in the end. I mean, in the *end* they go to court and get us out. But in between we have somewhere to live. It's better than it just *sitting* there for years.'

Liz was quiet. She said eventually, 'And when they *do* get you out?'

'We'll go somewhere else. But we'll probably have a few months. If we're lucky.'

'A bit *insecure*, Darren, surely. Waiting to get thrown out.'

He shrugged. 'You cannae have everything,' he said mildly. 'And it's better than Cardboard City.'

She stood up and carried their plates to the sink. She felt him watching her. She said, her back to him still, 'But that's not the choice, Darren, and you know that. The choice is *here* or your . . . squat.' She said it softly but her distaste still sounded in her voice. She turned. He was watching her solemnly.

'Liz,' he said, 'I cannae be a man and live off you.'

She raised her hands and laughed whimsically. 'What's happened to the Brave New World of male-female equality?'

He looked uncomfortable. 'I dinna understand.'

'No,' she sighed and leaned back against the sink. 'Look, Darren, forget that we're lovers. Forget I'm a woman and you're a man. Forget,' she paused, 'I'm older than you. If you can. If we were friends, just friends, like you and maybe Stephanie, and she had a place, and you hadn't, would you stay with her?'

'Aye maybe.'

'Then stay with me. There's nothing that happens when I pay the mortgage that makes you any less of a man.'

He nodded slowly and seemed to agree, though he looked neither convinced nor content.

The next day was Wednesday, but Darren was on the day shift. 'I'm sorry,' he apologized, 'I should be working with you, on the book. But they're short-staffed. They wouldn't take no for an answer.'

'It's fine,' Liz said lightly, and then added with a small smile. 'Anyhow, we've not been *that* productive the last two Wednesdays.'

'I'm sorry.'

'Don't look so guilty. I was a willing accomplice, if you remember.' She touched his shoulder lightly as he stood waiting to go out to McDonald's. 'As a matter of fact, I think I need some time *alone* with this book. I think maybe the time has come for some decision-making.' He accepted the answer, though not perhaps in quite the way it was meant, kissed her goodbye and went out of the door.

Liz went back into the kitchen, stretching lazily, enjoying the peace of a day to herself, cradled comfortably in the parenthesis of her lover's departure and return. The empty quiet of the flat was physically different from the emptiness of her weeks of solitude. She made more coffee and sat in the corner by the window, looking out over tiled edges of roofs to the thickening buds of a plane tree in a neighbouring garden. Esau came and sat on her knee, warm and sleepy and disdainfully indifferent to the striped kitten batting a napkin ring around the uncleared table. After a while, Liz got up and washed the dishes and went through to the living-room to try out a few yoga stretches before going to work.

She felt stiff and awkward, conscious of every defect of her body, a new awareness linked inevitably to the unthinking youthful perfection of Darren's. She decided simultaneously to pay some attention to her diet and to make a serious commitment to her yoga class. That at least would have the good effect of restoring her neglected friendship with Erica.

She relaxed down into *virasana*, legs folded back, arms outstretched over head on the floor and Jacob came and sat on her stomach. She had a sudden memory of Barry laughing at an identical occasion. She sat up, feeling odd and surprised, as if he had suddenly walked into the room. Unfolding her legs and setting the reluctant cat down on the floor, she got up and walked into the study.

The book awaited her like a reproachful spouse, tired stacks of paper, thumbed-over notecards, over-familiar photographs. She sat down at her desk, picked up her last chapter, read a bit and after a short while, put it down. She stood up, walked to the bookshelf, and took down Barry's first small volume, the little study of Thomas Hardy. She opened it to the beginning and began to read, leaning against the bookcase, smiling slightly.

The cats came in and began tumbling on the carpet, but she ignored them. As usual, when the kitten arrived, the skirmish stopped, the two Siamese overwhelmed by fascination with the striped intruder instead. Liz stepped over them, and returned to her desk chair, where she sat, still reading Barry's book. She curled up comfortably, her toes on the desk, enjoying his prose, so redolent of his spoken voice. After a long while, she closed the book, and got up and returned it to its place on the shelf. Then, with a quick determined step, she went out past her desk, through the living-room, and into the kitchen. In a drawer crammed with salvaged plastic bags and bits of string and paper, she found a roll of sturdy brown bin-liners, pulled one off, and separated it from its brothers with a pleasing snap. She shook it out, and carried it to the study, where she opened its flat mouth and began shovelling notecards, notebooks, and paper within.

She unpinned the orderly photographs from her cork board and chucked them in in a slithering heap. With both hands she carefully stacked Darren's questionnaires, but at the last instant she could not bear to feed them to the rustling brown maw. She carried them, instead, to the bookcase, and laid them carefully on top of a row of reference texts, glimpsing instantly their future residence there, dusty and dear.

She returned to her desk and with a grim but happy smile lifted the entire five chapter print-out and dumped it with a richly satisfying thunk into the depths of the bag. Light-hearted, she was searching her desk for escapees among the jumble of papers, when the door buzzer rang. She took the two looped handles of the brown bag, tied a big solid knot, and carried it, bloated belly banging on her knees, through with her to answer the door.

'It's Charles,' the voice said over the intercom, adding hesitantly, 'Charles Beatty.'

'Oh, Charles. How nice; come up.' She pushed the button to release the latch and then, kicking the bag into the corner of the alcove, opened her own front door.

He walked slowly up the stairs, well-dressed, but tired in his movements, shoulders hunched, older than his years. It took a long while for him to reach her landing and he looked weary when he arrived. He smiled, though, and said, 'Bet you hate those stairs.'

'Hadn't noticed them,' she said honestly, but he did not reply, because he had seen her then, clearly, in the light of the skylight.'

'Liz. Your *hair*.'

'Oh.' The haircut had slipped into history. She had forgotten that he had not seen it. 'Like it?' she said casually, giving the thick mass of curls a friendly flick with her hand.

'Oh, Liz.' His face was miserable. He said, 'It isn't you.'

270

She looked at him quietly for a long time as his face grew increasingly mournful. Then she said reasonably, 'Well, *I* think it's me, Charles. How exactly do *you* know different?'

He was taken aback by her answer, standing very stiff and upright. 'Well, I'm *sorry*, Liz. I didn't mean to offend you. But you did ask.'

She shook her head, smiling. 'Of course. Quite right. No, I'm sorry you don't like it, Charles, but I do. Maybe you'll get used to it,' she added cheerfully.

He looked, if anything, more upset by her easy dismissal of his criticism. But as she held the door open, he came in, ducking his head under the lintel. 'Sorry just to arrive unannounced, Liz, but I was just passing and I thought I hadn't seen you in so long . . .'

'Delighted you did, Charles. I'd been wondering what had become of you. Are you well? The girls?'

'Oh fine, fine. Everybody . . .' his voice trailed off. 'Are you working, Liz? I seemed to remember you worked at home on Wednesdays.' He paused and added quickly, 'With that assistant, what's-his-name, the one from McDonald's.'

'Darren,' she said clearly. She added, 'He's not here today. He's working there. Ten-to-six shift.'

'Oh. Oh I see.'

She took his coat and hung it from a hook in the alcove. 'Would you like coffee? Tea?'

He looked around the flat, as if not quite trusting she was alone. 'Tea would be nice.' He followed her to the kitchen, and sat down, at her invitation, at the table. The striped kitten popped into sight out of nowhere, and leapt on to his knee and immediately on to the table. 'Ow,' Charles said.

'Sorry about him. He hasn't learned about his claws yet.'

'That's new, Liz, isn't it?' Charles rubbed his knee.

'Darren's,' said Liz. There was a silence, and when she had filled the kettle, switched it on, and got out a teapot to formally enclose the teabags, she turned to face him and said, 'I think I ought to explain about that Saturday at McDonald's.'

'No need,' he said quickly.

'Yes, well, I'm sorry about that business with Darren. We were having a bit of a disagreement.'

Charles looked at her steadily and said, 'Actually, Liz, from where I saw it, you were having a lover's quarrel.'

Startled, she turned away, busied herself pouring boiling water into the teapot and then said, without looking back, 'Oh. Oh, I see, Charles. Well,' she paused then and faced him, 'you're perceptive.'

'I'm not *totally* opaque, Liz.' He looked sad and aggrieved. He sighed and said softly, 'So it's true, then.'

'True?'

'What Moira told me.'

'*What* did Moira tell you?' Liz demanded with a flash of anger.

He was quick to placate. 'Oh nothing *really*, Liz. I asked her, because she knows you so well I thought she might know what's going on. She just said you were *involved* with Darren. She didn't get specific and she wouldn't say any more. She said I had to ask you.'

'Are you asking?'

'I guess so.'

'We're having an affair.' She paused guiltily, her eyes on his shocked face. 'I'm sorry, Charles. It just happened. If I had known it was going to happen I would have let you know earlier. I promise.'

He shook his head. His eyes were bright. He said in a small boy's voice, 'I really thought you cared for me.'

'I *do*, Charles.'

'Oh *don't*,' he said angrily. 'Don't humiliate me any further.' He stood up. 'I'll just be off, now, Liz.'

'Oh sit down, Charles,' she said, so firmly, that like a small boy again, he did. She poured his tea and got milk and sugar for it, and while she fussed over him, opening a pack of biscuits and stirring the tea for him herself, she said, 'We've had a lovely time together, Charles, but there are other things in both our lives. You have your children. *And* Jane, for all your troubles. And I have my work, and my friendships. And I have Darren. I promise you *no one* is more surprised than I am how this has turned out.'

He drank a little of his tea and nibbled a biscuit. He said, with weary portent, 'Well, Liz, I only hope you know what you're doing.'

She sat down and faced him directly. 'Charles, I'm nearly forty. If I don't know what I'm doing now, I never will . . . Anyhow,' she half-turned from him, 'in my experience, when people say that, they really *aren't* concerned with the extent of my self-knowledge. What they *mean* is, they don't *like* what I'm doing.'

He looked about to argue, but then his gaze shifted away, down to the table and his well-manicured hands. He shook his head. 'I'm no good at this,' he said. 'Understanding people and the way they behave. I never was. All I ever wanted was just to be married and know where I stood.'

'I know, Charles,' she said gently, 'I'm sorry.'

They talked a little more, neutral talk about the girls and mutual friends. He was pleasant and even laughed a little at the acrobatics of Darren's kitten. Still, she was glad when he got up to go. In the doorway, as she was helping him into his coat, he said, 'I'm sorry. I never asked. How's the book?'

She grinned. 'That's it,' she said. She gave the brown plastic bag a sideways kick. 'That's it in its entirety.'

'What?'

'I've chucked it, Charles.' He looked, appalled, at the plastic bag.

'In *there*? You've thrown it out?' His voice was hushed. 'Oh, *Liz*.'

'Don't be so solemn. It was a good decision.' She laughed drily. 'A good *career move*.'

'But all that *work*.' He got suddenly angry. 'I could throttle that boy. Coming between you and your work. Getting you all stirred up . . .' His fists clenched.

She stared and then said very slowly, 'Charles. It was my book, my work, and my decision. I'm an adult woman of thirty-nine who has just reached an overdue realization that she's already in the one job she's really good at. I'm not a *writer*, Charles. I'm a *teacher*. I *love* to teach. I love young people. Darren,' she added, 'is just an extreme example of the case in point. I promise you,' she added with a giggle, 'I very *rarely* take my work home to bed.'

Charles stared, looking utterly shocked. 'I don't understand you,' he muttered. 'I don't understand you at all.'

She reached up and kissed his cheek. 'I know, Charles,' she said gently, 'but you're still a very nice man.'

Liz was apprehensive when she returned to Erica's yoga class the following night. Her body was still rebelling against her meagre practice session the day before and she was uncertain what welcome she'd get from Erica, or from John Harris.

John proved so phlegmatic in his response to her that she assumed first that he simply didn't care *who* she was sleeping with and later and more accurately that he did not know; Moira had not confided in him. Erica seemed cheerfully unchanged; glad to have Liz back, but less troubled by her absence than Andrew had inferred.

'You have been busy?' she said, arranging Liz's limbs in better order. And when Liz agreed, she said only, 'Andrew has been busy too. So much work, essays, his new book.' She sounded accepting, even sympathetic. She was attentive, spending extra time with Liz as she often had with John. John seemed now self-sufficient, his postures steady and sure. He was quieter, absorbed in the responses of his own body. His self-conscious flamboyance had faded. When he paused to talk to Erica after the class, he stood facing her, comfortably casual, hand on one hip, like an old friend.

The new sauna attendant was a preening red-headed Australian, who tried and failed to flirt with Erica and ignored Liz entirely. In the changing room, Erica undressed with school-girl precision, folding her garments neatly into her locker.

'I miss Darren,' she said. 'Darren was sweet. *He*,' she shrugged towards the outside door, 'is very boring.'

'I think it's a boring job,' Liz said neutrally.

'Darren was very sensible, quitting that job. How is he?'

'Oh fine, fine,' Liz said, still neutral.

'You are very good to him,' Erica said. 'Very kind.' Liz shook her head, feeling peculiarly hypocritical. 'Very kind,' Erica repeated. In the shower she said suddenly, 'You look different.'

'My hair?'

'Yes, that, but there is more.'

'Hmm?' Liz said. She looked down at her wet naked self. 'A bit fatter maybe. I haven't *done* anything for ages.'

Erica cocked her head sideways, but said nothing. She turned around under the shower, closing her eyes and letting the water flow luxuriantly over her face and breasts. Liz watched her, surprised. Erica looked different too, rounder and fuller breasted, as if, amazingly, in spite of everything, she was putting on weight.

In the sauna, Erica studied her as she lay down on the pine bench. She said then, 'You are having sex.'

Liz's head came up. She stared. 'What an extraordinary thing to say. How could you tell just looking?' She thought of Andrew again, but Erica only nodded, supremely confident.

'Is he a good lover?'

'Is *who*?' Liz said, coolly suspicious.

'Charles Beatty,' said Erica, 'of course.'

Liz laughed and sat up. She said cheerfully, 'I haven't the faintest idea. We've never made love.'

'Oh,' Erica said, surprised. Liz lay down again with a smug grin. Erica lay down too, looking puzzled. But a moment later she bobbed up, breasts bouncing. 'So then, you must tell me, who is it? Is it that man, who is he, who studies Africa? That would be nice for you, Liz.'

'No! And whatever you do don't ever *suggest* such a thing to anyone else. God! It would be all over.'

'Ah, a weapon. Come on, tell me now or I will tell *everybody* you are having mad wonderful passion with Africa eight times a week.'

'It's Darren MacPhee.'

'It's *who*?' Erica sat up straight and stared, her eyes ingenuous and wide. Then she giggled and buried her face in her hands. 'Oh, Liz,' she laughed helplessly, 'I *believed* you.'

Darren was home before her when Liz returned from the health club. The flat was brightly lit and smelled of curry. The cats greeted her lazily, fatly content. 'Oh, this is *nice*,' she said, as he came from the kitchen, barefoot, in T-shirt and jeans. She slipped comfortably into his arms, guiltily glad that she'd scuppered the Kensington squat.

'I like coming home to you,' she said. He looked deeply happy.

'I cooked a meal. It's maybe no' very good.'

275

'It'll be wonderful,' she said. 'How *very nice.*'

They ate together and after dinner Liz sat in the half darkened living-room while Darren rehearsed his audition pieces for Glasgow. She had moved the sofa up against the bookshelves to give him more space and she curled in the corner of it, a cat on each side, watching him. He did excerpts from *Macbeth* and *Midsummer Night's Dream* and a modern Scottish play she had not heard of, switching from one to the other with disciplined confidence. The kitten played about his feet and he ignored it for a while and then suddenly grabbed it and addressed a Hamlet soliloquy to its small whiskered face before dropping it into Liz's lap. She pinned it down with one hand, stroking her two Siamese alternately with the other.

'Do King Harry,' she said. He smiled, hesitated, and then came and sat beside her and recited the courtship speech in a low, sexy whisper, his hand toying with her hair and straying to her body.

She giggled, shoving the cats aside and drawing him closer. 'I'll have you anytime for that,' she said. 'I don't know about RSAMD.'

'I dinna think I'll give them the same,' he said. They stood up lazily, stretching and embracing and made their way to the bedroom, dropping a trail of discarded garments along the way.

In the night she dreamt an ordinary dream of friends and familiar situations and was woken from it by the telephone, thinking that it was morning and that the man beside her was Barry. 'Answer it, love,' she said sleepily. Darren's husky Scottish voice brought her instant awareness of time and place. It was the middle of the night, and Barry, as it turned out, was the person on the other end of the phone.

'Yes, sir. She's right here.' She sat up beside Darren, leaning over him to switch on the light. 'It's your friend from America,' he said. They blinked at each other in the brightness. Liz took the phone. 'Do you want me . . .' Darren whispered, gesturing to the door. Liz shook her head.

'Barry?' she said, into the phone.

'Liz? *What* time is it?'

'I don't know, Barry.' She glanced past Darren to the clock. 'Two.'

'You must be working *very* late.'

'Yes.'

'You and that assistant.'

'Darren.'

'Yes.'

'It's just as well,' Liz said brightly, 'since you're always ringing at these hours. You know, you *could* get one of those clocks that show two time zones . . .'

'Is everything all right, Liz?'

'Sure. Don't I sound all right?'

'You sound . . .' he paused, 'frenetic.'

'Well . . .' she drawled the word out trying to sound relaxed, 'you know . . . work, pressure . . .'

'How's the book?'

She blinked, glanced at Darren. 'The book . . . well, it's more or less *in the bag*,' she said evenly.

'Oh great. Well done.'

'Mmm.'

'Liz,' he paused and his voice turned weighty, 'I've called for a special reason. A very special reason.'

'Oh?' She worked hard at unfrenetic. 'What's that, Barry?'

He cleared his throat. 'Liz, what would you say if I told you I was getting married?'

She paused. 'Congratulations?'

'You'd say what?'

'Congratulations. You say, "I'm getting married." I say, "Congratulations."'

'Is that all?'

'It's the traditional response, Barry.' She paused. 'Would you like, Lots of Congratulations? Best Wishes? Felicitations?'

'Don't get sour, Liz.'

'I'm not *sour*, Barry.' Her voice sharpened. She was aware of Darren's troubled blue eyes watching her. She reached her hand out and caught his. 'What do you *want* me to say?' she asked reasonably.

'Oh nothing, nothing.' He sounded world weary. 'I only

277

thought maybe you'd be interested . . .'

'I *am* interested, Barry. I'm very interested. Who is she? The blonde girl, right? Is she nice? Do you love her?' She paused. Well of course you *must* love her, or you wouldn't *be* getting married would you . . .'

'Never mind, Liz, I knew you wouldn't understand.'

'*What?*'

'It's very special. Very important to me. I just wanted to share it with you . . .'

'Fine, Barry. Share away.'

'Oh, Liz. You're so glib. You Americans.'

'Americans! You're going to *marry* one, aren't you?'

'Yes,' he said gloomily.

Liz turned around in bed, facing away from Darren. She said slowly, uncertain awareness creeping into her voice, 'Barry, you do *want* to. I mean this *is* a free act . . .' He said nothing. 'Barry, she can't *be* pregnant, surely, can she?'

'Liz! For Christ's sake!' He sounded like a morally outraged adolescent.

'Sorry,' she said quickly. 'Just a thought.'

'Really.'

'Yes. Well. Barry,' she dragged the words out placatingly, 'isn't this *nice*. I'm so happy for you. Have you set a date?' He made no answer. 'Do I get invited?'

'I think that's rushing things a bit. We're just *thinking* about it.'

'I see. Thinking.' She looked at Darren and raised her shoulders in a baffled shrug. 'Well,' she said practically, 'maybe when you've thought some more you'll let me know what you've decided.'

'Yes,' he said gloomily. 'Look,' his voice was pointedly regretful, 'maybe I shouldn't have bothered you with this.'

'Not at all.'

'Well, I'll let you get back to work, or whatever.'

'Yes,' Liz said dutifully, 'back to work.'

'Bye, Liz. Love to everybody. And look, don't, you know, *say* anything . . .'

'Wouldn't dream of it. Bye, Barry. And love to . . . your . . .'

'Jackie. Her name's Jackie.'

'Love to Jackie.'

'Yes, Liz. Goodbye.'

She said goodbye and handed the phone to Darren, who put it down. He watched her gravely. She returned his solemn gaze and suddenly grinned. 'Well, love,' she said, sliding easily down the bed, her arms slipping about his waist, 'back to work!'

But after they'd made love, he was still as serious as before. She was warm and comfortable and ready to go back to sleep, but he lay beside her, chin propped thoughtfully on the palm of his hand, studying her. 'Do you love him, Liz?' he said.

She smiled gently. 'Yes. But it doesn't matter. He's gone, Darren.'

'I think he loves you too.'

'What makes you say that?' She sat up a little, curious. 'How would you possibly know?'

'From when I answered the phone. He didna like me being here. You know. With you.'

Liz laughed lightly. 'Well that may be, Darren, but he's seeing someone else and he sounds pretty serious about her.' He watched, expressionless. 'You heard me. He's talking about getting *married*.' She laughed again, still slightly astonished.

'Do you mind?'

'You're full of questions.' She lay down again, closing her eyes.

'I'm sorry.'

'Don't be,' she said, still with her eyes closed. She paused and said slowly, 'Yes I *do* mind, Darren. And it's awfully foolish. He's free. We agreed we were both free. And here *I* am . . .' She opened her eyes again, and shrugged her shoulders, looking up at him honestly.

'Aye. But this is only just now. And maybe you didna mean for it to happen.'

'When it *happened*, I meant for it to happen . . . and anyway, Barry and I have been apart for months, Darren. And I've been seeing Charles *most* of that time.'

'But no' sleeping with him.'

'How do *you* know?' she said, giggling. She pulled the duvet up close to her chin.

279

'I know.'

'Darren, you're so audacious. You amaze me.'

'Aye, and I'm right too.'

'You're right.'

They looked at each other solemnly and then Liz reached over him quietly and put out the light. They lay together in the darkness, comfortably, her head on his shoulder, her outstretched arm across his body. After a while, when she thought he was asleep, he said, 'Did you no' want bairns ever, Liz?'

Startled, she was silent for a while and then answered clearly. 'We couldn't, Darren.' She paused. 'Barry couldn't . . .'

He said softly, 'But *you* could.'

'Yes, I imagine so.'

'*We* could,' he said then confidently and after a moment in which she said nothing, 'I could give you a baby, Liz.'

'Darren . . .' She laughed a little, wanting to cry.

'What's wrong?'

'Nothing. That's lovely. Lovely.' She snuggled in closer and said, 'And how could I work?'

'You wouldna need to work. I'd work.' When she did not answer, he said hurriedly, 'I dinna mean at *this* sort of thing. I'm only doing this stuff because it gives me time free. I can get a *real* job in the building trade. I can make good money . . . there's *lots* of things I can do.'

She lay quietly, enjoying the security of his embrace, the young man's certainty of his voice. She said, 'Yes, Darren. Lots of things you can do I'm sure. And *one* thing you want to do.' He said nothing. 'What about that?'

The silence extended and eventually he said quietly, 'I dinna ken.'

'Well, I do.'

He was quiet again and then he turned closer to her, and laughed softly. 'Then I'll get a film part. We'll get rich . . .'

She laughed too, and after a while, he said solemnly, 'I guess it'll need to be soon, won't it?'

She tightened her arm slightly and kissed his shoulder. 'Goodnight, Darren,' she said.

He said goodnight, still sounding troubled, but as always he slept before she did. Liz lay awake, and with her arm still stretched across his flat stomach, suddenly remembered Barry struggling so hard – running, sit-ups, squash – to fight his little relentless roll of middle-aged flab. Her eyes filled with tears.

XV

North of Birmingham, she gave him the wheel. It was a grey wet April Sunday and they had left early in the morning, on quiet roads, and made good time. They had stopped for breakfast in a motorway café stocked with muesli and yoghurt and New Age awareness, and now were headed north again, up the rainswept M6. Darren drove steadily and evenly, an exact two miles per hour beneath the limit. She wondered if he was always so circumspect or whether her presence was an inhibition.

He slipped a tape on to the deck and the car filled with music, cheerful and unfamiliar.

'What's that?'

'Like it?'

'Yes, a bit.' She listened a little more and said, 'What *language* is that?'

'Gaelic. It's a Scottish group.'

'Do you *speak* Gaelic, Darren?'

He laughed loudly. 'You're joking,' he said. He glanced across briefly and shrugged. 'I like the music anyhow.' It accompanied them northwards.

When they crossed the border, Liz cheered. 'I'm really looking forward to this.'

'What? Glasgow?'

'Yes.'

'Have you no' *been* to Glasgow even?'

'Just once. When I was a student. I'm afraid I've never been back.'

'You didna like it.'

'I *did* actually. It's just that life never took me back there.'
She paused thoughtfully and added, 'Until now.'

Darren was quiet for a while and then he said suddenly,
looking straight ahead, 'I cannae imagine no' coming back
here. No matter what I did . . .' She was surprised by the
emotion of the words. In London he had appeared rootless,
his Scottishness a faintly comic misfortune. She had never
imagined it as something he might wish to reclaim.

'Have *you* been back, since you came to London?'

'A couple of times. I cannae afford the bus fare. I tried
hitching but it's a bit uncertain when you're needing to be
back for work.' He leaned back comfortably in the driving seat
of her car. 'This is luxury. I'll get soft.'

She smiled. 'I hitched that time I went to Glasgow. Barry and
I. It was the middle of the winter. We stood outside Highgate
Cemetery for hours and then we got a ride half-way to Wales
before we found we were headed the wrong way. We had a
lot of rides, but it took all night.' She smiled, warm and lazy
in the cosy little car, remembering the long, dark wet road,
long past. 'It was all different then. Rides were easier. People
were . . . less afraid.'

'Were *you* no' afraid?'

'What? Of hitching?'

'You know. Men . . . I know you had him with you, but
sometimes that's no help.'

'I never thought. Today when I think of my students doing
it, I panic. But then I never thought.' She smiled. 'Youth
is bliss.'

He looked across. 'Do you think so?'

'No,' she said at once. 'No, I think it's very hard. What
about you?'

'I dinna ken.' He shrugged. 'I dinna ken what else there
is.'

She smiled again, resting her head back, her eyes closed.
'Outside Newcastle our lorry driver stopped at a real old-
fashioned truck stop. What we call a "greasy spoon" in the
States. It was four A.M., the place was lively as day. It seemed
so American. Back then, everything in Britain shut down at
five. And they were playing all this country- and-western music
on the juke box. *Country-and-western*. I couldn't imagine what

it was doing there. What they *got* from it . . . *so* American. Cowboy songs. Trucker songs. Sentimental mid-western mush. I understand now. When you're young, you see all the differences. The sameness under things grows as you grow older . . .'

'Why did he no' marry you, Liz?'

'Who, Barry?'

'Aye.'

'Maybe you'd like to turn the question around,' she said, mildly enough, but he recognized the hint of reprimand at once.

'I'm sorry,' he said. '*You* didna want to, you mean.'

'No, Darren. *We* didn't want to. It was the way the wind blew then.' She laughed and said, 'It *was* a sort of ideal.'

'Would you marry me?' he said. She knew the question was real, not ideal, but he had left room in his tone for her to hide quickly behind the academic in her reply.

'I don't really see the *necessity* of marriage, Darren,' she said. 'I don't see what it changes.'

He looked straight ahead, overtook a lumbering lorry, settled back into his lane. 'Well, there's the church thing I suppose.'

'*Church* thing?'

'Aye, well you're supposed to really, right?'

'*Who* is, Darren? I don't go to church. You don't go to church. Who cares?'

'Well, I think I'd care eventually,' he said easily, 'I mean like if there were bairns and all . . .' She smiled, turning his tape over in the deck, looking at it briefly before playing the other side. She liked it, surprising herself.

'That's getting a bit serious about a slightly unlikely future,' she said evenly.

'Well, even without bairns. There's you and me. And it wouldna be right *always* would it?'

'Of course it would. Why not? Who says?'

He turned and looked at her and said clearly, 'The Church says, Liz.'

She met his eyes for the instant before they flicked quickly back to the road. 'Darren . . .' she said cautiously. 'You're not seriously telling me.'

'Aye, what? That I'm Catholic?' He looked momentarily belligerent. 'So?'

'You're *what*?'

'I'm Catholic,' he said plainly, adding quizzically, 'Did you no' ken?'

Liz sat silent in stunned amazement. At last she gathered sufficient words to say, in as controlled a voice as possible, 'Well, no, actually, Darren, I *didn't* know and if you'd like to stop and think about it, precisely how do you imagine I *would* know? I've never so much as heard you mention *any* church, much less the Catholic Church, ever. And as far as I know you've been nowhere *near* one as long as I've known you.'

'Aye, well.'

'What do you mean "aye, well"? Do you go to church or don't you?'

He shrugged. 'Sometimes.'

'Like when?'

'Sometimes.'

'When last?'

'Look, what is this, some kind of inquisition?'

'Darren, *you* raised the subject.'

'All right. All right. So let's drop it.'

'*No.*' She shook her head impatiently. 'You can't just *say* a thing like that and then drop it . . .'

'It doesna matter, OK?'

'What, you being Catholic, if you *are* Catholic? Or us talking about it?'

'It hasnae anything to do with you.'

'It certainly *has*, Darren. If you want to get *married* because of it.'

He was silent, and she left him alone to his driving, judging that the motorway wasn't the best place for a burgeoning argument.

After a while he said sadly, 'I didna want to marry you *just* because of being Catholic.'

She nodded and said gently, 'I know, Darren.'

'I love you.'

She did not answer. After a while she said, conversationally, 'You're a mystery sometimes. I think I know you and then you come out with something like that.' She was still a bit stunned.

He said, 'It's no' a big deal. It's just what I am.'

'*Were* surely.'

He shrugged. 'It doesna matter which, Liz. Aye fine, I'm no' going to mass or anything just now. But I know fine I *will* do, one day.'

'What? Go back?' She was irritated. 'But why, Darren? If you're happy enough without it now.'

'Aye, well, everyone does.'

'*No* they don't,' she said vehemently. 'And anyhow, even if that were so, *you* don't have to, just because everyone else does. You *can* break the pattern you know. It's possible to grow.'

'You mean just *stay* away?' he asked cautiously.

'*Yes*. You're a free individual, Darren. You can think for yourself.' She smiled encouragingly.

'How's that growing?' he said. 'At least I believe in *something*. How's believing in nothing better than that?'

Liz felt the crunch of rational against irrational that made debate impossible. She sighed and said, 'Perhaps it's not,' without conviction. He looked across as if he would argue further, but she said quickly, 'Are you happy driving still, or shall I take it again?'

'I'm fine. I ken the way, anyhow.' He nodded towards the city approach signs they were passing.

'Of course.' She smiled. The tape finished. 'I like that,' Liz said, playing it again. She was cheerful and light, but the shadow of argument followed them into Glasgow.

They slept on the floor of a flat near the art school; innocently, curled side by side in borrowed sleeping bags. The flat was crowded and chaotic, an enclave of students and hangers-on, in a decaying Victorian villa. People came in and out all night, flicked lights on, apologized, stepped over them, gathering belongings, seeking friends. A small dishonourable part of Liz yearned for a hotel room with a private bath, but she dismissed it as the voice of old age. And by morning she was already comfortable, wandering around among strangers with her toothbrush, slipping easily back into her hostel and bedsit days.

Darren brought mugs of instant coffee from the kitchen. They sat together on their sleeping bags, drinking it. He was nervous and quiet. They went out to breakfast and walked twice past the impressive façade of the RSAMD just to check it was still there. His audition was at eleven. At ten-thirty they were sitting in the pleasant student cafeteria, Darren with his scripts in front of him, Liz reading the *Glasgow Herald*. She looked up over it and gave him a small smile of encouragement. He smiled back, boyish and tense. She looked down at her paper. She felt remarkably at home; a room full of students, the easy functional comfort of institutional furniture. The trappings of the academic world were the same everywhere. Though it was odd to be there, on such familiar ground, in the unfamiliar role of outsider.

At the appointed hour, a scattered cluster of young people, fellow hopefuls, stood up from tables all over the room and made their way warily to the door. Darren rose also. He grinned. 'You can get me another coffee if you like. I'll be back in five minutes.' He laughed softly. 'Thank you very much, Mr MacPhee . . .' He bowed to her.

'Don't call us, we'll call you,' she said for him. She smiled then and added quickly, 'Just do what you did that morning in my office. Just that, and nothing more.' He nodded solemnly and left her. At the doorway he turned to speak to another young man, and then suddenly he was part of the group, remote from her, no longer his individual self, but one among many. She had a vivid sad sense of his belonging there, and not with her.

She waited uneasily for his reappearance, five minutes, and then ten, recalling his RADA audition and the sullen angry boy she'd met on the steps of the Central Club and wondering if maturity would now overcome disappointment. They were a long while, and when they did appear it was in a big, noisy group, loud with the relief of an ordeal survived. She did not see him at once among the cluster of animated faces, male and female, and then suddenly recognized him, talking at length to a blond bearded man, as if they had known each other for years.

They all stopped in front of the cafeteria line, fishing in pockets and handbags for money. The blond man glanced in her direction and said openly, 'Hey, Darren, is that great-looking woman with you your drama coach?' Darren smiled, looked up, and waved to her. She saw him shake his head in reply.

He pointed to the coffee cups and she nodded. 'She's not your *mother*, is she?' the blond man said incredulously, in a stunned but audible whisper.

There was a loud female laugh and a girl's strong theatrical voice said, 'Oh ridiculous, Jimmy. She's far too young.'

Liz ducked her reddening face behind her paper, caught in an innocent crossfire of flattery and humiliation. When Darren appeared in front of her, holding two cups of coffee, she found it hard to meet his eyes. When she did, she saw a new expression in his, a warily dawning confidence.

'How'd it go?'

'No' bad,' he said softly, his voice touched with surprise. 'They seemed to like it.' He paused. 'But they were real nice, anyway, so maybe it doesna mean anything.' He sat down across from her. 'They'll put up the names of the ones they want back in half an hour. Then we can go.' He said it with easy finality.

'Unless you're one of them.'

He looked surprised again. 'Aye. There *is* that. I dinna think I will be,' he said honestly. 'It was good though. I enjoyed it.' He met her gaze directly, smiling, thoughtful and self-assured, and her mind flashed suddenly to his first appearance in her office, bumbling and crippled by shyness. It was hard to imagine she was seeing the same person.

Liz stood at the back of the crowd that gathered around the posted list. She read the chosen names over Darren's shoulder and she saw his almost at once, and gripped his elbow with delight. He made no response, reading painfully slowly as always. She waited, containing herself with difficulty, until the sudden surprised tightening of the muscles of his arm told her he had seen it too. She flung herself on to his shoulder, embracing him. He was laughing, stunned and happy. Around them the crowd melted away, the majority drifting off with jokes and the light dry laughter of disappointment. There were six names on the list, his second from the bottom, and four young men and two women were left staring at each other in amazement.

'I think we should have lunch,' Liz said. 'They want you back at two.'

They found a café in a mall off Sauchiehall Street and ate

spring rolls and chips and talked in sudden frantic bursts of ideas, like generals of an unexpectedly victorious army, hastily reorganizing the campaign. Midway through, Darren said, alarmed, 'Christ, Liz, we'll no' leave Glasgow before eight, if we're lucky.'

'So?'

'We'll be awful late.' He looked worried.

'You working tomorrow?' she asked, surprised.

'No. But you?'

'It's Easter break, actually, Darren. And I told everyone I'd be two days. I knew we'd be all day, if you got by the morning.'

He nodded and then said warily, 'You mean you actually thought I might?'

'Of course.' She leaned back in her chair and smiled. 'Didn't you?'

He shook his head. 'No' in a million years,' he said honestly. He still looked worried, and she mistook the reason.

'You'll be fine, Darren. Just be yourself. And if they ask you to read, *tell* them you're dyslexic. They can understand that. *Tell* them.'

'Oh, aye,' he said, without feeling.

'What's wrong, Darren? You're not afraid, surely.'

'No. It's no' that.' He got up to pay and she sat still, allowing him. When he returned he smiled quickly, forestalling more discussion, and they went out together into the wet streets.

The afternoon session was long. Liz agreed to meet him at half-five and, leaving him on the steps of the college, turned back into the city. She bought a street map in a newsagent's, and set off like a tourist. So many years had passed since her last visit, and so much had changed, both in the city and in herself, that she had not one working memory of it left. She could not remember even where she had stayed, in a flat not dissimilar to the one they'd come from that morning, or who they had been with, or anything about the theatrical production they had attended in a big crowd of forgotten strangers. It might have been another city in another country, as well as another time.

This city was a surprise: lively and vibrant and self-sufficient. She realized, chagrined, that she had developed the Londoner's xenophobic snobbery that held all places outside the capital as poor imitations. Glasgow seemed quite happy to exist utterly independently, with no need to look south at all. Broad Scots voices met her in shops and cafés, Darren's accent becoming the cheerful norm. Mid-afternoon found her among the stylish shops of pedestrianized Buchanan Street, and at four o'clock she was drinking lemon tea in a café in Princes Square, while a girl played piano on the mosaic-floored court below. A small anarchic thought – that it would be possible to live in this city – flitted boldly across her mind. She sipped her tea, smiling to herself, imagining what Moira would have to say.

Out in the street she consulted her bulky refolded map and plotted her return, walking slowly so that she would arrive at the college just before the session ended. But her timing was wrong and he was sitting alone on the broad steps, waiting for her, his bookbag full of scripts beside him, elbows on his knees and chin on his hands. He looked solitary and she imagined disconsolate, and she hurried up the steps, filled with guilt.

'I'm sorry, I must be late.'

'We finished early,' he said. He had the same look of concern he'd worn at lunch.

She said uncertainly, 'How'd it go?'

He straightened up and got to his feet. When he spoke his voice was softened and uneasy, 'I dinna ken, Liz, but I think maybe I'm in.'

She stood still, stunned, and trying to match the happy meaning of the words with the troubled tone. 'You mean *accepted*?' she said.

'Aye. I mean, they've asked me to come back for a couple of days, in three weeks. So it's no' *settled* exactly. But they were – ' he paused and said cautiously – 'sort of keen.' He seemed to treat each positive word as a kind of dangerous animal, something that might turn on him in the end.

She said loudly to shake him out of his caution, 'For God's sake, Darren. That's *wonderful*.' He nodded, still warily. 'Well, isn't it?' she demanded.

'Aye. It is.' He looked down. 'It is.'

'So why aren't you happy?' she said, exasperated.

He half turned away, looking down the street. He said clearly, very adult, 'Because all at once it looks *real*, Liz.' He turned back. 'And if it is . . .' he paused and raised his vivid eyes to meet hers, 'where does it leave you and me?'

The question hung between them the rest of the day. The ghost at the feast, it shadowed the impromptu celebrations in the flat to which they returned that evening, and followed them out into the city streets that night, from pub to pub, and finally to a rock concert in a huge and dusty hall packed with Glasgow youth. The tickets were a gift from his friends, a reward for his success. Liz accepted with graciousness, concealing trepidation; neither crowds nor rock music being high on her list of enjoyments. Darren was thrilled. 'You'll love this,' he promised.

'Sure,' she agreed with a wan smile. At least, she thought, they would not need to talk.

A band was playing when they arrived, loud and discordant, and the jeans-clad young crowd jostled cheerfully around little pockets of spontaneous dancing. A second group followed the first, better, but unremarkable. Liz and Darren shared a lager and danced a little, glad of the noise drowning all conversation. The crowd grew and tightened until dancing was no longer possible. Liz felt crushed and wary.

There was a pause then before the main attraction. The lights came up, drab and grey, revealing the dark shapes around her as cheerful youngsters, ordinary and friendly. They closed in, expectant, pressing against her, but apologizing, oddly polite. The house lights dimmed into dark. Liz caught a nervous breath. A singing high chord grew out of the blackness, filling the waiting silence, and then light rose from the stage with a thunderous explosion of sound. Cheers answered it, and the crowd surged so close about Liz that she could see nothing but darkened moving bodies lit up in sudden flashes of changing colour. She struggled with her fear, only Darren's steady hands on her shoulders keeping her from panic.

She knew the music then; it was the group on Darren's tape in the car, new to her, but intimately familiar to their audience who shouted, swayed and sang along, waving outstretched arms in joyful unison. Beside her a lanky boy in denims raised a tall pole and unfurled from it a Scottish flag, swinging its rippling length over the heads of the crowd. Other flags appeared, across the hall, the blue and white saltire and the yellow and crimson lion rampant. They swayed with the music, bouncing with their dancing guardians, a buoyant, startling young nationalism.

Behind her, Darren sang along in his husky, happy, off-key voice. In front, a fat blonde teenager jigged up and down, stumbling, clasping her friends, staggering on the edge of hysteria. She spun around, eyes closed, pudgy lips parted in ecstasy. She opened her eyes, saw Liz, and flung her soft arms around her, embracing and dancing. Laughing, Liz danced with her and then detached herself and passed the chubby blonde to Darren. She clutched him too, with the same undifferentiated world-love. The crowd closed again, warm, united. Liz wavered between the welcome of their youth and the lonely detachment of her age. She stretched up on her toes, catching glimpses over the moving dark heads of lights, instruments, the dancing singers. Darren shouted 'Wait!' and knelt down beside her, ducking quickly between her legs, lifting her astride his shoulders.

'What are you doing?' she shouted back.

'Look!' he cried. He stood easily, holding her legs around his neck and linked beneath his arms.

'You can't,' she protested, but stopped. Poised above the darkened crowd, she saw clearly at last the sweeping, dazzling lasers swirling in stage mist, the silhouetted musicians, and their lead singer, transfixed and transformed by beams of white, a dancing, sweating god in a network of light.

'Oh!' she cried. 'It's *wonderful*.'

'Nice, eh?' Darren shouted. She clutched his shoulder for support, one hand on his thick curly hair, and he danced to the music, strong and sure beneath her. Her desire for him fused with the lights and the music and the flag-waving Scottish crowd. She slid from his shoulders and into his arms and they kissed passionately in an oblivious circle of young innocence.

It was three in the morning when they returned to the flat. It was dark, its occupants sleeping. They crept through the blackness to their mattress on the floor, and made love as silently as they could, falling asleep, guilty and glad, in each other's arms.

*   *   *

'So, Liz,' Moira said with her look of knowing assessment, 'how was Glasgow?' They were lunching together, a fortnight after Liz and Darren's return, in an Italian restaurant on Dean Street. It was posher and less convenient than their usual meeting place but, freed from her lecture schedule by the Easter break, Liz could choose her own time to get back to the stack of work on her desk. And Moira was celebrating a decorating success in Surrey with visible financial relief.

Liz studied the menu with deliberate care, smiling to herself, before she answered. 'It's *actually* quite a nice city,' she said.

Moira looked instantly aggrieved. 'It's in *Scotland*,' she said.

'What do you mean?'

'I mean keep your perspective,' Moira answered coolly. 'How's Laurence Olivier?'

Liz laughed, laying the menu down and looking candidly across the table. 'Better than he thinks,' she said.

'Did he get in?' Moira asked, incredulous.

'Not precisely.' Liz picked up the menu again. 'That avocado thing looks gorgeous.'

'What do you mean "not precisely"? Was he accepted, or not?'

'Or maybe the Parma ham.' Liz looked up. 'Mmm? They've asked him to come back next week.'

'What for?'

Liz shrugged. 'Oh, another interview.'

'Look, I don't believe this super-casual for a moment. This matters to you. To both of you.'

Liz set the menu down again. She leaned forward. 'We're just not thinking about it at the moment. He's working. I'm working . . . there's no *point* until it's certain. He still doesn't really believe it will happen. He still thinks they'll say no at the end.'

'And you?'

Liz sat back, thoughtful, and then said, 'I think he's in.'

Moira looked sceptical.

'Moira,' Liz smiled quickly, animated, 'I said at the beginning, he's very good. He's good out of proportion to what he is . . . who he is . . . like the talent is just *there* waiting for him to grow into it.'

'You're infatuated,' Moira said.

'No,' Liz said thoughtfully, 'no, I really think I'm not. Not about the acting.' She smiled secretively. 'About other things, maybe I am.'

Moira looked displeased. The waiter came and took their order and when he'd gone away again Moira slipped her little gold-framed reading glasses back in their case, snapped the case shut and said, 'Charles is really hurt.'

'I can't help that. We had no agreement.' Liz looked around the room, irritated.

'He thought you had an *understanding*.'

Liz looked back. She tossed her hair, in her new free way and said sharply, 'An understanding. Yes. The *understanding* that I'd fill in as part-time wife and part-time mother. Except of course when the *real* wife and mother needed his attention. And he'd supply dinners and theatre tickets and after a rather rigid little courtship we'd go to bed. Why? Because it's expected.'

'You make him sound like a shit. It's not fair. He's a nice man.'

'I *know* he's a nice man. I'm not blaming him. I'm not blaming Charles for anything. What I'm *blaming* is the expectations people have about my life.' She stopped, startled by her own anger and fearful of its effect on Moira. The waiter sidled in cautiously and slid her avocado in front of her, touched down in front of Moira with a green salad, and fled. Liz said, more softly, 'I didn't *expect* anything with Darren and I found a great friend and the best lover I've had in my life.'

'Better than Barry?' Moira asked brittly.

'The sex? Yes,' Liz said candidly. She paused. 'The friendship? How can I compare?'

'So it's true, all the propaganda about young men,' Moira said. She sounded tart.

'No,' Liz said gently. She smiled again, her private smile. 'However, any propaganda you hear about Darren MacPhee, I'd recommend you believe.' Moira looked baffled. Liz leaned forward and sipped from her wine. 'It's *who* he is, not what he is, Moira. He's kind and giving and though I doubt I deserve it, he's in love with me. That's what makes him a wonderful lover, not the fact that he can do it six times a night.'

'*What?*'

'Well, not every night.' Liz laughed. 'Look, sweetheart, I'm gathering rose buds. This isn't going to happen too many more times in my life.'

Moira raised an eyebrow. She began dressing her salad with great care, alternating layers of lettuce with dribbles of vinaigrette, and piling the whole into a neat mound, as if she were constructing a small compost heap on her plate. She said, looking down at her creation, 'I *suppose* if I weren't horrendously jealous, I'd be delighted for you. Which is what I *should* be, of course.'

'I really doubt you're jealous,' Liz said openly. She paused. 'You've been kind enough not to fall down laughing at my choice of companion, but it's been clear enough he wouldn't be *your* choice, *whatever* happened.'

Moira didn't look up. 'No,' she said. 'Though I do *like* Darren, Liz. I really do. No, there's something fatal that happens when you have children growing up. *Whatever* your age, they kick you into the next generation, irrevocably and for ever. I *couldn't* make love to Darren MacPhee. I could not do it. Which *doesn't* mean I don't get an itchy little twitch when I see his bum going by in those delicious skinny jeans.'

'Moira?' Liz said, startled.

'But *that's* not what I'm jealous of Liz. I'm jealous that you have someone in love with you. In love in that wonderful, hopeless, calf-eyed worship-the-ground-you-walk-on way. *That's* what I can't live without. I need to be admired and adored and nobody does.'

'John does.'

'Like fuck.'

'No. John *does*. In the real, true grown-up way that is the *only* way for love between adults to go. Like Barry loved me. And like Charles *still* loves his wife, I suspect. And,' she paused briefly, her voice dropping, 'like Darren and I will have to learn to do if there's ever to be a future for us.'

'And is there?' Moira said.

Liz hesitated. She said eventually, her voice uneven, 'I don't know.'

'It's not going to be easy, you know,' Moira returned suddenly to the attack. 'Him up in Glasgow. You down here . . .'

'No. That wouldn't be easy . . .'

Moira straightened up, laying her silverware down. 'Liz,' she said firmly. 'You won't go with him.' Liz said nothing. Moira's eyes narrowed ominously. '*Liz.*'

'I'm not sure.'

'Oh for *God's sake*!'

'I said I'm not sure.'

'After all this. After letting *Barry* go. After all that talk about career and independence and place and *friends*. Now you're going to drop it all, to drop *us* all and go running off to bloody *Glasgow* after a bloody little working-class toyboy . . .'

'Right, Moira. That's fine. Let's stop there.'

'Oh, Liz.'

'That's it. Just stop. OK?' Liz switched to the professional voice with which she quelled rebellion and argument in academia. It didn't work on Moira.

'Christ, what is this? Menopausal derangement? Would you like to try HRT? Or maybe a convent?' The waiter, approaching to clear plates, veered off suddenly and circled cautiously.

'Right, so what *would* be all right? Playing academic wifie-wifie in Wisconsin? Or draped in Laura Ashley with Charles in darkest Essex; *that* would be OK, wouldn't it? Just as long as it's *conventional*, it's just fine.'

'You're shouting.'

'Of *course* I'm shouting.'

'You've frightened the waiter.'

Liz looked up. The waiter fluttered behind a partition. She beckoned and gave him a steely smile while he whisked the plates away. She sat patiently, in silence, until he had returned with their main course and taken refuge again in the kitchen. 'Moira,' she said, 'you're a hopeless snob.'

Moira was unmoved. She tasted her chicken and said easily, 'If being a snob means being aware of real, tangible, insurmountable differences between people, then I'm a snob. What are you going to do in Glasgow?'

'I didn't say I was going.' Liz inspected her aubergine. 'There's a perfectly good university in Glasgow,' she added, casually.

Moira looked solemn. 'You really have thought about it,' she said sadly.

'Well, of course I've thought . . .'

'I mean *really* thought. Not just sweet romantic, "he and I beneath the eaves in a poet's garret."'

'Thin on the ground in Glasgow.'

'Oh shit,' Moira said.

'What?'

'I can't stand it.' She set her knife and fork down and blinked wet eyelashes. '*Everything's* falling apart. God knows *where* we'll all be a year from now.'

'Moira?' Liz said uneasily.

'Oh nothing. I'm just pre-menstrual.'

'That happens once a month. This seems something more.'

'I'm just so *tired*,' Moira said. 'I'm so tired of worrying and struggling and trying to keep things together.'

'What things? Money?'

'Oh yes, money. Damn money. I'm so sick of this recession. Thank God *somebody* still has *some* money left. If it weren't for this house in Surrey I've just landed, I don't know *where* the school fees would have come from . . .'

'Surely *John* is doing all right,' Liz said, privately thinking that recession or not, the money still had to go somewhere, and John was the sort of man with whom it was likely to end up.

'I don't know what John is doing,' Moira said.

Liz was quiet. She sipped her wine and then said cautiously, 'Surely you still talk about things like that.'

Moira tossed her head up defiantly. She took a quick sip of her own wine and said, 'Do you want to know what we talk about? Do you? We talk about *yoga*. About some benighted position he's finally achieved. With *Erica's* loyal help. We talk about running. Oh God, do we talk about running. I heard every single mile of that ghastly half marathon, *yard* by yard. *How* he paced himself. *Where* he met "the wall". How he got over it. Which bloody tendon hurt or didn't hurt. I could draw a map, I've heard it so many times. I'll tell you something, Nero may have fiddled while Rome burned, but when *London* next goes down in flames, it'll be surrounded by *bloody* runners, clipping four bloody seconds off their bloody best time.'

'Did he have a good race, Moira?'

Moira laid her hands flat on the crisp white linen and

looked ready to kill. 'He had a very good race, thank you, Liz,' she said.

'Do you still think he's having an affair?'

'I *know* he's having an affair,' Moira shot back.

Liz looked down, returned her attention briefly to her lunch and said without looking up, 'Hasn't it occurred to you that there's no way possibly he'd have the time? Or the *energy*? All that athletic stuff takes *some* toll, you know. And John isn't that young . . .'

'Oh, he may not be old Darren six-times-a-night MacPhee,' Moira snapped, 'but I'm sure he can still do his bit for England when duty calls. *Or* Switzerland,' she added sourly.

'I'm talking about mental energy,' Liz pursued seriously. 'The man is obsessed, from what you say. And not with other people's bodies. With his own. He's trying to prove something, and I don't think it has *anything* to do with Erica Pringle. Or actually, with you.'

'Oh I'm *long* out of the picture,' Moira said sadly. 'The closest we've got to sex in months is a discussion of the perils of jogger's nipple.' She grimaced and added, 'I imagine Erica's doing a bit better.'

Liz sighed and said patiently, 'So have you decided yet to *talk* to him about it?'

'When? While I'm pacing him around the paddock? Or standing on our bloody heads together in the bathroom.'

'You know what I mean.'

'What's the point?' Moira said defiantly. 'He'll only deny it.'

Liz looked serious. 'Do you really think he'd *lie* to you?'

'John's a *lawyer*, Liz.' Moira shrugged and half turned away, looking distractedly about the restaurant and other diners all wrapped in their own private worlds. She said, 'I'll need rock solid proof. When I have it, I'll confront him.' She paused and added with dignity, 'You were right, you know. I'd rather live alone than live like this.'

Darren went north on Wednesday, on the overnight coach from Victoria. Liz thought it a dismal way to travel, and poor preparation for two days of demanding work, but he was philosophical. 'It's no' busy on a Wednesday. I'll get a seat to myself and sleep.'

'And then perform?'

'I'll be fine.'

'I wish I could go up with you again,' she said, doubtful still. 'But there's so much on with the term just beginning.'

'I'm fine, Liz. I'll stay with my friends and I'll be at the college all day. I wouldna see you anyway.'

'It *would* be better if you travelled in the daytime.'

He shrugged lightly. 'I couldna get the time. They were no' thrilled as it was. And that's with me promising to be on at ten on Saturday. Hope to Christ the bus isna late.'

'With no sleep,' Liz said.

He grinned. 'You sound like a mother, woman. And how much sleep do I get most of these nights anyhow?'

'Different,' she said, suppressing a small smile. 'It's quality sleep.'

'Quality sleep?'

'I'll miss you,' she said.

She missed him more than she could have imagined possible a handful of weeks before. It disturbed her, the place he had found in her life in so short a time. On Thursday night she went to her yoga class, glad to have something to fill up the evening. John was not there.

Afterwards when they were in the sauna, Erica said, 'Poor John, he is working late. Things are hard just now.'

'At work?'

Erica shrugged. 'Yes, at work. But also . . .' She stopped, and looked down at her plain, unpainted fingernails, stretched out in front of her on the pine bench.

'If you mean things aren't right at home for John, you can say so,' Liz said quietly. 'I have a fair idea.'

Erica was still quiet. Liz sat up on the bench, adjusting her terry robe beneath her. Erica looked lovely and girlish, her face fuller and more innocent if anything. 'You are such good friends,' she said carefully.

'Moira and I?'

Erica nodded.

Liz said, with a heartiness she did not feel, 'Sure. But we're *all* good friends, aren't we?'

'She does not like me.'

Liz said nothing.

Erica looked up, blonde curls bouncing around her pink cheeks. 'It is all right. You can say you know. She must *tell* you surely. She has never liked me.' She ducked her head, girlish again. 'Always when I was at school, there were girls I really liked. Beautiful girls that I admired and I wanted them to like me. But they never did. They had special friends, like you and Moira, but not me. I do not know what it is I do wrong.'

Liz watched her steadily. She took a deep breath and said, 'Erica?'

'Mmm.' Erica still studied her nails.

'Are you in love with Andrew?'

Erica's head flew up, her eyes round. 'Of course,' she said, her wide sensual mouth firmed, as close to primness as it would ever manage. 'He is my husband,' she said.

On Friday night, Liz worked on lecture notes at her desk in the study, her eyes straying to the phone. She had formed the idea that Darren would call if he was successful, less from anything he'd said than from the memory of how Barry would behave. But the hour for his return bus arrived and passed. She pictured him on it, alone, travelling south through the night, with the mundanity of a day's work between him and the chance even to share his defeat. She felt sad and protective and went to sleep curled around the striped kitten for want of its master.

When the phone rang, waking her, at nine, she had a brief joyous hope that it was Darren after all, newly arrived from Glasgow, calling her before his work. But it was Moira; crisp, cool, and assured.

'I need your help.' She sounded very businesslike. Liz sat up amongst pillows and stretching cats, her bed a menagerie of grudging cohabitants.

'Sure,' she said, trying to match Moira's morning clarity with something resembling alertness.

'I'm sorry to wake you but there's very little time. I want to be in Bournemouth by two.'

'Bournemouth?' Liz pushed unbrushed hair away from her eyes and looked dimly at the clock. 'By two?' She put the clock down. 'Why Bournemouth?'

'Because that's where they're going. I've got the address and the phone number.' Moira's voice went hard. 'He left them by the phone. James Bond finally made his mistake.'

'John?'

'*And* Erica.'

'In *Bournemouth*?'

'I can't answer for my husband's taste in love nests.'

'You're saying they've gone *together*? What, to a hotel?'

'No. To the YMCA. Christ, you're thick.'

'You're wrong,' Liz said.

'I'm right. I heard him book it. And call Miss Switzerland to confirm. I told you he'd get careless when he didn't care about me any more.' For the first time her smooth, sure voice cracked, momentarily, but an instant later she was back in control. 'Are you coming?' she said. She paused and added quickly, 'I suppose I should bring my lawyer but since my lawyer is John, I think I'd rather have you.'

'I'm coming,' Liz said, firmly, 'I'm coming. But you're wrong.'

It was a windy, fresh spring day and the drive to the coast was pleasant. Moira, dressed exquisitely, made up to perfection, was brisk and efficient, as if the day's purpose was a demanding but perfectly manageable decorating assignment. At two-thirty they arrived at the address, an old-fashioned seaside establishment outside the town, approached by a long drive lined with fading, wind-battered tulips. A sign at the drive entrance read 'The Dunes Hotel and Water Sports Centre'. The latter, in fresher paint and more sophisticated lettering indicated a recent branching out to accommodate changing lifestyles.

'There it is,' Moira said drily, 'Shangri-La.'

'What's your alibi?' said Liz.

'What?'

'For being here. If you're wrong.'

'I'm not wrong.'

'Yes,' Liz said coolly. 'Well, just stretch your imagination a bit and think what a fool you'll feel if by some remote chance you *are*, and we find your husband here with a client.'

Moira shrugged her tailored shoulders, looked once across at Liz as she turned up the drive and said, 'A house, of course. A client of *mine*, just down that lane we passed a while ago.

301

I've come to do some measurements and you've come along for a day out in the country. Now we're going to have tea – ' she paused as they came out of a tunnel of privet before a pleasantly faded cream-coloured two-storey house – 'in this *charming* little hotel we've just happened to find.'

'You're pretty smooth,' Liz said with a nod of affirmation. 'Ever consider a life of crime?'

Moira smiled weakly, turning into the gravel forecourt. 'Well, I'll have to do *something* after this. Since I'm going to be a divorcee. Or a *widow*,' she added grimly. She sighed then. 'I never imagined I would end up like this; skulking about the countryside after a philandering man.'

'I never imagined I would either,' Liz said with a grimace. 'We're going to feel such idiots, you know.'

'Oh really?' Moira said, pulling up to park. She waved out her window. 'There's John's car.' It sat, silver-grey and guilty, beneath the fresh new leaves of a horse-chestnut tree.

Liz stared at it, a little stunned. She rallied bravely. 'It doesn't mean *she's* here,' she said.

'We'll see.' Moira smiled, a cheery executioner's smile.

Behind the rustic-hinged outer door, and the frosted glass inner ones, the hotel presented an entrance hallway of gentle mustiness, a decor reminiscent of illicit wartime liaisons, interrupted by the intrusion of a modern reception desk with telephone and fax. A stairway led up to bedrooms. Moira looked around and sniffed.

'Well, it won't be a total waste, whatever. This place is screaming for a decorator.' She walked to the desk and rang the bell. After a moment a young girl with French-plaited hair appeared from a doorway behind the desk. Moira greeted her with a bright professional smile. 'I *wonder* if you can help me,' she said, her voice honeyed. The girl looked respectful and attentive. 'I've agreed to meet a friend and I'm not *totally* sure I have the right address. Is there by *any* chance, a Mr John Harris registered here?'

The girl hesitated. 'I'm sorry, I've just come on . . .'

'Perhaps you could check the book?' Moira said helpfully.

But instead, the girl turned back to the inner room and called, 'Mrs Nelson? Are John and Erica here this weekend?' An older woman, pink-cheeked and tweedy, appeared in the doorway, while Liz watched Moira tap a peach-glossed fingernail on the fake wood of the counter.

'John Harris? Yes, they're in. I think it's seven and eight. Check the book, Audrey.'

Audrey bent her French-plaited head over the old-fashioned guest book. 'Here they are,' she said. 'Mr John Harris and Mrs Erica Pringle. Rooms seven and eight.'

'That's our Erica,' Moira said coldly. 'Straight and up front to the last.'

Liz leaned over her shoulder and said to the receptionist. 'That's two single rooms,' in a clear, careful voice.

'Yes, two singles,' Audrey said. She smiled and closed the book.

'*Two singles*,' Liz said pointedly to Moira.

Moira looked straight back and said, 'Well, of course. They keep *up* the pretence.' She turned back to Audrey. 'Are they in?'

Audrey offered to try John's room but the tweedy woman's voice floated from the inner room, 'They were in to lunch, but they'll be at the centre now.'

'Centre?' Liz said. She looked at Audrey.

'The water sports centre,' the receptionist said. She raised her eyebrows. 'Of course.'

Outside in the fresh salty air, Liz and Moira followed Audrey's directions, walking out through the lawns and rose beds to a path that led through a privet arch towards the sea. Liz walked comfortably in her trainers and jeans, Moira less so in heels and a slim skirt. She tottered briefly over an untended bit of gravel and said sharply, 'Why "of course" for God's sake? Who uses a water sports centre in this weather?'

'I think they're all year round, Moira. You can sail in the winter. And canoe. All sorts of things.'

'John doesn't sail. *Or* canoe.'

The path ended at another privet hedge, another arch, overgrown branches tossing in the sea wind. Beyond was sand, beach grass, the eponymous line of dunes. To the left stood a modern, attractive wooden building, surrounded by racks of canoes, beached dinghies, and a trailer full of flat white sailboard hulls. Three other boards were pulled up on the beach, beside a group of people in colourful wet-suits. Out on the grey choppy sea, two bright sails, one red, the other blue, flitted like summer butterflies.

'The Dunes Water Sports Centre,' Liz read aloud from the big modern sign on the side of the building.

'I'd rather guessed this was it,' Moira said grumpily. 'I don't *believe* people are going in the water,' she added.

'They've got wet-suits,' Liz said helpfully, but Moira was studying the small group on the empty beach. She walked awkwardly across the sand to the long wooden verandah of the building and, stepping around two canoes, mounted the sandy steps. A row of black wet-suits hung like bored commuters from a rail. Moira brushed past them, giving one an irritated shove, and approached the door.

'Where are you going?' Liz asked.

'I'm going to ask about bloody John,' she said.

'They're out there.'

'What?' Moira half-turned in the doorway. Her brow was wrinkled, preoccupied.

'They're there.' Liz smiled briefly and pointed to the open sea and the two flitting sails. 'Out there.'

Moira looked too. A pair of wet-suit clad figures, lithe silhouettes against the bright water, balanced easily on the skimming craft. 'John and Erica? *John?* Ridiculous.'

'Bet?' said Liz. She leaned against a wooden pillar on the verandah, watching the windsurfers. The water was rough, white spray splashing around the little prows. The sails veered, dipped; the two boards turned in unison and headed back towards the beach, bouncing and skipping on the waves.

'You can't possibly see.'

'No. But I'll bet anyhow.'

Moira peered seaward. 'That *can't* be John.'

'Why not?'

'John could never . . .' Her eyes narrowed with a first momentary doubt. The red and blue sails grew larger as the two surfers held their landward course.

'Well, you're going to find out,' Liz said. Her smile was spreading, as her conviction grew and with it her relieved amusement at Moira's consternation.

The wind was strong enough to pile a small surf of breaking

304

waves along the wet sand. The red-sailed board surged up on to the back of a long wave, rode it, slipped through and slid gracefully up on to the shingle. Behind it, the second sailboarder mounted the line of surf with a little jump, wavered, skipped like a flat stone along its frothy back, and landed well up the sloping sand. The two sails dropped and fluttered on the shore, and the two wet-suited figures dragged their boards up out of the surf and then turned to face each other. The one from the red-sailed board pulled off a close-fitting rubber hood, and loose, dry blonde hair bounced out into the sun. Moira stared. The second figure, a man, removed his hood and the couple walked together companionably up the beach.

Moira said, brittly, 'What was that you said about Erica? So straight she'd ask "Please may I have an affair with your husband" before she made her move?'

'She's waving,' said Liz.

Erica broke into a trot, waving one hand happily. 'Hi!' she called as she approached and, turning to her companion, 'Look, John, it's Moira and Liz!'

'Well,' said Moira, 'that's straight.'

John stopped walking and, still some distance off, stood watching them. When he resumed, his buoyant steps subdued, and drew closer, Liz saw his narrow face shadowed by a look of cautious uncertainty. His body was trim and attractive in the clinging rubber wet-suit, his stance wary. 'Moira?' he said, the uncertainty lapping over into his voice, as if his recognition might be faulty.

'Hello, John,' Moira said. Liz watched them both. Moira looked utterly self-possessed; John, increasingly baffled. To the side, Erica watched, simply curious.

'Hello, Moira.' He sounded stunned, but he said quickly, out of politeness, 'Hello, Liz.'

'Hi, John,' Liz said, and smiled suddenly. 'That was very impressive.' She waved to the water and the two beached sailboards.

His face brightened at once, 'Hey, did you see that?' Pride tumbled over his consternation. With a happy self-conscious-ness he turned to face Liz. 'Did you see that *wave*? Christ, I never thought I'd make that.'

'You did very well, John,' Erica said. John grinned boy-ishly. Erica turned to Moira and Liz. 'He is very good. He learns fast.'

'Oh he's a fast one, all right,' Moira said. 'I wouldn't argue that.'

'Moira?' John said, the uncertainty back, and with it his sense of logic. 'Hey, what are you two doing here, anyway?'

He instinctively addressed the question to Liz. Liz blinked and looked quickly at Moira. Moira stood with the palm of one graceful hand delicately balanced on her hip, her posture cast slightly awry by her sinking heels. She said, 'Just a happy coincidence, John. Liz and I were seeing a house I'm going to do just up the road. Then we thought we'd stop for tea at this *charming* little hotel. And just as I pulled in, Liz said, "Why look, there's *John's car*."'

Liz raised an eyebrow but said nothing. 'So,' Moira continued cheerfully, '*I* said, "what extraordinary luck. Perhaps John and his client will join us for tea."' She smiled charmingly.

Erica said, 'Client? Who is client?'

'You followed me,' John said indignantly.

'Followed? What absolute rubbish. I told you, we were passing and . . .'

'You *followed* me,' John said again. His voice was outraged, his eyes hurt.

Erica said, blithely oblivious, 'It *is* a nice hotel. We come here – what, John – three times, four times. The facilities are better here, really, though I *liked* Brighton.'

'Brighton,' said Moira.

'It is so lucky you find us here now, you see, because this is our last weekend.' She looked at John and smiled a warm, sentimental smile. He looked nervous. 'Shall I tell them why?'

'Maybe *not* just . . .'

'Yes,' Moira said, interrupting crisply, 'tell us why.'

Erica smiled, radiant, and laid her hands contentedly on her slick, rubber-coated stomach. 'I am pregnant,' she said happily, her continental lilt richly pronounced.

'Oh shit,' said Liz.

'You're *what*?' Moira's face paled, her mouth trembling.

'Perhaps you should explain, Erica,' John said hastily.

'Explain?' Erica looked at him blankly. 'What is to explain, John?'

Moira shook her head. She raised one hand in a fluttery gesture, half shielding her face, half waving John from her. Her eyes squinted shut and then, suddenly tearful, she turned and walked clumsily away.

'Oh, Moira, for Christ's sake,' John said loudly.

'I do not understand,' Erica said. 'Why does it matter I am pregnant and we go windsurfing together? It does not show. And now, I am stopping . . . so . . .' Her wide blue eyes widened further, and went suddenly cold. 'What is she saying?'

'She's *saying*,' John said, incredulous and furious, 'that I'm the father.'

Twenty feet up the beach, Moira stopped. She turned back to face them with battered dignity. 'Of course I'm not,' she shouted, teetering uncertainly in her awkward heels in the sand,

'Oh really. Oh?' John leaned towards her, shouting back. 'And what *are* you saying then. And *why* did you follow me? God, Moira, this is sordid. I never imagined you could be *sordid*.'

'*I'm* sordid? What about you and the Snow Queen here . . .'

'Oh!' Erica said. The blue eyes flashed. 'Oh, that is terrible. I am a married woman. My husband . . . oh! How can you think!' Her eyes filled and her lips trembled and she burst suddenly into hugely emotional tears, flinging herself on Liz's shoulder. 'You were my *friend*!' she sobbed.

'Oh, *look* what you've done,' John said. 'Moira, I can't believe you.'

'*What?*' Moira stepped closer, stumbled in the sand, and recovered. 'Believe *me*? *You* can't believe *me*? *You're* asking me to believe you've come down here all winter just to go *windsurfing*.'

'Yes,' John said, very calmly.

Moira spun around in the sand, raising her hands. 'Oh, *ridiculous*!'

'No, Moira,' John said, still calm. 'It's not ridiculous. Just because *you* don't understand it doesn't make it ridiculous.' He paused, drawing a deep breath. 'You haven't understood half the things I've wanted to do, as long as I've known you.

But it *still* doesn't make them ridiculous. Not doing yoga. Or running. Or learning to ski. I *did* want to learn to ski. And I *still* want to learn to ski.'

'I never stopped you, John.'

'You laughed at me.' His voice was hollow, as if he spoke from some well of deep remembered hurt.

'Well, for God's sake, John, if your ego is *that* fragile. Of course I laughed at you. You looked bloody silly.'

'Did I look silly just now?' John pointed to the sea.

Moira looked out to the two sailboards, their little bright sails rippling on the sand. She said grudgingly, 'No. No, I was very impressed.' She gave a small honest shrug. 'I never thought for a moment it was you out there, actually . . .'

'No,' John shouted, interrupting her. His calm broke in a flood of indignation. 'No. Because out there for once, for the first time maybe, I was doing something *by myself*. Something you hadn't authorized and approved and created. Something no one could say, like they *always* say about everything, from my First at Cambridge to my latest success, and I *do have* successes, "Well, of course, Moira's *made* John."' He straightened up, slim and wiry and tense with outrage. 'Well out there, just for a moment, on that wave, *I* made John.' He turned, with fine dignity, and walked away up the strand to the wooden sports centre building, Erica trailing uncertainly behind.

On the M3, somewhere nearing Staines, Moira broke her silence. 'He should have bloody told me. He still should have told me. What *was* I to think?'

'Would you have believed him if he had?' Liz said.

Moira was stonily silent again. Eventually she said, 'You're on their side, aren't you?'

'No,' Liz said, 'I agree he was foolish.'

'And me?'

Liz looked ahead up the motorway, thinking carefully for a long while before she answered. She said then, 'I think it's always a mistake to assume you know someone better than they know themselves.' She paused. 'Barry was utterly convinced, you know, that I was dying to return to America, in spite of the fact that I'd never once said anything of the sort. *Partly* it suited his purpose, partly it was just a kind of arrogance.'

'It hardly suited my purpose for John to be having an affair with Erica,' Moira said sharply.

'No.' Liz drew the word out carefully. 'But it did rather help if John was only interested in tending the garden and hosting dinner parties and, let's face it, making money to pay for a pretty lavish lifestyle.'

'*He* likes it too,' Moira protested vigorously.

'Yes. He does. But I suspect he'd *rather* spend some of that time and money on a skiing holiday in France.'

Moira sighed and looked gloomy. She negotiated a turn-off, heading into London. 'I suppose I'll have to go with him.'

'Look,' Liz said with a smile, 'it's not so awful. Lying around in front of a log fire with a good book and a glass of *gluhwein*. *You* don't have to ski.'

'And let him loose with some *other* Nordic goddess?' Moira demanded.

'For Christ's sake, do you never learn?' Liz threw up her hands in exasperation and then turned to face Moira, saying insistently, 'John isn't looking for Nordic goddesses. He's looking for self-fulfilment.'

'That usually ends up meaning sex,' said Moira.

'With some men it does. Not with John. *Surely* you see that now?'

Moira lapsed into suspicious silence. 'So,' she said after a while, 'if he's *not* getting it elsewhere, why doesn't he make love to me?'

Liz was quiet for a long time. Then she said cautiously, 'Maybe if you treated him a little more like a man, a little less like one of your children, he might.'

Moira said, hurt, 'I was only trying to look after him, to keep him from getting hurt. I didn't want him to look foolish and be laughed at.'

'Why should *you* care if *he* didn't?' Liz returned at once. Moira did not answer. Liz said, 'Let him make his own mistakes. He's your husband, not your Siamese twin.'

Moira said nothing more until they were driving through the streets of Fulham. Then she announced stiffly, 'I don't suppose Erica will ever forgive me, even if John does.' She looked sad and brittle in the streetlight, as she pulled up beside a line of parked cars. She reached across and squeezed Liz's hand. 'Thanks so much. It's been a perfectly hideous day and I'd never have got through it without you.' She paused, looking up at the windows of Liz's flat, lit up behind drawn curtains. 'Is Darren home?'

'He must be,' Liz said, watching the windows as well.

'I'm awful, Liz. I never even asked, how'd he get on?'

'I don't know. I haven't seen him,' Liz said, adding quickly, 'I guess I'll find out now.'

The flat was full of music, Darren's Scottish tape, playing loud enough for him to listen to it in the kitchen. He did not hear her enter. She stood in the alcove, watching him through the open kitchen door. He was cooking spaghetti and the air was full of steam. He moved about the kitchen, easily familiar. The striped kitten was sitting on his shoulder, balancing delicately, as he worked. Liz watched for a moment and then said, 'Don't drop it in the sauce. It'll taste lousy.'

'Liz!' He looked up, startled. 'I didn't hear.'

She stepped into the room and slipped into his arms. 'Hi, Darren. I missed you.' He kissed her and the kitten stepped haughtily on to her shoulder from his and then jumped off, digging in its claws. 'Jealous,' she said.

'Do you want some spaghetti? I didna ken when you'd be back but I made enough.'

'I'd love it. I'm sorry I'm so late.'

'I found your note. Did you have a nice day in Bournemouth?' He sounded mystified, but polite.

'I had a crazy day. Darren, how are you?'

'OK.'

She stepped back, holding him at arm's length. He looked troubled. She said, 'OK? Come on, love, how'd it go?'

'It went OK.'

'OK as in "come back next year and try again"?' she said gently.

He looked at her solemnly and shook his head.

'Worse?' she asked uneasily.

'They offered me a place,' he said. He was standing very quietly, his arms at his sides, like an apologetic child.

'They what?' she whispered, uncertain.

'They offered me a place on the course,' he said evenly.

She shrieked with delight, flung herself on to him, kissing him and laughing. 'Darren, that's wonderful. Wonderful. Oh, love, I'm so thrilled for you. So *proud*.' She paused, her eyes wet, and the room misty. 'When do you start? Next term, what is it, September, October?'

He shook his head. 'I told them no,' he said.

XVI

'Look,' Liz said wearily over the toast crusts and coffee grounds of a distracted breakfast, 'I don't want to hear any more about it. You're going. That's it. Final.'

Darren looked grimly up from where he had sat, head in hands, throughout. '*No*,' he said. His voice was ragged with the emotions of a night-long argument but just as unbudging as the evening before.

'Christ, are you stubborn.'

'Maybe.'

'Oh stop this bloody Scots macho crap. This isn't *you* talking, Darren.'

'Then who is it?'

She shook her head, throwing up her hands in exasperation. 'I can't see,' she said evenly, 'how a person can be so rational and sensible and open to discussion for months and then *suddenly* revert to this mindless recalcitrance.'

'You mean I'm no' agreeing with you any more.'

'But you *do* agree with me. You did. You . . . Darren, *this* is what this was all for . . . remember? *You* came to *me*. You wanted me to help you. Why? So you could get a place at drama college. So now it's worked. You've got your place. Now *how* can you tell me this isn't what you want?'

'You ken fine what I want.'

She turned away. Jacob stood up beside her on his hind legs and she lifted him on to her knee, stroking his long curved back, searching for words in the thick brown plush of his fur. She said, speaking with great care, 'It's perfectly understandable you should feel this way.'

'Stop it,' he shouted. She looked up, startled. 'Stop it. Stop talking like . . . some kind of teacher.'

She smiled wryly. 'I am a teacher.'

'No' here. No' with me.'

'All right, Darren. Fair enough. I'm not your teacher. But I *am* older than you. I've had more experience in *some* things, if not others.' She spaced her words out, timed to her stroking of the cat. 'And I do know how important it is to do the necessary things in life. *Like* education. And – ' she paused, looking up at him gently – 'how hard it is when emotions get in the way . . . I *often* have students in this situation . . .'

'Will you stop it, Liz,' he said tiredly. 'You're doing it again. Talking about us like you had nothing to do with it.'

'It's called professional detachment.' She stood up, smiled slightly, and set the cat down on the floor. She reached to clear their dishes from the table.

'Well I dinna want you detached.' He sat back, glaring at her in confused frustration. 'Do you no' *care* if I go away?'

Liz stopped, half-way to the sink, and turned to face him, the stack of dishes in her hands. 'I care.' He looked slightly mollified. 'I also care that you become what you're meant to be. Now, I want you to get on the phone this afternoon and tell them you're accepting this place. I know how these things work, Darren. They want you. They wouldn't have offered it otherwise. They understand young people's nerves. Tell them you've thought again and you want to accept. That's all.' She paused and added quickly, 'You can't throw away the first real chance you've had in your life.'

He looked up solemnly and said in a clear adult voice, 'Liz, *you're* the first real chance I've had in my life.'

'No.'

'Yes.' He met her eyes, his gaze unflinching.

She came back to the table, set the dishes down again and sat in her chair. She reached across the table and took his hands in both of hers. 'You can't make your life around me, Darren.' He started to protest, but she leaned forward encouragingly. 'You can't make your life around *any* other person. You have to be what you want to be first.' She smiled gently. 'I know what matters to you,' she said.

'How can you know better than me?' he answered at once.

She let go of his hands, and sat looking down at her own. She said, after a long thoughtful pause, 'Darren, do you want me to go with you?'

'I cannae ask that,' he said.

She shook her head. 'Do you want it?' she repeated.

'What do you think?'

'I don't know, Darren,' she said.

He sighed and got up from the table. 'If you loved me, you'd know.' He spoke honestly, with neither challenge nor bravado.

'I do love you.' She surprised herself, saying it.

He nodded solemnly. 'No' the way I love you.' He slipped his coat off the back of his chair and flung it over his shoulder, holding it by the collar. He turned to face her. 'It's all right. I ken what you mean.'

'Where are you going?'

'To work, Liz. I still have to work.'

'What about the college?'

'I'll ring them in the afternoon.'

'Darren, *really* it's best. You can't let this chance go by.'

'Right, Liz. I'll do it. I dinna want to talk about it now, OK?'

'OK, Darren,' she said quietly, 'whatever you say.'

He started to turn away, but stopped, and looked up suddenly, holding one hand raised. 'That's the door.'

'What, Darren?' she said distractedly.

'The door.'

'I didn't hear it,' she said.

He turned from her quickly. 'That's because they didna ring.' He dropped the coat on the floor and hurried past her, one hand balled into a fist. He stopped in the doorway, blocking her view. She heard the front door latch click, and the soft whine of its opening hinge, and caught her breath with a city-dweller's quick apprehension.

There was a moment's silence and then Darren said sharply, 'Who the fuck are you?'

'Excuse me?' The voice, plaintive and disorientated, was unmistakably familiar.

Liz's mouth fell open in silent amazement and then she dashed forward and grabbed Darren's arm. 'Don't hit him!' she shouted, pushing past in a small panic.

314

Darren looked baffled, staring first at her and then back to the doorway, where, rumpled and dishevelled, Barry stood, his Gladstone bag in his hand and on his face a look of jet-lagged misery.

'I'm sorry,' he said. 'My plane got in at six and there was just nowhere else to go.' He paused guiltily. 'I still had my keys.' He held them up, jingling apologetically.

Darren nodded slowly, assessing Barry. Then he turned to Liz. 'Is he your friend?' he asked. He sounded cautious.

Liz smiled. 'Well, friend enough that I'd rather you didn't flatten him. Not,' she added, 'that he might not deserve it walking in like that.'

'*Liz*,' Barry said sadly.

'I wasnae going to,' Darren said. 'No' really.'

'You should have rung the bell,' Liz said to Barry.

He looked stricken. 'I didn't think,' he said miserably. He was studying Darren with a mixture of bafflement and awakening dismay.

Liz smiled brightly. 'Well,' she said, 'since you *are* here, unexpected though it is, how nice to see you.' Barry nodded sleepily, still staring at Darren. 'Oh, Barry, this is my friend, Darren MacPhee,' she added cheerfully. 'Darren, this is Barry Poore. He used to live with me. I told you . . .'

'I ken who he is,' Darren said.

'Oh your *assistant*,' Barry brightened.

As they shook hands warily, Liz repeated plainly, 'My friend.' Their hands separated and they stood looking uncertainly at each other until Liz said, 'Darren's on his way to work. We'd better let him go.'

Darren turned to her quickly, and she nodded encouragement. He stepped past Barry to get his coat from the kitchen and returned, making a wide circle around him. He looked uneasily at Liz and then suddenly took her arm and propelled her into the living-room. 'Look,' he said, releasing her arm and shrugging towards the alcove where Barry awaited bemusedly. 'Are you a'right wi' him?'

'All right?' she asked vaguely.

'All right. Safe. Y'ken?'

Liz tossed back her head, laughing gleefully. Darren looked hurt. She tried to stop laughing, but failed. At last she said,

315

shaking her head, 'Thank you, Darren, but I'll be fine. I promise you.'

'I mean, I could stay if you like.'

'Go to work, love. He's an old friend. He's also really very nice. If he's still here when you come in, we'll all have a meal together. You'll like him.'

'Aye,' Darren said. 'Sure.' He drew back from her.

She said, 'Darren, he's just an old friend.'

Darren shrugged into his black coat. 'I have to go. I'm late.'

'Call the college,' she said. He nodded, and walked out past Barry without acknowledgement, closing the door heavily behind him.

'What a nice young man,' Barry said, after he'd gone.

'Delightful,' said Liz. They stared at each other in silence.

Barry set down the Gladstone bag and took off his tweed coat, hanging it by comfortable habit in the alcove, on a free peg between her beige trenchcoat and Darren's peaked cap and long white scarf. His hand brushed the cap. 'Liz?'

'Yes?'

'What's he doing here at eight A.M.?'

'Having breakfast.'

Barry looked uncomprehending. He stared in silence, and slow hurt gathered in his eyes. They blinked once behind his steel-framed glasses. 'Liz? That *boy*?'

'Do you want coffee before you go?' she said.

'Go?'

'To your hotel. You *are* going to a hotel, aren't you?'

'I thought . . .'

'You can sleep on the sofa, Barry, but I don't think you'll like it,' she said. She smiled and added gently, 'You really should have called.'

His shoulders slumped. He reached up to loosen the scarf around his neck; the red cashmere scarf she had sent for his birthday; but then his hand gave up, dropping defeatedly to his side. He looked utterly dejected, utterly exhausted. 'I'm sorry, Liz. I never thought. I never thought for a moment.' He sighed softly. 'It never occurred to me there might be someone here with you.' His back straightened. 'How utterly stupid of me. And completely thoughtless . . .' his voice trailed away.

'It's been a while, Barry. And you've gone *your* own way.'

He nodded quickly. 'Oh, I know. I know. You had every right . . .' The hurt look didn't leave his eyes. He said a moment later, 'Liz, is he really as young as he looks?'

'He's twenty-four,' she said.

His face registered another small shock. He bowed his head, scratching at his travel-tousled hair. He looked crumpled and miserable.

She said, 'Barry, would you like a little sleep? You look wiped out.'

'Oh, I'd love that,' he said. He looked up, abject. 'I'll sleep on the sofa.'

'You can have the bed. Look, I'll just go straighten it.' The hurt flicked through his eyes again. She hurried past him into the bedroom. Its tangled bedclothes shouted sex; ironically, they'd lain awake, loveless and deep in argument most of the night. She smoothed the sheets and straightened the duvet with guilty hands.

'Come in, Barry,' she called. He had followed her, a tired automaton, and was watching in the doorway. His eyes strayed helplessly to Darren's few belongings – trainers, a pair of jeans, a black jumper – scattered about the room. He said nothing. He sat on the edge of the bed and at once Jacob jumped out from under it and on to his knees.

'Oh my cat, my cat,' he said. He wrapped his arms around it, hugging it, dog-like, to his chest.

It looked around at Liz and blinked haughty eyes, but sat patiently. 'I think he's actually glad to see you,' she offered kindly.

Barry closed his eyes, hugging the cat, and then lay down on the bed, pulled his feet up, and rolled over, his back to her. 'I'll wake you at one,' she said. He mumbled something, already half asleep, and she went out and softly closed the door.

She let him sleep until two and when she woke him, it was with a fresh cafetière of coffee beside the bed. He woke up with a smile, as if he had forgotten his circumstances. He took the coffee cup she offered and she sat down on the end of the bed. He watched her and the smile slowly faded. He said cautiously, 'I like your hair.'

She said, 'Why are you home, Barry?'

He sat up straighter on the bed, kicking off the shoes he'd slept in. He stretched his toes, in white sports socks. He looked well, slimmer, very fit. 'I thought it would be nice to see everyone,' he said noncommittally.

Liz nodded. She said, 'Pity you didn't let me know. I could have arranged some things.' She paused. 'I don't suppose you'll have terribly long . . .'

'Oh, I have a while,' he said in the same easy voice. Liz absorbed that. She said, 'Our Easter break finishes this week. I suppose they're different over there.'

'Oh yes. Very different. Quite an elaborate system, actually.' He looked vaguely around the room as he spoke, his mind elsewhere.

'When do you go back?'

'I'm not sure actually, Liz.' She looked up from her coffee, puzzled. He said, 'I'm not sure I'm actually going back.'

'Barry?'

'Lot of complications with the work,' he said abruptly.

He paused and looked directly at her. 'It's a very strange place, you know.'

'The States?' She smiled quietly.

'Yes. The students . . . they're *very* independent. Or something. Demanding.' He shook his head, puzzled. 'You know they actually *censored* Shakespeare.'

'Censored?'

'Yes. They took a vote. I was lecturing on *Merchant of Venice* and they took a vote and decided *not to do it*. Because it was anti-semitic.'

'Well . . .' Liz said, 'some people have . . .'

'Oh, of course. Of course. But not to *study* it? Then they balked at *Othello* because it was racist. And then they threw out *Shrew* because it was sexist.' His face was solemnly outraged.

Liz giggled. 'I suppose *Lear* was ageist,' she said, laughing.

'Yes!'

'No.'

'Yes.' He pushed his hand up into his hair and looked grim.

'That's half the syllabus, virtually.' She was still smiling. He said, 'It's not really funny, Liz.'

'No, I suppose not.' He shook his head.

'There was more. I wasn't *totally* happy with the faculty either. Things aren't quite as they were presented.' He talked quickly, stringing together a solid fence of words.

Liz said, 'I thought you were getting married.'

'So did I. She traded me for a roller-skate.'

'What?'

'Joke. She was a little young, Liz.' He met her eyes and looked away, briefly confused, but he regained his stride in a moment. 'She took me home to meet her parents. Her dad was the same age as me. Big Chicago lorry driver. Thrilled to bits about it, as you might imagine. I was lucky to get out of there alive.'

'You're joking.'

He looked down. Jacob and Esau had climbed back up on to the bed and were licking each other. He watched them a while and said, 'A little. Actually,' he paused and smiled whimsically, 'I got on fine with her dad. We talked about mid-life crises. Only in America are there lorry drivers with mid-life crises. Jackie got bored and went off with her brothers. I saw the writing on the wall.' He tickled one cat, dejectedly.

'Did you sleep with her?' Liz said. He did not look up.

'I hadn't the heart. It would have been like deflowering Tinkerbell. Christ I feel a fool, Liz.' He sat, knees drawn up, big hands folded across them and bearded face resting on his knuckles, boyishly disconsolate. She reached to touch his shoulder with her hand but in the same moment Darren's kitten dropped unannounced from the top of the wardrobe, on to the pair of Siamese curled by Barry's knees. The bed exploded in claws and fur.

'Christ!' Barry shouted, flinging his legs out of the way. 'What's *that*?' Brown and striped cat shapes sinuously intermingled, hissing and yowling, and fell off the bed with three soft thuds. The kitten streaked for the kitchen; Jacob and Esau pursued.

'Perez de Cuellar,' said Liz.

'Who?'

'The UN Secretary . . .'

319

'I know who Perez de Cuellar is,' Barry said sharply.

'It's Darren's kitten. His name is Tiger, actually. He's the peacemaker.'

'That was peace?'

'Sure. They don't fight with each other any longer.' She paused, straightening the duvet. 'Now they just fight with him.'

'Great improvement.' Barry rubbed a scratched knee.

'I didn't think so either.'

'Darren lives here,' Barry said solemnly.

'At the moment,' Liz said. 'He needed a place.' She was conscious of being deliberately casual. 'He was looking for another . . .' She stopped. 'I'm not sure what his plans are now.'

'Liz, is this *serious* with this boy?'

'He's a man, Barry.'

'I'm sorry. I didn't mean . . .'

'And of course it's serious. I'm not casual about sex. I never have been. You know that.'

He stared at her, his open face, lined with tiredness and confusion, unable to disguise his dismay. 'I suppose I'd better go,' he said awkwardly. 'Find that hotel. Or somewhere.' He looked around the room as if baffled by its very familiarity.

She said quietly, 'Perhaps Moira and John could have you stay. For a while. Or Andrew Pringle?'

Barry shook his head. He said honestly, 'I couldn't face them, Liz.' He stood up, bending over and finding his shoes again.

She nodded, getting up from the bed and going to the door. At the doorway she turned and said, 'Barry, I have a friend with a flat in Butler's Wharf. I'm sure he'd let you stay. You might get on quite well. He's a nice man.'

'I'm not sure,' Barry said. But he looked interested.

'I'll make some lunch and then I'll give him a call,' Liz said. She went out to the kitchen and he did not protest.

Charles answered the phone sounding warily surprised. 'Liz? What's up?' There was a new distancing in his voice.

'Charles, I'm going to be a real shit and ask a rather unfair favour. *Please* feel free to tell me to piss off.'

'Oh, Liz, I'd never . . .' The voice softened into remembered kindness.

'Wait till you've heard it,' she said. 'Charles, are you spending a *lot* of time in the flat?'

He was briefly silent and then answered with a note of cautious reserve, 'Well, on and off.'

'On and off?'

'Ah, I've been spending a bit of time in Essex.' He paused again and then added quickly, 'I'd been meaning to tell you, Liz, but we've been out of touch.'

'Tell me what?' she said, puzzled by his persistent sense of duty.

'I've been with Jane, Liz. We've been trying a reconciliation . . .'

'Oh, Charles. How nice for you.'

'Do you mean that?' he said eagerly.

'Of course. It's what you wanted, isn't it?'

'Oh yes.' He burst instantly into relieved honesty. 'It's *just* what I wanted. When it happened I wanted to tell you right away, but it seemed a bit rum . . . of course, it's not a *full* reconciliation. We're taking it slowly. Step by step. The girls are thrilled of course . . . oh, I must tell them you've called. They ask about you often.'

She was surprised, but he was too genuine to doubt. 'So, Charles,' she said carefully, 'do I take it that you're giving *up* the flat?'

'In the long run, I suppose I will. Right now it seemed wise to hang on to it. It keeps the pressure off Jane. I don't want her feeling shut in by me all over again. I stay here the odd night.' He laughed softly. 'I've actually grown a little fond of it. Moira's dove-grey bloody walls.' He stopped suddenly. 'Why, Liz?'

'I have a friend who's back unexpectedly from America needing a place . . . just for a week or two while he,' she dropped her voice, 'sorts himself out.'

'Of course, Liz,' he said at once. 'There's a sofa bed, anyway, for the *odd* night I'm in town.'

'Is that you or your excellent manners speaking?' she asked.

He laughed. 'I can't tell,' he said. 'I think that's half my trouble, Liz. Please. Send him over. You were such a good friend all winter. All those bloody cheeseburgers. It's the very least I can do.'

She found Barry in the living-room, trailing his red cashmere scarf around the floor for the amusement of Darren's kitten. She had written down Charles Beatty's name and address and handed them to him. He sat cross-legged on the floor, the scarf across his knees. He read it carefully, and thanked her, then continued to sit staring at the kitten which had climbed on top of his Gladstone bag and was worrying the paper luggage-tags.

'When does Darren get back?' he said.

'About six, tonight.'

'I'd better be away before then.' He looked morosely at the address before putting it away in his wallet.

Liz felt a surge of pity for him. 'Yes, you'd better,' she said.

When Darren returned that night, he rang the doorbell. She opened the door, expecting Barry back, having forgotten something, and jumped with surprise.

'Lost your key?' she said mildly.

'No.' He looked shy. 'I just thought maybe . . .'

'Barry's gone, Darren.' She stepped back and he followed her in. He nodded. He slipped out of his black coat and hung it on its peg, dropping his rucksack on the floor. He looked about with alert wariness, like his kitten, newly arrived. Liz went into the kitchen and switched the kettle on. When Darren appeared in the doorway, she said, 'You hungry?'

'I ate at work.' She looked surprised. He added quickly, 'I wasnae sure . . .'

'Darren. You live here. There was nothing not to be sure of.'

'Aye,' he said, without conviction.

'Barry's gone to stay with my friend Charles,' she said. 'You remember Charles?' She smiled quickly.

'With him?' Darren sat down at the table, looking stunned. 'You sent him to stay with *him*?'

'Sure.' His eyes were incredulous. She filled the cafetière and said, looking at it, 'Did you call the college?' He did not answer and she looked up sharply. 'Darren?'

'I called them.'

'And?'

'Fine. It's fine. I mean, I'll have to see about getting my grant and all, but it's fine.'

Her face relaxed into a happy smile. She set the cafetière on the table and sat down across from him, reaching out and taking his hands. He turned them to clasp hers, but did not look up. Still smiling, she studied his big, workman's knuckles. 'You're going to be great,' she said.

'Liz?' He raised his eyes and she met his clear, honest gaze.

'Yes?'

'If I wasna here, would he stay with you?'

She smiled and answered casually, 'Oh probably . . .' Hurt shuttered down the openness of his face. She added quickly, 'He'd sleep on the *sofa*, Darren, but he'd probably stay.'

'You love him.'

She shook her head. 'He's an old, *old* friend.'

'You love him.'

She bent down, eyes on their joined hands. 'Yes.'

On Thursday evening, Darren was working until eight. Liz was alone in the flat, in her tracksuit, doing a few preliminary stretches before her yoga class, when the buzzer rang for the street door. She answered it and Barry's voice, tentatively cheerful, came over the intercom, 'Liz, can I come up to see you?'

'Sure,' she said, reaching for the button. Then she stopped. 'I thought you had your keys.'

'I have.'

'Well?'

'May I use them?'

'Oh for God's sake, Barry.'

He came up and rapped lightly on the door of the flat before opening it with his key. She was waiting in the alcove.

'Ten out of ten for effort, Barry.'

'Well I *did* learn my lesson.' He looked around, rather as Darren had done.

She said, taking his tweed coat, 'He's out at work.'

Barry nodded and smiled cheerfully. He looked composed and energetic, recovered both from his flight and the shock of his arrival. 'He won't mind?' he said airily.

Liz gave him a sharp look. 'Of course not. Did *we* ever mind each other's friends?'

'Oh no, no.' He smiled again. 'Only I thought this might be different . . .'

'Why? Because he's young? Because he's working-class and Scots? Do you really imagine me with a jealous lover?'

Barry ducked his head and held up one hand. 'Sorry.' He stepped into the living-room, found Esau curled in a cushion, uncurled him and picked him up. 'I keep putting my foot in it,' he said.

Liz shrugged and answered lightly, 'Just don't make assumptions, OK?'

He nodded, chastened, and she left him and went to make coffee. When she returned, he had wandered into the study, still carrying the cat. She found him looking down at her unnaturally tidy desk. 'How's the book, Liz?' he asked. He seemed to be seeking some sign of it among her stacks of class essays.

She handed him his coffee cup and looked straight at him. 'I chucked it,' she said.

He said nothing. He did not protest, as her other friends and even Darren had done, and he did not look totally surprised. 'Why?' he said quietly.

'Because you weren't here.'

He laughed. 'Oh come on, Liz, I wasn't *that* much of a slave driver.'

She smiled, sitting on the edge of her desk, looking up at him fondly. 'No. But you were my chief motivation.'

'To please me?' he said wonderingly. 'Surely not.'

'To *be* you, Barry.' She flicked the corner of a sheaf of papers, gently. 'You were my only rival. The only one I cared about. Moira was beautiful and successful and a wonderful mother and wife, but we weren't rivals. I didn't want to be her. I wanted to be you. Ever since we first met. You studied, so I studied. You lectured, so I lectured. You wrote, so I wrote.'

'Well of course you wrote. You had things to say.'

'Nothing original. Not everyone does. I'm a teacher, Barry. I love to teach and I do it well.' Her eyes strayed to Darren's dog-eared stack of questionnaires lying on the bookshelf. 'Actually, I do it very well.' She looked up and met his eyes, her own warm and kind.

324

'What happened between you and that boy . . . you and Darren, Liz?' he asked.

She smiled whimsically. 'Lessons in life?' He looked startled. 'Nothing I *intended* to happen,' she said quickly. She paused, removing and replacing the cap of a pen. 'He wants to be an actor, Barry. And he comes from the sort of background where no one in a thousand generations, as Neil Kinnock would say, has set foot inside a legitimate theatre. Or a library,' she added. 'Or a museum, a gallery, a university . . . I wanted to help him. He was so honest and awkward and courageous somehow. Most people would have given up years ago with all the strikes he had against him.' She dropped her eyes, studying the pen. 'I do admit that I was also intrigued by the challenge. But I never intended any *harm*. And I never imagined the degree of involvement.'

'He fell in love with you,' Barry said. She nodded without raising her eyes.

Barry leaned against the bookshelves. 'A bit irresponsible, Liz.'

'What?'

'Young, impressionable man, thrown into a dependent relationship with a woman like you? You should have seen that coming a mile off.'

'Barry, I don't go around expecting men to fall in love with me,' she said vigorously. 'I never have.'

He looked severe. 'You should have headed it off, Liz. You'll hurt him.'

She looked up sharply. 'You're assuming a lot,' she said, adding quietly, 'as always. Has it occurred to you that maybe he'll hurt me?'

'I can't imagine . . .' He stopped, baffled. 'Do you *love* him, Liz?'

'Yes. I do.'

'Oh. Oh, I see.' He kept his eyes on her face, swallowed once, and nodded. He said nothing, seemed unable to say anything. She turned away and stood up, her fingers trailing idly across the papers on the desk.

'How are you getting on with Charles?' she asked.

He swallowed again and then said, 'Oh,' in a dry, hollow voice, 'oh splendid.' He seemed relieved then at the change of subject and added brightly, 'He's a tremendously nice

325

bloke.' He paused and asked curiously, 'Where'd you meet him, Liz?'

'I told you. At Moira's. One of her lame ducks, remember?'

'Oh.' Surprised recollection crossed his face, and quick reassessment. '*That's* who he is. That's the bloke . . .'

'We went out for a while.'

'Oh I *see*.' Barry nodded, a little uneasily. 'He doesn't mind . . .'

'What, about you?' she paused. 'Or about Darren?'

'Well, either,' he said lamely.

'He has a wife, Barry.'

'Yes, yes I know. I met her actually.'

She stopped in the doorway to the study. '*Did* you? What's she like?' she asked quickly.

'She's charming. A really nice woman.' He followed her out of the study and into the living-room. 'A bit like Moira to look at.'

'Oh really?'

'Yes, a bit of a stunner.'

'I see.' Liz absorbed a small twitch of childish jealousy. 'I know their daughters, of course,' she said.

Barry stood in front of the mantel, idly touching familiar objects. He moved Andrew's book aside and said casually, 'Pringle's paperback out yet?'

'Next month. He's deep into another.' Barry's fingers reached the small bronze cat from the British Museum. He picked it up and then set it down quickly, as if by some instinct, and said nothing. 'Ah, well done, old Andrew.' She could see his mind was on something else entirely. 'Charles is thinking of giving up that flat, actually.'

Liz settled on the sofa beside the curled up kitten, and drew up her feet. 'Yes, he said something . . .' She stretched her arms over her head and closed her eyes. 'I gather there's a reconciliation on the cards.'

'He offered it to me, actually.'

Liz straightened up, alert. She waited, but he said nothing more. 'Well?' He watched her quietly, leaning on the mantel. 'Maybe worth considering?' she said cautiously.

He shrugged. 'I doubt I can afford Butler's Wharf,' he said morosely.

'Of course you can. On *your* salary . . .' Barry smiled whimsically, running a hand through his tousled hair.

'I haven't got a job, Liz.'

She blinked, startled by the idea which she had failed to consider. 'Oh *they'll* take you back . . . or someone will have you. You're well thought of,' she said honestly.

He put his hands in his trouser pockets and looked down at the floor. 'I'm not so sure of that,' he said. He prodded the carpet with his foot and the kitten jumped down to bat his shoelaces. He watched it kindly. 'Anyway,' he said, 'I don't really care.' He looked up, eyes candid. 'I want to write, Liz. I . . .' He hesitated shyly. 'I started a novel . . . oh I'm sure it's bloody awful, but . . .'

'Why should it be bloody awful?'

He shrugged and gave her his whimsical smile again. 'Because it's mine? One more middle-aged academic bursting into print. Oh shit, Liz, it's what I wanted all my life. What my parents wouldn't hear of. My tutors steered me away from. My friends smiled indulgently and changed the subject . . .'

'You never told me.'

'No. I never told you. I never dared, Liz.'

'Why?'

'In case you laughed. I could ignore the rest of them and still know one day it would happen. But, if *you* laughed, that would be the end of it.'

She smiled slowly, watching him, then she got up from the sofa and crossed the room, and put her hands on his shoulders. 'I'm not laughing.' He grinned, embarrassed and glad and she reached up and kissed his cheek. 'I think it's a terrific idea,' she said.

At the door, as he was leaving, he said suddenly, 'Liz, can I ask a special favour and borrow the car tomorrow? I'd sent all my stuff to the university and I'd like to shift it down to Charles's flat . . .'

'Barry, it's your car.'

'I gave you my half,' he said honourably.

'Well, have it back. For God's sake, Barry. And we'll have to work out something about the flat as well.'

'No.' He shook his head solemnly. 'But if I could use the

car tomorrow it *would* be handy.' She picked the keys from their hook in the alcove and tossed them to him. He tossed them back. 'I've got my own, still,' he said, with a small guilty smile.

Erica's green leotard, sleek as ever across her narrow hips, revealed the slightest imaginable pregnant bump in the front, which she had chosen to embellish by tying her pink sash over it in a big ostentatious bow. She stood at the side of the hall, limiting her demonstrations of the postures to a few careful stretches. At intervals, she stopped to explain, 'Of course, I cannot do this *asana* now, because I am pregnant.' The words rang out cheerfully and each time she gave a happy smile. John Harris watched, proud as a new father.

After, Liz asked, 'Can you sauna?'

'A little while is fine,' Erica said. She had the solemn medically-conscious manner of first-time mothers. They went through to the sauna suite together. The Australian attendant leered dutifully. Erica strode by, exasperated. They undressed together, Erica proudly showing off her minuscule stomach, and went through to the showers.

'*Hi*, everybody,' a sultry voice called over the rush of water. Liz stepped out of the shower and crossed to the carpeted lounge full of wicker and potted plants. Moira Harris lay stretched on a padded deckchair in a new turquoise robe. 'Thought I might find you here,' she said airily.

'Moira, how nice,' Liz said. She went and sat at the end of the chair and they exchanged kisses. She looked up and saw Erica following her warily. Moira smiled and offered her a corner of the chair, but Erica remained standing, her loose robe hanging open.

'My heavens,' Moira said cheerily, 'who would have believed it. You actually *show* already.'

Erica blushed happily, looking down. 'I do, don't I,' she said. 'I wonder now, when will Andrew notice?'

Moira blinked. 'Notice? You haven't told him?'

Erica shook her head. She sat down then, on the very edge of Moira's chair. 'I didn't think that was necessary,' she said.

Moira sat up straighter, neatly covering her legs with a

turquoise flap. 'You didn't think consulting your *husband* was necessary?'

Erica shrugged, pushing up her blonde curls with one hand. 'What difference is it to him? I do everything for the children. If we have one more, I will still do everything. He has plenty of money . . . and anyhow, he *likes* children.'

Moira looked pale, 'I hope so, sweetheart,' she said.

Erica leaned back, looking down fondly at her little naked bump. 'He has his job and his book and his politics. I want something too.'

'A baby?' Moira said, slightly disapproving.

'Well, why not?' Erica returned forcefully. '*Always* I am wanting children. Of course we *have* the children . . .'

'But they're his.' Moira gave a wise little toss of her head.

Erica looked up, indignant. 'They are mine too. But they are growing up. Soon they will be away to school. Surely there is room in that big house for a baby. So I asked the children.'

'You asked *who*?' Moira said.

'The children. Surely it would not be right to have another baby without asking first the older children.'

Moira laughed incredulously. 'It never crossed my mind to ask mine. If it *had*, Rachel would have vetoed Clare *and* William, right off.'

'Oh she wouldn't,' Liz said reproachfully.

'Oh she would.'

'But anyhow,' Erica said, 'that is different. You are their mother. I . . .' She paused, wistful, 'I am, you know, outside.'

Liz said quickly, 'No you're not, Erica. You're Andrew's wife.'

Erica shrugged. 'I am not their mother,' she said evenly. 'I think they love me, but who knows? Maybe they do not. So I ask, and you know what they say? "*Two*. You must have *two*, Erica. One for each of us."'

'I tried that once with puppies,' Moira said. 'We ended up with seven.'

'Seven?' Erica's eyes widened.

'They bred. Never mind, Erica, it shouldn't be a problem.'

She leaned forward confidentially and said then, 'What *I* want to know, is how did you manage it?' She paused while Erica looked blankly back at her. 'I mean, you always led us to *believe* sex was notable by its absence.'

Erica smiled wisely. She stood up and stretched her arms over her head and then wandered barefoot across the room, her loose terry robe fluttering about her knees. She looked back, her eyes crinkling. 'I was clever,' she said. She came back to the deckchair and sat again, midway down its length, comfortably intimate. 'At first,' she said, leaning forward, 'I was *not* clever. At first I moped about and pleaded and said, "Don't you love me?" all the time. And he said always, "Of course I love you, but go away, I must work, I must study, I must write." And I moped more and he worked more and it got worse and worse. And I got so miserable, I thought, I will go away home to Switzerland, since he doesn't love me any more. But then I thought of the children and I could not go. So *then* I got clever. I thought, so, if he does not want to love me when I love him so much, let us see what it is like when I don't. So I stopped.'

'You stopped loving him?' Moira asked, startled.

'I stopped *telling* him. So then, he would say, "I am working", and I would say "fine". "I am going away for the weekend." I said, "Bye, bye." "I want to go to sleep early." "Night, night."'

'Did he like it?' Liz asked.

'Yes, at first. At first he is very happy. No problems. No trouble from Erica. All is peaceful.' She smiled, remembering. 'But then, you know, he starts to ask, "Must you go away this weekend?" And I say, "But I have a seminar." And he asks, "Do you mind if I work, or shall we sit and talk?" And I say, "Oh no, you must work. It is very important." And then *I* say, "This bed, Andrew, is no good. I cannot sleep. It is bad for my back. I want single beds. Much healthier." And he is puzzled, but yes, we take from the guest room the single beds and we put them in our room. And so, that night we go to bed. And it is very quiet. And then I hear Andrew, "Erica?" "Yes?" "Are you . . . you know, sleepy?" And I say, "Yes, Andrew, very sleepy, good night." And the next night, he asks again, "Erica, are you sleepy?" And

I say, "Oh yes, Andrew, very, very sleepy. Good night."'
She started to laugh and rocked back on the lounge chair,
arms folded across her newly round breasts. 'And the *next*
night . . .' she laughed raucously, her head flung back. 'So in
the morning, he is very pleased with himself, but his back is
so sore, he walks like this.' She stood up, bending over and
hobbling around the room. Moira burst out laughing. Erica,
seeing her, smiled happily. Then the smile faded and she lifted
her chin firmly. 'So you see, it was not *John* I was thinking
of at all.'

'Oh no,' Moira said at once, flustered. 'Of course not. I never
actually thought . . .' Liz hid her face in her towel.

Erica looked solemn. 'You see, I would never do such a
thing. Always when I am a little girl, my father, he is away
and my mother sits by herself and sometimes she cries.
When I find her crying, I say, "Mama, what is wrong,"
and then she laughs and says nothing, there is dust in
her eyes. I think, this is strange, this dust in her eyes
whenever my father goes away.' She sat, upright on Moira's
lounger, her feet firmly planted on the floor. 'Later, I know
about the mistresses. My father is handsome, bold, I admire
him and so when he confides in me, I am proud and
I pretend to agree, yes, of course, he must have these
women. My mother understands, he says. He is so vigorous, he is a man, he has *needs*. But I think always of
the dust . . .' She lifted her head abruptly. 'Never. I never
do such a thing.' She stood up. 'I will sauna now,' she
said.

'Erica.' Moira got up from the lounger too. She wrapped her
dressing-gown around her and tied the belt firmly. 'I'm sorry.
I've been a complete cow.'

'Oh no,' Erica said. 'It was only natural . . .'

'No, Erica. It was swinishly awful. But I would still like to
be friends. Any chance?'

'Oh, Moira,' Erica said. 'I want so *much* to be friends.' She
bit her lip, her eyes dewy. 'I am sorry. I am crying all the time
now.' She sobbed suddenly.

Moira enveloped her instantly in motherly arms. 'Of course
you are,' she soothed. 'You're *pregnant*.'

Erica sobbed happily and nodded. 'It is very emotional,' she

331

said. They walked together, Moira's arm around her waist, to the sauna. Liz followed, smiling to herself, behind.

The flat was dark when she arrived back home. She looked at her watch in the streetlight outside her door and read nine-thirty. She looked up again at her unlit windows, a little surprised. Perhaps he'd worked late for some reason, or met some friends. She climbed the stairs, turned her key in the lock and pushed open the door. The cats surrounded her, clamouring in the darkness, and she switched on the lights, pushing them gently aside. As she stepped through the door, her boot kicked something that slid and jingled across the floor. The striped kitten jumped on it at once. Curious, Liz lifted the kitten in one hand, the object, paper-wrapped and metallic, in her other. The paper was loose and the interior fell out and landed at her feet, brushing by Esau's weaving back. He jumped and then reached his nose to sniff it. She pushed him aside. A bunch of door keys lay glinting on the carpet. She thought at once of Barry, exorcising his guilt still, and she smiled. Then she straightened up and her eyes fell on the row of hooks in the alcove, oddly bare.

She was wearing her trenchcoat, and Darren's black wool coat went to work with him as always, but his peaked cap and the long white scarf were gone as well. She resisted the urge to go into the flat, check the bedroom and living-room. She knew in any case, what she would find. Carefully, she unrolled the crumpled paper that had contained the keys.

He had written the note from memory, word perfect, and spelled atrociously:

> 'To say to thie, that I shall dye, is true – but for thy luv, by the Lord, no; yet I lov thee to'

She crumpled the paper in her hand, sat down on the floor amidst the mewing cats, and cried. The two Siamese battered around her, thudding their sinuous backs against her shoulders. She pushed them away and hunched over her knees, sobbing. The striped kitten wormed under the arch of her legs and climbed up between them, claws digging through her tracksuit. She clutched it and sat leaning up against her sports bag, her head bowed over it, wet face buried in its fur. It purred, oblivious of her sorrow, and then the significance of its continued presence struck home. She raised her head, looked up at the bare coat hook and down at the small striped cat.

'Darren, you *shit*!' she cried aloud.

Liz was sitting alone, at two the next afternoon, at her bare kitchen table, morosely stirring milk into a solitary cup of coffee, when Moira rang. She got up to answer the phone listlessly, and stood leaning against the kitchen wall, cup in hand, glaring at Darren's kitten which skulked guiltily about as if personally responsible for its master's defection.

'Liz,' Moira said severely. 'I'm appalled.'

'What? How'd you know?' Liz said uncertainly.

'How'd I know what?' Moira's voice shifted swiftly from condemnatory to suspicious.

Liz regained caution and said only, 'Appalled at what?'

'The perfectly rotten thing you did to Barry.'

'What?'

'It wasn't very nice for Charles *either*. Bloody convenient for *you* of course. Packing the pair of them off together like so much left luggage, but *really* . . .'

'Now wait a minute, Moira . . .'

'Erica's a bit shocked too.'

'Erica? How does Erica know?' Liz said testily. 'And how do *you* know, anyhow?'

Moira was silent. Then she said stiffly, 'Well, since my *friend* didn't deign to tell me last night, I had to find out through the grapevine. Barry met Andrew in Bloomsbury. *Andrew's* appalled as well,' she added weightily.

Liz sighed. 'I'd have told you eventually,' she said. 'If you *have* to know, I would have told you last night. But I thought I'd wait for a private moment. I needn't have bothered.'

'Your friends are concerned for you. *And* for Barry.'

'Fuck my friends.'

'Liz?'

She sighed again. 'Sorry. Look, Moira, I'm not in the best of moods.' She teetered on the proud edge of putting the phone down and then relented. 'He's left,' she said. She heard Moira's sharp intake of breath.

'Oh, Liz.'

'Don't say you're sorry if you're not.'

'I am sorry.'

'He's left his bloody cat.'

'You like cats,' Moira said helpfully.

'Within bloody reason. Christ, I can't afford any more men in my life. I'll end up with a bloody cattery.'

Moira drew in a listening breath. 'Why, Liz?' she asked softly.

Liz sighed. 'He didn't say, Moira. He left . . .' She paused and swallowed. 'He left a lovely note. A lovely sad note.'

'Don't you *know* why?' Liz was silent and Moira said meekly, 'I thought you were really happy together.'

'We were,' Liz said. She watched the kitten sadly. It leapt up to a chair and then on to the table where it sat delicately washing its ears. 'Time got in the way. His future. My past. He was right to go. I know that.' She paused and said softly, 'Only, I wish he'd said goodbye.'

At seven o'clock, when she was disconsolately rooting in cupboards for the ingredients of supper, the door buzzer sounded. She thought it would be Barry, returning the car he had borrowed in the morning, but the voice over the intercom was soft and female and distantly familiar.

'Liz? It's Stephanie. Do you remember me?'

'Of course,' Liz said, surprised. 'Come up, love, it's the third floor.' She pushed the door release and then went out and stood on the landing. Stephanie came running up the stairs, light-footed in little thin shoes, long dark voile skirt trailing a rain-dabbled hem. She was carrying a square wicker basket in one hand, swinging it easily as she ran. She arrived panting, her glossy black hair tumbling over wide mascaraed eyes.

'Hi, Liz,' she said shyly. Clusters of gold earrings sparkled

334

with rainwater. She shook her head like a puppy, casting a light spray.

'Come in; you're soaked. Would you like coffee?' She shook her head again. 'Tea?'

'I can't stay. Darren . . .' She stopped. 'I suppose he's told you,' she said.

Liz paused in the alcove, turning to face the girl. 'Not a lot,' she said drily.

'He's going to Glasgow tonight. He has all his things but he asked me to collect Tiger for him . . .' She paused uneasily, 'Didn't he say?'

'Not to me, Stephanie.'

'Oh.' She looked crestfallen and confused. 'He should have . . .'

'I think he's had a lot on his mind,' Liz said gently. 'How is he travelling? Do you know?'

'The night coach. I'm to meet him at Victoria. With Tiger.'

Liz drew back slightly. 'Are you going with him, Stephanie?'

Stephanie blinked honest worried eyes. 'Me? With Darren? Of course not, Liz. I mean, I thought you . . .'

'Never mind,' Liz said, quickly ashamed.

'I'm just bringing him Tiger.'

'Of course.' Liz turned and said quietly, 'I'll go get him for you, love.'

She found the cat asleep on her bed. It had managed to make itself look extraordinarily small and vulnerable, curled in a tight ball, nose tucked under one paw, and circled by its long striped tail. From a source of intense annoyance all day, it became instantly a dear possession. She thought with dismay of the wicker cat basket Stephanie held.

'Well, come on, you,' she said, 'your master wants you after all.' She picked it up complete and it remained momentarily asleep in her hands, but then woke and unwound, making a huge wide yawn. The two Siamese got up from their own hollows in the duvet and looked disdainful. Liz carried the kitten through to the living-room, where Stephanie waited, crouched in the pool of her circling skirt, beside the open basket. 'Here he is,' Liz said.

'Oh he's *grown*.' Stephanie reached up and took the kitten

335

in her hands. It was wide awake, tail swishing. She cuddled it, and then lifted it over the basket. Four paws shot out horizontally and claws connected instantly with the wicker rim. The kitten hung suspended, a small furry trampoline. Stephanie unhooked paws one by one, and the kitten replaced them in order. She tried two together and it closed teeth on her hand.

'Ow!' She let go and it bolted under the sofa.

Liz lay down flat and scooped it out. 'I'll do it.' She turned it over with a no-nonsense hand, held it over the basket, dropped it in, and slammed the lid. It meowed pitifully and unconvincingly. 'Ignore it,' she said to Stephanie. 'It's a dramatist.' She leaned over the basket and peered in the little barred wicker window. One sideways yellow eye looked out. 'Hope you like RSAMD,' she said. She stood up and Stephanie picked up the cat basket gingerly. The kitten sat in one corner, tilting it sideways, and began gnawing at once at the bars of the window, crunching loudly.

'I hope he doesn't get out,' Stephanie said nervously. In response the kitten flipped over and hung from the lid, jiggling at the catch. 'Oh!' Stephanie cried. 'Maybe I should tie it . . .' She held the latch with one hand, balancing the basket with the other. Her eyes were wide with distress. 'I'm not used to cats,' she said.

Liz watched her, edging awkwardly to the door, a moment longer, and then said wisely, 'Stephanie?'

'Yes?'

'Shall I do it for you?'

She looked instantly hugely relieved. 'Oh, Liz, would you?'

'Sure. Give it to me. What time is his bus?'

'Nine,' she said. 'Scottish Citylink.' She held the basket a moment longer and added guiltily, 'I told Darren I would.'

'I'm sure he won't mind,' Liz said, not sure in the slightest. 'I'll explain. Promise.' Stephanie released the cat basket, handing it and its rustling occupant back to Liz.

'Oh thanks so much. I was so afraid I'd lose him on the Underground . . .' She was backing towards the door, as if fearing the offer withdrawn.

'No problem,' Liz said as Stephanie slipped out of the door and fluttered down the staircase in her trailing skirt. 'I'll drive him.' Then she closed the door behind the girl and remembered that Barry had the car. 'Oh *shit*,' she shouted to the caged cat. It slipped the latch, wriggled from under the lid, and fled behind the fridge in response.

Victoria Coach Station was cold and cavernous, hazed with diesel fumes. Crowds of young people, dripping from the rainy night outside, gathered around heaps of brightly coloured rucksacks. They looked lively and cheerful, impervious to the weary sordidness of their surroundings. Liz picked her way through them, cradling the wicker cat basket in her arms. The lid, which she had fastened with kitchen string, was now secured with the belt of her trenchcoat after an escape attempt on the District Line. The kitten had given up chewing his way out and was now bleating with rhythmic and miserable regularity. Girls and boys in jeans and shell-suits looked disapproving as Liz passed.

'Shut up, you little bastard,' Liz whispered. 'Try that crap with Darren and I'll have your ears on toast.' She jiggled the cage savagely and won a satisfying scuttle of claws.

The big Scottish Citylink overnight coach was waiting at its stand, surrounded by a crowd of young Australians, three or four Scottish students and a pair of stoical Glaswegian grandmothers in tweed coats. Darren was sitting alone on a railing, his feet on his rucksack, his back to her. The long black coat trailed down to the wet pavement and his white scarf was wrapped around his neck in two careless loops. She came closer and stepped around the railing. He sat still, remote and unaware, his chin on one hand, his fine profile turned towards her. She saw him suddenly afresh, as if she was meeting him ten years hence, a handsome, distinctive, charismatic man. She shifted the wicker basket to her other hand and walked to his side.

'Going far?' she asked.

His head came up and his eyes opened wide. 'Christ!'

'Just running a little errand for Stephanie. She said you wanted this.' She held up the basket, smiling wryly. He stared, silent. 'You did want this?'

'Oh. Aye. Aye, I wanted it. I mean,' he ducked his head, 'I couldn't just leave him.'

'I thought you had. I could have throttled you.'

'Did you no' get my note?' He jumped down off the rail.

She set the cage on the ground. He faced her and she smiled gently. 'I got it, Darren.' She paused. 'It was lovely, but I think I'd have preferred it face to face.'

He turned away. 'I thought he'd say it better than me.'

'You don't have to be Shakespeare to say goodbye, Darren.' He nodded, looking down at his feet. 'Will you manage?' She lifted the cat carrier and held it out to him.

'Aye, sure.'

'Where are you staying?'

'I dinna ken yet.' He took the cage and peered through the bars. 'Hi, Tiger,' he said. It meowed sadly. 'He looks cold.'

'He's not very happy in there,' Liz said. Darren set the cage down on the pavement and crouched beside it. 'Darren?'

'Aye?' He did not look up.

'Shall I keep him for you?' He raised his head, uncertain. 'Just now, anyhow. You can have him back whenever you like. When you've found a place.'

He turned away. 'That's what he did,' he said. 'I canna do that.'

'He's not that bad, Darren, honestly.'

He looked up, meeting her eyes. His own were yearning and sad. 'I didna want to be like that. I wanted to be different for you. To look after you and no' leave you and – ' he paused – 'to love you. Really love you. No' just take things from you and go away.'

Liz laid her hands on his shoulders. '*Didn't* you love me, Darren?'

'Aye, I did, I did,' he said desperately. He paused and swallowed hard. 'I do.' She leaned forward and kissed him and dropped her head on to his shoulder. He clutched her hard for a moment and then let her go.

She stood up and lifted the cage. 'Anytime, Darren. Whenever you want him back.'

'Aye, Liz.'

'You'd better load your things. It's time to go.'

'Aye.' He did not take his eyes off her. She lifted his small sports bag and he took up his rucksack and they went together to load them in the hold. At the steps of the coach he turned to face her, holding her lightly at arm's length. 'I'm sorry, Liz.'

'For what? The best winter of my life? I wouldn't be.' She laughed richly, and raised her hand and lightly brushed his messy forelock of hair. 'Get that cut,' she said, 'it looks like shit.' He laughed and kissed her and climbed awkwardly up the stairs, his back to the driver, jostled by a cluster of giggling girls. He tried to stand where he could see her, but the crowd forced him back, the doors closed, and the big coach pulled noisily away. She thought she glimpsed him through a window and stood waving through the smoky air at the darkened glass, until the coach turned out of the station and drove off into the night. Then she lifted the wicker basket with Tiger and walked out in search of a phone.

Charles answered on the first ring. He sounded buoyant and happy and she could hear him shouting cheerfully for Barry across the little studio flat. There was some loud male laughter and then Barry came on to the phone.

'Liz, look, I'm sorry about the car . . . I got tied up. I'll bring it right around.' He sounded abject and eager to please.

She said quickly, 'It doesn't matter. But I'd actually prefer if you brought it to Victoria.'

'Victoria?'

'The coach station. Never mind why, but I'd like a ride home.' She peered into the wicker cage which rested awkwardly on the shelf beside the phone.

There was a brief baffled silence from his end. Then, realizing she wasn't going to explain, he said, 'Of course, Liz. Right away.'

He had brought his bafflement with him when he arrived, but also his good manners. He hopped out to open the door for her. Liz seated herself with the wicker cat basket on her knee. Tiger had gone to sleep, curled in a corner, tufts of fur sticking out through the canework. Barry got back behind the wheel. He looked at the basket but said nothing.

'It's Darren's kitten,' she volunteered.

'Oh. The kitten.' He glanced at it once more and then pulled away into the traffic. 'Vet?'

'No.'

He didn't say anything more until they arrived in front of the flat. He edged in behind the white Volvo, switched off the engine and sat for a moment, hands on the wheel.

'Look, I'm sorry about the car.'

'It's all right, Barry. I told you. Anyhow, I *still* say it's half . . .'

'I'm sorry about everything, Liz.' She looked at him quizzically, but he still sat staring at his hands. 'I'm sorry for barging back into your life the way I did. And – ' he paused – 'I'm sorry . . . I'm sorry for the whole damn thing. Hellish mistake. Worst bloody mistake of my life.'

The car filled up with silence. Rain pattered persistently on the roof and the windows misted, blurring the stark streetlight. Tiger awoke and walked around his wicker cage, rocking it on Liz's knees. Barry waited a little longer and then said resignedly, 'Charles Beatty's offered me a pretty good rental deal on the flat. I think I can just about stretch to it.' He paused and said carefully, 'What do you think?'

'I think you should probably take it,' she said evenly.

He sighed. 'Yes. I imagine so. Of course, it's not a permanent commitment.'

'No. Of course not.'

'Charles would understand . . .'

'I'm sure you can work out something suitable,' she said abruptly.

He heard the finality in her voice and said, 'Yes. I'm sure.' He waited a moment longer. She opened her door. He opened his then and got quickly out into the rain and went around the car to help her. He took the cat basket and followed her through the front door, and set it down in the tiled foyer. 'Shall I take it upstairs for you?'

'It's light, Barry,' she said, lifting it, 'thanks.' He hesitated. 'Would you like to take the car again?' she asked. 'It's a filthy night.'

He shook his head. 'I'll get the tube.' He turned to go, and then stopped, looking around the familiar space, his forehead wrinkled in confusion, as if he couldn't quite grasp how he got where he was. He turned back. 'You wouldn't fancy a curry would you? Only – ' he paused again, almost shyly –

'Charles and I were whipping one up. Plenty for one more. Two, even,' he added quickly. 'The two of you, I meant.' She smiled. His descent into bumbling boyishness revived a Cambridge image; Barry in ill-fitting dinner suit, hovering at her door, two May Ball tickets transforming their comfortable friendship into romance.

'That's very kind, love. And as a matter of fact, it sounds terrific.' She was aware suddenly that she hadn't eaten since lunch.

'And Darren?' he repeated kindly.

'Darren's not here,' she said quietly. 'He had a star to catch.'

'What?'

'The night coach to Glasgow. He's going home.'

'Liz?'

'I'm fine, Barry. Come on, let's have that curry.'

'Because of me, Liz?'

'You?'

'Because I came back. Did I ruin this for you?' He sounded anguished.

She laughed gently. 'Barry, I'm thoroughly capable of ruining things for myself. Give me credit for some initiative.' She laughed again, twirling the cat basket.

'I can't believe you're finding this all that funny.'

'Oh, he'll be back one day,' she said lightly. 'I've kept a hostage.' She held up the basket. 'It worked with you.' She grinned and started up the stairs. 'Hey, Barry, my feet are wet, my cat's cold and I'm starving. Let's get this show on the road.'

He waited for her at the foot of the stairs. She appeared five minutes later, divested of Tiger and newly dressed in red leggings and a black sweatshirt with the name of a Glasgow theatre group stencilled on the back. She was carrying her damp tan trenchcoat over her arm, and her hair, freshly brushed, bounced in a glossy tangle of youthful curls. She was smiling brightly and looked suddenly like an attractive stranger, someone he'd like to know. The image triggered a ripple of memories and he puzzled over it as he helped her into the coat. As she opened the door, a picture sprang into his mind, vividly clear.

341

'I've got it!' he cried.

'Got what?' She half-turned, widening her eyes in curiosity.

'The Bridge of Sighs.'

'What?'

'Cambridge. I was crossing the bridge and you came running from the Backs. In a black sweatshirt and jeans. Your hair loose. All wet. It was October and pissing down.'

'Barry?'

'It's where we met. I've remembered it!' he cried triumphantly. 'I said, "Who are you?" I had to know. You were so lovely. And you said . . .'

'Get out of my way. I'm late for my class.'

'You didn't,' Barry protested, hurt and insistent.

'No,' Liz smiled brightly, 'but I should have.' She stepped out into the wet night and turned to face him abruptly. 'The truth is,' she said, 'I don't remember what I said, but I suspect I stammered something hopeful and idiotic because I'd been watching you for months and *finally* you'd noticed me.'

'Surely not.' Barry followed her onto the pavement, his brow lined in confusion.

'Oh, very likely.'

'But, Liz,' he persisted, 'I thought *you* couldn't remember meeting *me* either. You always said . . .'

'You don't imagine I was going to confess being hopelessly infatuated ever since I laid eyes on you.'

'When was *that*?' he asked, baffled.

'A party. Nothing significant. You chatted to me for about ten minutes and then went off with a blonde.'

'A blonde? Me, Liz? I never . . .'

'Victoria, she was called. Never mind.'

'I *chatted* to you?'

'And then you forgot. And then for some reason I'll never fathom you fell all over yourself for me on the Bridge of Sighs.'

Barry stepped backwards towards the car, and then stopped, leaning on its wet roof and oblivious of the rain making dripping tendrils of his hair.

He said warily, 'You remember it all, don't you?'

'Every bit.'

342

He ducked his head. 'I've never been very good at remembering.'

'No.'

'That first time . . . the party . . . you're not making it up . . .?' He sounded faintly hopeful.

''Fraid not, Barry.' He looked up, his eyes meeting hers.

'You must think I'm a shit,' he said vigorously. She tilted her head, rain touching her cheek.

'No,' she said thoughtfuly. 'Not usually. Why?'

'For what you just told me. Meeting you. And then *forgetting* you? So that I didn't even remember . . . surely it's a bit humiliating.'

She shrugged. 'It's *realistic* Barry. It happens to everybody. It happened to Moira and John. Remember, at that godforsaken dinner party, Moira with her heroic image of John the Great Debater? Never mind the man had worshipped her since the day they met punting. He failed to register until she saw in him the thing she could love. *That's* what she remembers: the man fitting the image of her dreams.'

'And me?' Barry asked uncertainly. 'Am I doing that? Was I?'

'You tell me.'

He leaned against the car, looking down at his wet trainers. 'I can't remember,' he said sadly. 'I just see a picture of a beautiful girl in the rain.' He paused, shifting his feet once, and looked up again. 'Liz,' he said plaintively, 'do you *really* wish you'd brushed me off?'

'I wish I'd had the courage to be honest. To say, sorry, I'm *late*. I *was* late. And I missed that class.' He started to protest and she said quickly, 'I'm not blaming *you* Barry. I'm blaming me. And I wish I'd had the courage to remind you. To say "very romantic, but actually, we've met."'

'I'd have died of embarrassment.'

'I know,' she said gently. 'I knew that then. And so I accommodated. I protected you, and lost a little bit of me. And that's how it began. Me accommodating, chipping off any rough edges that didn't suit your picture of me. No wonder you ended up thinking you knew me better than I knew myself. I lost a *lot* of me in seventeen years. It made me resentful. And it made you arrogant.'

343

'I'm sorry.'

'It wasn't your fault. I was willing accomplice. And I wasn't even aware.' She paused. 'Not at the time.'

He sighed, looking down at his feet again, the white trainers sodden and grey. He said softly, 'You know, all the way home, on the plane, even before that, really, from when I made up my mind to leave . . . I was just heading for one place . . . here. You, me, the flat, our cats, our friends. Like I'd been in some time-warp and I could just step right back in through one of those windows in space.' He raised his head, water dripping onto his collar, and faced her bravely. 'It's not going to be the same for us, is it?'

'No, Barry. Never.' He winced and looked away. 'But who's to say it won't be fun?' she said. She touched his wet sleeve, and when he looked back she was smiling, her eyes wide and challenging, as she stood before him in the rain.